### Entangled

"*Entangled* is a simmering slow burn romance, but I also fully believe it would be appealing for lovers of women's fiction. The friendships between Joey, Maddie, and Gabriella are well developed and engaging as well as incredibly entertaining...All that topped off with a deeply fulfilling happily ever after that gives all the happy sighs long after you flip the final page."—*Lily Michaels: Sassy Characters, Sizzling Romance, Sweet Endings*

"Ms. Brayden has a definite winner with this first book of the new series, and I can't wait to read the next one. If you love a great enemies-to-lovers, feel-good romance, then this is the book for you."—*Rainbow Reflections*

### To the Moon and Back

"*To the Moon and Back* is all about Brayden's love of theatre, onstage and backstage, and she does a delightful job of sharing that love... This is not a story with plot twists and unexpected developments. Brayden set the scene so well I knew what was coming, not because it's unimaginative but because she made it obvious it was the only way things could go. She leads the reader exactly where she wants to take them, with brilliant writing as usual. Also, not everyone can make office supplies sound sexy."—*Jude in the Stars*

"Melissa Brayden does what she does best, she delivers amazing characters, witty banter, all while being fun and relatable."—*Romantic Reader Blog*

### Back to September

"You can't go wrong with a Melissa Brayden romance. Seriously, you can't. Buy all of her books. Brayden sure has a way of creating an emotional type of compatibility between her leads, making you root for them against all odds. Great settings, cute interactions, and realistic dialogue."—*Bookvark*

### Beautiful Dreamer

"I love this book. I want to kiss it on its face. I also want to go to Dreamer's Bay, so I can eat the donuts, hang out on the beaches, and maybe even join in on the Saturday night cornhole game with Devyn and Elizabeth. Instead, I'm going to stick *Beautiful Dreamer* on my to-reread-when-everything-sucks pile, because it's sure to make me happy again and again."—*Smart Bitches Trashy Books*

"[A] perfect summer romance, the kind you want to take to the beach to enjoy as you soak up the sun and sea breeze."—*Rainbow Reflections*

"*Beautiful Dreamer* is a sweet and sexy romance, with the bonus of interesting secondary characters and a cute small-town setting." —*Amanda Chapman, Librarian (Davisville Free Library, RI)*

### Love Like This

"I really have to commend Melissa Brayden in her exceptional writing and especially in the way she writes not only the romance but the friendships between the group of women."—*Les Rêveur*

"Brayden upped her game. The characters are remarkably distinct from one another. The secondary characters are rich and wonderfully integrated into the story. The dialogue is crisp and witty."—*Frivolous Reviews*

### Sparks Like Ours

"Brayden sets up a flirtatious tit-for-tat that's honest, relatable, and passionate. The women's fears are real, but the loving support from the supporting cast helps them find their way to a happy future. This enjoyable romance is sure to interest readers in the other stories from Seven Shores."—*Publishers Weekly*

"*Sparks Like Ours* is made up of myriad bits of truth that make for a cozy, lovely summer read."—*Queerly Reads*

### Hearts Like Hers

"*Hearts Like Hers* has all the ingredients that readers can expect from Ms. Brayden: witty dialogue, heartfelt relationships, hot chemistry and passionate romance."—*Lez Review Books*

"Once again Melissa Brayden stands at the top. She unequivocally is the queen of romance."—*Front Porch Romance*

"*Hearts Like Hers* has a breezy style that makes it a perfect beach read. The romance is paced well, the sex is super hot, and the conflict made perfect sense and honored Autumn and Kate's journeys."
—*The Lesbian Review*

### Eyes Like Those

"Brayden's story of blossoming love behind the Hollywood scenes provides the right amount of warmth, camaraderie, and drama."
—*RT Book Reviews*

"Brayden's writing is just getting better and better. The story is well done, full of well-honed wit and humour, and the characters are complex and interesting."—*Lesbian Reading Room*

"Melissa Brayden knocks it out of the park once again with this fantastic and beautifully written novel."—*Les Reveur*

"Pure Melissa Brayden at her best…Another great read that won't disappoint Brayden's fans. Can't wait for the rest of the series."
—*Lez Review Books*

### Strawberry Summer

"This small-town second-chance romance is full of tenderness and heart. The 10 Best Romance Books of 2017."—*Vulture*

"*Strawberry Summer* is a tribute to first love and soulmates and growing into the person you're meant to be. I feel like I say this each time I read a new Melissa Brayden offering, but I loved this book so much that I cannot wait to see what she delivers next."—*Smart Bitches, Trashy Books*

"*Strawberry Summer* will suck you in, rip out your heart, and put all the pieces back together by the end, maybe even a little better than they were before."—*The Lesbian Review*

"[A] sweet and charming small-town lesbian romance."—*Pretty Little Book Reviews*

### First Position

"Brayden aptly develops the growing relationship between Ana and Natalie, making the emotional payoff that much sweeter. This ably plotted, moving offering will earn its place deep in readers' hearts."
—*Publishers Weekly*

# By the Author

Waiting in the Wings

Heart Block

How Sweet It Is

First Position

Strawberry Summer

Beautiful Dreamer

Back to September

To the Moon and Back

*Soho Loft Romances:*

Kiss the Girl

Just Three Words

Ready or Not

*Seven Shores Romances:*

Eyes Like Those

Hearts Like Hers

Sparks Like Ours

Love Like This

*Tangle Valley Romances:*

Entangled

Two to Tangle

## Visit us at www.boldstrokesbooks.com

# TWO TO TANGLE

*by*

## Melissa Brayden

2020

# TWO TO TANGLE

ISBN 13: 978-1-63555-747-3

This Trade Paperback Original Is Published By
Bold Strokes Books, Inc.
P.O. Box 249
Valley Falls, NY 12185

First Edition: November 2020

**CREDITS**
EDITOR: RUTH STERNGLANTZ
PRODUCTION DESIGN: STACIA SEAMAN
COVER DESIGN BY JEANINE HENNING

# Acknowledgments

Food is a big part of my life and I'm thrilled about it. In fact, I've always considered myself a proud foodie. When at a restaurant, I long to try everything on the menu. Potlucks are my favorite because of the extensive sampling opportunities. While I'm not a bad cook, I don't get to flex my culinary muscle as much as I would like, making this story a satisfying one to pen. I got to live in the food world for a little while and loved it. And oh, the research! I shall not complain. Oh, no. Never.

It's an interesting time to write a book, when the world is quarantined and shut away. It turned me inward, and I think that influenced my characters' paths as well. The internal, personal journey became the crux of the tale, and I found myself writing what I hope is a more grown-up, reality-based struggle. I hope you'll enjoy exploring the themes in the book, and perhaps you'll drink a glass of white with some homemade carbonara as you read.

I had my hands full this go-round, and I want to say thank you to Bold Strokes, Rad, Sandy, and Cindy for having my back and extending grace and flexibility. What a top-notch group of professionals I work with. I got a lot of pep talks from my pals in the writing world. Special shout-outs to Nikki, Georgia, and Rachel for checking in on me and keeping me afloat, to Paula and Carsen for the glass raising, and Fiona and Kris for the laughs. Ruth Sternglantz, my editor, did a fantastic job of shepherding me through the process of making this a stronger book and Jeanine Henning's cover offered great inspiration. The proofreaders continue to amaze me with their diligence, and Stacia Seaman is a fantastic quarterback, putting it all together. Readers, thank you for your messages and kind words as we traverse these difficult months together. Books really do have a way of bonding people and I'm so grateful to be a part of such a tight knit community. To many more. Double cheers!

For anyone who's ever felt like a secondary character
in their own story

# PROLOGUE

G abriella Russo believed fully that the smell of fresh coffee and baking bread was enough to steal a person's heart and never give it back. Each morning that she walked into the Bacon and Biscuit Café for her twice-a-week fix, she was reminded of the sentiment. After a deep and satisfying inhale, she approached the counter. She scanned the menu even though she practically knew it by heart after living in town for eight months now. Finally, she beamed at blond-haired, blue-eyed Clementine Monroe, who stood patiently at the register, poised to take her order. Her eyes looked a little more slate colored today. Pretty.

"Is it a honey bacon and butter biscuit kind of a day?" Clementine asked, rattling off Gabriella's standard order. "They're fresh out of the oven, and that bacon is perfect. Frankie has outdone himself on the grill."

Gabriella quirked her lips to the side in indecision. "It's tough today. I was leaning toward maybe the jalapeño bacon, but no. I think I have to stick with my go-to." She pointed at the menu posted above the counter. "Question for you. Is the apricot jam purchased or made in-house?" As a chef, these were the questions that overwhelmed her brain when she came in contact with any kind of food or its preparation. These were the details she craved, that got her excited and ready to head to work and create her own food and flavors.

Clementine sighed. "No. Mr. Rothstein purchases the jam commercially." The look on Clem's face said that she didn't much agree with the owner's decision. From their conversations since Gabriella had moved to town, she surmised that Burt Rothstein was a business owner going through the motions, in contrast to Clementine, who had a real passion for the place. She and Clem had become acquaintances, given that they were about the same age and both carried a passion for food.

She'd shared with Gabriella that she imagined running a café of her own one day. "I wish he sourced locally or let us make it in-house. Frankie and I have been working on recipes, but he shoots down the idea every time."

"Huh. Well, that's a shame about the jam. I'll stick with my order. Not a branching out kind of day."

"Coming up," Clementine said and disappeared to assemble the to-go bag.

"Lookie over there," a woman's voice said. "That's the pretty little chef from the food truck thingy over at Tangle Valley. You know, the one they hired on once Jack Wilder passed?"

Well, well. Gabriella knew the voice. It belonged to Thelma McDougall, one of the four little old ladies who made up the gossip squad in the town of Whisper Wall, Oregon, nicknamed the Old Biddies. They were equal parts charming and trouble, wrapped up in a bundle of girl power. Gabriella adored and feared them. The rest of the town seemed to agree.

"Oh, my, yes. I forget her name, but I always call her the pretty one out there. Just a real looker," Maude Berkland, another Biddy, said in her recognizable vibrato. Gabriella kept her back to them, not wanting to interrupt their fun even if they were way too loud to be discreet. There were only a handful of tables in the café. Surely, they knew she could hear them. Right? You'd never know it, though, and this wasn't exactly unusual. She ran into them most any morning she dropped by the Biscuit. This was apparently their morning gathering spot, where over coffee and fresh-baked bakery items they discussed the ins and outs of whoever passed through the shop.

"From what I hear," Janet, another Biddy, informed the table, "she's from some big Italian family from the Northeast. No husband. Likes the ladies."

"Nothing wrong with that," Birdie said sweetly. All four Biddies, present and accounted for. "I used to like a lady here and there in my day."

"Oh, you did not," Maude said, making a scoffing noise from the back of her throat. "You're just trying to show off again. You're always doing that under the pretense of playing coy. You're not the coolest one here, Birdie."

"Well, I just might be," Birdie said sweetly. "You don't know."

Gabriella smothered a grin and waited patiently for her order.

"I like the food she makes in that truck a whole lot," Janet said to the other Biddies. "Gonna mosey over and see if she's making that homemade pasta with the killer sauce at lunch. The kind with that fresh cheese on top. I'm a sad little addict for cheese. All kinds. My doctor has opinions, but I just don't care."

"Get me some wine while you're there," Maude commanded. "I like the red kind. Three bottles should do it."

Clementine showed up with the greasy white bag containing Gabriella's order from heaven. Gabriella held it up and felt herself beam. "Now my morning can start right. See you soon, Clem."

"I'm betting on the day after tomorrow. You can't stay away long," Clem said with a grin and went to work stocking the pastry display case that showed off a variety of muffins, breads, and even a few cake doughnuts. None of those compared to the wonder of their biscuits, however. Those things put them on the map for good reason. Sweet Lord.

As Gabriella passed the Biddies, she offered a wiggle of four fingers. "Sausage rigatoni, arancini, roasted mushroom ravioli, and a prosciutto and goat cheese salad. All on the lunch menu today. Plenty of that special cheese you like, too, Ms. Janet. Come out and see me."

The Biddies practically glowed at the invitation, chattering back over one another.

"Sounds marvelous."

"Good to see your beautiful face, sweetheart."

"My mouth is watering at that list."

"I need some of that special cheese."

With warm biscuits and bacon in her bag and a skip in her step, Gabriella hopped in her forest-green Jeep Wrangler and drove home to Tangle Valley Vineyard, quite possibly the most beautiful place on Earth, to start her workday. It would begin with food prep. Until the restaurant she would oversee as executive chef was ready to open, she worked out of Jolene, her trusty bright blue food truck, with the mission of feeding the patrons of the vineyard as they stopped in for a tasting, tour, or wine purchase. Business at her truck had been booming, and she was thrilled she'd made the move to Oregon when she'd been offered the position at the soon-to-be restaurant.

This morning, she followed the winding road past the quaint sign announcing the vineyard until she sat at the top of the hill that overlooked the expanse of land below. It was springtime, and that meant everything was taking a big stretch and waking up from the winter slumber. Greens, yellows, and pinks popped all around, temperatures were beginning to rise, and everything had a fresh, new feeling. There was a buzz in the air, and she, for one, relished the anticipation of all that was to come in the next few months. Grinning, she surveyed the barrel and tank rooms down the hill to her right, where her best friend, Madison LeGrange, made magical things happen to grapes. Just past them sat the rustic but modern tasting room, where Joey Wilder, who'd recently inherited the place from her father, served the guests. If you followed the path farther onto the property, you'd come upon several cottages, set aside for those who lived and worked on the grounds. The second one down was hers, and she adored it. Across from the tasting room and adjacent guest patio, she caught sight of shiny blue Jolene, and the building just behind it? Well, that was the site of the vineyard's soon-to-be brand-new restaurant, name still to be decided. She needed to seriously narrow down her favorites for Joey. Though she'd been given the reins creatively, Joey did still own the restaurant, after all, and would want a say.

Gabriella's days at Tangle Valley were peaceful, fun, and full of great potential. But first? Biscuits and bacon for breakfast while she prepped for lunch service in a friendly food truck. She'd tune in to her favorite morning radio show on which Darby the Tator Tot kept them laughing and in good company. Maybe she'd dance a little with Tator Tot as she worked.

Her life sparkled and she had no complaints at all.

# CHAPTER ONE

The sheer satisfaction that came from the perfect bite of food was better than sex. Gabriella was damn sure of it. It scored better than air-conditioning on a sweltering day, the thrill of a roller coaster ride, or a massage when your muscles ached. A flavorful, well-balanced bite took Gabriella to pleasure-filled heights like nothing she'd ever known. The only thing better was the knowledge that she was the one who'd prepared the dish.

Tonight, that was her happy reality.

She sat back in her chair, alone in her cottage, and enjoyed the payoff. The chicken scaloppine she'd whipped up practically fell off the fork, accentuated by the richness of the sauce composed of wine, lemon, butter, and her own little addition of grilled pancetta. "I like you very much," she said to her next forkful. "Near perfection." Another bite. "You're going in the book, too. That's how special you are." Gabriella paused her meal and made her way to the drawer where she kept her cooking notes. She found the scaloppine page and jotted the details of the slight adjustment she'd made to her sauce, upping the wine quotient and dimming the butter. The results had yielded an amazing flavor balance that didn't grow too rich the more you ate, which, in her experience, tended to end a good meal early. She sipped the crisp Tangle Valley chardonnay, made just yards away from where she sat. Gabriella had been in her job as resident chef of Tangle Valley for eight months now, and though it had been a bold move to leap from upstate New York and a more urban existence to a small wine town in Oregon, the decision had been good for her soul.

The town of Whisper Wall was quaint beyond all measure and had taken Gabriella back to basics, giving her the space to create her food, breathe all the fresh air, and enjoy a slower pace. She'd not been happy in the months leading up to Joey's job offer. Her life had been riddled with work drama, romances that never really went anywhere, and the uncomfortable stress from both. Her brain had been in overdrive, and it felt like she was losing valuable years to the grind. But ever since she'd arrived in town, she'd felt herself slowly begin to relax, and that had been much needed. She felt like a different human being now, a focused one ready to achieve her goals in both work and personal fulfillment.

Two knocks, then a voice interrupted her flow. "Excuse me, chef person. What smells amazing in here?"

She grinned, recognizing Joey's voice. "That would be chicken scaloppine with a side of lemon butter spaghetti that has already knocked my socks off."

"You're sockless?"

"That's what I'm saying. This food steals socks, and I'm not even ashamed to gloat about it."

"Wait." Joey frowned. "How did you do this so quickly?" She pointed in near accusation toward the open kitchen and the pots and pans on the stove. "I saw you close down Jolene less than an hour ago, and now you've constructed an entire mind-blowing, sock-stealing meal? Impossible."

"Very possible. That was ninety minutes ago, to be precise, but I also took a shower." She showed off her partially wet hair with a quick toss.

"What kind of witchcraft is this?" Joey asked, regarding Gabriella with suspicion, her blue eyes narrowing.

She took another bite and pointed at Joey. "Why are you here? You're never here at dinnertime. Aren't you supposed to be canoodling in after-hours splendor with your beloved?" Gabriella melted. Joey and Becca were the cutest couple.

"Right? I should be. I'm missing any and all canoodling." Joey sighed and sat down. Gabriella wordlessly walked over a plate of food, which Joey accepted. Their shorthand had developed nicely over the last few months of living and working in such close proximity.

"Then what gives?"

"Becca is staying late at the resort because some fancy-pants guests are having a special dinner in the restaurant that she needed to be there for. That leaves me alone." She brightened. "Well, not anymore. I thought I'd come see you."

"Anytime." Gabriella gestured with her chin to the plate. "Tell me the truth. Thoughts?"

Joey paused mid-bite. "I don't even know what this dish is, but I'd be willing to enter into a committed relationship with it. If it has family members, I'd love to meet them."

"Chicken scaloppine. Plenty of family. You have my blessing."

"Then we're officially in love."

Gabriella relaxed into a smile. Exactly the kind of thing she liked to hear about her food. She finished her own plate and carried it to the sink while Joey launched into an update on all things restaurant related. Vendor lists, staffing advertisements, and dining room design.

"Looking at a timeline," Joey said, "I think we can safely hope to open in early summer."

"Fantastic. Any thoughts on a name?" Gabriella asked. They'd batted around a few ideas with an Italian theme to match the menu, even going as far as to consider naming it Filomena's after Gabriella's maternal grandmother back in Positano, Italy. But somehow that didn't feel grounded to the vineyard itself.

"Not yet. You?"

Gabriella held up a cautionary hand. "Hear me out. I know we've tossed around lots of fancy names that give the tongue a fun workout, but I'm feeling like maybe we lean into simple."

Joey thought on it. "I like simple."

"What about…Tangled?" She let the word linger in the air for a moment before continuing. "Not only is it a great name for a restaurant all on its own, but when people talk about it in the community, everyone will remember its origin and location."

"It does seem like good branding." Joey hesitated. "But I wanted the restaurant to feel like yours, too, not just an extension of the Wilder family. This project belongs as much to you as to me."

Gabriella warmed. "It means so much that you're including me in so many of the decisions."

Joey shrugged. "I know wine and how to sell it. I stay in my lane and leave this part of the business to you. I love Tangled if you do."

Gabriella grinned. "I think we have our name." Goose bumps sprang up on her arms the way they always did when something felt right. This did.

"Done. Also, I have a date for construction," Joey said, prompting Gabriella to halt mid dish scrub.

"Finally?" Her heart rate escalated, the excitement taking hold. "I thought we'd never get there. Don't get me wrong—I love cooking in Jolene." She came around the counter to address Joey fully. "But once that beautiful building with all the natural light is remodeled, I plan to set more than just my kitchen on fire." She shook her head, lost in a daydream about all she planned to serve. The menu was still in draft form, but it was coming along. The scaloppine had just made the cut.

Joey seemed to enjoy her celebration. "I have a feeling this town isn't going to know what hit them once we open this place and you get to work. Napa who?"

"I love the way you think." Gabriella placed a hand on her hip. "When do we start demo?"

"Ryan has us on the calendar for two weeks from tomorrow."

Gabriella had met Ryan Jacks, the owner of the remodeling outfit, only briefly, but she seemed knowledgeable and ambitious. Two great qualities. She also happened to be drop-dead gorgeous. Not an awful perk. But Joey's update tossed her into an excited flurry. "Ack! I feel like there's so much to do." She turned and made a lap around her kitchen island. "Isn't there so much to do? I should grab a broom. Something."

"I'm not sure jogging through your kitchen with one will help." Joey met her gaze and tried to steady her with a calm tone. "All I need from you is your opinion on the plans as we move forward. Like I said, I want you to be in the driver's seat. I've got wine to pour all day."

Joey didn't just own the vineyard, she also served as manager for the tasting room and had her hands full on a daily basis. Gabriella appreciated her ability to delegate rather than micromanage. "I'll be there every day. I'll oversee the whole thing. I know what I need and what I want."

"And please make sure you speak up as we go." Joey frowned. "Though I'm not sure that's a problem for you. You can be a spitfire."

Gabriella brushed one shoulder. "I grew up in Jersey, JoJo." She rolled her shoulders. "Speaking up is not a problem."

The door to the cottage opened a second time, and Madison entered and grinned at Joey. Her deep blue eyes sparkled. "I saw you come in and not come out again. I was jealous of the friend time, so here I am. Tada."

Gabriella automatically handed her a plate, which Madison set to filling at the stove without missing a beat.

"We've settled on a name for the restaurant," Joey told her proudly.

Madison looked over her shoulder from Joey to Gabriella in anticipation. "Is no one going to tell me? I'm feeling jealous again."

"Tangled," Gabriella said, smiling proudly.

Madison took a moment with the word, nodded, and visibly melted, which was the best kind of progression. "I really like it, you guys. I'm not just saying so either." She kicked her hip out as she pondered her words. "It's sophisticated and obviously on brand, right? Why didn't we think of that before? It's perfect."

The declaration made Gabriella stand even taller than her five feet three inches. She valued Madison's opinion. After all, if it wasn't for Joey originally offering Madison the job as winemaker, and Madison then recommending Gabriella as chef, she wouldn't be here. That Madison was also her ex-girlfriend hadn't complicated their working relationship at all. In fact, they got along way better as friends than they ever had as a couple. "I'm so happy we all agree. How's the chicken?"

Madison nodded. "Better than most things I've experienced." That was another win. Madison wasn't a gusher or someone who leaned toward hyperbole, but rather an individual Gabriella could count on for an honest opinion. "I'd come back for it tomorrow."

"Unfortunately, me and my two guests have killed the whole pan."

"Does it bother you that we just barge in?" Joey asked with a half wince. "I can try to announce myself in advance more often. Stomp down the path outside real loud so you hear me coming."

"I'm not doing that, the stomping," Madison said, pointing at Joey with her spoon and a smile. "But I think you're used to me."

Gabriella folded her arms. "I like things the way they are, but thank you for asking," she said pointedly to just Joey and gave Madison an elbow in the arm as she passed.

"Ow," she heard her murmur, yet it didn't stop her cheerful meal consumption.

"You two are always welcome to pop in and eat my food. In fact, I demand it."

"Where's Becca? She didn't pop with you?" Madison asked Joey. Becca Crawford was the chic, yet warm general manager of the Jade, the multi-million-dollar resort located just up the road from Tangle Valley Vineyard.

Joey got that starry look in her eyes, the same one she got each time she thought about, looked at, or even considered a sentence that contained mention of the woman she loved. "Working late. Alas."

"Wow. Lots of that lately. She must be exhausted," Madison said.

Joey nodded and eyed the chocolate cake on the back counter. "It's been a busy month with tourism picking back up before the seasonal hires start in June. Sometimes I feel like we're two ships, you know?"

"Cake, JoJo?" Gabriella asked, lifting the less than perfectly frosted dessert. She'd made it herself the night before, but her baking skills, while better than most of the population's, still lacked the heart that her cooking came with. The cake looked beautiful, but she knew better. The frosting hadn't folded as effectively as it could have. The flavors didn't pop, which was a downer. She'd continue to practice.

Joey lifted her shoulders. "I mean, if you're *offering*." She dragged out the last word and gave her blond hair an innocent toss.

"Maddie?"

Madison grinned. "Always in for chocolate cake. Is there red?"

"There is. Joey restocked me yesterday, which I have to say is a fantastic perk of this job. Free wine? Sign me up."

"Well, if you're pairing food, you need to be constantly reminded what you're working with. The least we can do is keep you drowning in wine." She straightened. "I'm thinking the dolcetto would be great with the cake."

"You would be right," Gabriella said and sliced up three pieces while Joey busied herself pouring the wine.

"So Ryan will be on and off the jobsite for Tangled, supervising her crew. But she has other sites to oversee as well." Joey paused mid-pour. "God, I really like the sound of that name. Right this way to Tangled," she said in the most sophisticated of voices. "Have you eaten at Tangled? The food is to die for."

"Have I eaten at Tangled?" Madison laughed like a snooty rich person might. A guffaw, really. "Only every week, darling."

The two of them guffawed together, and Gabriella laughed along, in the best of spirits. Not only were her friends funny and warm, but she was on the precipice of something truly exciting, a restaurant that she would usher into the world from day one of construction to selecting the kind of napkins they'd offer their guests.

Joey turned to her. "You realize that you're going to have to force yourself to meet regularly with Ryan Jacks, devastatingly sexy contractor. She might toss that dark hair around and show off her dimples while she puts in a backsplash. I pity you. So hard on the eyes."

Gabriella pretended to fan herself. "I'll have to find some way to survive." A pause. "So, Ryan is in charge of all the renovations?"

"Yes, we've hired her company, which, the way I understand it, is essentially just her. She's the draw, and she'll subcontract out the rest of what she needs. She claims she has the best guys, and the reviews are good. She's right, but they all mention her specifically."

Gabriella's interest was piqued. "What does she call her company?"

"Level Up Contracting."

She grinned. "Clever. I like it when people try."

Madison tapped a finger in Gabriella's direction with a knowing grin. "You've got such a crush already, and she hasn't even started work."

"No."

"Yes."

"Maybe," Joey said, weighing in. "But that just means you have a pulse because everyone talks about Ryan, drools over her, longs to be in her presence. It's always been that way."

"You guys went to school with her?" Gabriella asked.

Joey squinted and looked to Madison for a consult. "Yes and no. She's around three years younger. Yeah?"

"Sounds about right," Madison said.

Madison and Joey were both thirty-one, which likely put Ryan in her late twenties. Gabriella, at thirty-four, felt like the wise soul in the room.

"But I've heard a few stories," Madison supplied from behind her wineglass.

Gabriella turned. "Like what?"

"When it comes to women, and that is where she spends her time, she's said to be hard to pin down."

"Well, if I looked like her and was in my late twenties, I'd probably be sowing a few oats myself. Wouldn't you?"

Madison thought on it. "I feel like I came out of the womb a forty-year-old."

"That's because you did." Joey shook her head. "I don't understand why anyone would prefer to date multiple people when you could be missing the chance to find your one."

Madison rolled her eyes. "I don't think hard-core in-love people who spend more time in the bedroom than out of it are allowed to weigh in. Your thoughts are disqualified due to starry-eyed bias. Take a seat, Wilder."

Gabriella laughed. "Gotta side with Maddie on this one. Take two seats."

"Fine. I'm lovesick and owning it. Speaking of which"—Joey pushed the last tiny bite of her cake into her mouth—"I'm going to head back to the Big House and see if Becca's home, so we can be starry-eyed and biased as a twosome."

"It's because I alluded to sex, isn't it?" Madison said. "Now it's all you can think about."

Joey balked. "I'll say hello first," she said with a grin over her shoulder. "I hope she's wearing the white dress shirt today. I really like unbuttoning the white dress shirt."

"Too much information. Get out of here before the place explodes with giant hearts," Madison called after her.

When they were alone, Madison straightened. "You seem really excited to get things moving on the restaurant."

Gabriella shook her head. "You have no idea. It's the reason I'm here."

"Good. I just wanted to make sure." Madison dipped her head as if about to confess something. "I feel a certain amount of, I don't know, pressure to make sure you're happy out here. You're a long way from home, and dragging you out here was my idea."

She covered Madison's hand with hers. "You're off the hook. For the first time in years, I can breathe, and that's because I'm here and have you to thank. It's been really nice. This," she said, gesturing to the room around her, "is exactly the kind of pace I needed. Slower. Less drama. It's what I never knew I wanted for my life." She stood taller with a grin. "Aside from missing my sisters, my family, I've never been more at peace."

"Good." Madison relaxed her shoulders. "You've seemed lighter. Glad I wasn't wrong to suggest you take the job."

She smiled ruefully. "Well, I know how you hate to be wrong. Dear God, the shame."

"If this is a reference to the green *coffee* maker incident of years past, I still claim I was right. My tinkering with it did nothing to harm that machine. I still believe it was being dramatic."

"Oh, I know." She laughed. "And I refuse to have that argument with you again. The fantastic part? We broke up, so I don't have to."

Madison leaned back against the counter and sipped her wine. "Did you ever imagine we'd be so great at the whole friendship thing? It's honestly refreshing. Our maturity. Our growth."

"I'm impressed with us."

"Same. We rock." They clinked glasses. "I came in and stole your dinner, dessert, and vino, and now I have to head to the barrel room and put the wine to bed."

"Well, make sure it has a blanket and a glass of water."

"If that will balance its acidity, I'm all for it."

As head winemaker for the vineyard, Madison's job was an important one that demanded a lot of hours. She had to be an artist, an innovator, and a chemist in one. The combined skill set put Madison LeGrange on the map in the industry as a young winemaker to watch. She was known in her field, and highly respected as someone who'd accomplished a lot by the time she'd turned thirty. She could have had her pick of a lot of vineyards, so it was noteworthy when she'd chosen this one, a smaller operation but one near and dear to her heart.

"Me and these empty plates hold no ill will," Gabriella said. "Oh, are we all doing a movie night later this week? Once the restaurant work starts, we lose our makeshift movie theater." They'd been using the unoccupied building and the giant white wall. Seemed fitting to say farewell.

"Good point. I vote for a Bond flick."

Gabriella winced. "Again? No. I vote for a rom-com this time. I need to laugh and cry in quick succession, back and forth like a maniac. Lets me know I'm alive."

"Do we have to?"

"Wasn't Loretta's daughter in an indie one from last year?" Carly Daniel was the only child of Loretta Daniel, their coworker in the tasting room. Joey and Madison knew her from back in the day when they'd grown up in the same town, but Gabriella hadn't had the pleasure. She imagined she'd be starstruck as hell if she met her, given how much she loved Carly's work.

"Yes, but it's all mushy."

"The entire point, Maddie. Time to meet your feelings. Say hello once in a while."

"Let's let Joey and Becca decide."

"Okay, but those two are in love. They're peanut butter and jelly on warm toast, adoring life and its splendor. What do you *think* they're going to go with?"

"Damn. Carly Daniel rom-com it is. I'll bring extra wine for the suffering party."

"'Night, Maddie. It's okay to cry. I want you to work on it."

She laughed and rolled her eyes. "'Night, Gabs. Be good."

Gabriella started on the ever-present dishes while listening to the one local radio station counting down the hits.

With a hop in her step now, Gabriella spent the rest of her evening on her front porch, looking out over the darkened vineyard she'd grown to adore. She made a list of ideas for the running of the restaurant, tweaked her working menu, and then finished up with a little reading. A romance novel Joey had recommended by Parker Bristow. The cover was bent and worn in from Joey's and Becca's devouring of the story, which, she had to admit, was sucking her in as well. It had been a little while since she'd experienced a romance of her own, but honestly, the book was an excellent substitute for the unavoidable stresses that came from relationships. The quiet of the night around her made the best backdrop for her evening and on a larger scale served as the perfect metaphor for her life. Calm, quiet, simple, and easy. The tranquility Tangle Valley delivered was something she would never quite get used to, and thank God for that.

# CHAPTER TWO

R yan Jacks stood on her wooden deck in the early hours of the morning, looking out over the quiet ripples of Lake Tillman. She still wore her low-rise gray sweatpants and a black sports bra as she sipped a warm cup of black coffee following her morning run. This was her favorite part of her day, when Whisper Wall had yet to wake and the sun rose peacefully over the water. She'd pushed hard today, demanding more of her body, stealing an extra mile beyond her usual five and following that up with a few hundred crunches and as many push-ups as she could manage.

Luckily, the day ahead would be a mellow one. She had the painters coming to the Sherwood Circle job, so she'd swing by, touch base, and make sure the colors were consistent with the sample the client had selected. She had some drywall to demo on Ruby Lane and needed to swing by Tangle Valley Vineyard to do some preliminary measurements in order to start work there in two days. That should be a fun job. She liked Joey Wilder, the spunky owner of the vineyard, a lot. Joey'd been three grades older in high school but was known for being well liked. Plus, Joey came out and had a girlfriend at a young age, which in a lot of ways paved the way for Ryan's own self-discovery. She'd always thought a lot of Joey for that. Maybe Ryan would even stick around and buy a glass of wine after knocking off for the day. Beyond that? Who knew what that Friday evening would bring? But that was exactly how Ryan preferred things—go with the flow, very few plans. Maybe she'd hit up someone local for some one-on-one time or take a ride to Portland for a sweeter nightspot than the town of Whisper Wall could provide. The options were endless.

At her side, her big dumb dog Dale whined quietly. Dale was a golden retriever mix of some sort, who she'd rescued five years earlier. Dale had slept soundly through her run and now demanded his breakfast. Typical. "Yeah, yeah, I'm getting to you. You're lucky you're good-looking and such a great kisser." She leaned down so he could swipe his tongue across her cheek. "Okay, that one was a little sloppy, but I forgive you."

She filled the dish, kissed her dog's head as he gobbled it down, and hit the shower, which was a recent remodel job of her own that came with a rainfall showerhead she would never take for granted. Her lake house had been the first real investment she'd made for herself since Level Up began to take on more and more clients. She'd gotten to the point where she finally had to start turning down jobs, simply because she wouldn't be able to give each one her firsthand attention. If she couldn't do her absolute best, she didn't take the gig. Maybe eventually she'd hire a project manager or two on a full-time basis. Would have to be the right person, though.

As she let the hot water run down her body well past the time it took her to get clean, Ryan caught sight of Dale charging in a circle, always intent on catching that damn tail. He'd yet to do it, but she had to give him points for tenacity. Twenty-five minutes later, with her lunch in hand, she turned to him, only to find him fast asleep. It happened to be his default. "Ready for work?"

Dale knew the question well and raced for the door, probably looking forward to truck time, when he could pop his head out the window and feel the air rush past his fur. At the Sherwood house, Dale investigated the overgrowth of wildflowers in the backyard as she signed off on the paint. On Ruby Lane, he fell asleep in a sunny spot along the sidewalk, making her subcontractors walk around him on their way in and out of the house. When they arrived at the winding road marked with a Tangle Valley Vineyard sign, Dale put his paws on the dash as they ascended to the top of the hill that overlooked it all. Ryan stole a moment to look down on the beautiful green farmland below, rows of vines, buildings for winemaking, and of course, a nice spot for visitors to take in a glass or embark on a whole tasting experience. With spring in session, the vines had clearly woken up from their winter snooze. Having grown up in wine country, Ryan still never got used to the beauty around her on a daily basis. "Now that's a view," she told her dog and gave his head a good ruffling. "You be nice to these people. We like the owner, and she has wine."

She drove down the hill onto the property and straight to the vacant building that would become the new on-site restaurant. It was a medium-sized job, and Ryan had been able to offer a fairly good bid for the majority of the work, with things like finishes and flooring to be decided as they moved forward. Joey told her that the executive chef, Gabriella somebody, would be her point person for those kinds of decisions and to be on the lookout for her. They'd met briefly when Ryan had first come out to the property, but Gabriella wasn't from around here, which made her interesting.

The building itself was quite beautiful with original oversized windows she hoped they'd be able to keep with a little restoration work. What was more, the space was flooded with natural light, which would make the lunch service pop. She stood in the doorway with Dale at her side and surveyed what was essentially one very large room that they'd be separating into a kitchen, a bar, an expediting area, and a dining room complete with workstations for servers and front-of-house staff. She imagined light fixtures, paint colors, art on the wall, and tables and chairs dotting the floor once they were finished, a practice that always got her excited and eager to get to work. Transforming an otherwise nonfunctional space into something beautiful was what made her get into the business in the first place. "Monday, this is ours," she told Dale.

"I can't wait."

She turned at the sound of a female voice, only to find Gabriella, the chef. Wow. She remembered her being pretty, but now she was reminded of the reality up close. She blinked and took in the thick dark hair, big brown eyes with some of the longest lashes she'd seen, and subtle curves that accentuated her petite frame. Ryan determined she had her by a good four inches and, now that she got a better look, saw that those eyes were hazel. "Oh, hey." She smiled. "I hear you'll be my contact on the ground? Ryan Jacks. We met a few months back."

"I remember. Who is this gentleman?" Gabriella knelt to look Dale in the eyes. He, of course, practically melted, sinking to the floor and offering his belly. Such a player. Ryan resisted an eye roll.

"That's Dale. He's inhaling attention right now."

Gabriella sank farther and gave his tummy a good feisty rub, which earned her points. None of that gentle, dainty petting some women went in for. "Well, of course he is. He's a good boy and knows it. Good boys need affection. Good boys need rubs."

With that, her dog leaped up and licked the hell out of Gabriella's face and chin because, clearly, she understood his plight. Impressively, Gabriella didn't seem to mind and even laughed. She seemed to have no trouble with a dog slobbering all over her gorgeous face and ruining her makeup. More points. "Sorry about that. He gets a little excited when people love on him. Knock it off, D. Give her a break."

Gabriella straightened. "Nah, he's good. Just saying hello." She placed her hands on her hips and exhaled. "Ryan Jacks."

Something about the way Gabriella stated her name had Ryan's full attention. She blinked and remembered her purpose. "Yeah, and you're Gabriella. Good to see you again. I'm just here to take some more measurements," she said, indicating her laptop and tape measure. "Already covered the big stuff. This will be for some of the minor nooks and crannies in the space. That okay? I don't want to get in your way."

"More than okay," Gabriella said, beaming. Her smile was infectious in all its vibrancy. Genuine, too. "I'm ready to turn this building into a living, breathing establishment. Joey estimated three months."

Ryan hesitated. Time estimates were hard, especially given how many variables were out of her control. There could be discoveries along the way that added time, or worse, stop their work altogether. Sometimes subs didn't show up or turned in work that had to be redone by her, or the weather didn't cooperate. Generally, Ryan did her best to help manage the client's expectations. "That's the goal, and I emphasize *goal*. Construction sometimes has a mind of its own. I've got my best people lined up, though, so we're in good shape."

"I'll pay you a million dollars in ravioli to have this place ready to open by early summer."

Ryan met what were definitely hazel eyes. Striking ones. Her cheeks felt hot. "You don't have a million dollars in ravioli."

"I could get it."

Okay, that made her laugh. She liked Gabriella's spunk. This woman was going to be fun to work with. "All right, but I'm holding you to it. So is Dale." Her dog stood up as if to agree.

"Dale can already have all the food he wants from my pan. That's a given."

Ryan winced. "He's a pig. Don't go there."

"Too late," Gabriella said, stroking his chin. "He's my buddy and he's gonna make sure you finish. In under three months." Some of the playfulness had fallen from her tone, and Ryan understood that she was hard core when it came to that timeline. That part would be less fun to navigate.

"Like I said, we'll do our best." She paused, studying Gabriella, who had been wearing a chef's coat the first time she'd met her. Today, she wore cropped denim jeans and a pink and purple plaid shirt. The top two buttons had been left open, offering a glimpse of smooth skin beneath. She looked away. Not on the job. Well, sometimes on the job, but maybe not today. She could at least *try* to be good. "You're a new transplant, right?" Ryan asked, moving herself back on track. "Everyone mostly knows everyone around here."

Gabriella nodded. "Less than a year."

"Where from?" Ryan asked, depositing her laptop on a rickety stand holding a projector, which seemed odd in this room.

"Jersey originally, but the Finger Lakes more recently. I worked in a prominent restaurant in wine country there. Used it to really find my own flavors, after starting my career in New York City following culinary school."

"Impressive. And now you're a West Coaster." She wondered about that story, imagined hearing it over a whiskey neat late one night. Maybe under the stars. "You like it here? I wish there was a little more going on, myself."

"I love it. I prefer the slower pace. So we're different that way." A wistful look came over her. "People here actually look you in the eye when they speak to you. Wait for your response and actually listen. Not like they have somewhere more important to be." She shook her head. "Trust me. Worth it."

Ryan grinned. "There's always Portland if you want to get crazy sometime. Call me up. I'll take you." Ryan nearly swore at herself for going there, but with Gabriella, she couldn't seem to help herself.

Gabriella raised an eyebrow that was hard to interpret. "I'll keep that in mind," she said conservatively. "And that's our movie projector I saw you eyeing. This room has been a makeshift theater for my friends and me. Last week was *Terminator*, so naturally I'm a badass this week."

"Well, don't kick my ass while I work or anything."

Gabriella chuckled. "I'll do my best, but just watch yourself is all." Ryan smiled, really liking this woman. "Other than that, I'll let you work in peace. I have a grill to fire up for lunch service. See you Monday?"

"I'll be here bright and early with a sledgehammer."

"Intriguing," Gabriella said quietly, then seemed surprised to have said it out loud. Ryan smothered a smile. "Gonna go now. Food is imminent."

"You're a good chef."

She paused. "Ryan. I'm the best chef. Stop by my truck one day."

"Sold. Bye, Gabriella…?"

"Russo. Bye now, Ryan Jacks."

Ryan went to work, taking quick measurements and adding the notations to her spreadsheet, all the while preoccupied with the last ten minutes of her life and how much she'd enjoyed them. Maybe it was because Gabriella was someone new, or because she was so beautiful, or sassy. Probably all three. Regardless, Ryan carried their exchange with her straight through dinner. Then she kissed Dale good night and headed forty minutes away to Portland, where she could lose herself in a throng of people, drinks, and loud music. She followed a woman to her apartment next door and had a little harmless fun before grabbing a cup of coffee and heading home in the wee hours.

Inside, she felt hollow. As the streetlights flew past and the road grew darker the farther she got from the city, that feeling only multiplied.

Nothing new for Ryan. Yet, at the same time, she felt it more intensely now. Would this always be her life? She sighed and turned up the volume on the radio, anything to drown out how much she disliked herself right now. There had to be more.

## CHAPTER THREE

The sun was taking its time today. Perhaps it had slept in.

Gabriella had been up a full hour before she watched it peek out from behind the hills in the distance while she nursed her second cup of black tea. She hadn't slept much overnight. It felt like her own very personal Christmas morning, and she was bursting with anticipation. For now, she'd still work in the food truck and had a dynamite menu planned for the day, full of bites and dishes that had her eager to cook and use up some of this extra energy. Today was the true realization of something big, however. Tangled had been the reason she'd dropped everything and hightailed it to Oregon wine country. A quiet location to make her own food and have control over her own restaurant? Sign her up. At last, the kickoff to all of it had finally arrived.

"Well, look who's bright-eyed and bushy tailed like a flashy little squirrel this morning," Madison said, as she came down the path. Their cottages, while not next door, weren't separated by too long a walk, and Madison passed Gabriella's every day on her walk to work.

"The day is finally here, and it's true, I'm a damned happy squirrel. I fully admit it."

Madison squinted. "Specifics needed. Is it a moon landing? Santa Claus? The stork?"

"You know very well it's restaurant day. We start construction. Well, the contractors do, and I think your parents should talk to you about where babies come from."

Madison moved past it. "Maybe when I'm older." She took a seat next to Gabriella on her porch steps. "Hey, I talked to someone about you in town yesterday."

"Oh yeah? Who's that?"

"Clementine from the Bacon and Biscuit. I stopped by for a butter biscuit."

"Who doesn't? They're probably illegal. They'll declare it any day now."

"Right? God stamped *Approved* on those things personally. Anyway, she told me that her softball team is looking for a player. Steve-O from the garage broke his foot. I declined because—"

"Obviously."

"Hey." Madison accompanied this with a pained look.

"What?"

"Words ruin lives."

Gabriella closed one eye. "I think we can both agree that you're not the most athletic. Not a huge leap. But also don't do any leaping because you'll fall. I've seen it." She frowned. "Ouch."

"I was a mathlete once upon a time." Madison leveled a stare.

"And it shows."

They exchanged a smile and moved on to business. "So how about it?" Madison asked. "Want to be their missing player and complete the team? I told Clementine how much you loved your high school glory days, and she's very interested."

"I do miss it." Gabriella felt lighter just thinking about those times as the nostalgia surfaced. She'd played third base for the Jasper High School Rockets, with her younger sister, Mariana, on shortstop. Those had been some of the best years of her life. They'd missed the state tournament by two runs and had their souls crushed like twigs, but she wouldn't undo it. "You know what? Yeah. I think I'll talk to Clem about the team. As long as it doesn't take away from my gig here, I think that'd be a fun thing to add to my weekly schedule. Plus, I'd get to know more people around here."

"*Bam.*" Madison stood. "I'm now the superhero matchmaker of the day and can go make wine with pride."

"Make it real good, too. We need the best wine possible to pair with the amazing food I plan to whip up this summer once I open."

"All right." Madison sighed. "Because you said so."

Ninety minutes later, Gabriella's heart leaped at the sight of Ryan Jacks's maroon truck pulling onto the property as she sliced zucchini strips inside Jolene. If she peered out the back window—and okay, *she did*—she could see the building that was soon to be Tangled and Ryan and Dale exiting the truck. A half an hour later, two more vehicles pulled up alongside Ryan's, and she watched four strong-looking men in dusty jeans make their way inside. It took everything she had not to race over there just to watch, but she vowed to give them some time to get settled. Instead, she focused on her lunch service. Today, seventeen-year-old Chelsea would be her sous chef in the truck. Whisper Wall High School had a growing culinary program, and Gabriella had eagerly signed up to be a spotlight professional as well as a mentor. Interested students applied to work in the truck for a small wage, class credit, and the experience of working alongside an established career chef. Currently, she had about four or five students who rotated as part of the official internship program, and they had wildly different personalities and skill sets. Chelsea was a talkative firecracker with knife skills that needed some work.

"The thing is, guys are, like, dumb anyway," Chelsea exclaimed exuberantly as she sliced zucchini into strips that could have been a little more uniform in Gabriella's opinion. "Geoffrey Johnson, he's this one guy. He acts like he's into you one minute, and then the next, he's staring at Rachel Marie's ass and your heart is on the floor like a loser, you know?"

"Oh, that's awful. High school isn't easy, but you have to know that everything is temporary," Gabriella said, as she seasoned the batter for the zucchini fritti. "About six more," she said with a nod to the cutting board.

"I mostly like Brandon Newton, though, who runs track and likes to draw, because he doesn't care about things like labels or name brands. I feel like we could go to the mall and really live our lives."

Gabriella nodded obligatorily. "Mall living. So important. Maybe a little thinner on those slices."

"God, I love the mall," Chelsea opined, swinging her knife wistfully. "I wish it were closer because clothes sold in a big group is the only way to go. You have to comparison shop to have any hope in this world."

"Yep. Just watch that knife. It should be below your shoulders at all times."

"Oh, sorry. Have I told you about Chase Henderson? He's insane. There was this one time with mice when things really got out of control."

The conversation went on like that through lunch service, and though Gabriella was grateful for Chelsea's help, the teenager could maybe brush up on her professionalism in the kitchen. Something they could delicately address when it came time for class evaluations, a thought she didn't relish. She much preferred giving praise, but if her culinary education had taught her anything, it was that criticism was more attention getting.

However, on the bright side, the constant chatter had kept Gabriella's curiosity about the construction just a hundred yards away tamped down. Didn't mean she didn't plan to peek in on the progress once she closed shop for the day at four. Just casually breeze by like a lookie-loo at an open house.

"Hope I'm not interrupting," she called into the space that now resembled an actual construction site. Whoa. Chunks of drywall lay all over the floor, which was covered in plastic sheeting. The dividing wall, which luckily had not been load bearing, was halfway gone. Ryan grabbed a loose piece of the wall with her bare hands and tossed it to the floor, removed her mask, and grinned. Okay, that was a look right there. Gabriella's breath caught as Ryan stood before her in soft-looking faded jeans, a gray and white ringer T-shirt, and a really sexy ponytail that showcased a gentle wave in her medium-length dark hair, shorter than Gabriella's and maybe two touches lighter. The dimples that appeared in both her damn cheeks were not to be glossed over either, nor was the sparkle in her blue eyes. She carried a passion for her job, and it showed.

"Not interrupting. What do you think?" Ryan held out her arms to showcase the utter destruction. "Not exactly pretty, but demo day rarely is."

"No, no. I would say not. So, that's where the bar will go?"

"Yep." Ryan ran her forearm across her forehead, and Gabriella swallowed at the pleasant hum it sent to her midsection. That was too sexy for the afternoon. "I have an order in to a carpenter I know. She's already secured a gorgeous shipment of mahogany that she's setting aside for us. Knock-you-over beautiful. I think you'll love it."

"I do already." She shifted her weight, wildly aware that she was not behaving like herself because there was a hot-as-hell woman doing impressive things with her hands in her new restaurant. Was she Chelsea all of a sudden? Did she need mall living? "Anything I can do?" she asked, looking around nonchalantly.

"Yes. Can you write me up a detailed list of things you see as must-haves? Any extra outlets not on the plans, storage needs, extra working space here or there. You understand the flow of service a lot more than I do, so if you could help me get inside your brain a little, I could tweak what we have on paper to match your needs more specifically."

"Customization. I like it. I will make a list this afternoon."

"Stellar."

"You've never worked in a restaurant?" Gabriella asked, as two guys hacked away at the wall, making holes with the backs of hammers and dragging away the wreckage.

"I delivered pizzas for Pizzamino's a couple years in high school."

Gabriella squinted. "Really? Well, that's something, I guess." But now she was imagining someone with the sex appeal of good-with-her-hands Ryan Jacks showing up on her doorstep with a piping hot pizza, which wouldn't be the only thing that was warm. Her mind had devolved into the exposition of a pornographic video. She could only laugh.

"You okay?" Ryan asked. That dimple again. *Je-sus.*

"What?"

"I asked if you'd tried it. Pizzamino's? The way they crisp the pepperoni should go down in some sort of pizza manual."

"I've had their meatball and onion pie, but you've now elevated the pepperoni to the must-try list."

"It's that easy?" Ryan passed her a lazy grin.

"When it comes to food, I'm a sucker every time. I can't be stopped."

Ryan shrugged. "Can't imagine why you'd want to be. I'm someone who thinks life is meant to be lived. Chase your pepperoni dreams."

This was going really well. Too well, which meant Gabriella should move them out of it. Less focus on sexy Ryan and more focus on the restaurant. "Any issues today?" She slid her hands into the back pockets of her jeans.

"Billy was fifteen minutes late, but we let it slide."

A guy wearing a ball cap tipped the brim in their direction.

"Good God, Billy," Gabriella said in exaggerated horror.

"My daughter Wrigley's teacher wanted to chat when I dropped her off," he said with a wince. "Good thing I still have a job." He hooked a thumb at Ryan as if to indicate how awful she was.

Gabriella turned to Ryan with an outstretched hand and mock exasperation. "You're giving this man a hard time for being a good father?"

"I just like to harass him for kicks. Don't worry. He gives it back, the bastard."

Another proud tip of the ball cap from Billy. These two were fun together. She felt like she was beginning to understand the dynamic of Ryan and her crew, who'd likely worked alongside one another for years. "Ah, well, I'll leave you to it then." She turned to Ryan. "I'll stop by in the morning with that list."

"I'd appreciate it. It'll be a mess in here, so prepare yourself. Everything is temporary."

"Can't wait. Yep." She hooked a thumb behind her and rocked on her heels. "Let you good people work now."

She wasn't sure, but she thought she caught Ryan's eyes lingering an extra beat before she turned to go, and that little detail prompted goose bumps from head to toe. Had she imagined that? No. It had happened. She chuckled at how easy she was. A good-looking kid with a hammer and she was drooling? How cliché. Gabriella sighed. How long had it been since she'd had sex again? Probably had a lot to do with it. She shook her head, not sure she could count that high. "Get it together, Russo," she commanded in amusement as she made her way to the parking lot. It appeared maybe she needed a healthier outlet for her, ahem, extra energy.

"Excuse me. Freeze. Where are you off to?" Joey asked her, as Gabriella strolled past the tasting room. Joey stood on the outdoor patio gathering a foursome of empty glasses from a table. "Was gonna see if you wanted to try Loretta's batch of peach sangria. You'll notice your whole day gets better." She shook her head. "Happens every damn time. That's why spring is my favorite."

"I don't think sales get any more convincing than that. I'll be back for that in a few. Gonna pop in and see Clementine. I think it's time I sign up for softball."

Joey grinned. "Ah, yes. Hot dogs, snow cones, and cheering incessantly at the town softball games. Another sign spring is in the air."

Gabriella smiled back ruefully, remembering her traitorous body's reaction moments ago. "God, you can say that again."

❖

Great day for a white wedding. At least according to Billy Idol on full blast. They had the radio station set to classic rock, and once Gabriella left, Ryan cranked up the volume for proper working conditions, confident they wouldn't see their client for the rest of the day. In her experience, they generally checked in once, and after that happened, Ryan and her crew could relax into their workday and focus on the fun part.

She loved music and wasn't married to any one genre. In fact, she allowed her mood and the work at hand to determine what they listened to. Demo day called for the heavier stuff and got them amped to tear stuff apart. Billy turned his cap backward as he laid into the drywall. She joined Billy, and Lonzo and his guys handled the demo on the adjacent wall, working in tandem just like they had for years now. The weather was nice, and with the door open, a nice breeze floated through the room.

"You gonna work your magic on the chef?" Billy asked. "I saw the look you got when she smiled. I know it well."

"I don't even know what that means," she answered and grabbed hold of a pesky piece of drywall, using her foot to brace as she pulled. Finally, the damn thing came free, causing her to stumble back.

Billy flashed his impression of a sexy face. She'd seen the tragic thing before. "You were flirting. I've seen it a million times."

"Yeah. So?"

"She's hot, and from the way she stared at you, I'd say she plays for your team. Otherwise, I'd have brought the heat." More of the sexy face. There should be a protective order against it.

Ryan rolled her eyes. "The heat? You mean from the frozen corn dogs you live on?"

"When my kid stays with me. I also add veggies." He smoldered to punctuate.

"You're right. Corn dogs and green beans." Ryan mimed a burned hand by shaking it. "Too hot to handle."

"Hey, we can't all have the same game. It would get fucking boring. You have your looks, your charm. I have frozen foods on a Thursday to woo my prospects." Billy smiled and patted his Winnie-the-Pooh tummy, the only part of him not in decent shape.

"She's gonna hit that," Lonzo said without turning around. He was the oldest of the three of them and no-nonsense in his approach. He'd listen to the two of them banter, and then finally throw his two cents in. "Calling it now."

"Too crass," Ryan scoffed. "She's a smart and beautiful woman. Words matter, Zo. Don't say that."

"You don't like it, call it whatever you want. Worked with you too many years. Know your ways. Hell, they work. Why change 'em?"

She could admit that there had been a time in the years after high school when she did view her various hookups as accomplishments or conquests. Sounded awful now. A decade had passed, and, well, call her more mature, but the practice felt misguided now. Didn't mean Ryan didn't enjoy herself out there, but she respected the women she got together with and hoped they respected her right back. A consensual, adult evening full of good conversation and a little fun afterward was not a bad thing. She happened to like sex. Still, the people mattered more these days.

"You goin' to the Scoot tomorrow?" Billy asked, moving them past it.

Patsy's Boot and Scoot was a bar and dance hall just on the edge of town, tucked away from the tourists that flocked to Whisper Wall for wine and relaxation. The Scoot was for locals and about the only late-night joint in ten lonely miles. Tuesdays were two-dollar beer nights and gaining in popularity. "I'll probably check it out."

"Nina has the kiddo, so first round's on you," Billy said and grabbed his final chunk of drywall.

"Me and the single dad out on the town," she said. "Please wear a plaid short sleeved shirt. And tuck it in."

He looked at her, incredulous. "It's my signature going-out look. How could I not?"

Lonzo snickered, but she knew he'd likely show up, too. "Punks."

They got back to work and went hard for several hours, but the conversation had Ryan thinking back to Gabriella Russo and her professed dedication to trying the best of every kind of food. Ambitious and fun. She grinned as she started cleanup for the day.

"What in the world are you smiling about?" Billy asked. "Dust everywhere. This is gonna take an hour."

"Don't you worry your pretty little head about me." She grabbed a broom and tossed him one. "Nothing to see here."

"Sure, boss," Billy said, knowingly. "Just a woman who loves to clean so much, she gives it her smolder."

She got to work. "Don't be jealous."

# Chapter Four

Peach sangria on a warm day had to be about the most refreshing drink on the friendly face of the Earth. And that wasn't hyperbolic at all. As someone who'd traveled through Spain on a food trip in her early twenties, Gabriella was a fan. And this particular batch, prepared by Loretta Daniel herself, a staple of the Tangle Valley tasting room for decades now, hit the spot.

Gabriella stared at her half-full glass. "This stuff is liquid crack. I might have a second glass and it's a weekday. Don't tell my priest."

Madison frowned. "You have a priest?"

"No. But I wouldn't want him to know."

With the tasting room now closed, Joey, Gabriella, and Madison could relax with Loretta after a long day at the wine office. If only there were wine secretaries and personal assistants to wait on them. One could dream.

"Recap time," Gabriella said. "I made zucchini fritti, a vegetarian carbonara, kickass meatballs, and toasted ravioli. Sold out of all but the fritti. What did you do?" She tossed the question to Joey.

"Poured about six hundred tastes, met with our distributor, visited three of our local wine shops, and called your priest to turn you in. Go," she said and passed the baton to Madison.

"Worked all morning with Bobby on disbudding to remove as much weight as possible from the vines. We then lifted and trellised the good vines. The afternoon had me checking in on the tanks personally. One at a time. We're getting well acquainted. The pinot is coming along nicely. I also gave a tour of the barrel room to a seventh-grade class. Gabriella's priest stood me up for lunch, but there's always tomorrow. Loretta?"

Loretta, their surrogate mother, smiled wearily. "People. Sangria. People. Sangria. And repeat. I also ate an oatmeal cookie from Knead Me on my break. Those guys are my new best friends. I'd send a box of 'em to the priest, but I can't give away what I need for myself. Bless me, Father, for I am selfish."

"Well, that calls for a cheers. We all killed it today," Joey said, initiating the clinking of glasses. Gabriella sipped the cool, sweet glass of sangria as the door across the room opened. Since they were officially closed, everyone swiveled to see who might be approaching.

"An executive walks into a bar." Gabriella said the words as Becca Crawford, Joey's girlfriend, appeared in a muted maroon business suit that had her looking like a million bucks, per usual. With sunglasses perched on top of her head and a small smile on her lips, she looked like an ad for an expensive car, one Gabriella would totally buy. She wondered what it took to look that sophisticated and put together.

Joey's attention rose like a dog who just heard it was dinnertime. "Va-va-voom," she said as Becca approached with a soft sway of her hips. "The Jade Resort's loss is my gain. You're here. With me."

"Hi, baby," Becca said. She leaned across the bar and placed a soft kiss on Joey's lips. The two of them were so perfect together it made Gabriella's insides turn to Jell-O with every loving look they passed. She believed in love when they were around. Oh yes, she did.

"Hi," Joey replied. "Loretta's sangria made fresh. Want some? The visitors went nuts for it. I had to fight them off with sticks."

"Painful. Your specialty, I hear?" Becca asked Loretta, whose cheeks went pink with pride.

"Well, yes." She tossed a towel onto her shoulder, and her green eyes sparkled. "I've spent a few years perfecting my recipe. I think brandy is the key, and in the right balance to fruit."

Madison offered Loretta a fist bump, which she accepted. "Woman after my own heart."

"Hey, I passed Ryan Jacks's truck on the way over here," Becca said. "How did the first day of construction go? Exciting."

All eyes shifted to Gabriella. "Starting to look like a crazy disaster area, which I suppose is the point, so I'm going to go with successful?"

Joey nodded seriously. "The real question is did you see Ryan Jacks actually wearing a tool belt?"

"A woman doesn't tool and tell," Gabriella scoffed. "Ryan was very professional. She did give me a much appreciated pepperoni endorsement that earned her street cred, however."

"Pizzamino's," the group said in near unison.

Gabriella blinked. "You have to stop holding out on me. We've talked about this."

Becca pulled out her phone like a boss, dialed, and waited. "Hi, we'd like to order two large pepperoni pizzas to be delivered to the Tangle Valley tasting room."

Gabriella turned to Joey with conviction. "Listen to me. This is why you can never let her go. Did you see the response time?"

Joey melted. "I don't plan on it. She's kind, smart, and gets important things like pepperoni in a pinch done."

"There's pizza coming," Gabriella announced to the vastly empty room.

Becca clicked off the call. "Twenty minutes."

"You're getting an awesome Christmas present," Gabriella said, pointing at her.

When the pizza arrived piping hot, Gabriella beamed. While it wasn't her mama's dough, or her own for that matter, she liked what Pizzamino's had done with the pie. The pepperoni, as Ryan promised, was crispy and flavorful. She planned to chat up their kitchen later in the week and swap tricks. She made a mean pizza, but the perfect pepperoni crisp eluded her, and she didn't want to lie awake for weeks trying to figure out why.

"Hey, how did the softball thingy go with Clem?" Joey asked, once they'd gathered around the table for their impromptu meal. Pizza paired with sangria certainly didn't suck.

"Oh, you're doing it?" Madison asked, dabbing the sauce from the corner of her mouth.

Gabriella sat taller as a shot of excitement hit like lightning. "Yep. I stopped by the Biscuit during their lull and talked with Clementine about the team. Muskrats is an interesting name, but I'm working it through. They can be feisty when called upon, I imagine."

"Have you seen their logo?" Joey made a little muskrat face.

"Oh no."

"Oh yes," Madison said, enjoying this. "Please make that exact face every time you're at bat."

Joey made the face again. It was remarkably accurate and disarming.

"You have to stop that," Gabriella said, laughing. Then all four of them made the face, and it was forever seared into her memory. "Well, I'm a Muskrat now, so you're going to be looking that way a lot."

"Not a problem," Joey said and made half her fist into a tiny paw shape. "Total battle cry. I'm ready. When's the first game?"

"In a week. I'm third base." She made a *yikes* face. "I guess I should practice. I already missed the team's one and only. Is this league competitive?"

"Does Al Roker have sexy glasses?" Loretta asked emphatically around a slice.

Gabriella squinted at her friends for help. "Does he? I don't know this stuff."

Joey took over the explanation. "It's a pretty competitive league. Slow-pitch. Four coed teams all named after various rodents. No one is clear on why. The Muskrats, the Otters, the Prairie Dogs, and the Gophers."

"Technically otters aren't rodents," Madison said, raising a finger. "They're from the order Carnivora, which—"

"They're close enough," Joey said. She turned back to Gabriella. "Two teams emerge to the championship game, which is what everyone talks about. One becomes the season winner and is revered across Whisper Wall for eight months before we do it all over again."

Gabriella blinked. "I want to be revered across Whisper Wall. Held upon shoulders. Sprayed with the most expensive of champagnes."

"I see a lot of third base outs in the future," Becca said, raising her sangria. She gestured to Gabriella with her glass. "Also? That face is a lot more formidable than the muskrat one."

"Well, we'll be there to cheer you on," Joey said.

Becca nodded along. "Wouldn't miss it. Sky loves outdoor sports." Becca had adopted her dog Skywalker from a rescue ranch on the outskirts of town. They'd hit it off in a big way, and he'd become a kind of fixture at the vineyard lately. The Tangle Valley mascot. Guests loved him, and he loved them back.

"Oh, you need to drop him by the remodel sometime. Ryan brings her dog to work. Dale. He has the sweetest eyes and most rubbable belly. Sleeps a lot, though."

Becca furrowed her brow. "I can't believe you're cheating on Sky."

"I was scouting him friends. He'll be thrilled. If he can find a way to wake Dale."

They clinked glasses. "You're actually right. I'll swing him by."

Madison sat back in her chair and folded her arms. "Like you're not practically living in the Big House."

*Hey, wait.* Joey didn't argue with the insinuation that Becca and Sky had all but moved into her recently inherited home, handed down by her grandparents. Gabriella let her mouth fall open. "Maddie's right. You two are officially shacking up."

"I wouldn't say *officially*," Becca said.

"When was the last time you stayed at your place?" Madison asked.

Loretta waved them off. "You leave these two gals alone. They're in love and it shows, and if they want to pretend they're not shacking up when they are definitely shacking up, well, then we won't stop them."

"I can get behind that," Madison said. She worked well with logic.

Joey wasn't fazed. She tucked a blond strand of hair behind her ear and grinned proudly. "You don't have to. We're totally shacking up. Unofficially."

Becca laughed. "Guess the cat's out of the unofficial bag."

"More like two cats in the sack," Gabriella shot back. "Too much?"

Joey laughed. "It's perfect." She looked at Becca with such affection in her eyes that it made Gabriella's heart thud. "We're happy. Why not admit that to the world?"

"I couldn't agree more." Becca leaned in for a kiss that pulled a collective *awww* from the others.

Gabriella remembered those days, happy with someone new, excited for what was to come. The problem? It always seemed to fizzle or, worse, flare with unnecessary drama. Her first girlfriend had been insanely jealous and threw fits of rage when Gabriella so much as spoke with other women, a requirement of her job. Her second needed constant attention. Then there had been her and Madison, two people who were too different to appreciate each other's perspective when it came to matters of the heart. Madison was all logic and reason, and Gabriella led with her passion. It was a no-go. Any other minor love interests along the way had only made life harder. For Gabriella, life on her own was good. No, great, and this time, focusing on just herself was the goal. No complications. No weird or disappointing dates. No conflict or broken hearts. Gabriella found the pursuit of love and all things romantic exhausting. That didn't seem to be the case for Joey and Becca. But then, they were different. Maybe their search was over, and they were the real deal. In fact, she felt more and more confident of that by the day.

"To shacking up and sinfully good sangria," Gabriella said sincerely.

"You forgot crispy pepperoni," Loretta said, raising a happy slice. "And I'll never forgive myself for it. To all the things!"

They cheered each other and enjoyed a lively dinner as the sun began to set over the grapes of Tangle Valley on a brisk day in spring. Gabriella's heart swelled. This feeling right here? Content. At ease. Relaxed. This was exactly what she'd come to Tangle Valley in search of. She could breathe easy, and for that, she was grateful.

# CHAPTER FIVE

Patsy's Boot and Scoot sat like a beacon of neon on a stretch of land set apart from the rest of civilization. Country music escaped from its walls anytime a patron opened the door. To find it, one had to travel down a lonely dark road until the Scoot's bright lights lit up your path—a neon image of Patsy, looking voluptuous and welcoming from back in her heyday. Ryan parked her truck in the dirt lot and hopped down, taking note of the impressive number of vehicles already there. Gonna be a rowdy one at the Scoot. The new Kacey Musgraves song drifted her way. Ryan caught the door and made her way inside, taking in the familiar combo smell of French fries and beer. The bar, behind which hung a million different brightly lit signs, was well stocked and always full of people sipping and sitting.

"Well, look who made it," Billy said, when she took a spot next to him at the bar. He had a drink in front of him and his ball cap turned customarily backward.

"I couldn't let your one night out go to waste," she said and smacked his shoulder. "What are you drinking?"

He grinned. "Hard apple cider."

"You are not."

"Yes, I am. It's delicious, too. Like a hug from an apple."

She stared at him. "Don't say that sentence to anyone else, okay? I mean that."

"Two scraggly people out and about," Lonzo said, arriving next to them and wearing his actual boots. There wasn't a country bone in his body until he showed up at the Scoot. Then you'd think he was raised in Nashville. He gave each of their heads a squeeze-shake combo as he sailed past on his way to the dance floor, boots ready to go. Ryan knew better than to try to hold any conversation with the guy when he was ready to cut loose. For a guy maybe twenty years their senior, he could sure shake his ass.

"Dark brew for ya, Ry?" Patsy asked as she approached, bright red lipstick in place. She owned the place and came with a personality as tall as her hair. Though she was old enough to be Ryan's mother, she behaved more like a sassy aunt who had no problem shooting her mouth off when guests got out of hand, and flirting with whoever, wherever. As was customary, she grabbed Ryan's face across the bar and gave it a squeeze, which was Patsy for *Glad to see you.*

"I'll take one, yeah. Since my buddy here has the cider all covered."

"Don't you make fun of my Billy. He's taking it slow like a good boy."

He held up his timid little drink and grinned proudly like a kid who'd just received high marks from a teacher. She shook her head at him, secretly adoring the hell out of the nerd. They'd worked together six years now, and when you spent that much time with a guy, you learned to trust him, depend on his solid presence. She and Billy had a friendship like none other she'd known. He was a keeper.

Patsy slid a local vanilla stout her way, and Ryan took that first remarkable sip. She didn't get much further than that when someone said her name from behind. Oh, hello. She knew that voice. She'd heard it in the throes on more than one occasion.

She swiveled around to find Heather Leonard grinning at her, perfect teeth on display. Her top was low-cut as always, but her hair was different than last she'd seen her, slightly shorter and recently highlighted. Ryan prided herself on noticing those kinds of details because they mattered. She sent Heather an appreciative grin. "I really like your hair."

"You have good eyes. Had it done this afternoon." Heather gave it a subtle toss as her tongue wet her bottom lip. "We should dance tonight. Come find me when you're through?" She gestured to Ryan's beer, which Ryan held up in response.

"I'm there." They held eye contact for another couple of beats, and next to her she heard Billy chuckle quietly with his back to the whole scene. Once Heather moved on, she turned to him. "What? I'm just sitting at the bar."

"You've been here three minutes."

"No way. Four."

"Doesn't matter. They're already showing up. Who are you going home with tonight? And don't say no one. My money is on Shana from the little café in the grocery store. The one who always puts the heart in your cappuccino foam. She's got it bad."

"Who says I'm going home with anyone? I'm actually pretty tired. Long week already."

He laughed into his beer.

"Knock it off. I'm not that awful."

"Who said anything about awful? Hell, I'm impressed. Fucking jealous over here. I don't get cappuccino hearts. I wish I had your game, which honestly seems to consist of smiling and existing."

"Drink your juice." She turned back to her beer, unfortunately knowing that what he said was likely. She'd probably dance and chat and finally accept some sort of offer, only to do it all again next week. The whole thing lacked heart. She'd never felt it more than recently.

"If it isn't the destroyer of walls."

Ryan turned to her left at the declaration and saw none other than Gabriella Russo, the chef from Tangle Valley, standing next to her stool. Only she looked different than she had the few times they'd seen each other this week. She was out of her chef's coat and comfortable shoes. Her dark hair, which she often wore halfway pulled back, fell across her forehead to her shoulders, which were partially visible in the green sundress. A surreptitious glance down showed off strappy sandals and beautifully polished toes—turquoise. Ryan found herself in a state to which she was unaccustomed: lacking words. Gabriella grinned and watched Ryan likely resembling an idiot. In desperate response, she nodded and lifted her beer. By the time she finally came up with something to say, by the grace of God, Patsy had already ambled over and taken center stage.

"The best chef in the west is here," she crowed, then looked down the line and saw Joey and Madison, too. "Aw, shucks, it's the whole damn gang. What did I do to earn this? No one told me. Come here, sweetheart." Patsy reached across the bar and squeezed Joey's face and then each of the others'.

"We're here to scoot. Girls' night," Joey told her.

"Our executive hottie is missing. She working late?" Patsy asked.

"Yes, hotel hours and all. But we had a lovely morning to make up for what would be a late night." Joey grinned and slipped into an impressive shade of strawberry. Ryan enjoyed seeing Joey Wilder hot and heavy with someone new after the town obsessed about her being left at the altar a few years back. Happy and carefree looked good on her. Not as good as that sundress on Gabriella, though. She blinked and stole another luxurious glimpse. When her mouth went uncharacteristically dry, she took another swallow of beer.

"Cat got your tongue tonight, Ryan Jacks?" Gabriella asked with a side of sass. The group seemed energetic. Rowdy, like they were already in the midst of a fantastic night out together.

"I'm just decompressing from a very successful day making your dreams come true. You can thank me later."

Gabriella's eyes went wide. "I'm not going to argue with the dreams part. You might have to wait a while on the formal thank-you. It's going that well?"

"I had the electrician in there today, taking a look at what we'll need. He sees no major issues. Just some rewiring for the kitchen specifically to pass inspection."

"That's what I like to hear." She touched her newly delivered draft beer to Ryan's longneck, then craned her neck around Ryan. "Good to see you, Billy. I like your shirt. How's your daughter?"

"Thank you. She's starting on algebra early," he said, beaming. "She's really smart." Gotta love the guy and his big heart.

"Aw, that's the best. You must be proud of her."

He touched his chest. "I really am. Her mom is, too."

"You should see the kid. She got the best from both parents." Ryan turned more fully to Gabriella. "Will you be dancing tonight?"

"You know, the night is young, and I'm going to play that one by ear."

"Maybe I'll see you out there."

Gabriella nodded but didn't say anything for a minute. "Yeah, well, you never know." She offered a smile but it was delayed. What the hell did a delayed smile mean? Ryan couldn't tell if she'd made an impression, or if Gabriella was merely tolerating her. Five minutes into a conversation with Billy about whether or not they should bring in Doug D. for the paint job at Tangle Valley, and Ryan realized she wasn't fully listening. Hell, she was replaying her damn exchange with Gabriella Russo and keeping track of where she was in the bar. In this particular moment, she happened to be standing on the edge of the dance floor, chatting animatedly with Clementine. Ryan focused on her beer, and then Billy, and then Gabriella again, and then her beer.

"Are you even in there right now? What the hell, Jacks?" Billy asked.

She swiveled to him. "Of course. I'm just enjoying the music. See?" She grooved to the beat. The song was something from years ago, but she bopped her head to feign interest. "I can't help it if I'm moved by the tunes of yesteryear, Billy. I can't be held down."

"You're a damn liar. Two seconds ago, you told me I could take your truck to Mexico and leave it there."

She blinked and grinned. "Did I?"

"Straight up."

"I'm not that attached to it is all."

He inclined his head toward the dance floor. "I don't know who's on your mind, but they got a firm grip. Is it the chef?" He shook his head. "She's really pretty, Ry. Another level. I like her, too. She's quick."

Now that Billy had broached the topic, she leaned in, eager for an outside opinion. "This is the thing. Are you ready?"

He rolled his shoulders. "Put me in, coach. Born ready."

"I can't tell where I stand. If she'd be into it or not, you know? She's playful, but maybe she's just being friendly." Ryan shook her head. "It's weird."

Billy snorted. "Best day *ever*. Since when has Ryan Jacks been on the ropes about a woman and her feelings?" He leaned in. "It's not weird. It's how the world works. You've just had it different than the rest of us, but no more. Fuck, yeah." He slapped the bar, enjoying this too damn much.

She scoffed, "Who said anything about feelings?"

He stole a glance at Gabriella and her friends and didn't have the decency to be discreet. "She doesn't seem like the hookup type to me. She's put together. Smart."

"Smart people like to have fun, too."

"I guess there's only one way to find out. Work your magic."

Billy tipped his hat to her, content to keep his barstool warm. She knew him well enough to know he was the kind of guy who just liked being around other folks and having a brew. He didn't need to go hard and, in fact, turned in by ten p.m. most nights they went out. Ryan was the adventurous half of the duo. She stepped off her stool, downed the last of her beer, squeezed Billy's shoulder, and headed toward the action. She was ten feet from Gabriella and smiled when their eyes connected. She needed something clever to say, but for whatever reason, her brain cells abandoned her. Should she say something about cooking? No. She knew very little. The restaurant? They shouldn't only talk about work. Where were the good words? She felt her smile dim. Her stomach hitched weirdly, and she was hyperaware of the volume of the music. The sweat began to prickle the back of her neck from all the people, and she craved more space. Gabriella tilted her head, a questioning look crossing her features. Ryan opened her mouth to at least say the word *hey*, when Heather Leonard appeared, wrapped her arms around Ryan's waist, and kissed her cheek.

"Time for that dance? I've missed you." Another kiss to the cheek.

Normally, Ryan would have grinned and given Heather a squeeze or her hair a nuzzle. Tonight, she froze, as did Gabriella, whose lips parted subtly at the display in front of her. After a beat, she lifted her beer to Ryan and turned back to her friends. No. God. *Disaster.* Heather gave her arm a tug, and Ryan followed her blindly to the center of the dance floor where they joined a two-step in progress. It got worse. Heather was pretty handsy tonight, running hers lightly across the front of Ryan's black shirt, down her back to her ass. When the music finally shifted, Ryan took the opportunity to disentangle herself from Heather, who'd turned into a one-woman TSA agent. She hadn't made it off the dance floor before Lana McCarver grabbed her for a slow dance. Both of them in one night? Lana was a sweet girl who'd left her husband eight months ago. In her own personal quest to discover more about her sexuality, she'd taken an interest in Ryan and her abilities in the bedroom.

Lana leaned in. "You look fantastic."

"I could say the same about you." Lana's shoulder-length dark blond hair was down, her lips glossy.

"I haven't seen you out in weeks," Lana whispered. "Any chance we could steal some time soon? You're probably busy, but I miss our one-on-ones, you know?"

Ryan did know. Lana was ambitious about making up for lost time now that she'd found this part of herself. Sex—that's what Lana missed. She wasn't interested in a relationship, but she very much liked no-strings action, and Ryan had very much liked Lana and their arrangement. "I've been slammed at work and crashing most nights, but yeah, I'd like that."

"Then I will be calling you soon. Unless, of course, you're free later tonight. Am I that lucky?" She leaned in close. "I will make it worth your while. It's been too long, and you know what I'm like."

Ryan hesitated. That seemed like a plum offer. Any other night, Ryan would have capitalized and headed back to Lana's place, but apparently some kind of screw had come loose and she hesitated. "Tonight's not the best for me." A lie. She was wide open. What the hell?

"No worries," Lana said and slipped her fingertips behind Ryan's hair, lighting touching the back of her neck. "I know you have your hands full." She glanced at Heather, who eyed them like an impatient predator.

"Oh no," Ryan said, squashing the Heather assumption. "I'm just tired. I'll probably head home before too long and catch up on sleep. Alone. It's not like that."

"You know that none of that matters to me, right?" Lana asked. "You see other people, and I'm fine with that. I'm a big girl."

That was the great thing about Lana. She was kind and came with very few expectations. She knew Ryan liked to have fun, and maybe that was part of Ryan's appeal. Lana could explore herself, her wants, her desires without worrying about getting herself into something she wasn't even clear she wanted. Ryan smiled as the song wound to its end. "Trust me. You're someone I can always be up front with. I don't have other plans."

"Okay then." She leaned close to Ryan's ear. "Call me soon, and we'll have a two-person party."

Ryan nodded and Lana left, leaving her alone on the dance floor as the music shifted. She headed back toward Billy, passing Joey, Madison, and Gabriella, who were situated at a tall table along the perimeter of the dance floor. In other words, a front row seat. As she passed, Gabriella raised her eyebrows in what seemed to be appreciation. "Nice work out there," she said with a friendly smile. "You know how to juggle."

Ryan laughed, wildly aware of her own behavior and uncomfortable seeing it through Gabriella's eyes. "Thanks, I think."

When she arrived back at the stool next to Billy's, he greeted her with high-pitched laughter. "I gotta say, that was entertaining as hell. More of that, please." He pretended to draw on an invisible whiteboard the way a coach would map out a play. With his finger, he tracked the action on the board. "First we had a Chef Gabriella meetup that was sideswiped—literally, I might add—by a Heather swoop-in, followed by a Lana sneak attack at the end." He clapped her on the back. "This is your life, my friend. I am merely an engaged spectator, waving at your wild ride from the safety of the ground, clutching my beer and pearls."

That was her cue to look smug or laugh along with him. She couldn't seem to. "Just not feeling it tonight. I'll kill one more with you. Then how about we get out of here? Call it a night."

His smile faded. "You okay? Not enjoying the loop-de-loops?"

She shrugged. "You know me. I'm always okay." She wasn't,

though. She felt done with all this. Ryan raised her finger to Patsy's barely legal bartender and grinned like Ryan Jacks would, trying to own the mask. "One more round for us, and we'll close out." She passed Billy a look. "On me."

"Shucks, Jacks. You shouldn't have."

❖

At seven a.m. sharp, Gabriella's alarm erupted in a soothing song most likely recorded on top of a mountain by a band of monks with long flutes. That was what she imagined, anyway, as she let the music bathe her in peace. She smiled in greeting at the new day, gave her shoulders a lift, and exhaled. With relaxed muscles, she pushed herself into a sitting position and rearranged three fluffy pillows behind her, poised to wake up slowly and take in the view from her bedroom window.

Green grass sloping downhill. A healthy spattering of wildflowers. An old oak reaching up and out as if to shake hands with the sun.

Sweet Lord, she'd never get used to this beauty. If she angled all the way to the right, she could catch a glimpse of the tangled vines and their green grapes, ripening to purple for the next harvest of pinot gris. Madison had some sort of special project going on that would allow them to keep the good buds and lose the bad ones. There'd been folks in the fields for days now, working on each individual vine, providing lots of attention. Madison was not one to cut any corners, so the days had been long.

Gabriella gave herself a squeeze and blinked happily. The first ten minutes of every morning mattered to her. She used the quiet to wake up her thoughts, take stock, and prepare for what she had ahead. In fact, she made it a point not to speak in those ten minutes, to herself or anyone else. Those minutes should be sacred and her mind quiet. She had the rest of the day to be loud and opinionated.

Six more minutes.

Wearing her customary sleep attire, a T-shirt and panties, she tossed an arm over her head and allowed her thoughts to drift back to the night before at the Scoot. She grinned when she remembered Joey working so hard to teach her how to line dance, a skill she picked up pretty damn quick if she did say so herself. Then there were the two out-of-town guys who tried to pick up Madison because she looked fantastic. They'd been relentless until she finally told them that her husband would be arriving any moment from axe-throwing practice. Finally, her mind shifted to sexy Ryan Jacks, who clearly had her hands full with the wanton women of Whisper Wall. She was obviously a hot commodity and enjoying every minute of it. Why shouldn't she? Ryan was young and so good-looking it almost hurt to look at her. She'd dressed casually for the bar that night in dark jeans and a simple black shirt that would look plain on anyone else. On Ryan, it more than worked. It was all she needed. With that gorgeous dark hair that hung past her shoulders and dreamy blue eyes that contrasted with her tan, Ryan could make a nun rethink her life choices. Gabriella grinned because Ryan had been so incredibly cute when she opened her mouth to speak and then paused, like she'd forgotten the most important of things.

Three minutes.

A new understanding struck. Her heart was thumping, and her palms itched. Thinking about Ryan Jacks had apparently gotten her unexpectedly keyed up. What in the world was that about? But she knew and resisted the self-recrimination. Like the rest of the universe, she found Ryan off-the-charts attractive and was paying for it now. She shifted in bed, acutely aware of her body's newly awake sensitivity. She remembered Ryan's gaze connecting with hers at the bar and those startling blue eyes dancing. Where had those eyes come from? Unexpectedly, she imagined Ryan's gaze on her now. Everywhere. She swallowed. Her panties were now wet, and she lightly touched herself on the outside of the fabric, prompting her eyes to slam shut. Too many pleasing sensations hit. She checked the clock with one eye, realizing that she needed to get a move on. No more minutes. Plus, Ryan Jacks was not the wisest person to fantasize about. In fact, given what Gabriella had witnessed the night before, the woman should have caution tape draped all over her. She wasn't for the faint of heart, and Gabriella was no player. She wasn't going to beat herself up for her little Ryan crush, but she wasn't going to indulge or fantasize about the woman any further either. Too many more important things to concentrate on.

After showering and prepping for the day, Gabriella walked the perimeter of the property along the row of quaint cottages en route to Jolene, where she would start prep for the day's service, beginning with the fettuccini she'd been itching to roll out. She'd finish with the creation of an ingredient assembly line for a crowd favorite, the Goodfella—a slider topped with salami, pepperoni, prosciutto, mozzarella, roasted red peppers, and her famous vinaigrette. She worked quietly with the exception of an occasional *bam, huzzah,* or *what-what.* Cooking simply required sound effects. It had always been her way. She was not at all aware that her body was still turned the hell on from earlier. Nope. She hadn't noticed at all. Sigh. If only she could find the off switch and stop thinking about sex.

Some sort of power tool roared to life behind her in the distance. Interesting. She checked her watch. Way too early for Ryan, yet she caught sight of her maroon truck peeking out from the side of the building. Curiosity got the best of her, and Gabriella paused her work and took the short walk to the jobsite just in time to see Ryan, alone, sanding a column complete with the sexy goggle things to protect her eyes. Yeah, she was definitely a sight for Gabriella's already exacerbated state.

She swallowed back the burst of lust and watched a moment, unsure whether it was rude to interrupt someone wielding a power tool. They'd not covered that in any of her schooling. She didn't have to wonder for long, however, as Ryan saw her there and grinned. Dammit. The dimples. The eyes. All of it. She wore faded jeans, a white T-shirt, and her dark hair up in a high ponytail. Ryan silenced the sander and raised a hand. "Hey." Such a simple word, but when Ryan said it, she felt it.

"You're early." Dumb observation. What did it matter? She ordered her brain to return to the regularly scheduled version of herself without delay. She'd fake the confidence she was used to having if she had to.

"I know. I have another commitment this afternoon, so I need to knock off early and didn't want to short you on time."

"Isn't that unusual for a contractor? I've always imagined you guys did what you wanted."

Ryan blinked because that probably sounded insulting. "It's not unusual for me. I make sure I put in the time. You're actually my second stop today." She gestured to the road with her thumb. "Checked on a job of mine a couple miles from here on the way."

"I didn't mean to insinuate you were lazy or less than dedicated. Sorry it sounded that way."

Ryan shrugged. "I'm good."

"Okay."

Dammit. Had she made it weird? Should that matter? She was the client, after all, but rapport mattered to her. In fact, Gabriella appreciated the way Ryan seemed to care so much about her job. It spoke to her character, her work ethic. "When did you get started in the business?" She held up a hand. "I'm probably distracting you."

Ryan shook her head. "Nope." She hesitated. "Hard to say exactly. I started apprenticing when I was seventeen and went full-time after graduation, learning all I could along the way. I was a day worker first and opened up my own operation six years ago."

"I forget you're a kid."

A pause. Ryan grinned. "Except I'm not. At all."

She raised an eyebrow. "Twenty-seven?"

"See? Way off. I'm twenty-eight." Ryan looked at her in victory.

"A baby."

Ryan scoffed, "And you're what? All of thirty? So much time on me."

Gabriella tried to stand taller than her small frame allowed. "Actually, I'm thirty-four."

"Which is so super different."

"Oh, you're a smart-ass," Gabriella said with a hint of fire. "That's six years of life on you. Of wisdom." She caught herself before saying *maturity* because that seemed unkind.

"Good thing I'm advanced for my age."

Gabriella laughed until her gaze landed on something that snagged her attention away from the topic. "Wait a sec. The shape of that column is not what we talked about."

Ryan surveyed the column in front of her. "It's incredibly close."

Gabriella came father into the room and stood next to her. "Not close enough."

Ryan sighed, which she didn't love. "What's the issue exactly?"

"What's the issue?" she repeated, incredulous. "Look at the curve at the base. The sketches you sent over before we started had no curve. You can't just change what we decided."

Ryan turned to her. "Very minor in the scheme of things, and I think it adds a little flavor. The sketches are a guide, but sometimes I get pulled a little this way or that way when inspiration strikes. It's one of the things my clients like about my work. Joey and I actually talked about that very quality when she hired me." Ryan was downplaying this when it was anything but minor.

"Yeah, well, this is too important to me to defer to your inspiration, okay? Joey handed control to me, and I have a very specific idea of what I want this restaurant to be. I'm the client."

"You're the client," Ryan said with a tight smile, but it was clear she was stifling what she really wanted to say, and that irked Gabriella.

"I say what goes."

"Right. I think you just said that in different words."

Gabriella blinked, feeling heard, but patronized, too. Her cheeks heated and her brain sped up. She didn't like conflict, but she also didn't shy away from it when it was something that mattered. Fun and fearless. That's how her mother had always described her.

"You're definitely in charge," Ryan stated, then paused, scratched her eyebrow, and looked at the ground. "Just, that doesn't mean you always know what's best."

"Oh, and you do? With your vast restaurant background."

"I have a little experience about which details make a room pop." She held her hands up and shrugged, as if minimizing what she seemed to feel passionately about. "But if you want to lose the very regal curve, we can go with a standard column. Boring is fine with me."

Gabriella blew out a breath, frustrated now and second-guessing herself. "You really think it'll be boring?"

"I believe you've already pointed out that it doesn't matter what I think, right? You're the client."

Oh, that just annoyed her more. Gabriella pinched the bridge of her nose, now overthinking the whole column thing and realizing how behind she was on her food prep for lunch. "Leave it for now. Let me marinate on it. I think I'm just concerned that you're pivoting from what we discussed, and that has me a little freaked out about what else you're going to pivot on."

Ryan seemed to relent, her gaze finding Gabriella's. "I will be sure to check in with you when a thought like this one occurs."

"That's all I'm asking."

"Right. Got it, boss. No creativity."

She squinted. Ryan was annoyed. She could tell, and that, in turn, annoyed her. "You don't have to call me that."

"Ms. Russo. I apologize."

"Gabriella is fine." This was getting worse by the moment, so what did she have to lose? She decided to speak her mind now that anger fueled her courage. "Also, I don't know if you noticed, but there are a few water bottles, soda cans, things like that along the steps outside.

Can we maybe get those cleaned up?" She tried to sound brighter, friendlier when she said it. Courage didn't always last.

"Understood. I'll get on it. Tell the guys less mess." She looked at the column and back to Gabriella with a sigh. "Anything else?"

Gabriella pursed her lips. Regret fired. "No. I'll, uh, let you get back to work."

Ryan nodded, forced a polite smile, and flipped on the sander, ending any chance of further conversation, which was probably for the best. As Gabriella walked back to the truck, she pondered it all. Where did Ryan get off going rogue and pivoting from their agreed upon design? The challenging smile had also gotten under Gabriella's skin. You know what? So did Ryan's casual behavior with those women the night before. She tried to shake it off as she got back to work, but Ryan had definitely irked her. Gone was the lust of this morning, and in its place, irritation rose and stayed with her throughout the lunch service. She rolled out her pasta with extra force. She seasoned her sauce with excessive vigor and tossed her pizza dough a little higher than normal.

That helped. What would also help? The softball game she had on her schedule for later that afternoon. She'd slug a few softballs into oblivion, hammer a couple throws from third to first, and help right her state of mind.

She plated a slice of prosciutto and arugula pizza and handed it to a customer with a smile. Ryan Jacks was someone Gabriella needed to move to the back burner of her brain. In fact, done. Banished. Life was too short for good-looking young things with way too much confidence for their own good.

# CHAPTER SIX

Ryan arrived at the duo of ballfields with her bat bag over her shoulder and Wayfarers on her face. Perfect day for a little softball, and she, for one, could use the release. Her four-mile morning run had long worn off, and her muscles were ready for a little action. She could also use the distraction. Her day had gotten off to a rocky start with that run-in with Gabriella Russo, who maybe wasn't so sweet after all. Sassy was a better word for her. A spitfire. Opinionated, too. Something about her had Ryan perpetually on her heels, and that left her out of sorts and wildly uncomfortable. Okay, and a little pissed off. She knew the column shape was perfect for the space, but she'd swallow her opinion in the future and keep her damn head down.

"You ready to take out a few Muskrats?" Billy asked, turning his cap backward as he leaned against the dugout. "Pick 'em off like little bitches?"

Ryan winced. "Harsh."

"I know. Trying something new. No?"

"Not really you. But to answer your first question, yes. Been dreaming about this game all afternoon. How'd it go at Ruby Lane?"

"Homestretch. I bet we wrap up tomorrow. Next day at the latest, and then I'll head back to you at Tangle Valley. Did you see Wrigley is here?" Billy turned and waved at his daughter in the stands, but it was Ryan Wrigley pointed and waved at. She hurried to the fence and blew the little girl a kiss. She caught it and blew one back. Their own little game. Wrigley was seven going on sixteen and into all the latest clothes and trends, and anything girly. Ryan tried her best to keep up and spoiled her rotten whenever possible.

"You think your dad's gonna make it on base today?" she called to Wrigley.

Wrigley stole a glance at Billy and shook her head sadly. "Probably not. Didn't last time."

"Hey!" He looked between them. "Have a little faith in me, please. I don't come to your soccer games and predict your failures to other second graders."

Wrigley laughed and so did Ryan. They double-teamed him a lot.

The rest of the Otters were already warming up on the grassy area next to the diamond, throwing pop flies and grounders and cheering for each other to get the energy up. Ryan had joined the Otters as their first baseman three years prior, and after winning the championship last season, she was ready for a repeat. Sure, there were only four teams in the league, but a championship was a championship, and in this town, bragging rights mattered.

She stole a glance at the Muskrats in their bright yellow uniforms warming up on the other side of the diamond. The Otters wore red, which Ryan couldn't help think might be part of their success. Red meant business. Yellow was…cute. She warmed up with Billy, making sure her arm was loose and chattering up the group for morale.

"Looking good, Billy."

"Get at it," he shouted back. She snagged the grounder and fired a missile back, landing it squarely in the pocket of his glove.

"Nice one," he yelled and gave his hand a small shake from the force of her throw.

"You're killing it, Brenda Anne. More like that," Ryan shouted to their right fielder, as she easily caught a pop-up. "Go hard, Constance," she called to the local veterinarian chasing down a wayward ball. "That's the way to hustle." Ryan loved her team and reveled in anticipation as she headed to the dugout before the start of the game.

"You all set?" Powell Rogers, the used-car salesman, asked her. He served as both their coach and pitcher and wore his Otters ball cap perched extra high on his head, as always. She swallowed a smile because it just looked so tiny up there.

She did a couple jumps to loosen her calves and nodded. "Let's give 'em a game."

He tipped his hat and turned to the team who'd gathered in the dugout. As he went over the lineup, the Muskrats took the field first, the infield taking turns throwing to first base one at a time. Ryan focused on Powell, who had her down fourth in the lineup, batting cleanup, likely because she often hit the sweet spot with her line drives and managed doubles, triples, and the occasional inside-the-park homer.

"Remember—Muskrats aren't Otters. You hear me?" Powell asked loudly. The group picked up their cue.

"Muskrats aren't Otters!" the team chanted back in unison, their standard practice. "Muskrats aren't Otters! Muskrats aren't Otters! Down with the Muskrats. Otters win, win, win." Their hands flew to the center and up again on that last part. Ryan rolled her shoulders just as the Muskrats' third baseman beamed a ball to first in her peripheral vision. Whoa. She swiveled, blinked, impressed by the speed. Since when had Bruno, the wine guy from the Jade Resort, picked up that kind of skill? He'd always been an easy target, missing most of the balls sent his way and struggling to connect with first. No, this was someone new. She squinted at the much smaller third baseman. Definitely not Bruno. The dark ponytail coming out the back of the cap confirmed it. The player adjusted her cap, and Ryan paused midbreath. "What in hell?" she murmured.

"You seeing what I'm seeing?" Billy asked, his fingers through the chain link of the dugout's fence as he watched the action on the field.

She turned to him in shock. "It looks like our client is a Muskrat."

"And has fucking ferocious chops. Where was she at the season opener last week?" Billy asked, incredulous.

Ryan sighed. "I'm guessing she's replaced that one guy who turned his ankle. They probably adjusted the field positions for her. Moved folks around." Sure enough. There was Bruno out in center field, kicking grass.

Billy whistled low when Gabriella hopped straight into the air and caught an overthrown ball like a jackrabbit. "What the fuck? Did you see that?" He pointed for emphasis. "I mean, did you *see* that?"

Ryan sighed audibly. Internally, it got her the hell going. "Lucky us."

"This could be bad."

"Don't you worry at all." She scoffed, "They're the Muskrats. They lose. It's ordained." Ryan shook off any intimidation. Couldn't let the other team get in her head. What was harder to banish? How amazingly hot Gabriella Russo looked in a softball uniform, all focused, making crazy catches like a badass. The pants alone looked made for her. It was perplexing. This game day version of Gabriella was nothing at all like her everyday persona, which was decidedly softer. She glanced in the stands and, sure enough, saw Joey Wilder and her girlfriend along with Madison LeGrange. They were making strange little mouse faces at Gabriella, who laughed and made one right back. What the hell? Too late. The game was on.

Two batters scored hits and made it onto base. Great start.

Ryan grabbed a bat and stretched with it before stepping into the on-deck circle and taking a few warm-up swings. Moments later, she was up to bat with two runners on at first and second. She let the first pitch go, always preferring to take her time. Make the pitcher pitch. The second was outside. On the third, she swung fast and hard, savoring the crack of the bat. Nothing the hell like it. The cheers from the crowd fueled her dash to first. Peripherally, she saw Gabriella dive for the ball, stop it, touch her base and hammer it to first a tenth of a second before Ryan landed there. Dammit. Double play. She blinked, swallowed, and fumed, trying to absorb what happened as she walked back to the dugout. As she passed third, Gabriella waved. "Sorry about that, Ryan. Great running, though. Really. Way to hustle."

Ryan nodded back, still half stunned.

The game went on like that. The Muskrats, usually a mildly competitive team, had renewed energy today. Maybe Gabriella's presence and prowess had inspired the rest of them to give a little bit more, run a little faster, swing with more courage, believing they now had a shot.

The Muskrats were last at bat, but luckily, still down by a run. Gabriella strolled to the plate. She was petite but confident as hell at the same time. The way she swung the bat a few times before the first pitch showed off her stellar form. Her last at bats had all been base hits, so Ryan prepared herself to get the damn out this time and end the game with a win. Gabriella swung on the first pitch, and the ball sailed over the heads of the infielders but dropped in just shy of the outfielders in left, giving her time to race to first where she landed safe and sound. She'd also advanced two runners, one who took home. Tied game.

"Hi," she said happily to Ryan once she'd arrived safely on her base. Too much damn pride on display in that beautiful grin.

Ryan exhaled, defeated. "You're trouble."

"For the Otters? Oh yes. You should prepare your pretty face."

Gabriella trash-talked, too? This was new. It had also not escaped Ryan that half the crowd was now doing that little mouse face, which Ryan had determined was actually an impersonation of a feisty little muskrat. "Oh, I'm just fine."

Gabriella looked up at her and their height difference was evident. "You sure about that?"

Ryan wasn't clear whether Gabriella was alluding to the game or Ryan's libido. The possible insinuation derailed her before she rebounded and found her tongue. "Nothing I can't handle," she said as the bat cracked and Gabriella took off to second. The view was too good to pass up, and it cost Ryan the stop, which cost them the out, which lost the Otters the game. "Fuck me," Ryan mumbled as the winning run landed on home plate.

"Oh, she got to you," Billy said with a laugh. He tossed his glove in the air as he made his way in from the outfield. "They said it couldn't be done, but they were wrong. Ryan Jacks has met her match. No, I think she might have been *outmatched*. It's brutal, sports fans."

"Shut up, Billy."

"Beer while we watch the next one?" The Gophers and Prairie Dogs would face off next, in a showdown of orange and blue. She personally had always carried more respect for the Dogs, but that was because the Gophers tended to give up when they were down, making them the weakest team of the four. Maybe this season would be different. She was ready to find out.

"Good game, slugger."

Ryan knew the voice. A chill moved through her as Gabriella approached from the other dugout, ball bag on her shoulder. She dropped it on the bleachers next to Ryan. "Are you using the nickname to tease me?"

"A little. But you played a solid game, and I wanted to be sure you knew it."

"You mean until that last play?"

"I wasn't going to point that one out," Gabriella said with a noticeable twinkle in her eye. Oh yeah, she was savoring the win.

Clementine approached and clapped Gabriella on the back. "What do you think of our new ringer?" she asked Ryan, glowing about her find.

She shrugged. "She had a good first game out."

Clementine smiled, her blue eyes knowing. "The first of many. Come by the Biscuit tomorrow," she told Gabriella. "Free breakfast item for the winning team."

"Hey, we never get a free breakfast when we win," Ryan pointed out. Billy nodded emphatically. He was obsessed with their cinnamon sugar biscuits.

Clementine made a sad face. "Aw. That's because you're not a Muskrat." At the mention of the word, several around them in the stands responded with the newly introduced Muskrat face. Joey Wilder looked rather proud of the trend. Yep, the ringleader. "But stop by anyway, Ryan, and I'll make sure we have some of that jalapeño bacon you love."

"I'm feeling better already," Ryan said with a victorious grin. "I'll be there."

"Just bring your credit card," Gabriella said. That inspired laughter from the group.

Clementine headed out, and Gabriella shook her head. "Don't worry. Your charm is still limitless. I'm sure Clementine is not immune."

"Clem? No, no, no. Strictly friends and neighbors."

"Mm-hmm."

Gabriella turned back to her cheering section. The friends squealed and clapped her on the back in celebration of the victory while Ryan sat there off-kilter and not sure how to right herself. She hated the loss, but the disdain that hung over her felt like more than that. She zeroed in on what it was—the annoyance that Gabriella would think there was even a kernel of something between her and Clementine. It said a lot about Gabriella's impression of her, which likely stemmed from the other night at the Scoot. Unfortunately, that night was a pretty standard one in Ryan's life, which she had mixed feelings about now. She saw herself through another's eyes, namely Gabriella's, someone she liked and admired, and wished she was known for something other than her way with women. She stared at the dirt, numb, as conversation continued around her. So who *did* she want to be? The question was an important one lately. Also unnerving. She looked over her shoulder at Gabriella and her pals a few rows higher on the bleachers. Gabriella laughed at something Madison said, and Ryan caught herself grinning along from afar. She wanted to join in their conversation. Had it been anyone else other than Gabriella, she would have climbed up there to do just that. Instead, she accepted the beer Billy handed her and cheered on the new game, all the while glancing behind her to see how Gabriella reacted to each out, run, or misstep.

"You've got it bad," Billy told her as they headed to the parking lot after the game. "You couldn't even focus on that last inning, and the ridiculous Gophers were actually rallying. That woman has you hooked."

She decided not to push back and faced facts. Billy was right. "I like her a lot. So much that I'm just not myself, and it's starting to freak me out. What the hell am I supposed to do about it?"

He stared at her. "You're asking me? Aren't you the seasoned one at this kind of thing? I've literally had two girlfriends my entire life, and one of them is now my ex-wife."

She leaned against the tailgate of her truck and faced him. "This is different than meeting a woman at a bar. I can do that with my eyes closed, but Gabriella"—she dropped her volume when she said her name, not knowing who was around—"is different. She sees through it all. Through me. She's not a pickup. She's…different."

Billy pulled his face back, for the first time seeming to understand that Ryan wasn't just being Ryan. "You're interested in more with her. Didn't see that coming."

"I know." She nodded. "Maybe a date. A real one?"

"No sex," he cautioned.

"Okay. Got it. Because it's not a hookup." She paused. "None?"

"Absolutely not."

She nodded wholeheartedly. "That makes total sense. How long do people wait, when it's not a hookup?"

He looked skyward, and about as unsure as she was. "Well, respect is key. So at least a few dates. Maybe more."

She nodded enthusiastically, on board. "Got it. I just really want to get to know her. Find out what she likes on a baked potato. Does she like exercise? Movies? That kind of thing. Is that weird? Feels like it is."

He laughed. "The novelty."

She accepted his amusement. "I'll give it a shot. Tomorrow."

When Ryan arrived home at the lake house, she dropped to the floor next to Dale, who lay in his customary spot on the living room rug, on his side, as if no longer living. His preference. He had full access to all her comfy furniture yet chose the coolness of the hardwood for his slumber. Sensing her arrival, he stood, walked a few inches, and swiped a tongue across her face. "Thanks, pal." Dale then lay back down and stared over at her expectantly. That was because this was usually the part where she updated him on her day while he hovered just shy of a brand-new nap.

"Well, we lost the game, and I'm crushing on the other team's third basewoman." He blinked. "She's also my client. Kind of. You made out with her once or twice." He lifted a paw. "No, no, no. Don't be jealous. She might like you more than me." He settled back in and sighed.

She sighed, too. "You and me both, buddy. This stuff is harder than it looks."

❖

It was Tuesday morning, and Jolene was hopping. Gabriella swayed her hips to Demi Lovato, her fake best friend who often kept her company when she worked. Currently, that meant plating a goat cheese torta with crispy shallots for a couple visiting the vineyard from Idaho. She hoped they liked Demi. The head-bopping wife seemed to confirm it.

She handed the small plate to Mr. Idaho and smiled. "Please let me know what you think when you're done. We have a restaurant going in right over there," she said, gesturing to the future site of Tangled, "and this guy just might make it onto the menu if enough people like it. Oh, and it pairs well with the chardonnay in your hand."

"Well, it looks simply beautiful," Mrs. Idaho said, raising her wineglass in thanks. "I'm going to put it on Instagram right now. I'm a new Insta addict. I've got all the filters. Woohoo!"

"Tag us!" Gabriella said as the couple headed to a picnic table to dive in.

"You bet I will," Mrs. Idaho said and gave her hips a shake as she walked. Yeah, she'd had a couple of glasses. More power to Mrs. Idaho on her vacation.

Gabriella tossed a towel on her shoulder. The lunch rush had been more than decent, and she'd finally hit a lull and could breathe. She was taking a few moments to straighten her workstation and reset when the next customer arrived. "What can I get for you?" she asked while giving her counter a quick wipe. She looked up, and everything slowed down. "Well, well. Ryan Jacks, as I live and breathe." She made a playful show of fanning herself.

The dreamy smile appeared. "It smells amazing in there."

"Doesn't it? My life's work."

"You need some sort of medal."

"I never turn away jewelry." She laughed. "And what can I do for you? A consult? Tell me you didn't completely redesign my restaurant on a whim. Are we about to have another fight?"

"Let's save it for later."

"Deal."

"I'm actually here for lunch if that's okay. I usually bring my own, but after several days of downright jealousy watching the tourists eat your food, I thought I'd give it a try."

She took out a twenty and surveyed the menu, which was written in Gabriella's own handwriting on a chalkboard out front. Her selections changed daily, and the flexibility kept Gabriella excited for each new day. She planned on the restaurant having a similar fluidity. Staples on the menu, but floating specials.

"Put that away," she told Ryan. "I'll make you up a sampler plate. I can't have the person who's transforming my dream space light on blood sugar."

"Okay, but let me pay," Ryan said. Her dark hair was down today, which was new at work. The only time she'd seen it down was at the Scoot when the temperature in the room went up three degrees the second Gabriella noticed her at the bar. It was a good look and allowed her to see the slight waves in Ryan's hair that she imagined were natural. The gentle curl complemented Ryan's skin perfectly.

"Your money is no good as long as my restaurant is in your hands." She went to work on Ryan's plate. The torta, a couple bites of toasted ravioli, a side of the pickled vegetables, an arancini ball filled with her famous white wine risotto, and an eggplant caponata. Everything she was serving today. "There."

Ryan stared at the plate. "It think it's too pretty for me to eat."

"Is not. Dig in. Food is meant to be enjoyed, savored. That's an order from the head chef of this amazing blue truck."

Ryan looked around and leaned in. "Are there other chefs in your blue truck? How do you know when to boss them around if they're imaginary?"

"Shut up," Gabriella said and pointed with her spatula. "You can't question blue truck logic." She relaxed and gave in to the logic. "Sometimes there's an intern about, just not today."

Ryan nodded, her eyes dancing. "I like the coat." She gestured with her chin to Gabriella's white chef's coat, which looked like it had been to cooking battle with the food and lost. The ravioli had been an adventure.

She grinned, cocked her hip, and placed a hand on it, in a playful mood today. Maybe it was that softball win hanging on, or the beautiful weather indicative of spring, or the high she got when Ryan paid attention to her. She wasn't proud of that last part. "This old thing? You must be into tomato."

"Deeply." Ryan shrugged. "I think that's just your passion on display. It's hot...out today." Ryan smothered a grin. She was beyond smooth and proud of herself.

Gabriella laughed and sidestepped the insinuation. "My passion on display. Gonna use that." She dropped her vegetable scraps into the trash and gave her cutting board a good wiping down as Ryan watched through the truck's service window. She had her food but didn't seem to be going anywhere. Gabriella didn't mind.

"Have lunch with me if you haven't eaten."

Gabriella paused. Eat with Ryan? It was true that she hadn't had a moment to grab lunch for herself yet, something she normally did on the fly, and this *was* an opportune time. No line at the truck and she hadn't seen any new cars drive onto the property. She met those deep blue eyes and shifted her weight, ignoring their effect. "I guess if we're fast and eat at the table closest to Jolene."

"I'm sorry. Jolene? Who is that?" Ryan glanced behind her at the couple eating their lunch. "Do you have an imaginary friend we should talk about? Invite to lunch?"

"Jolene," Gabriella said as if it was the most obvious thing in the world. She grinned and smacked the inside of the truck above the window and went about making herself a quick plate with extra ravioli just because. "She's my girl. My ride or die. My cook or be cooked."

Ryan relaxed into a grin as Gabriella hopped off the truck, nailing the landing and spilling nothing. "You've named your truck. Of course you have."

"Can you imagine someone not naming their food truck?" She took a seat across from Ryan at one of the tables nearby, as outrage at the notion took firm hold. "You'd have to be a barbarian."

"That person must be cold and dead inside." Ryan likely didn't mean it, but Gabriella appreciated the show of solidarity and the conviction with which she proclaimed it. "Wow. Okay," Ryan said and took a minute to study her plate, midbite.

Gabriella frowned. Surely, Ryan didn't hate her food. But her midsection tightened in concern. Did she bite into something hard? Was the ravioli too hot? She'd just fired it. "Is something wrong?"

"What is this?" Ryan asked, gesturing with her fork.

"That's an arancini ball. Fried risotto. Not a fan?"

Ryan's standard grin was noticeably absent, which didn't bode well. "Uh, the opposite. It's…" She shook her head. "Fantastic."

Gabriella relaxed. "I have more."

"No. I need to spend a little time with the rest of this plate first."

She laughed. "I like your approach. A little bit of everything. But then we know you have game."

"Doesn't mean I don't know a good thing when I see it." She met Gabriella's gaze, and they stared a moment. Was that a reference to her? Sweet Lord, she had not been prepared for veiled flirting over lunch. What was she supposed to do with the comment? She decided to enjoy it and smile.

They ate in silence, listening to the tunes floating from Jolene. Ryan was seemingly lost in her relationship with the food, until she finally raised her satisfied, gorgeous face to Gabriella. "Does this mean you're no longer mad at me about the whole column disagreement?"

"Still mad. I just hide it well. You're no longer bent out of shape about the beating your team took?" She made a point of putting on the most sympathetic face possible.

Ryan outdid her. Her face fell and she looked like a dejected puppy. "Not yet."

She laughed. "Too soon?"

"Way too soon."

"Well, you'll get another crack at it in not too long when our teams meet again. I checked the schedule."

"Oh, so you were casually wondering when you might see me in my uniform again and had to look it up."

Gabriella nearly spat out her food at the accuracy of that statement, almost like Ryan had been spying on her. "No," she sputtered, recovering. "Just making sure my schedule was free for all the runs I plan to score on you."

"If you're looking to score…" Ryan's mouth tugged to the left.

"I'm not," Gabriella said simply and returned to her food. Ryan was fun, good-looking, and cheeky as hell, but she also came wrapped in a jumble of red flags as far as Gabriella was concerned. She couldn't let things go too far. She wasn't a tease.

"I think I just offended my lunch partner," Ryan said and closed one eye. Her face was surprisingly red. Gabriella was not expecting the vulnerability and was thrown yet again. This was all so new from Ryan, and it softened her heart.

"Revelation. I'm not easily offended," Gabriella said. "Angered?

Sure. I'm one of four girls who grew up in a small apartment. We fought for what we wanted. You saw that with the column reaction."

Ryan's eyes went wide. "Oh, did I ever. You're a go-getter."

She winced. "I have a spark of a temper and have been known to launch into the Italian my grandmother used to speak to me as a kid. Never really been described as a wilting flower."

"Trust me. I'm aware after last night's game. No one would mistake you for anything wilting."

Gabriella laughed. "And I'm a fantastic chops buster. You'll notice I give it back just as good as you dish it out."

Ryan sighed, and it was clear she was unsettled. Something hung over her, and it was more than the softball loss. "I guess it's my turn to offer a revelation."

Gabriella cut into her ravioli. "I'm listening."

"I tend to tease you that way because I like what I know of you so far." She exhaled slowly as if relieved to have just said it. "A lot. More than maybe I should." She shook her head. "It's a thing."

"Oh." Gabriella wasn't sure what to do with that. She liked Ryan a lot, too, but she wasn't about to go all the way there. She couldn't. Dreamy eyes and a physique to die for were fun. But Ryan was a kid on a playground, having the time of her life, hopping from girl to girl. She, on the other hand, was settled and old and comfortable and boring. Okay, well, not ancient, but definitely not in the same place as someone like Ryan Jacks. Nor did she want to go back there.

"If it's a client-contractor issue, I get it. But the job is only temporary."

"Not the job, and what you said was…sweet. Really, it was, but—"

"No, no, no. Don't say I'm sweet like some kind of gentle pat on the head to the neighbor kid across the street." She covered her eyes.

Was Ryan embarrassed? Where was the swagger?

"What is going on right now? Did I hurt your feelings?" Gabriella leaned in.

"No. Absolutely not." Ryan dropped her hands. "I just happen to think you're pretty great, even though you yelled at me, and wanted to hang out. You don't, and that is one hundred percent okay and allowed."

"We can hang out," Gabriella said. "In fact, we should. I can't guarantee I won't be bossy." She paused, feeling the need to manage expectations. "But we're not going to wind up in bed. I should be up front about that."

A pause. Ryan got that cheeky look on her face again. "Are you sure, though? It could happen even if we aren't expecting it."

She closed her eyes and shook her head sagely. "It won't."

Ryan laughed, the mood light again. It seemed whenever they circled back to flirtation, they relaxed, enjoyed themselves. Gabriella supposed it was harmless enough and fun, but she was happy she'd been direct. "Fine," Ryan said. "No sex. But if you change your mind, that's okay, too."

"Oh, you apparently didn't get the widely circulated memo that I'm the most stubborn person on the planet."

"Oh, I can attest to that." Gabriella turned at the sound of a familiar voice. Madison.

"See? Listen to my ex-girlfriend. I never waver."

Ryan raised an eyebrow, her expression dialed to shock. "Oh, wow. You two used to…"

Madison nodded. "We used to. Yes. Back in the day."

Gabriella watched Ryan take in that information, looking from Madison to her and back again. If Gabriella wasn't mistaken, Ryan deflated.

"I had no idea based on how tight you two are now."

"It was in the lesbian rule book," Madison said. "Be friends with your ex—so we had no choice but to make it happen." She turned to Gabriella apologetically. "Can I steal food? I have a meeting with my crew in twenty and want to make sure I don't pass out."

"Of course."

Gabriella stood, but Madison waved her off. "I can plate. I've been watching you do it for years. Sit. Enjoy your date."

Gabriella tried not to wince. "Not actually a date."

"She's right," Ryan called after Madison. "She likes me but thinks I'm too wild and childish."

"I never said childish."

"You thought it." Ryan's eyes sparkled in challenge. Why did she have to be so damn sexy? And why did they have the best give-and-take rhythm? It was frustrating when you got right down to it, the look-but-don't-touch ideology.

"It's possible it crossed my mind," Gabriella conceded. "In a purely affectionate way."

"Until I screw up your columns."

"Then we go to war."

Madison's eyebrows rose as she climbed down the truck steps, listening to them. "All right then," she said, holding up her plate of food. "I'll leave you two to figure all this out."

"Wait. No. You can join us if you want," Gabriella said, sliding over.

Madison stared at them as something unnamed crossed her features. "Generous. But I'm gonna pass. I have to eat fast anyway." With that, she darted, and Gabriella stared after her, perplexed.

That was weird. When she looked back at Ryan, she found her lost in her plate once again. Gabriella watched her delicately cut into her next bite with true reverence. It was obvious that Ryan really liked food, which made her Gabriella's people.

"Did your parents cook a lot for you growing up?"

Ryan looked up. "Still do. My mom, I mean. My dad's not in the picture. Left when I was three. Plus, I hear he's an asshole."

"I'm sorry." She meant it, too. Something hit her square in the chest as she imagined a tiny Ryan wondering why Dad wasn't around anymore.

Ryan didn't seem fazed. "Your folks still together?"

"Yes, and bickering like children in the most lovable way possible. She wants him to listen more, and he wants her to talk less." She laughed. "It's a cycle."

"Sounds fun at least."

She paused. "But food has always bridged the gap in pretty much any conflict in my house. When someone was angry? They cooked. Happy? More cooking. I loved how it brought people together, all that food. Maybe that's why I took such an interest. It's a powerful tool."

Ryan grinned and looked down at her empty plate. "You can count me as one of the people grateful that you did."

"More? Because there's always more. My motto."

"Trust me when I say I'm desperate for seconds, but if I give in, I'll be napping in the sun next to Dale instead of sanding the sides of your beautiful server station."

"I think I'm in favor of the sanding." She stood. "Thanks for inviting me to eat with you. One of my better lunches of late."

Ryan stood, too, which showed off the height she had on Gabriella. "Keep an open mind, okay?"

Gabriella furrowed her brow. "About the restaurant?"

"Me." But she didn't say it with the standard bravado. In fact, there was nothing playful in her delivery in the slightest. She appeared downright nervous, and that humility sent a potent shiver up Gabriella's spine. Her limbs broke out in goose bumps.

She blinked. "Well, I think I try to go through life with an open mind."

"That's all I ask. See you soon, I hope."

Gabriella noticed a tugging that came on fast and insistent, the kind that made her want to kiss Ryan one minute, protect her from the world and herself the next, and pummel her the third. That wasn't normal, was it? Kissing and pummeling? But, oh, did she feel them both. She watched as Ryan set out on the short walk to the jobsite. She opened her mouth to call after her, to prolong their time together for just one more memorable minute, but the selection of which words were appropriate eluded her. There were no good ones. Ryan wasn't for her, and she just needed to get that through her stubborn brain and have a good, stern talking-to with her traitorous libido. It was out of control and influencing way too much of the rest of her.

When she went to bed that night, she spent some time writing in her journal. With pen in hand, she explored the sensations she'd experienced in Ryan's presence and wrote about her confusion with regard to the tugging. Maybe facing the details head-on would help her let them go. Why had this person been sent into her life? What lesson was Ryan there to teach her, because as her Grandma Filomena had often explained, important people walked into your life with a lesson. That meant Ryan had a greater purpose, and her powerful debut on the scene was not a coincidence. Maybe they were meant to be friends, and Gabriella should embrace that tug a bit more. See what she could learn from Ryan and what she could impart in return. She was older and wiser, after all. She set her journal aside, switched off the lamp next to her bed, and slid beneath the cool sheets nestled snugly in the Spring Cottage.

She struggled to fall asleep, though, because she felt different somehow. Unsettled, as if she'd missed an important detail, or forgotten something huge on her weekly to-do list. She tossed and turned, attempting to settle in, but nothing she tried brought her much sleep. Something was tapping her incessantly on the shoulder, beckoning her. She just had no idea what.

## CHAPTER SEVEN

R yan estimated that she had a couple months left on the Tangle Valley job, and it was time for Joey and Gabriella to pick out the remaining fixtures and finishes. Ryan was not a professional designer, but she did come with thoughts of her own, built on experience, and did her best to guide her clients when it seemed like they were making inconsistent choices.

The three of them had arranged to meet at four o'clock that afternoon in the tasting room, knowing that guest traffic would be winding down and the food truck—correction, *Jolene*—would be closed for the day after late lunch service. Ryan arrived first and smiled at Loretta. She and Carly had been friends through high school and still talked here and there on social media.

"Well, look who the devil drug up and dropped at Tangle Valley." Loretta leaned across the counter and kissed Ryan's cheek. "Took you long enough to pop in here after working these weeks on the property. Not yards away, even. I'm offended—except I'm not."

Ryan grinned sheepishly. "You're a VIP around here, Loretta. Didn't want to bother you."

"Since when?" Loretta asked.

Ryan leaned on the bar. "Talked to Carly a couple weeks back. She said she might pop over for a visit later this year. That still happening?"

"Yep. And she's flying me to the Caribbean for a trip with her and her girlfriend's family."

"Get the hell out. Really?"

Loretta nodded and her green eyes sparkled. "I'm a jetsetter now. I've already started my packing list and it's months away." She grinned and her cheeks got red and happy. It was clear how very much she loved her kid. Though her hair was more gray than not these days, there were still glimpses of the blond she shared with Carly. "How's your mama? We need to get together for our twice a year coffee date soon. Is she giving herself time to be a human being?"

"She's busy this time of year. School district has all those state tests she has to get her fifth graders ready for. I need to stop by and see her."

"Yes, you do," Loretta said, gesturing with a wineglass. Her mom was a sweet, funny, and opinionated woman, obsessed with crossword puzzles and the Food Network, but a consummate worrier when it came to Ryan, her only child. "And I'll give you a bottle of the pinot noir to take with you. My treat. You two can kill it together and toast my good name." Loretta laughed jovially, and Ryan was filled with warmth.

"We'd both like that."

"I'd give anything to have Carly closer. So I'm more than jealous of you two in that sense. Really happy to see her settling down, though." She sighed as if basking in it all. "Lauren, the girlfriend, has made all the difference in her life. You need a Lauren. That's what I say." More emphatic wineglass pointing.

Ryan grinned. She'd seen the change herself. Carly thought things through more these days, seemed more grounded now, happier. "They seem so great together. The two of them." Ryan had seen photos of Carly and Lauren online just a few days back. Not only were they a gorgeous duo, but they looked at each other with such love. Ryan had to wonder what that must be like. And if it happened to her, would she change for the better the way Carly had? These were thoughts she'd never tried on…until recently.

"Please tell me I haven't missed any good gossip," Joey said, arriving behind the bar from the back room. She had her blond hair down today and parted on the side. Since taking up with Becca, she, too, seemed to sparkle more. Love, man.

"A ridiculous amount. And we're not going over it again either." Ryan folded her arms.

"Well, dammit," Joey said, grinning at her.

"Ready to make a pretty slick restaurant?" Ryan headed to an open table, set a few books of samples she'd picked up from various vendors on the floor, took a seat, and opened her laptop to the folder with additional photos. They'd not get through everything today, but they could at least get most of the details worked out, so she could be sure the orders were placed in time.

"Born ready, but I'm just here as a consultant. I'm likely going to defer to Gabriella. She knows more about upscale dining in general and, let's be honest, has better taste than most other people and nearly all animals."

"Nearly all?"

"Have you met Skywalker?" Joey waved off the topic. "It's a whole thing. I'm just saying he excels at pillow arranging."

"I'm ready, everyone," Gabriella said, practically bursting into the room with overflowing energy. She might as well have been mid-song like the lead in a truly happy musical. "I've been waiting for today. I almost didn't sleep as my brain chirped away with ideas, and visions, and concepts."

"Oh my," Joey supplied. "Sorry. Couldn't leave that hanging. Cinematic blasphemy and all."

"Oh my is right," Ryan murmured. They turned to her. Joey raised an amused eyebrow. Damn. She thought she'd said those words in her head. She hadn't. They'd been out loud because Gabriella was out of her chef's coat and wearing jeans, those strappy shoes that wound up her ankles like temptation on a stick, and a green top with a neckline that made everything about her...pop. Joey passed her an approving grin, but Gabriella luckily didn't seem to have heard the utterance. "Ready to get started?" Ryan asked, moving them forward.

Gabriella rubbed her hands together and took a seat. "Let's do it."

They settled in and got to work. Ryan's main focus today was countertops, cabinetry, and knobs and handles. Gabriella seemed to know exactly what she wanted for the place and scoured the books and photos like a pro, narrowing down her choices, explaining how they fit into her concept.

"*Bam,*" she'd say, when she found one that she liked. Ryan would flag the bammed sample as they moved forward. "Bam," she'd say to another. "Bam, and bam." She shimmied her shoulders as they progressed.

"That your bam dance?" Ryan asked.

"It is now. Bam." Ryan flagged another with an amused shake of her head. "What? Bam is empowering," Gabriella said. "You should try it sometime." She flipped the page of the counter lookbook. "Bamalama to that sexy one right there. How *you* doin'?" She flipped the page. "Bam to that precious soul."

Ryan raised an eyebrow and silently flagged it. God, Gabriella was cute when she got going.

"What about these cabinets?" Gabriella asked sometime later, flipping the book around for Ryan to see. "They're the most perfect set. I don't think I could have dreamed up a more perfect match for what's in my head."

Ryan winced and studied the specs. "Big for the limited space behind the bar, though."

"Can't we just make more space?"

She shook her head, going over the plans from memory. "Doesn't really work that way, unless you want to go with fewer cabinets than we talked about." She sighed. "Even then you're pushing the depth out farther than would be comfortable."

"Could we do it anyway?" Gabriella asked, unrelenting. Much like the column conversation, she was not giving in.

Ryan blinked, loving the firecracker side less than just moments ago. "If you know how to invent more space."

"Not really my job to do that. I make the food. You invent the space."

Ryan blinked again, the pointed comment landing. They were at a standstill, and frustration flared. "You're pushy."

Gabriella held up a finger. "Respectfully ambitious." They stared at each other. Joey looked from Ryan to Gabriella. Music from an old Western played eerily in Ryan's brain.

"Is there anything we can do to compromise here?" Joey asked, intervening, the voice of reason. "Or is it a complete no-go?" The question was aimed more at Ryan as the expert in the room.

Ryan sighed. "Not on the budget you have me on. I'd have to knock down that half wall to expand the bar area."

"How badly do you love those cabinets?" Joey asked Gabriella.

Gabriella exhaled and slid a thick strand of hair behind her ear. Her eyes softened. "I can find others. They're just everything I imagined. The finish, the rounded edges, and the intricate design in the center. They say Tangled to me."

She wasn't wrong. The cabinets would look great in the room. Watching Gabriella relent twisted Ryan's midsection uncomfortably. She couldn't stand it. The sad acquiescence. The pout Gabriella tried to conceal.

"But you know what?" Ryan said, trying to fix it. "There are plenty of other choices here." She flipped back to some of Gabriella's earlier picks, though it was clear they excited her less.

"Yeah. That one could work." Gabriella turned her head to the side, studying the runner-up.

It was only another moment or two before Ryan cracked. "Let me see if I can move some things around in the budget and take care of that half wall."

"Don't reduce your fee," Joey said quietly.

Gabriella's gaze shot up. "No. I wouldn't want that either."

"I'll work it out," Ryan said, feeling better having made the decision. "Don't worry about it."

Joey and Gabriella exchanged a look.

"Ryan, I don't want to put you in a difficult spot, just because I'm not being flexible. I'll adjust."

"No," Ryan said, closing the book. "You're right. Those are the best cabinets for the space, and you're getting them."

"I don't know what to say. Thank you."

Ryan nodded, wondering how she was going to make this happen, but determined nonetheless. They hadn't gotten to knobs and handles, but it was well past the time they'd set aside to meet, so they'd come back to it.

"Time for a glass of wine on the house?" Joey asked Ryan, as she packed up.

While the offer was nice, her conversation with Loretta earlier had planted a seed. "No, but thank you. I'm gonna swing by my mom's. She mentioned that she'd have a pot of shrimp creole on the stove today."

Gabriella, who was halfway to the door, turned back. "She makes creole?"

"The best I've ever had."

"Does she use fresh shrimp? Where does she get hers?" This seemed like a hugely important question to Gabriella. Joey waved and sneaked away to avoid interrupting.

Ryan laughed. "Why don't you come with me and you can ask her. The pot is huge and can feed an army."

"No, no. I was just curious about the shrimp." She paused and seemed to rethink her whole course. "You know what? I take it back. Bring on the shrimp and the mom. I'd love to go with you if you're serious."

"As a bad haircut on a Friday night."

"Okay." Gabriella shook her head with a laugh. "Not messing around then."

Ryan held up the keys, nervous as hell, excited as hell, and happier than she'd felt in a while. "I'll drive."

Dale, who'd been lounging on the steps of the Big House with

Becca's dog, Skywalker, stood and fell into step with Ryan when she passed, tossing a half bark over his shoulder, perhaps in a farewell to his napping buddy. Sky whined quietly.

"I'll follow you, buddy," Gabriella said. "You seem to be the one in charge here."

"He's not."

"Says, you lie."

Ryan chuckled. "He would."

Dale hopped in the truck's tiny back seat, and Gabriella joined Ryan in the front. "This truck suits you," she told Ryan, resting her cheek against the back of the seat.

"Yeah?" she fired up the engine. "It helps to be able to haul my tools and equipment around."

Gabriella's eyes darkened, which caught Ryan off guard. "The tools also suit you," Gabriella said, but quieter this time. Interesting development. Was Gabriella hot for tools? Did Ryan need to carry her hammer in her back pocket for emergencies? She'd do it.

"Yeah, well. I've always enjoyed working with my hands." She drove them off the property and, in her peripheral vision, saw Gabriella exhale slowly. She smothered a satisfied smile. Maybe she had an effect on Gabriella after all.

Well, well.

She pulled her truck onto the tree-lined streets of the small suburb just to the west of town center. The house she grew up in was a modest one-story that was well kept with a variety of colorful flowers blooming in the bed in front, most all of them yellow. Her mom had a thing for the color. The sidewalk was neatly swept and a bit curvy, which had always been fun for scooter riding growing up. Ryan didn't bother waiting for her mother to answer the door. Instead, she knocked twice and let herself in, calling out, "Just your only child, here unannounced."

"Well, hey there, sweet girl," her mom called back. "Get in here. I haven't seen you in a week."

"I brought a friend from work," Ryan said, following her mother's voice down the hall to the small kitchen off the living room.

"Even better. Bring him in. I've got plenty of food, and you know I like company."

Ryan stood in the archway above the small kitchen and smiled. She lowered her voice. "Technically, a she."

"Oh," her mother said and grabbed a dish towel to dry her hands as if the new development changed everything. It made sense. Ryan didn't bring women home. Ever. Her mom stood straighter and beamed as Gabriella joined Ryan in the archway.

"Hi, there. I'm Gabriella. I'm crashing."

"Well, look at this! I just assumed you had Billy with you." She beamed at Ryan like she'd brought home an A on her spelling test. "This is such a nice surprise. I'm Joanna Jacks. Welcome, welcome, welcome. Come in."

Gabriella didn't hesitate and headed straight for her mother. "It's so wonderful to meet you." She didn't go in for a handshake or rest on her heels or her warm hello. Nope. Gabriella pulled her mother into a full-on hug, which was happily returned. Ryan rolled her lips in to cover the smile.

"Aren't you the sweetest?" her mom said. She passed Ryan a happy smile and looked like she was already bubbling with questions. Ryan shrugged back.

Finally, Gabriella released her and grinned. "I just happen to come from a family of huggers. Can't seem to leave it behind. We're a tactile people."

"You're stunning," her mom said, and then laughed. "Is that okay to say? I never know these days with how PC everything has gotten. So much is off-limits."

"Thank you," Gabriella said. "Totally okay."

"And you work with Ryan?" her mom asked, looking from Ryan to Gabriella.

"Not exactly," Gabriella answered. Ryan liked the rose lip gloss she wore today. It drew attention to her lips, which happened to be perfectly shaped. Not the kind of thing she should be focused on right now, however. But how would they taste? "I'm a client."

Ryan abandoned the daydream and jumped in. "We're remodeling one of the buildings out at Tangle Valley. It's soon to be a restaurant, and Gabriella's the head chef."

"Oh, I've heard about you," her mom enthused, eyes bright. "You have that famous food truck out there right now. Helene! The third-grade teachers at my school love it."

"You mean Jolene, but yes. I don't know how famous we are, but it's good to hear folks are talking about us."

Her mom was off and speaking a mile a minute now. Ryan couldn't say she was surprised they were hitting it off so quickly.

"Everyone is. I've been meaning to visit one Saturday."

"Well, you have to," Gabriella enthused.

"Now that I know the chef, I'm inspired. My friends said that line is long if you don't get there early."

"It can be, but I move pretty fast."

"I like her, Ryan. Thank you for bringing her to me."

"In that case, how do you feel about us staying for dinner?" Ryan asked, knowing the answer well in advance. Her mother was proud of her creole recipe and would be thrilled to show it off.

"I say grab a bowl. Oh! And I have some fresh bread cooling on the rack." She clapped. "This is such a nice surprise. We could open some wine."

Ryan held up the bottle. "From Loretta. She misses you."

"Oh, bless her. We need to do a cards night, us girls. I've been in the mood for one."

Her mom dished out three bowls of shrimp creole and sliced the bread. The warm butter she placed on the table had Ryan's mouth watering. The kitchen smelled like heaven in Oregon. The only thing better was how happy Gabriella seemed and how easily she fit in to their evening. Startling, actually.

"This is so good," Gabriella whispered to Ryan, as her mother carried over last-minute additions like salt and pepper and extra napkins. "Thank you for bringing me."

"You're welcome," Ryan mouthed back with a wink, hoping two seconds later that it didn't come off as obnoxious.

They dug in. Her mom and Gabriella chatted about anything and everything: the food, the simmer time, the stock her mother had used, favorite brands of spices, and Gabriella was even kind enough to answer a few cooking questions and directed her mom to the best website for fantastic pots and pans.

"How long have you lived in Whisper Wall now?" her mother asked. "And why hasn't my daughter brought you by sooner?"

Gabriella looked at Ryan and smiled. "A little under a year. As for Ryan, probably because I can be feisty and annoying when she's trying to work. There was a column dispute. And a cabinet one just earlier. A softball trouncing, too." Gabriella winced. "She's probably not quite recovered from that one."

"Oh, the game I missed. You were beaten?" She turned to Ryan in sympathy.

Ryan's competitive spirit fired. "Total fluke. The Muskrats had some easy breaks. It won't be happening again."

Gabriella lowered her spoon. "It was quite the game, Joanna. The Otters fought hard, but it wasn't hard enough." She winced. "I look forward to a rematch and shutting them down again."

Joanna practically choked on her mouthful, clearly enjoying Gabriella's tenacity.

Ryan sat back. "Or we'll see the Muskrats back to their hole."

"This has taken a turn," her mom said and took a bite of shrimp. "But I can't wait to hear how it plays out."

Ryan stared at Gabriella, and she stared back in challenge, which was awesome. The more time she spent around Gabriella, the more she liked her, even the parts that pushed her damn buttons. It turned out she really liked having her buttons pushed, especially by someone so formidable.

"How about a quick game of something?" her mom asked, after they'd polished their bowls from seconds.

Ryan looked to Gabriella. They had always been a game family, but that habit didn't always transfer to others. "What do you think? Do you need to be home? Your call."

Gabriella didn't miss a beat. In fact, her eyes shone brightly with enthusiasm. "I'm obsessed with games. What are we playing?" She cracked her knuckles.

They answered in unison. "Phase Ten." It had become their obsession the past couple of years, and Ryan had been bested by her mother the last three times they'd played. No more. As they gathered around the small table in the front parlor, affectionately referred to as Game Central, Ryan was off to a strong start, laying down phase one and pulling glares from the other two opponents. Halfway through, her mother shocked them all and pulled herself into the lead, winning three rounds in a row and on her way to another win.

"Joanna, how are you managing this?" Gabriella asked, with a bewildered look. Ryan's eyes lingered on her for a beat too long, and Gabriella flicked her gaze to Ryan's and grinned. Caught. A moment of heat passed between them. Ryan wasn't mistaking it either. Gabriella's eyes moved over her face to her neck, down to her chest, while her mother studied her cards, paying them no mind. Ryan swallowed.

"All in knowing whether to draw or pick up from the discard pile," her mother said. "But beyond that, you two are on your own. I'm on my own mission." She glanced up and caught them staring at each other. "What? Am I missing something?"

Gabriella picked up her cards quickly, rebounding. "Your mom's as competitive as you are."

Ryan lifted a shoulder. "I suppose I learn from the best."

"Good thing I'm here now to give her a run for her money." She made good on her word and took the next two phases easily, leaving Ryan stranded with cards in her hand. The game continued like that with the three of them laughing and trash-talking until eventually her mother emerged as the victor.

"You two kids have to work harder," her mother said with the sweetest smile on her face, like an assassin you didn't see coming. She fanned herself with a wayward card.

"She's a shark," Ryan said.

"A sneaky one," Gabriella echoed. They cleaned up the game, and Gabriella grinned. "I loved tonight. In fact, it was one of my favorites since I've been in town. A home-cooked meal and a competitive card game? Unstoppable."

That apparently called for a hug, and her mother wasted no time offering one. "You come back here for my homemade chili with or without Ryan. Your invitation is standing because I like you a lot."

Gabriella held her by the elbows and looked into her eyes earnestly. "Listen to me when I say that I will be on your doorstep, cradling a bowl. You have my number now. Call. Or I'll call you."

Oh, they were a force now, and it had only been their first meeting. Ryan wasn't exactly surprised. "All right, you two. Break it up."

"I like her," her mom said, pointing at Gabriella. "Did I mention that?"

"No. And we have to leave," Ryan said. "Ready?"

"Until next time," Gabriella said as they exited the house.

Once they were back on the sidewalk and heading to the truck, Gabriella turned to her. "Hey, I don't know why you did it, but thank you for inviting me. I had the best time."

"Yeah." A pause as the world slowed down. Now that they were alone, things felt different. Heavier. Wonderful. Electric. "Me, too."

They hopped into the truck and flipped the radio to mellow tunes, content to listen to the music as they drove with an anticipatory energy floating between them. Halfway through the drive, she heard Gabriella begin to sing quietly along. Ryan looked over, surprised because her voice wasn't just pretty, it was beautiful—angelic yet full.

"I like to sing," Gabriella said sheepishly when she saw Ryan watching her. "It's a thing. Ignore me."

"I don't think that's possible," Ryan said, her eyes on the road. She shook her head. "I had no idea you could sing like that."

"Just for car rides and the shower."

"Which is a shame."

Gabriella turned in Ryan's direction, resting her cheek against the seat as she'd done on the drive over. It was becoming a move Ryan associated with only her. "What's something you're good at?" Gabriella asked, as they made the turn past the Tangle Valley sign and up the hill that would reveal the darkened vineyard in just a matter of moments.

She decided to just say it. "I like to make furniture. Just for fun, though. Nothing too serious. People seem to think I'm good at that. Maybe I am. I don't know. Did you see the bench on my mother's porch?"

"The wooden one with the slightly gray finish?" Gabriella's jaw dropped, and she sat up. "I did. I admired it on the way in. Gorgeous. You're telling me that you made it?"

Ryan nodded, feeling a little embarrassed to have revealed that. She didn't talk about her side projects much, but for some reason she wanted to share that part of herself with Gabriella tonight. She put the truck in park in front of the cottage, and the cab went quiet. The radio off. The engine cooling. Just them.

"What else do you make?"

"Rocking chairs, tables. A dresser once. A couple of trunks."

"You have to let me see some." Her voice was quiet when she said it, and Ryan could only see part of her face. The shadows somehow made everything feel safe, relaxed, and low stakes.

"Come over sometime. Soon."

"I will, and I might bring some cash with me. I have a cottage that could use a few unique touches." She exhaled. "I like getting to see this side of you. You're a talented kid."

"There you go again. I'm not a kid."

"Right. You're not." Her tone was unconvincing and laced with pacification.

Ryan sat taller. "One day, you're going to change your mind about me."

"I'm afraid I already have," she said with a soft smile.

A pause. "Don't be afraid."

They looked at each other in the darkened truck for an extended beat. She could hear the sounds of her own heart beating and Gabriella's soft breaths. This moment mattered.

Gabriella shook her head as if pondering a point. "I liked being with you tonight. I felt like I was where I was supposed to be. Is that strange?" She held Ryan's gaze.

Ryan shook her head.

"This might be the wine talking, making me speak too freely, but I think we were meant to meet, Ryan. I don't know why, but I can't shake the feeling."

"Maybe we were." Another pause. "I've never taken anyone but Billy to my mom's house."

"Is that true?"

She nodded.

"Well, then consider me honored." She popped open the door. "Thanks again for taking me, Ryan. And for the ride. Will you be on-site tomorrow?"

"My guys will be in first thing. I'll join them midmorning. Gonna get the paperwork taken care of on the orders we need."

Gabriella held the door and smiled. "I'll stop in before the lunch rush and see how things are going, in that case. Maybe hassle you and tell you how to do your job. Kinda my favorite."

"I'll count on it." The anticipation of seeing Gabriella again already sent a shiver from her toes to her shoulders. "Just don't get all fiery."

"Have you met me?" She hopped out. "No promises."

The truck door slammed, and Ryan sighed, watching Gabriella, the pint-sized ball of charisma, walk in front of her truck to the stairs that led to her cottage, her dark hair swaying behind her.

"What is happening?" Ryan whispered to no one. She wasn't exactly sure, but her world had tilted dramatically ever since taking this job. She longed for things she'd never once imagined she'd care about. She craved time with Gabriella, conversations with her, and more. Her phone vibrated in the cup holder and tore into her thoughts. Reluctantly, she checked the readout.

*Come over. Now. I'll take care of you.*

Lana McCarver. They'd not shared an evening together in months now, and she was clearly in the mood. It was the perfect time of night for Ryan to jet over to Lana's place for a little fun and still make it home for a decent night's rest. There was nothing at all holding her back.

She began to type. *So sorry. Not gonna make it tonight. Exhausted.*

She turned off her phone and tossed it onto the passenger seat. She smiled as she drove through town and straight home. She'd figure it all out later. Because this? Didn't feel so bad. She slept hard that night. The last thing she saw in her memory before drifting off was a pair of beautiful hazel eyes.

# CHAPTER EIGHT

"Holy hell. Have you been over to Tangled lately?" Joey asked with her eyes wide, giant fuzzy slippers on her feet, and her mouth agape. She was the last one to arrive in the old barn that evening, and thank God she'd arrived because she was the one who had promised to bring the wine. Luckily, she clutched two bottles, always in favor of variety. It was their friend night to kick back and chill, push aside anything too pressing with regard to the business, and unwind. With their usual meeting spot now under construction, they'd chosen the old barn as the next best location for flicks.

"Are you wearing pajamas?" Madison asked, squinting. "Why are you wearing pajamas? It's not even eight."

"No. Just fuzzy pink slippers. Brenda Anne got them in at the Nifty Nickel and said half the town is wearing them, and that means I had to give them a flex." She lifted one bunny-clad foot, and Gabriella grinned in appreciation.

"Those look so comfortable. I'm calling Brenda Anne after this and demanding the hookup. Maddie, you need a pair. We'll all wear bunny slippers everywhere we go."

Madison frowned. "Not really a bunny kind of person."

"Yes, you are," Joey deadpanned. "Get over yourself."

That seemed to work, and Madison offered a small smile. "Maybe if they had brown ones. With eyebrows."

"You're the weirdest human," Joey said, perplexed. "But you folks are off topic. The restaurant. Amazing. Picture-perfect. Sleek, yet homey enough to fit in on the grounds."

"I stopped by this afternoon. They're doing a killer job. I love it." Gabriella grinned and her heart swelled. The place wasn't even open yet, but she was so proud of it she had trouble sleeping. "We could feasibly do a soft open in ten weeks, you know. We're that close. We'd need the inspections to go through and the permits to process, but Ryan says things move fast in Whisper Wall red tape land."

"She would know," Joey said. She blinked rapidly, which signaled her brain had taken off. "Everything would have to line up, but maybe we could link it to our chardonnay release party for the wine club members. Make the VIPs feel special. What do you think?"

Madison nodded. "Would certainly draw attention to both the release and the opening if we paired them."

Gabriella sat up. "I love the concept of a whole event. We can publicize the hell out of that."

"And it's a really good batch," Madison said, sitting taller. "I can't take full credit because your dad did most of the work," she said to Joey, "but damn, the slate minerality slays me with every taste. It's sophisticated and has lots of personality."

Joey beamed. "Sounds like Becca."

"Me?"

"Baby. You're here." Becca stood in the doorway, still wearing her work clothes and a smile, looking gorgeous as always. Joey's eyes sparkled at the sight.

"Saw the note on the counter and didn't want to miss whatever this is you're doing in bunny slippers," Becca said, studying Joey's feet. "You've never been sexier." The two exchanged a kiss.

"We'll need to get you a pair," Gabriella said. "I'm ready for the dish. You always hear the best gossip at that resort. Well, you and Loretta. What do you have for us?"

Becca nodded. "What can I say? When people relax, they like to talk. A lot."

"You can't sit in this dusty barn in those." Joey looked aghast and gestured at the room and then at Becca's expensive, probably designer, suit.

Becca ignored her and took a spot on the floor next to Joey, her back against a bale of hay. "Can, too. Dry cleaning is a booming business for a reason. I'm a hearty patron."

"Only you would unwind in a Chanel suit and rock it like a boss," Madison said with a laugh into her glass. "I like your style, Crawford. I want to be you when I grow up."

"As long as I can stay up late and learn how to make kick-ass wine," Becca said and raised the glass Joey had just handed her.

"Deal."

"Dish?" Gabriella asked, eager to know all and looking around in earnest. "Where's the dish?"

Becca didn't hesitate. Gabriella appreciated that. "Well, Lucinda from the Dark Room, that chocolate shop off Main, has a thing for Powell from the used car dealership."

Gabriella squinted. "Oh, the guy with the baseball cap perched on his head? He's an Otter, and thereby my mortal enemy."

She and Joey made the muskrat face because it was required. Joey looked skyward. "That means Ryan is your mortal enemy, and I heard from the Biddies that you had dinner with Ryan and her mother last week. A detail you neglected to mention." Joey looked overly mystified. "So strange."

It was true. Gabriella hadn't shared her evening with Ryan with her friends. She wasn't exactly bent on keeping it a secret, but for a reason she didn't understand yet, she wanted that night to be hers for a little while. But leave it to the Biddies to stay one step ahead of her. "How do they do it? We were in a residential neighborhood. How do they know so much of what goes on in this town? It's insane."

"Says the girl who just begged me for the dish." Becca seemed to be enjoying all this from behind her glass.

Gabriella pointed at her. "I can own that, and I don't begrudge a single Biddy her thirst for gossip. In fact, I'm impressed with their prowess. The difference is I don't pass it around to anyone who will listen. I keep it here." She touched her heart reverently.

"But you're not denying it, then? Dinner with Ryan and her mom?" Madison asked the question in a way that had Gabriella's radar pinging. She didn't sound like herself. What was that about?

She answered honestly. "I did go over there to try her fabulous shrimp creole, and then we stuck around and played a card game. It was fun." There. She'd just put it all out there. No need to hoard the Ryan details, confusion on her end or not.

"That's great," Joey said. "Joanna is the kindest. She was my fifth-grade math teacher, you know. Maddie's, too. We used to get in trouble for talking."

Gabriella laughed and would have loved to have known the two of them back then. Little Joey and tiny Madison, making plans for their eleven-year-old afternoon. Madison didn't look as caught up in the nostalgia as Joey did. In fact, she didn't seem to be listening to the conversation at all.

"You also had lunch with her," Madison pointed out, yanking Gabriella back into the Ryan conversation.

"Yeah. She loved the food, and then we both went back to work." She kept her tone light and unaffected. She left out the part where they flirted here and there in a playful manner.

"Oh. So it's a thing now? You two?" Madison asked, squinting. Why did this feel like a tense conversation all of sudden? Was this an ex-girlfriend thing? If so, she had not seen this coming. Maddie wasn't the jealous type, but her brows were drawn down and her lips pursed slightly. Gabriella knew her well enough to understand that something had her rattled, and she had a feeling it was her spending time with Ryan Jacks. Dammit. Weren't things complicated enough? She and Madison had managed to avoid every traditional pitfall since their breakup.

"We are most definitely not a thing, but I like hanging out with her. We smack-talk softball and cover details about the restaurant." She decided to go there. She leveled her gaze on Madison. "What? Does that upset you?"

"She's bad news. Always has been," Madison said automatically, clearly fired up and not doing that great a job at hiding it.

Joey held up a hand. "Okay, hold on. I wouldn't go that far. Ryan likes to have fun. That's all. But she's kind."

"Too much fun," Madison countered. "She uses people and moves from one woman to the next like a round of Duck, Duck, Goose. I would just hate to see you get caught up with someone like that. You're too smart to."

Gabriella forced a smile and cradled her wine, absorbing the mild insult. "I'm not getting *caught up*."

"Not what it looks like from here." Madison shook her head, seemingly affected by this conversation more than called for. She stood. "I didn't mention it before, but my head is killing me. I'm gonna call it a night. Head home and take something. You guys enjoy." And with that Madison set down her glass and hightailed it out of the barn, leaving the rest of them staring after her in surprise.

Gabriella blinked. Her chest hurt. On top of that, annoyance flared. "What was that about?" she asked the room, grappling to understand what had just happened.

Joey sighed. "I think she cares and is feeling…I don't know, protective of you."

"Or jealous," Becca added, with an apologetic look to Joey. Was this something they'd discussed? "I don't know Madison as well as either of you, but that's what it felt like from here." She tapped her nails on the outside of the glass, the clinking the only sound in the room.

"There's nothing going on with Ryan and me," Gabriella said.

Joey took a moment. "Yet."

"No, Jo, it's not like—"

Joey cut her off. "You don't have to convince me of anything, and you're welcome to change your mind at any point about Ryan. Or not, even. You have my friendship and support." She looked over at Becca and took her hand. "You were there for me when I needed someone, and I'll always be there for you."

"That makes two of us," Becca said and kissed Joey's hand.

"I appreciate that." She downed the last of her wine and gave it some thought before turning back to her friends. "I think what's happening for me is that I'm making a new friend, and I like it."

"Then I like it for you," Joey said. "She makes you smile and glow, and that matters so much."

"She also makes me fume."

Becca raised a knowing eyebrow and exchanged a look with Joey.

"What?" Gabriella asked.

"It sounds familiar," Becca said with a grin. "That's all."

"No, no, no. You fell in love with Joey. She's your person."

"Yes. She is. But we also wanted to murder each other a lot early on."

Gabriella scoffed, laughing off the impractical comparison, because she knew what this was with Ryan and what it wasn't. She let the empty glass press against her cheek, contemplating the smile, glow, and fume combination. She'd experienced two of the three together in various combinations. But the whole group? All together? She wasn't sure what to do with the new discovery. It had her thinking about one person in particular, though, and missing her. Actually *missing* her. What in the world was happening exactly? In a way, it felt like there were forces behind the scenes at work, moving them all around, inching her and Ryan closer together one millimeter at a time. In fact, maybe it was time that she admitted she was no longer in the driver's seat, and sat back and enjoyed the ride.

❖

There weren't many days spun together as beautiful as that Thursday at the end of April. Sunshine, blue skies, and the gentle caress of a refreshing breeze had Ryan energized and ready for the game. She'd run an extra mile that morning because she was keyed up even before work began, just thinking about playing ball. She arrived early to take in the end of the first game to find the Muskrats completely wrecking the Prairie Dogs in a 7–1 beatdown with twelve minutes left in the fifty-minute timed game.

Three batters into the inning, Gabriella strode to the plate in her bright yellow uniform looking like a wound-up stick of dynamite waiting to go off. She slung the bat over one shoulder and back again as she walked, repeating the action several times like a badass. She adjusted the bill of her cap almost in challenge to the pitcher, which had Ryan bursting with pride and wrestling with lust. From her third row seat on the bleachers, she surveyed the stands around her. Joey and Becca were there screaming for their friend. Madison, too, though she was always a little quieter. She clapped and smiled along, though, seeming to enjoy the game.

Ryan returned her focus to Gabriella, who let the first pitch go, a ball. She passed on the second pitch, too, this time drawing the strike, and then another. Damn. Before the next one, she looked over her shoulder to the stands, her eyes settling on Ryan. She wasn't sure, but she thought she caught half a smile before Gabriella turned back and slugged the hell out of that softball, line driving it right past the shortstop's glove, running like hell, and earning a double. Holy hell, she was a force. Ryan shook her head, smiled, and turned to enjoy the moment with Gabriella's friends. After all, the teams weren't rivals today. Joey tossed her an air five, which she returned, but Madison sent her a cool stare before moving her gaze back to the field. Huh. Ryan wasn't sure what she'd done but wondered if it had anything to do with Gabriella and their history. She made a mental note to tread carefully with Madison and see if she could maybe befriend her, or offer reassurance that her intentions were pure. Ryan understood the hesitation, though. Hell, she hadn't exactly proven herself when it came to long-term intentions, so her battle was uphill at best. But if she was being honest, Madison unnerved Ryan right back. She was Gabriella's ex and always put together, polished, and sophisticated. Ryan was none of those things. If Madison was the type of woman Gabriella was drawn to, then Ryan might be out of her league. She deflated.

"Well, look which Otter the cat dragged in," Gabriella said. The game had ended, and the Muskrats improved their record. They were stepping up this season, and Gabriella was a big part of that momentum. Clementine handed her a beer, and she accepted.

"Just scoping out the future competition," Ryan said, pulling herself out of it. She gave Gabriella's bill an affectionate shake. "You looked great out there. Your swing has me envious." She shrugged, humbly facing the truth about her own skills. "Mine lacks follow-through."

"I can give you some pointers if you want."

She liked that idea, her face heating like an idiot. She didn't give a damn. "I'd love it."

"I'll stick around after," Gabriella said over her shoulder with a killer smile. Ryan exhaled slowly. It's like the world had created a woman with everything she never knew she wanted, and all parts of Ryan were affected. How was she supposed to play ball now? Her mind moved too fast, her cheeks were likely red, and she had that tingly feeling all over that she still hadn't gotten used to. Somehow, she managed, motivated by the knowledge that Gabriella was watching, making Ryan want to play her best ball. She managed to pull a handful of outs at first base and got on base twice herself, scoring on one of her drives. The win against the Gophers was an easily fought battle. After a short team meeting about the upcoming schedule, the Otters broke, and she spotted Gabriella speaking with her friends as they gathered their belongings.

"How about that swing? You ready?" she asked as Ryan approached.

"Should I be nervous?" She added a grin.

"Nope. I was watching yours tonight. It's not bad. A little low, but I think it's a hips thing giving you trouble, too. Not just your follow-through."

"How do you know so much about softball?" she asked, squinting. Gabriella had taken her hat off and let her hair down. It was a little wild from being kept up through the game, and that now translated to unencumbered and sexy as hell. Something Ryan decided to try to ignore, but her midsection already felt wobbly, and that tingle across her arms and shoulders seemed to have doubled. Her mouth was dry even though she'd just downed a bottle of water.

"It's something to do in Jersey to stay out of trouble. Kids hanging out around our apartment building tended to wind up worse for it." She shrugged. "I've always been more of a rule follower."

"It suits you. The rule following."

"Says a non rule follower."

Ryan made sure to appear shocked, confused, and offended. None of which she was. "You don't know that."

"Oh, please," Gabriella said with a laugh. "Cheated on your taxes?"

"Maybe some of my nights hanging with Billy weren't exactly business meetings."

"Speeding tickets?"

"I get out of those," Ryan said simply.

"Because of the way you look."

"Nope. It's my charm."

"Trust me. It's both. Doesn't mean you didn't break the damn law."

Ryan widened her eyes. "You're swearing at me now. It's getting serious."

Gabriella held her gaze but didn't say anything. She seemed amused until the glimmer in her eyes faded into something sincere. "Yeah. Maybe."

Ryan's game had been the last of the night, and most of the crowd had shuffled out of the complex. The snack bar dropped its window closed, and they were alone on the side field with enough light from the fluorescents bleeding over to see by.

"What about that swing?" Ryan asked, reminding them of the mission at hand.

Gabriella straightened, all back-to-business now. "Show me your stance."

Ryan picked up a bat, faced the front as if preparing for a pitch. She felt Gabriella's gaze on her and that had an effect. On a lot of things.

"It's here," Gabriella said, touching Ryan's hip. Ryan rolled her lips in at the contact. She experienced a recognizable stirring in her lower body, shoved it to the side, and remained still, attempting to listen. Gabriella moved behind Ryan, her body close and her voice quiet. "If you just adjust your hips back a bit, like this, you'll level more force into your swing. You gotta keep your follow-through, though."

"Hips back, and more follow-through," Ryan repeated.

"Let's see it."

Ryan blinked, still recovering from the moment prior. Gabriella's hands on her hips. The heat of her body from behind. "Right. Uh, the swing." She took a moment to reset her stance, hips back as instructed, and swung through. It was an easy enough fix, and she could see how it added to her momentum.

"Yes. Like that. See?" Gabriella said, clapping. "It's subtle, but it really will make a difference."

Ryan grinned, straightening. "I have to point out that you just handed your opponent a much stronger hitter."

Gabriella pointed at her face, which was steely and focused in a near glare. "Do I look nervous?"

"You look beautiful," Ryan said without pause. "I'm not sure there's much you could do to change that."

Gabriella's lips parted slightly at the compliment she didn't seem to expect. It took a moment for her to rebound, and when she did it was with a cheeky grin. "Charmer."

"No." She shook her head seriously. "Sometimes I'm charming. Tonight, I'm just me."

Gabriella looked skyward, and a moment later, Ryan understood why. The first drop of rain hit her arm, the second her shoulder. Gabriella frowned. "Uh-oh. They said showers later tonight, but I thought we had time." The sentence had barely fled her lips before the heavens opened up in a full-on storm.

"Whoa," Ryan said, wincing with the assault of huge drops.

Gabriella let out a little scream, followed by a laugh. "Get your stuff! Hurry!" They scrambled with hats and bat bags and gloves. But it was too late to save themselves, and they both knew it. The rain had drenched them in a matter of seconds, and they laughed their way in defeat to the parking lot, hopping into Ryan's truck for shelter.

With soaked clothes and wet hair and faces, they looked at each other in shock. "That wasn't supposed to happen," Gabriella said, still laughing, because what else could they do?

"Oregon for you. Are you as drenched?"

Gabriella nodded, pulling her yellow wet shirt away from her skin as rain pelted the windshield with force. "Beyond."

"Yeah. Me, too." She attempted to see through the glass with little success. "I can try and take you to your car, but I'm not sure either of us should drive anywhere until it eases." The intensity of the rain only seemed to be increasing, providing a lively soundtrack.

Gabriella winced in apology. "I was hoping you'd give me a ride home, actually. I came with my friends."

"Oh. No problem at all." Was it wrong that she liked that Gabriella felt like she could count on Ryan for that sort of thing without even having to ask? Because she could. "We should maybe wait a few minutes. See if Mother Nature leaves us a window to escape."

"Sending her good vibes now." Gabriella looked over at her. "You played great today," she said quietly.

Ryan faced her. "You, too. The line drive you caught." She shook her head, remembering the little hop that had propelled Gabriella into the air and back down again with the ball and the out. Her signature move. "You continue to shock me out there."

"Why is that?"

"Girls I crush on don't tend to be such badasses. They're nice enough and smart enough and amazingly capable people, but you? You dominate everything you set out to do, it seems."

Gabriella blinked. "You have a crush on me?"

"Please. You know I do." Then she realized something. She'd insinuated as much but had maybe never said the words out loud.

"I knew you liked to flirt with me. They're different."

Ryan exhaled slowly, realizing she was now wading into deeper waters. Didn't matter. Here went nothing. "Like I said, I think about you a lot. You're fun to be around, and you call me on all my bullshit." She laughed. "All of it. You're friendly and warm and confident and so beautiful that when you walk in a room, the rest of the world stops." Gabriella hadn't said anything, so she continued. "That's new for me, and it has me, well, not always knowing the right thing to do or say. I'm sorry about that part. I think that—"

She didn't get to finish because Gabriella's lips were on hers as the world skidded to a glorious, mystifying pause. Gabriella had leaned across the center of the cab and caught Ryan's mouth, pressing her soft and surprisingly warm lips to Ryan's. Just as Ryan had a chance to absorb what was happening, Gabriella pulled back an inch, met her eyes briefly, before going back in, this time determined, hungry, and hot as hell. Ryan didn't hesitate to return the kiss, lost in a haze of shock and lust. Her hands slid beneath Gabriella's jaw, cradling her face as they kissed each other with the built-up tension she'd been drowning in for weeks now. She wasn't alone there. She knew as much now. She could feel it through every second of that kiss. Gabriella's wet hair tickled the top of her hand, and everything in Ryan's body screamed for more. She slipped her tongue into Gabriella's mouth, pulling a murmur of appreciation. She'd fantasized about kissing this woman, but the reality was so starkly different. It rocked her, amounting to so much more than she could have imagined or even hoped for. Suddenly, she wasn't chilled from the rain. In fact, every part of her was warm, alert, and on fire.

"Wow," Gabriella said, pulling her face back. For a moment, the only sounds in the truck were the rain and their joint attempt to find air. "I should apologize. Right?"

"Don't you dare," Ryan said.

Gabriella swallowed and took a moment, as if sorting through her thoughts. Ryan could identify. Hers raced. "It's not a good idea, Ryan. You? Me? C'mon."

"We're adults."

"In very different places with entirely different wants, needs, and trajectories. I'm not the hookup type, and I don't want to be."

"I know that." Ryan studied the ceiling, as thunder struck. "I don't know what place I'm in." She shook her head, trying to explain and failing to locate the words she needed. "But it's somewhere new. I want things I've never even thought about for myself before, and I wish I knew how to communicate them. But I'm not sure I even understand it."

Gabriella nodded. Thank God she didn't discount Ryan's feelings right off. "How about this? Why don't we work on our *friendship*? Something a little more practical, and I will try not to maul you in any more thunderstorms."

"No. I'd rather work on other things," Ryan said with a grin, doing her best to be persuasive. She just wanted a chance to prove she wasn't a consummate player who would disregard Gabriella's feelings. She didn't have to be that, didn't want to be.

"Ryan." Gabriella covered her eyes with the heels of her palms, and for the first time, Ryan witnessed her struggle.

"Hey, it's okay. I get it. I see what you see, okay? I don't fault you."

"It sounds awful when you put it that way." Gabriella held out her hand and let it drop in defeat. "I'm trying to keep my life simple right now. Do I happen to find you ridiculously attractive?" She pinched the bridge of her nose. "God, yes. And do I now know you have the best lips on the planet? Unfortunately, I do. Dammit. Hold on." She reached for Ryan, finding her lips. With a laugh, Ryan happily obliged, sinking into the wonder of Gabriella's mouth, letting her take control and relishing the power of her kiss. Her skills were not just good, but expert level. If only the damn cup holders weren't in the way. She leaned halfway across anyway, hoping to ease the burden for Gabriella, anything to keep the kiss from ever ending because it was the most exciting and wonderful place to be.

"Good God," Gabriella whispered against her mouth.

"I don't see any reason to stop doing this," Ryan murmured and kissed her again. Deeply.

"Just for a moment longer," Gabriella gasped out a beat later, then went in again, angling her mouth for better access. Damn, the things this woman was inciting in Ryan from her head to her tingly, impassioned toes. And finally, and tragically, Gabriella pulled away again. She closed her eyes, and then opened one sheepishly. "I attacked again."

"There are better words for it."

"Still. I'm horrible."

"Don't say that," Ryan whispered and placed her thumb over the lips she would be dreaming about tonight and for many to come. "Here's the plan. We're not going to talk about it at all." Which was entirely preferable to deciding the whole thing had been a mistake, something Gabriella had a tendency to do, she'd found.

"Okay," Gabriella answered, in the shortest sentence Ryan had ever heard her construct.

"We're going to drive you home and make no decisions about anything. Nothing to stress about. Nothing to overthink. Light as a feather."

"A feather," Gabriella repeated. "No stress." Her fingertips touched her swollen lips, as Ryan drove them out of the parking lot in considerably less rain. "Ryan?" she said finally.

Ryan passed her a smile. "Yeah?"

"That was really good. Too good."

She nodded, a huge smile taking shape. "I won't ever forget it."

When they arrived back at Tangle Valley, they didn't kiss each other good night. In fact, they didn't say much at all. That thrum of palpable energy still passed back and forth between them like the best kind of tether. For a moment, they just stared at each other, lost in whatever spell had been cast the moment Gabriella's lips had descended on Ryan's. Finally, Gabriella relaxed into a grin, nodded once, and hopped out of the truck. In a few moments, she was gone inside the cottage. What had transpired between them remained, however, and wrapped around Ryan like the most wonderful of blankets. The world felt different now. Music sounded new. Trees were more beautiful in their darkened glory. Alive. Vibrant.

Full of so many breathtaking prospects.

Ryan's heart soared.

# CHAPTER NINE

Were you canoodling with an Otter in the rain last night? Tell it to me straight."

Joey's question stopped Gabriella mid-onion-chop because of its specificity. Joey stood outside her window that next morning with a huge grin on her face, almost like she'd uncovered a lost treasure. Gabriella continued to slice as she pondered the best maneuver here. In fact, prep work was the absolute best remedy for Gabriella's head when things got complicated up there, which was why she'd hurried out to Jolene first thing, after her ten minutes of silence, of course, to slice Italian sausage, roll out her pasta, and dice vegetables in large quantities. She could always make use of leftovers later. Grandma Filomena, whose name she carried as a middle name, used to drive home the importance of leftovers regularly. "More food, more happy," she'd say.

Gabriella paused, finally settling on a response. "There was rain. There was an Otter. And there was some kissing." Back to chopping. Peppers next. Much to do. She imagined Joey's eyes lighting up because, let's be honest, this was good fodder. "But wait a sec." She raised her gaze. "How did you know so much?"

"About that…" Joey pointed at her. "One of the Biddies opened a Biddy Instagram account. I have no idea who taught those women how to use technology, but they're off and running with it, snapping photos like mad and tossing them up there willy-nilly. They might be out of control. This morning, there's a photo of you and Ryan from last night, cozy behind a bat. Very cozy." Joey shrugged. "I know the rain started up shortly after we left, so I imagine you got caught in it together, which I happen to think is very romantic sounding."

Gabriella's mouth fell open. "There's a photo?" It came out like a squeak.

"Don't sweat it. It's a really sexy photo." Joey fanned herself.

"I'm not interested in that kind of attention." She gestured to herself with her knife. "It's a situation I don't even have a handle on. I certainly don't need other people speculating and whispering about it." Her blood pressure rose as the reality descended. "I moved here to focus on my food. Keep life easy and relaxed and simple. Now I'm Lustful Linda behind a bat."

"Who's Linda?"

"I made Linda up, Joey. Follow me. But I'm here now."

"Sorry. Got it, Linda. But don't make it personal. It's part of life in Whisper Wall, unfortunately. That's what people do here. Drink wine and talk about each other. All day long. Then they get up and do those two things again."

"I guess I need to give them less to talk about."

Joey sighed. "Gabs." A pause. "Linda. Whoever you are. If you like Ryan, I don't see the point in pretending you don't."

"Of course I like her. She's funny in that sly, underplayed way she has, and knowledgeable, and kind. You should see her with her mom, JoJo. They're great friends. Plus, yeah, there's some crazy chemistry there that makes me want to kiss her clothes off. None of that is the point." She realized she'd gotten a little loud.

Joey blinked. "I'm not sure if you're aware of this, but you're wielding that knife like it's your third hand, and maybe we could set it back down now for the safety of all."

Gabriella looked at the knife and let it fall onto her cutting board with a thud. She placed her hands on her hips. "Sorry. I just have a lot of opinions on the topic."

"I see that. I think you could have less. Maybe stop trying to have it all figured out. That advice comes from someone who desperately did that once, only to crash and burn."

"You sound like Ryan. She wants us to think about it less."

"Is that an awful idea?"

Gabriella raised her knife and sliced clean through a red pepper in a whoosh. "Maybe not."

"Good." Joey pointed to the overwhelming piles of chopped vegetables. "I'm going to leave you now before the army you must be expecting arrives or I'm accidentally cleaved to death as you process your emotions via vegetable."

"Well, at least come back later, and I'll make it up to you with some amazing lasagna fritti. I cook my best when I'm conflicted. Knock your blond locks off."

Joey brightened. "Suddenly, I'm feeling much better and balder." She glanced up the hill with an exaggerated gasp. "Would you look at that? A pickup truck approaches. Must be time for someone's workday to begin. I wonder who. Ta-ta."

"Ta-ta?" Gabriella called as the truck drew closer. "Since when do you say ta-ta?"

"Since you canoodled with an Otter. I'll be back in a couple of hours for that fritti."

Gabriella swore quietly at her friend, who was enjoying this struggle way too much. As Ryan's truck passed by en route to Tangled, Gabriella made sure to focus on the work in front of her. Not on its beautiful driver. What was next? Oh, yes, spices—and weren't they a lot of fun? A spice party indeed. Captivating. Toss a little oregano here. "Shazam," she called out. A bit of garlic there. "Wham." Basil, next. "Whoopah." All intuitive, no measurements needed. When she looked up, the truck had passed and she could breathe again. That was, until she remembered the heat level of that kiss the night before, how everything in her had woken up and reached for Ryan in the most primal form of yearning. Her knees felt it now, as communicated by their Jell-O-like state. She closed her eyes for just a moment and let her memory transport her. She remembered Ryan's fingertips touching her cheek. Ryan's hands cradling her face. Ryan's tongue exploring—

"What are you thinking about?"

Gabriella's eyes flew open, and her hand fluttered to her heart. Ryan stood in front of her looking like a jeans model. "Jesus in overalls!"

Ryan quirked an amused eyebrow. "Really? Did he wear those?"

"Listen, I don't know. It's the kind of thing that flies out of my mouth when someone terrifies me. They never make sense." She exhaled slowly and felt the traitorous smile tug at the corners her mouth because Ryan was standing in front of her, and, God, she was happy to see Ryan. Too happy, but she refused to police herself right now. She couldn't after that sizzling flashback that still had her lower body awake and paying too close attention.

"Hi back. How is your morning going?" Ryan asked. She was sunny today, which was nice, but all she wanted was for Ryan to take her in the back of Jolene before the world arrived.

"Oh, standard. Meat, veggies, knives. All the rage."

"Well, I don't want to interrupt, but I brought you this." She set a coffee cup from the Biscuit in the service window. "Clementine says you take your coffee with two creams and two sugars."

She stared at the coffee cup, touched. "Clementine is right, and you're thoughtful."

"Have a good day, Gabriella. I'm off to work."

"Wait." She craned her head through the window. "That's it? You just stopped by to smile and drop off coffee?" There was no mention of the night before, no poring over details, or what they should do about the fact that everything felt different now.

"Exactly," Ryan said over her shoulder, showing off those damned dimples. "Stop by when you're done, and see what you think of the floors. They should be finished by this afternoon."

"I will do that." Excitement sparked…for a lot of reasons. She let herself revel in every single one of them for a change. "Oh, and Ryan?" she called.

"Yep?"

"You look amazing today. Have a good one."

"Thank you. Wow. Already happening," she said, walking backward an extra beat or two before heading off to start work, where she'd use her hands to transform a blank canvas into all that Gabriella had been dreaming about. Well, all she had been dreaming about until right *now*.

❖

Tangled was beginning to shine and sing. The progress stole her breath. That was Gabriella's immediate impression when she stopped by the jobsite after finishing service for the day. Ever since that morning, when Ryan had popped by with coffee, she'd been waiting for the chance to peek her head in. She'd detoured to her cottage first and cleaned up, changing out of her work clothes and into something a little more fashion-forward and flattering, selecting her slim-cut jeans that Joey said made her ass look amazing, brown sandals with the cute heel that added a couple of inches, and her favorite turquoise top that flowed a little at the hemline. All the while, very aware of the fact that this was not normal behavior for her. This was the Ryan factor, and she felt like a pebble in the current, as it swept her swiftly along. Nervous and exhilarated in combination. That was her.

She took in the partially completed dining room. The place felt new and charming and open and welcoming. She imagined the tables she'd selected dotting the dining room and complementing the pending charcoal and gray accented floor tiles wonderfully. Ryan had recommended they lay the tiles at an angle for a pleasing effect, and Gabriella knew her judgment was accurate. The main portion of the construction was mostly complete, showing off the open concept she'd imagined, where the kitchen was visible to the diners over an extended countertop that segued into the bar that would serve Tangle Valley wines, Oregon craft beers, and maybe a few choice spirits, also local. The lighting fixtures hadn't gone in yet, but the kitchen was structurally in place, waiting on appliances and supplies. Ryan, as far as she could tell, was on schedule and moving along at a swift place, which in the land of contracting seemed unusual. Gabriella was beginning to think that Ryan was prioritizing Tangled above other jobs on her behalf, a gesture she was more than grateful for.

"It's not a restaurant yet, but it's inching its way there." Ryan appeared from the kitchen behind Gabriella, carrying a broom. Her hair was down, but she had a baseball cap on backward that was way sexier than it should have been.

"It's like I can see it all so clearly now. The guests will check in here." She raced over and demonstrated a welcoming gesture from the host's stand. "The bar with the tall shelves over there." She ran over and pretended to pour a drink with panache, and then set to pointing. "The grill, the walk-in, the server paths. Everything."

Ryan seemed to enjoy the show, her eyes bright. "Please come demonstrate the different stations every day after work."

"Now that you've requested as much, I just might." She let her hips sway a little bit extra as she walked toward Ryan. "What's next?"

"Staining and paint tomorrow. Cabinetry arrives Monday. The ones you wanted, by the way." Ryan slid her hands into the back pockets of her jeans, which were dusty and faded and looked perfect on her.

"The half wall is gone. Whoa." How had she missed that?

"Told you I'd figure it out."

"And you did." Gabriella's heart felt like it might burst at any moment. "I'm more than impressed with the progress you've made. Every day I come in here, it's a new surprise. It's starting to feel real."

"Trust me now?" Ryan took the broom and went to work on the new floors, clearing them of dust and debris from the installation.

"It's not that I didn't trust you. It's more like I'm a relentless control freak when something matters to me. I gotta have my hands everywhere. Even places they don't belong."

Ryan raised a saucy eyebrow but respectfully moved on, pausing and pointing. "You? No way." She went back to sweeping with a smirk on her face. "I love the top, by the way. And the view." But she wasn't looking at Gabriella's top when she said so, which meant she'd noticed it in the course of their conversation. That realization had Gabriella feeling warm and satisfied. Even a little alluring, standing there in her heels. The shirt *did* have a generous neckline. She had zero regrets about it now.

"This old thing?" She winked, feeling coquettish and liking it.

Ryan stopped and rested on her broom. "I don't think you have any idea of the power you carry. It's not fair." She shook her head and went back to sweeping.

"I wish I could say the same back, but I think you're well aware."

Ryan didn't seem fazed. She took the ball cap off and let her hair tumble out of it in a movie Gabriella would hold on to and play back again later. "You're different. With you, my confidence is"—she shook her head—"unrecognizable, lost, and confused. Wandering in the desert looking for water. Stranded on an island with a lone volleyball. Floating through space unaccounted for."

Gabriella raised a hand. "Now you're just being dramatic," she said with a laugh. "Which in my experience is very unlike you."

"See? That's exactly my point."

She leaned against one of the columns she'd grown to like so much. "How do you account for it? Because we're so different?"

"We are, and we aren't. I like food, kissing, and seeing a project come together. So do you."

Gabriella nodded. "Oh, you're highlighting our common ground. We also both have fingers and toes."

"This has taken an interesting turn."

"It always seems to." Gabriella folded her arms and smiled. There was that ping-pong chemistry again, flitting back and forth. God, it was addictive.

"Do you want to keep logging body parts? We can discuss all of them. I certainly have favorites."

Gabriella grinned but said nothing because she could see that game taking them to forbidden places, and that unnerved her.

"I have a feeling we have even more in common than we realize," Ryan said like a know-it-all.

Gabriella reached for the broom, understanding that this cleanup session was the last step before Ryan would leave for the day. The least she could do was help out. "Well, we can both sweep as well. Another commonality. Let me have a turn, so you can finish up."

Ryan handed her the broom and gathered up a few stray tools Gabriella couldn't identify if her life depended on it.

She felt Ryan regarding her from across the room. "Let me ask you something about your job."

Gabriella pushed the broom and on the last shove lifted her leg like an ice skater gliding after a jump. "Go for it."

"Do you ever feel frustrated working in a truck for all of these months, given your skill set, your training?"

Gabriella shook her head automatically and paused her sweeping-ice routine. "The minute a chef starts to think like that, they've lost themselves. If you want to make amazing food, you have to step outside of your comfort zone, get creative, and roll your sleeves up." She gestured in the direction of the truck. "I worked in a truck for the first time one summer about ten years ago. Some of the best down-and-dirty culinary education I've ever had. Some of it better than the fancy institute that trained me." She looked around the room behind them. "Am I ready to get back into a full-sized kitchen and elevate the dishes I've spent time out there developing? Hell, yeah, it can't happen fast enough. But the back-to-basics refresher has been invaluable."

Ryan had been listening intently, having paused her work. "I admire that. Not allowing yourself to be above a valuable experience." She nodded. "I'm going to remember that one."

"The ego is a horrible roadblock on the road to achievement. That one is from the fancy institute." She slid a strand of hair behind her ear. "I don't want that to happen to me, you know?"

"Somehow I'm not worried. Speaking of ego, I'm about to check mine."

Gabriella raised a brow. "Dangerous."

She took a breath and walked the distance to Gabriella. Up close and personal, Ryan did not disappoint. Her skin was practically flawless, and those expressive blue eyes were so easy to get lost in, dreamy as they were. "There's a place on Center Street, Truth or Dare. Heard of it?"

"Of course."

"Good. They have developed a very impressive list of craft cocktails, and their head mixologist is hosting a gathering to launch his latest find, a Ginger Snap Smash. He took a trip to New York and apparently fell in love with it at this up-and-coming bar in the city. Anyway, he's bringing it to Truth or Dare, and I thought maybe we could meet up there. Try one out."

"Hmm. You want to hobnob with me in public. Possibly get ginger-smashed."

"Could be fun."

Gabriella hesitated at how formal this sounded. Near date caliber. Was she prepared to open this door officially?

Ryan watched her as she contemplated. "Okay, you're not saying anything, and now my fragile ego has crept back in place." She rocked back on her heels in overexaggerated anticipation. "You can say no. I will be devastated but understand."

"When is the event?"

"Tomorrow night at seven."

A pause. "Okay."

"Okay?" Ryan blinked and squinted as if waiting for the catch. There wasn't one. She'd decided to go for it. The event sounded like something she'd love, and there would likely be lots of people from town there. Spending time with Ryan was a bonus she didn't let herself get hung up on because honestly it was the biggest lure.

Gabriella raised a shoulder, trying to keep things light. "I figure if we can make out in rainy parking lots, we can certainly grab a drink together. See you tomorrow, Ryan," Gabriella said, handing off the broom as she passed. With a hearty pat to Dale, who lifted his head in gratitude before retiring to his sun slumber, Gabriella headed home.

Excited.

Nervous.

But also excited some more. She closed her eyes and smiled as she walked the winding path home. Her heart was reaching, that was for sure, and she wasn't sure she wanted to get in its way.

# CHAPTER TEN

Truth or Dare was already packed when Ryan arrived at five minutes to seven. She wasn't one to show up to social occasions early, but she made the extra effort because tonight felt like a big deal. She'd changed her outfit three times because all of a sudden she apparently owned nothing she liked. Also a new development. Her stomach squeezed uncomfortably as she watched the crowd, prompting her to roll her shoulders to release the pent-up nervous energy as she scanned the room for any sign of Gabriella. She hoped she'd like the event, and that they'd have fun. Lots of familiar faces had come out to the launch, but no sign of Gabriella yet. That was good. Ryan could figure out how to relax and be a regular human being before she arrived.

The bar, which had only been open a handful of months, was pretty swanky for Whisper Wall. Leather-backed booths flanked the perimeter, with a large open space at the back of the room for mingling, wine, and cocktails. That's where the action of the event was tonight.

"Hey there, Ryan Jacks," Monty Murphy said in his crisp white shirt and jeans.

She grinned and gave him a squeeze. As one of the two cowboys who owned the Moon and Stars Ranch, he did a lot for the town's dog population, fostering and placing them in the best homes. She beamed, always happy to see the cowboys. "So they'll just let anybody in this place?"

"Well, we heard you were going to be here, so we snuck in. Plus, I need a quote for a new shed."

She laughed. "You never stop the work out there, do you?" She'd put in a deck for him and his partner, Stephen, a few months prior. She'd always liked those guys, especially since they were the ones responsible for bringing Dale into her life. Gay cowboys on a ranch, fostering rescue dogs? Easy to like.

"We're a work in progress. Oh, and you got a date looking around for you," he said, gesturing vaguely over his shoulder to the bustling room.

That sent a bolt of energy. "Thanks. I guess I better find her."

"Which one is it tonight?" Stephen asked, joining them with a gleam in his eye. He was the cheeky one, prone to teasing.

Ryan could handle it. "No, no. Not like that."

"No?" Monty asked, intrigued.

She shook her head and brought her tone down to sincere. "I'm slowing down a bit, and maybe that's a good thing." It was a boring answer and went against her reputation, which people tended to have fun with, using it to clap her on the back or tease her.

His smile faded a tad. "Well, good for you. I think that's pretty awesome."

"It is," Stephen said and raised his glass in her direction. "The new Ry."

She made a *yikes* face. "I guess so. For now, I better go find my date. Can I bring Dale by soon to roughhouse with your pack?"

"We'd love it. Maybe we can hear more about the changes you mentioned too. I'll grill some steaks."

"Cool. See you soon," she said with a nod and set out to find Gabriella, which proved much harder than she'd anticipated.

"Truth or dare," a female voice said in her ear from behind. A cocktail, what Ryan imagined to be the Ginger Snap Smash, snaked around in front of her. She accepted the drink and turned, already knowing it wasn't Gabriella. She'd planned to wait, so they could try the drink together, but actually, a little fortification first might calm her nerves.

"Hi, Heather."

"Hey, there," Heather said in her trying-to-be-sexy voice. Her blond hair, roots showing, was extra wild and curly tonight as if she was making a statement. She wore a black cocktail dress and stilettos. Well, okay. She knew who she was dealing with. Heather Leonard had two speeds. Regular Heather and Flirtatious Heather. It was clear who'd come to play tonight. Her boobs had as well, as she'd pushed the girls up and put them on display with a neckline that didn't mess around. She averted her eyes from the show, focusing purposely on Heather's face.

She squeezed Ryan's hand. "You've been MIA lately, and trust me, I've been looking."

"It's been crazy. Work is busy, and I've been going straight home." She took a long sip of the cocktail, which was pretty amazing. Refreshing with a kick. So she took another drink. Strong, too. "How have you been?" It was a polite thing to say. Heather was a CPA, and that meant she was just coming off her busy season and likely looking for a little fun and relaxation. Ryan was one of her favorite diversions, but that simply wasn't going to happen. In fact, she was shocked how little interest she had.

"I've been able to breathe again," Heather said. "Thank God."

Ryan quirked her head. "What do you mean?" Another sip of the cocktail, which she would definitely be having another of because this one was gone. She scanned the room anxiously for Gabriella. Instead of relaxing her, the alcohol had her even more convinced that tonight was high stakes. She cared about how it went more than she'd allowed herself to reflect on fully. She just craved time with Gabriella. It's all she'd thought about all day. Her stomach felt off, though, and her cheeks warm. Wait. There she was. Gabriella was making her way into the open section near the bar. The cowboys must have assumed Heather was her date. She tracked Gabriella, who stopped to speak to Clementine, looking like the breath of fresh air she was. Dark jeans, brown booties with a heel, and a sleeveless white blouse. Classy, sexy, everything. Ryan caught herself smiling automatically because the night just got better.

"Remember my dad?" Heather yanked her back to the conversation. "The one I don't really talk to? Passed away this week, out of nowhere. It brought up a lot of unresolved emotions for me, you know? I've been struggling with these battling feelings."

Ryan's attention swiveled back to Heather and her proclamation because it was awful and unexpected. "I'm so sorry. I had no idea."

"And because I freaked out and didn't call in while we're in the middle of busy season, they put me on probation at work, and it feels like I'm being watched like a hawk."

"Oh, that's terrible," Ryan said, downing the rest of her drink. Heather signaled for another one, which wasn't ideal because she had a date to get to and didn't have time for another with Heather. A stolen glance at Gabriella and she saw her speaking with the cowboys, laughing along at some joke. Gabriella turned and caught Ryan's gaze across the bar and smiled and waved four fingers in greeting. Ryan raised her drink and smiled back. But Heather was still talking. No, emoting. She went on about how gutted she was that she'd not reached out to her father before he died, and how she felt like the world was moving against her now. Ryan nodded, and the minutes ticked by. She was halfway through her second Smash and feeling the heady results. The room seemed too small, and she could no longer see Gabriella through the throng of loud, talkative people, shoulder to shoulder. She absently realized that Heather had a hand on her waist as she talked, no, *shouted* above the din. The whole night had gone wildly off the rails.

"God, I'm just so glad you came tonight. I had a feeling you would, and that you would understand all of this." She placed a kiss on Ryan's cheek, which made her wince. "You're a good listener, sweetheart."

She took a step back, reclaiming control. "I'm sorry you're having such a hard time. Truly." She gestured behind her. "I do need to speak to a friend I was meeting here, though."

Heather straightened, a near bristle. "Oh?"

"Yes. Please excuse me." Ryan held up her second Smash, which had just arrived. "Thank you for these. I owe you."

"Many ways to pay me back. I'll be over here."

Ryan nodded, not sure what to do with that. She gathered her courage and hoped to salvage what was left of the evening, traversing the crowd until she found Gabriella toward the front of the room, standing by herself. She closed her eyes, feeling awful. "Hi. Sorry about that." She swallowed and waited for a response.

"Sorry about what exactly?" Gabriella asked. She was smiling at Ryan but it wasn't real. She knew Gabriella's real smile. It made her eyes light up and crinkle, and her face transform into a glow. This smile was plastic, for show only.

"For taking so long to come over. I got caught up in a dramatic thing."

"Seemed like it. Heather, right? She was at the Scoot a couple weeks back with you."

"Not *with* me."

"Details." She handed Ryan her empty glass. "Thank you for introducing me to this. Fabulous drink. These guys know what they're doing. But I'm tired, and I think I'm going to go."

"Go? What? Why?"

"I've been here for close to forty minutes, Ryan, and this is the first time you've spoken to me."

Her defenses flared, whether justly or not. "Well, then, why didn't you just come over and talk to me?"

Gabriella dipped her head and looked up at Ryan, her expression darkening. "It looked a little too cozy for three. But I did learn about a new cocktail," she said, pointing at the empty glass. Ryan's spirits hit the floor. "And tonight was educational. I'm glad we did this."

She closed her eyes, willing it all to stop, for time to go backward so she could make tonight everything she was hoping it would be. "Don't. Please. There's a decent explanation for this. Heather needed a friend."

"She definitely needed something, and you were there." A pause. "Good night, Ryan. Enjoy whatever it is you have going."

Gabriella didn't seem angry. Resigned was a better word, as if she'd just received the bad news she'd expected all along and was rolling with it. Ryan felt like crying, which was something she rarely did. As Gabriella headed straight for the door, Ryan took stock. Yes, Heather had needed a friend, but Ryan should have handled that whole thing better. Nerves and alcohol had interfered with her decision making, and she'd fallen back into what she'd always known, what was comfortable, and shit, now what? How did she recover from this nosedive she'd allowed herself to plummet into? Her head swam and self-recrimination fired, but Ryan was determined to fix this misstep if it killed her. She hightailed it out of the bar into the parking lot where she saw Gabriella climbing into her green Jeep Wrangler.

"Wait, please."

Gabriella looked up patiently.

"Can we talk before you go?" Ryan asked.

Gabriella sighed. Luckily, however, she closed the car door and walked the five steps until she stood in front of Ryan. "Sure we can," she said maturely.

"I'm sorry tonight didn't go how we planned."

"Me, too." She nodded, and for the first time, Ryan caught the sadness in her eyes. She wasn't just mad and resigned. She was hurt. "You need to know how tonight made me feel. You invited me to the cool kids' club and ignored me the whole time. I picked out my outfit, took a deep breath, and showed up here *for you*, only to be made to feel less important."

God, that slashed at her. She tried to defend what was probably indefensible. "But you have to understand, Heather needed—"

"I hear you. Heather needed. I do. No major crime was committed here, and you and I are good." She winced as she explained further, "But I fear there will always be Heathers with needs out there that you'll tend to when called upon. I'm not a stand-in-the-background kind of girl. I know my limits and can save us both a lot of time and effort by acknowledging them."

Ryan shook her head. "I screwed up. That's what this is, but it's not some kind of forecast."

Gabriella paused. "Isn't it, though?"

A car pulled up behind them, and they turned. Damn it all to hell. Heather eyed Ryan through her open car window. "How about that repayment? Hop in?"

Ryan closed her eyes, wanting the pavement to swallow her up. So not helping.

Gabriella laughed quietly. "See? This is your life, and I'm an idiot." She gestured to the car. "You know what my life is? *20/20* on the couch with popcorn. We're just not suited. See you at Tangled, okay?" She offered Ryan an *everything is fine* shoulder pat and headed for her Jeep.

Ryan didn't even try to stop her this time. She could not have come up with a more fucked-up way to end the night. Gabriella thought the worst of her, and she'd blown her chance at what seemed like something real. Something important.

Left alone with just Heather, she turned. "Not tonight, okay?" That's when she heard the words and what they implied. That there would be other nights in the future. "Actually," she said, taking a bold step forward, "I think maybe it's best we just focus on the friendship side of things. I'm not available for anything more."

Heather pulled her face back and frowned. "What's going on?"

"I think it's just time for me to chill out a little. Focus on a slower pace for my life." She was admitting a lot to Heather. She didn't let too many people in on the regular. Tonight, it seemed important to be open and honest. If only she'd started the night that way. Better late than never.

"Who are you, and what have you done with my sexy Ryan?"

She frowned, not liking the implication. She shrugged. "Just me, trying to do what feels right."

Heather rolled her eyes, and Ryan felt small. It shined a light on how little she knew Heather outside of their flirtatious banter and late-night hookups. "Have fun with that," she said and rolled up her window, effectively cutting Ryan out of further conversation.

When Heather peeled out of the parking lot, drawing stares and showcasing her anger, Ryan was left alone, embarrassed, but with a startlingly clear handle on who she wanted to be and which parts of her she wanted to leave behind. Something significant was playing out in her life, and she damned well better pay attention. Very much aware of the precipice on which she stood, Ryan was determined to shed old habits.

She walked to her truck, shaking her head along the way. Gabriella or not, she was heading somewhere different, and she was set on making it there. "Don't you dare screw this up," she murmured. "Don't you dare."

"What do you mean she didn't really speak to you?" Madison asked. "I thought Ryan invited you to the event on some kind of pseudo date? Not that I thought it was a great idea." It was late morning, and Gabriella swung by the barrel room to say hi to Maddie before finishing up prep for lunch service. Her culinary assistant today was Jace, who'd already cut himself twice with a paring knife while slicing zucchini, so she probably shouldn't leave him for too long.

Gabriella thought back on the whole cocktail launch debacle with a pit in her stomach. "Me, too, which is why the whole thing surprised me, but not entirely." She shook her head as if trying to land on the right words to explain. "Ryan means well. I know that part. She didn't plan to blow me off, but she got caught up with that Heather person because that's what Ryan does, gets caught up with pretty girls. A little time with this woman, a little time with that one." Gabriella raised a shoulder. "I just don't want to be the *that one* in any scenario. And that's precisely who I became."

"Thank you." Madison nodded wholeheartedly. "That's what I've been saying all along. Why would you ever want that?" She leaned against the side of one of the racks and brushed a wavy strand of dark blond from her eyes. She'd likely had a long day already, and it was only ten a.m. "You deserve so much more, and it makes me want to tell the Biddies all about this and let them go to war with Ryan Jacks online."

Gabriella's eyes went wide. "No, no, no. Let's not release the blue-haired hounds just yet. Ryan is just being Ryan. I should maybe start to expect less."

Deacon, Madison's assistant winemaker, approached. He was working full-time at the vineyard while finishing up his degree in Portland. "If you're talking about the account that gang of ladies started, there's already a photo from last night of you and Ryan in a tense-looking conversation in the parking lot of Truth or Dare. Over a hundred likes." Madison turned to him and his eyes went wide. He held up his palms. "None of them were mine."

"How do they do that?" Gabriella asked. "Nary a Biddy was there last night."

"A network of spies. Recruits," Madison said, in just as much awe as Gabriella. "I wonder if they're paying for photos like real-life tabloids. They're more sophisticated than we thought."

"Are they here now?" Gabriella whispered, looking around the barrel room slowly.

Madison glared at their surroundings. "One has to assume they're everywhere. My thoughts? Kick Ryan to the curb, and focus on all the good stuff you have going on. Tangled is shaping up, and once it opens, you're going to be too slammed to worry about what Ryan Jacks is running around doing."

"Good point."

"So it's a plan?"

"Most definitely."

"Go team."

She high-fived Maddie. "Nailed it." Gabriella straightened, renewed. "Better get out of here and toss some pizza dough. Service starts in an hour, and Saturdays are usually hopping. The Jade has been practically bussing all their guests here."

"I'm gonna stick around and audit acidity levels. A little less people centric."

"Which is why you love it. Thanks for the pep talk, Maddie," she said over her shoulder. "Be nice to the wine."

"Anytime, Gabs. And remember the plan."

She tapped her temple. Turned out, she didn't have to. Ryan kept to herself that day. No coffee delivery, lunch invitations, or requests for consults. Her truck sat in front of Tangled, and Gabriella spotted Dale taking his normal midday snooze.

The next day was the same, and so was the day after. She received a few questions via email addressed to both herself and Joey, which she answered promptly after visiting Tangled after-hours. The renovation had continued to make great strides and looked less like a jobsite and more like a restaurant. She stood in the center of the soon-to-be dining room late that Wednesday, marveling at the rapid change.

"Well. What do you think?"

Gabriella turned, surprised to see Ryan standing in the doorway, arms folded and a conservative smile on her face. Everything in Gabriella leaped to attention. She was instantly energized and realized just how much she'd missed Ryan. Dammit. "The paint colors really complement the floors. Especially the complexity of the texture on the back wall."

"I thought the same thing." Ryan came farther into the room, and Gabriella's spirit hummed as if she'd just come alive after days of meandering through life, something she wasn't even aware she was doing. Double damn. "I also think keeping the original windows and enhancing with the custom sills was the right call. The light in here is insane and will make for a gorgeous lunch service on the weekends, with the guests overlooking the vineyard."

Gabriella closed her eyes and imagined it, doing her best not to sway to the imaginary music in her head. The first restaurant with her vision, her design, and her menu. She felt a little like Cinderella looking forward to the ball. When she opened her eyes again, she felt Ryan's gaze on her. She attempted a smile but couldn't deny that everything warmed.

"I want to apologize for the other night."

Gabriella raised a shoulder. "You don't have to. We're good. I told you that."

"It doesn't matter that you forgive me for acting like an ass. It matters that I acted like one, so you might have to put up with my apologizing a lot."

She nodded, and it seemed like the tension in the room evaporated some. "I can handle that."

"Good. I'm sorry, by the way. Again." Ryan smiled. "And with that, I will leave you to bond with your new baby. Back in the morning."

"See you then," Gabriella said. She watched Ryan leave and then exhaled. Ryan hadn't attempted to put them back on the track they'd been on. She hadn't flirted or flashed her playful grin that made Gabriella's stomach feel like she was on a wonderful roller coaster. For the best.

But the coffee was back the next day. Hmm. The still hot cup sat on the ledge of her closed-up truck when she arrived for lunch prep. She didn't make a big deal about it but accepted the gesture as a waving white flag.

*Plumbing, electrical, and HVAC tomorrow*, a text message from Ryan read the following day. *Also, I'm sorry. Did I mention that? Dale said hey before he went back to sleep.*

She smiled. The space Ryan had given her along with the small gestures and hard work began to soften Gabriella's heart. She caught herself watching for Ryan's truck each morning, wondering what kind of day she had, and how her mother was doing. Okay, she also tried to imagine what Ryan was wearing that day. She could admit to being a hussy on occasion. She wasn't dead.

"What have you been up to?" Gabriella asked, when Ryan stopped by for a to-go order of calamari later in the week.

"Well, to start, a lot of equipment delivery. And when I say a lot, I mean it. You guys have a complicated existence back in that kitchen. Then the dishwasher didn't fit. My fault. So I had to rework some of the spacing, which maybe set us back forty-eight hours, unfortunately."

"Ah, I see." A pause. "I meant *you.*"

"Oh," Ryan said, her mouth in the shape of the word. "I've been okay. Doing a lot of thinking. Some staring at walls."

"I saw that you guys had another great run against the Prairie Dogs."

"They did put up a scrappy fight, though." The dimples appeared and all felt better.

"Well, they are prairie dogs. I wouldn't mess with one."

Ryan met her gaze. "Didn't see you there."

"I left after my game."

Ryan nodded, seeming to absorb the step back Gabriella had taken. "Did I mention I'm an idiot and very sorry?"

"You're not and you did. Well"—she held up her thumb and forefinger—"a little bit of an idiot." Her heart loosened another notch, and she relished sharing space with Ryan again. It felt like a soft blanket and a really potent shot of whiskey all in the same stroke.

"The thing you said the other night, about watching *20/20*?"

Gabriella frowned, vaguely remembering the reference.

"It stuck with me."

"Big fan of the show? Amy Robach doesn't mess around."

Ryan swallowed. "No. I've only seen it a couple of times, but the idea of watching it with you, a quiet night, a good glass of wine"—she gestured to the vineyard behind them—"sounds better to me than just about anything else I can come up with."

"Well, I'll be sure to invite you over to my enthralling couchfest sometime."

"This weekend?"

Gabriella paused. She'd not meant the invitation to be literal, but what was she supposed to say now? This was not at all part of her plan to take a step back from Ryan's magnetic pull. "Um, maybe. Let me look at what I have going on."

"Fair. I ambushed you." Ryan smiled.

"I can handle it," Gabriella said, brushing off the reflex of concern, and heading to the door. "In fact, definitely come."

Easy. Done. Not a big deal in the scheme of life. This was the perfect opportunity to embrace a newfound dynamic between them. She was emotionally mature and grounded in what she wanted in life, so why the hell shouldn't she hang with Ryan, whose number she now had? It had nothing to do with how much she'd missed even their short interactions over the past couple of days. She'd pop some popcorn, slather it with butter, and they could watch some edge-of-your-seat interviews with politicians or, if they got lucky, try and solve a cold-case murder. She was pretty sure it would turn out to be the ex-boyfriend, which put her way ahead of the game.

"Yeah?" Ryan said, looking surprised and relieved to have not crashed and burned. "Friday, then?"

"Um, okay. Yeah. We can relax after a killer workweek, have some snacks, and I know where there's wine."

"Bound to be around here somewhere." Ryan was now a puppy with tons of energy. A really cute one, too. "What can I bring? Is there a protocol? I want to get this right."

"Listen, don't stress. Just bring yourself, and well, I don't dress up, so…"

"Casual clothing it is. God, I'll have to scour my closet," Ryan said, furrowing her brow in mock sincerity.

She laughed. "Hey, you can't make fun of my comfy couch night. That's rule number one of comfy couch night."

Ryan touched her chest. "And risk banishment? No way. I finally pulled the invite after a lot of missteps."

"Good point."

"And now I'm going to get out of here before I completely ruin this or you change your mind. My track record is not great."

"Another valid point. You can bring one of your girlfriends if you want. I have extra popcorn." She tossed Ryan a cheeky look.

She winced. "I deserved that but will politely decline. Lock up for me?"

Gabriella pulled the key from her pocket. "On it." She watched Ryan walk toward then past her out of the restaurant, taking in the hint of vanilla that she now associated only with Ryan. She stood alone near the bar and placed her hands on her hips. The cool, casual, breezy woman who'd just invited Ryan over to her home receded slowly, leaving one who was smarter and annoyed she'd given in to what she longed for over what was intelligent. After hearing the truck drive away, Gabriella locked up and took the shaded path to her Spring Cottage where she plopped onto the steps to watch the trees sway gently in the comfortable breeze.

It was only a few minutes before she heard rustling in the vines a few yards away. She blinked and craned her neck because she thought she heard voices. There, down the path, she saw Bobby step out from the field and offer a hand to none other than Loretta Daniel, who smiled at him and gave him what could only be described as *the eyes*. Gabriella gasped and covered her mouth. What was she witnessing? But the heated look they exchanged as they waved farewell told her everything. Loretta headed back up the path to the tasting room, and Bobby, her neighbor, strolled in her direction toward his cottage. Scandal among the vines! She looked for someone to tell. No one. Dammit. She watched in shock as he passed, nodding to her and offering his usual half smile, quiet guy that he was.

"What a day, huh?" she called to him as he approached, trying to remain normal. Did she look normal? She felt her eyes might be wide, and her voice might be shrill and loud. First, she invited Ryan over, and now Bobby and Loretta were sneaking around? What the what?

He nodded his agreement. "Gettin' hotter, too." He talked about the weather a lot, so she seized the topic.

"Moving toward eighty degrees, I hear." But her mind was elsewhere, and confusion reigned. Maybe if she opened up to Bobby, he'd open up to her. Plus, she could use it, quite honestly. Bobby was always such a good listener. "I know you're busy and tired, but here's the thing, Bobby. I'm being dumb again."

He blinked, took off his ball cap, and scratched the back of his neck.

"I am the captain of my own ship. I chart the course, and I decide what's good for me and what's not. I mean, right?" She realized she wasn't making a lot of sense, but when she tried to express herself, that's what came out.

"Ah. Yep," he said, shifting uncomfortably. This was not the kind of thing Bobby, in her experience, generally said much to. He was more of the silent, head-down, and get to work type, enjoying a brewski on the porch of his cottage after a long day in the fields and maybe a ball game on TV in the evenings. He didn't involve himself in much interpersonal conflict, which was maybe why he was her perfect sounding board.

But it felt like she'd opened some kind of vault, and it all came tumbling out. "I'm also perfectly capable of sorting things out as I go. I can have a good time if I want to, or take the smarter route and live a chaste nunlike existence until I'm ninety-two."

His eyes went wide, but bless him, he stood his ground.

"Ryan Jacks is younger than me. Wilder than me. And probably a bad bet. I shouldn't get mixed up with her, right? No matter the feelings I'm dealing with."

He shifted his weight. "Um. Well. She's nice enough. Helped me unload my equipment the other day when my guys were off in the back acreage."

Gabriella softened. "She is kind, isn't she? I think that comes from her mom and how she was raised. Never rude or cruel. At least not intentionally."

"Sounds about right. Went to school with Joanna. She was smart and real nice, too."

"Have you ever struggled where matters of the heart are concerned, Bobby?" She raised an eyebrow and waited for him to unleash on her in the same manner she had.

He took a moment, appearing uncomfortable. Finally, "Nah."

Gabriella blinked and slowly sat upright from her relaxed position. Well, that wasn't what she expected to come out of his mouth. "What about *Loretta*?" she asked, peering over at him.

"Oh no. Nothing to do with Loretta," he said, popping his hat back on his head. "She was just helping me strip some of the buds in the field."

"Mm-hmm," she said.

The hat returning to his head meant he was done with the conversation. With a quiet nod, he headed off down the path to his cottage, leaving Gabriella mystified, keyed up, and downright confused about so many things around Tangle Valley.

# CHAPTER ELEVEN

As the credits rolled on the makeshift screen they'd erected in the large barn, Gabriella wiped her eyes and looked over at her friends, who each came with a different brand of reaction across her face. *Splendor in the Grass* had been their movie that night, and yes, this one had been her choice, a favorite of her mother's, who loved a good heart twisting.

"I don't get it. Natalie Wood deserves better," Joey said with a frown. "This is not okay."

Madison stood up and pointed at the screen as the familiar theme music they'd heard through much of the film played achingly. "That's it? They just go their separate ways? He *loves* her. This is crap. It makes no sense. I demand an immediate refund."

Gabriella's heart hurt, too. But she'd been prepared for it. Her friends were new to the film. She tried to explain. "But Warren Beatty is now settled into his new life. Too much time has passed. He has to farm his land and keep that child in diapers, and there's spaghetti for dinner, so he can't chase the past."

"I think I get what Maddie is getting at, though," Becca said, but with a lot more composure. "It's tragic that they didn't fight hard enough for each other, and now look at them. Regretsville town mayors, both of them. Though it's all his fault. I have to say."

Gabriella contemplated the meaning, liking the part of movie night when they talked it out. "Maybe this is a sharp reminder that some things you think are meant for you just aren't."

"In some cases, but I think these two were different," Becca said, gesturing to the screen. "This was their great love, and they blew it. Now they have to live a subpar existence, settling for less because they didn't go after what their hearts truly reached for, messy as it would have been."

The words swirled and settled squarely on Gabriella's shoulders, burdensome and troubling. Because surely that wasn't what she was doing in her own life, was it? Not being open-minded enough to see what might be right in front of her just tied in a messy bow?

"Stop with the wisdom," Joey said. "It's annoying when you're always right."

"Can you put that on video?" Becca held up her phone, and Joey distracted her with a kiss, grabbing the phone and lowering it. Madison still stared hard at the screen as if attempting to work a puzzle she carried a lot of resentment for.

"You okay?" Gabriella asked, touching her shoulder.

Maddie seemed to shake it off. "Yeah, just depressing, you know? The one that got away is a bitter pill to swallow. Makes you think." She attempted a laugh but the mirth didn't quite achieve authenticity. "Where's a good shoot-'em-up movie when you need it?"

Gabriella sighed. "For once, I might actually agree with you."

Madison held up her phone, mimicking Becca. "Can I get that on video?" And for a moment, Gabriella recalled a time in life when the two of *them* were that same type of couple like Joey and Becca, happy and playful and looking forward to more. While the relationship hadn't blossomed the way she'd hoped, she still had a handful of fond memories from those days.

"Not a chance."

Madison exhaled loudly. "Next movie night, something a little lighter."

"*Wizard of Oz*," Gabriella said, her spirits lifting.

Madison didn't hesitate. "No."

"*Frozen.*"

"Definitely not."

"You seem stressed, Maddie."

"Don't do it," she warned.

"Let it go."

Madison closed her eyes in defeat just as Gabriella launched, full voice, into the song, chasing Madison out of the barn and into the night with her serenade as their friends laughed.

She hadn't told any of them that she'd invited Ryan over the next night. Part of her felt embarrassed about her inconsistent, waffling outlook. Another part of her wanted to figure this out on her own without the rest of the world weighing in. The movie and Becca's assessment weren't far from her thoughts as she settled into bed that night.

She didn't want to be that person, the one who let something potentially wonderful slip through her fingers because, like Warren Beatty, she was too stupid to know what she had.

"Don't be Warren," she murmured to herself as sleep slowly descended.

❖

Darkness draped the vineyard when Ryan pulled onto the property and drove down the hill then around the perimeter to Gabriella's cottage. She wore her soft jeans and an off-the-shoulder blue slouchy sweatshirt that was perfect for chillier evenings. Arms covered, a shoulder out. A nice combo. At least, she hoped. Comfy couch night seemed specific.

She knocked on Gabriella's door and grinned when she answered. Gabriella wore calf-length stretchy workout pants, a pale pink hoodie, and nothing on her feet but blue toenail polish.

"Hi," Ryan said quietly. She wasn't sure why quiet was the way to go, but it seemed as if the theme warranted calm and tranquil, reminiscent of the way people spoke at day spas. She held up her offering. "I brought popcorn."

Gabriella grinned and snatched the jar of kernels. "Gifts are not necessary but will never be turned away. Come in, new guest. Welcome to the Spring Cottage of Tangle Valley, where comfortable dreams come true."

"That's quite the promise." Though she'd passed the cottages many times, Ryan had never actually been inside one. Gabriella's house was so very her. An open floor plan with the kitchen and living room joined as one. A yellow and sage color scheme that felt warm and happy. On the walls hung large framed photos of vibrant flowers, interspersed with still lifes. Breads, wineglasses, and an empty outdoor café. Along the entryway, Ryan spotted smaller family photos. One of them featured Gabriella with three other women she had to be related to.

Gabriella followed her gaze, pointing at the frame. "My sisters. I'm third in the lineup. Teresa, Angela, me, and that right there is my younger sister, Mariana. She's cheeky."

"It's like three variations of you, but not quite you," Ryan marveled. "That's crazy."

"Genetics. You should hear us all in one room." She frowned. "Correction, you should avoid it. We can get pretty loud when we all get to talking at once. You have to top the other three, you know?"

"I think this is something I need to experience."

Gabriella winced. "At your own risk."

Ryan stretched. "Okay, I'm ready for this. What do we do now? I want to get comfy night right. I can't screw around and miss out on the full experience."

Gabriella pointed to the sofa. "Take a seat and cue up the show. We have a few minutes, so I'll pop this corn. How do you feel about clarified butter and maybe a little grated parmesan on top?"

Everything in Ryan sighed in massive appreciation of Gabriella's suggestion. "How do I feel? I feel like you're a genius, and this might turn out to be the best bowl of popcorn I've ever had."

She hadn't been wrong. After a million *pop, pop, pop* sounds from the pan, Gabriella whizzed around in the kitchen with a couple of fun sound effects like *wham, kapow, boom,* and *voilà*. She presented a big silver bowl and plopped it into Ryan's lap before joining her on the comfy cream colored couch with the sage blanket lining the back. Ryan took a bite of a hot buttery kernel and slid right off the couch onto the floor. She wasn't prone to emotional demonstrations, but the popcorn warranted the physical melting. It was hot, fluffy, and dressed with the perfect amount of warm butter and little flakes of parmesan cheese, which she'd never had before on popcorn.

"How is your popcorn this good?" Gabriella opened her mouth to answer, but Ryan held up a hand. "No. I get it. This is what you do for a living, but I was braced for fantastic already, and I still fell off the couch."

"I don't think I've sent anyone to the floor with popcorn before. I will need to put this in my diary later."

"I can't tell if you're kidding. You keep a diary?" Ryan asked, returning to her chair, intrigued by the idea of Gabriella's innermost thoughts poured onto the page. What she wouldn't give to read them, to get inside her head for just a moment.

"Yep, and this is going in there. Popcorn fanfare and all."

Ryan laughed, and the *20/20* anchor with the dark hair and handsome face appeared. Gabriella snapped her focus to the television like a soldier at attention, so she did, too. It wasn't easy, however, with Gabriella's feet tucked beneath her in such a sexy manner. When their hands brushed against each other in the popcorn bowl, Ryan got a tiny shiver like a middle schooler. She'd learned not to be surprised by the things Gabriella did to her, things no one else ever had, and just enjoy them, even when they had her feeling off-kilter.

*20/20* didn't mess around either. Apparently, a jealous college student had stalked and killed his own girlfriend on the grounds of their university. They knew he'd done it but couldn't prove it. "That's infuriating," Ryan murmured, as the detective in charge was interviewed.

Gabriella pointed passionately. "This happens so often. Juries these days expect DNA, and when there's none to present, prosecutors hesitate to bring charges. It's rampant. I know this from my comfy nights on this very couch. Murder is my jam."

"I've been missing out," Ryan said in jest, but she was every bit as enthralled as Gabriella now. Comfy night was both fun and educational. Okay, a little bit tension filled, too, but the desirable kind.

"You should see last week's. I think I still have it."

"Cue it up," Ryan said with conviction, taking another blissful bite of popcorn. She caught Gabriella staring at her happily. "What? Why are you passing me this brand of smile?"

"I can't tell if you mean it. Do you really want to watch another one?"

"Do Otters take Muskrats to school on the ball field?"

Gabriella gasped at the unexpected smack talk and snatched the bowl of popcorn in punishment, but Ryan caught the side and pulled it back into her lap, along with part of Gabriella, whose lips were now surprisingly close to hers. The struggle for the bowl was placed on hold as their eyes connected. For Ryan, it wasn't even a decision, and Gabriella must have agreed because they both leaned in across the bowl, slow enough that it was purposeful, a clear decision. Ryan dipped her head lower and captured Gabriella's mouth in a kiss that was soft, tentative, sweet. They were testing the waters. But, hell, that didn't last. The kiss caught fire and escalated to hungry in a matter of amped-up moments. The evening news had taken over on the television, but it all seemed to fade into the background, leaving Ryan aware only of the sounds of their uneven breathing and the need to get as close to Gabriella as humanly possible. Without breaking the kiss, Gabriella expertly set the bowl on the coffee table, which was wonderful because there was nothing between them now, and their hands were free to roam. And they did. She pulled Gabriella closer as she pushed her tongue inside Gabriella's mouth, overwhelmed by the sensation. Her entire body felt warm, her skin tingled, and her center ached the more they kissed. Either she'd hauled Gabriella there fully, or she'd climbed into Ryan's lap herself. Didn't matter. She now had fantastic access, and nothing had ever felt better. As they kissed, she slipped her hands beneath Gabriella's pink hoodie, pleased to find no T-shirt underneath. She ran her hands up the warm skin at the small of her back, which only upped her need. She swallowed, steadying herself, feeling her longing take over in a manner she wasn't prepared for, but did her best to go slow and keep her wits about her. She wanted to be attentive and respectful, but if given permission, she'd have Gabriella on her back in three seconds flat, so she could worship her body properly.

Picking up on Ryan's cues, it was Gabriella who pulled down the zipper on the front of her hoodie, revealing smooth skin and a black bra that offered more than a generous glimpse of what was beneath. Good God. Gabriella Russo smiled, and Ryan's eyes feasted. Gabriella had full breasts, the tops of which said hello. With her arms around Gabriella's waist, Ryan kissed the center of her chest and traced the outline of her bra before diving in, kissing all around it. She felt Gabriella's hands tangle in the back of her hair, and that sent a shot of heat straight downward, the ache between her legs becoming ever more pressing as the seconds ticked by. She pulled the hoodie down Gabriella's shoulders, bringing the fabric to her elbows. No woman on Earth was this beautiful. She brushed her lips reverently across one shoulder, kissing down, zeroing in on those breasts until something tugged at her. She blinked, realizing it was the sound of a knock. Two seconds later, the door to their left opened, and Madison walked in.

"Hey, I was wondering if you—" The words died on her lips and she let her head drop, averting her eyes. "Oh. Okay. I'm so sorry. My bad entirely." She turned and immediately headed for the door as Gabriella struggled to get her top back into place.

"Hey, Maddie. It's okay. Wait a sec."

Ryan held her position on the couch, realizing this embarrassing moment in history was best handled by Gabriella. She closed her eyes, lamenting the end of the make-out session and feeling awful about the awkward walk-in both for Gabriella and Madison, who she reminded herself was the ex, making this doubly awkward.

She let her head drop onto the couch as her body continued to scream with desire. She was learning one thing for sure. Life at Tangle Valley was never boring.

❖

Gabriella was horrified, embarrassed, and concerned as she chased after her friend, her own clothing still askew. Madison had made it past the porch and to the pathway lit with the yellow twinkly lights when Gabriella caught up to her. "Maddie. Wait."

Madison placed her palms against her eyes and gave her head a shake. "I'm an idiot for walking in on you. So sorry. It was rude of me. Will never happen again."

"No," Gabriella said, coming to her. "One hundred percent my fault. I like our walk-in policy. I don't want it to change, because that's who we are. I just should have locked the door, and I would have if I'd known that I'd—that we'd—that there'd be something to—"

"You know what? Let's not." Madison said it with a bite that hadn't been present in her voice moments before. She was clearly still processing.

"What's going on?" Gabriella blinked. "Hey, are you angry with me?"

"Not angry. No. This whole thing is just a really dumb move is all," Madison said, seeming to embrace her newfound agitation. "We've been through this, Gabs. That woman is all over the map, and careless, and you know it, and yet, you allow her to…" She shook her head.

"What?" Gabriella said, now feeling defensive. "I'm trying to figure it out. I don't claim to have all the answers or always make the right decisions, but I'm doing the best that I can." She exhaled slowly. "I'm just looking for a little support from my friends."

Madison scoffed, shook her head, and looked back up at the cottage with disdain. "Yeah. I don't think you have mine anymore. Not for this." She tossed her chin toward the door. "Guess you better get back in there."

"Are you serious right now?" Gabriella was floored. It didn't fit or make sense. She called to Madison's back as she walked the path back toward the front portion of the property. "Madison."

"Not right now," Maddie said, holding up a hand without looking back.

Gabriella sighed, confused and shocked by the events of the last five minutes. Her head swam with warring emotions, and the two wildly different scenarios vied for her focus. In the absence of an opportunity to have a beneficial conversation with Madison, she gave her head a shake to clear it, took a fortifying breath, and remembered where she'd been earlier. In Ryan's arms. Their lips pressed together. She'd liked it there very much, and what was more? She'd had such a nice time before they even laid a hand on each other.

When she arrived back in the cottage, she found Ryan waiting patiently, right where she'd left her. She gestured behind her to the door. "Gotta remember that doors have locks for a reason. We're pretty informal around here. I'm really sorry about that."

"No, I'm sorry." Ryan touched her chest. "She's your friend, and that was probably a lot for the both of you. Probably more so given past history."

"Yeah, maybe so."

Ryan chewed the inside of her lip, which was a new move. Maybe it was what she did when she was stressed. "Should I go? You can tell me to go kick rocks, and I will."

The fact that she offered and was willing went a long way. Gabriella tucked her leg beneath her and sank into the couch next to Ryan. She stared at the ceiling wordlessly, trying to let everything settle. "No. I don't want you to go, but I also don't think you should stay over."

"Yeah, I get it. The mood's shot."

Gabriella smiled at Ryan. "Look at us. Like two children disappointed that the school canceled our field trip."

"You're good at analogies."

"I've heard that before."

Ryan sat up, away from the back of the couch. "No. Who tells people that?"

Gabriella followed her up, laughing. "Well, you, for one."

Ryan laughed and leaned back. "Good point." A pause. "She doesn't like me. Madison. Am I right about that? You can say so. I'm resilient."

Gabriella scrunched an eye closed, not sure if she fully believed Ryan was. She carried vulnerability behind her eyes that gave her away. "More like she doesn't like you for *me*."

"Because of what she's heard about me."

Gabriella nodded.

"Well, I guess that makes her a good friend." She rested her cheek against the back of the couch, deflated. "But if I could tackle that?"

"Please," Gabriella said, giving her the floor.

"If I've been carefree when it comes to having a good time, it was

only because it was something mutually agreed upon between parties.
I've never led anyone on, or made promises I couldn't keep."

Gabriella mulled this over. "You're saying you were a player but
very open and honest about that."

Ryan quirked her lips, considering the statement. "Yes, but it
sounds better when I say the two consenting adults thing."

Gabriella laughed. Ryan was immeasurably cute, which just
complicated things infinitely. She was irresistible when she showcased
the cute side. "Are you trying to say that this is different?"

"As a belly dancer and a federal judge."

Gabriella tilted her head. "That makes no sense."

"I know. Weird stuff comes out of my mouth around you because
you're smart and pretty, and I can't help it."

Cute again. She stole a soft kiss, careful not to let it progress
farther. This felt like an important conversation, and Gabriella didn't
want to derail it. She gave Ryan the space to continue.

"I'm not into hookups," Gabriella said. "So tell me why we're the
judge and not the belly dancer."

"Because it's early between us, and I already feel terrifying
things."

"You do?"

Ryan nodded, and Gabriella glimpsed the fear. Interesting. "Do
you?"

Gabriella wasn't sure she wanted to show her cards. Yet here they
were having an open, honest conversation. How could she withhold
when Ryan was offering such transparency? She nodded, letting her
barriers down. "Yeah, I think it's safe to say there are feelings involved.
Feelings I've tried to push to the side. Tonight shows how successful
that little practice has been."

"I can stop holding my breath now," Ryan said with a shaky grin.
"That could have been really awkward."

She took Ryan's hand. "You're not alone. Promise."

"The thing about us? We're not two consenting adults with no
strings. I could do strings." Ryan swallowed. "I want strings."

Gabriella passed her a skeptical look. "Really?"

"Yeah. I don't think I could do this any other way." She touched
a strand of Gabriella's hair that framed the side of her face. "I also
want to know so much more about you. What you do first thing in the
morning. What your least favorite dish might be, given you've been
exposed to so many."

Gabriella met her gaze sweetly. "Have you ever tried monkfish?"

"I can't say I have."

"Then you are very lucky indeed." She sighed. "My turn?"

Ryan nodded and waited patiently.

"One step at a time, okay? No one is asking for a myriad of strings, but—"

"I'm not gonna see other women, Gabriella. I'm just not. I only want to see you. That simple."

Gabriella looked away, her heart aching at the push-pull with her brain. "I keep wanting to shove you away, and dammit, I've tried." She paused. "But what if you're Natalie and I'm Warren?"

"I'm Natalie now?" Ryan squinted. "How much wine have you had?" She laughed. "Would you like more?"

Gabriella shook her head and tried to refocus. "No. Listen to me. I came to Tangle Valley to simplify my life. Lose the fast pace, the drama."

"I hear you."

She realized that somewhere along the way, she'd grabbed hold of a fistful of fabric from the bottom of Ryan's soft blue shirt. "But I don't want *simplicity* at the cost of something that could be *amazing*."

She watched Ryan's face transform and soften. In fact, everything about her did. "You think we might be amazing?" Ryan asked quietly, and the most sincere, perfect, and defenseless smile took shape on her lips.

"I'm saying that I don't know why we met just yet, but we did for a reason."

"I think so, too," Ryan said, pressing her forehead to Gabriella's. She kissed her softly, and Gabriella let out a happy sigh.

"See? Now that felt like everything."

"Because it was." Ryan took a steadying breath. "For now? Even though I don't want to, I'm going to go. But I can guarantee that I'll be back, and we will put that amazing hypothesis of yours to the test." She stood. "Even if you are a Muskrat."

Gabriella, on cue, did the face, and Ryan laughed, hauling her in by her elbows for a final toe-curling kiss to cap off their evening. The way their mouths fit together so effortlessly astounded. They had yet to have a single moment of awkward contact that required adjustment or nervous laughter or any of the physical missteps you'd expect when people were new at this together.

"The way you kiss," Ryan said, closing her eyes and taking a minute. It made Gabriella feel beautiful and sexy, and she loved every moment of it.

"I thought maybe it was just you and your moves."

Ryan shook her head. "Definitely not." She closed her eyes and smiled, as if attempting to recover but maybe not wanting to. "I can safely say that comfy couch night gets the full five stars. Heading over to Yelp to write it up now."

"Oh, then I'll need a website," Gabriella said, following Ryan to the door and checking out her perfect ass as she did so. "I hear it reoccurs."

"Thank God." Ryan hit the porch. "Oh, my mother says hello and demands you come by."

"Will you be there?"

"You can assume that I'll be wherever I know you'll be."

Gabriella laughed, leaning in to their new strings-attached plan. Letting herself enjoy their new unrestricted dynamic, terrifyingly heady and delicious as it was. "Part of me doesn't want you to leave. That part wants to take you right back inside."

Ryan hesitated. "The old Ryan would have leaned in to that uncertainty and persuaded you to invite me back in, and she'd have been good at it."

"You're not going to do that?"

Ryan shook her head. "Good things are worth doing right. We have time. I'm not going anywhere."

"Good. Me neither." With her index finger, Gabriella pointed at her mouth. "But maybe for the road."

Ryan's response was immediate and came with a slow grin. She practically leaped into Gabriella's space, which made the air around them spark to life as they kissed in the small shred of moonlight. Alone on her porch, she watched the most beautiful creature she'd ever met stroll past the sleeping vines of Tangle Valley to her maroon truck, leaving behind a promise of so much more to come.

Gabriella touched her swollen lips and grinned, clinging to the memory of that kiss for a few seconds longer. Comfy couch night had never felt so good.

❖

A couple of days later, and Ryan didn't know what to do about the messages hitting her phone. Since she'd stepped back from her usual nights out, her inbox had been getting a workout. Heather Leonard had definitely faded away after she'd declined her invitation at Truth or Dare, but Lana had doubled her efforts, as had a variety of other women who hadn't seen Ryan out much lately.

The quantity of messages alone alerted Ryan to the fact she'd been playing the game way too hard. Perspective was everything, and she didn't full-on regret her past because it had brought her here, but she winced when she saw her behavior in the stark light of day. She was a sex-positive person for sure, but there came a point when you just needed more. At least, she did.

"What are you staring at?" Billy asked and sat down next to her on the brand-new steps in front of Tangled. The craftsmanship was fantastic, and she planned to use that same subcontractor on many more jobs. This place was really beginning to come alive.

"What do I do with this?"

She turned her phone around, and he read the message on her screen out loud. "*Come out tonight. Worth your while.*" He looked up at her and quirked an eyebrow. "Who's *Brianna from Portland club*?"

"Got me. I have a vague memory of dancing with her a few times one night. That was all."

He pointed at the phone. "More than a vague memory to Brianna from Portland."

"I know." She shook her head. "There are a lot of these kinds of messages coming in."

"Yeah, because you've stopped showing up at your spots and showing off your hair and dimple thingies the women are always talking about. Your public is calling you." He pointed at her phone again. "Literally."

"Yeah, well, I only seem to want to show up for one woman these days."

"I know, and it's the strangest fucking thing. Peter Pan grew up and wants to read the paper and knit, sipping tea from a damn cup and saucer on a vineyard. Dinners out on Tuesday at six p.m. sharp. Home by seven thirty."

She smacked him one. He didn't flinch. "Knock it off." A pause. "Plus, I don't knit."

"I'll amend the fine print."

She sent him a wink. "But seriously, when we're together? Nothing boring about it."

"I believe it. I've seen her. I've *met* her."

Ryan marveled. "Right? She's different. So what do I do about this?" She lifted her phone, needing outside guidance.

"Can I give it a shot?"

"Knock yourself out." Maybe Billy had the magic touch for saying no. For her, it was a new, unflexed muscle.

He narrated as he typed. "*Fuck. Off. I'm. Taken. Bitches.*"

She laughed. "Effective, yet I don't see that really working out well for anyone. I'd like to keep my tires inflated if at all possible."

He erased his work and tried again. "*Wrong. Number. Who. Dis?*" He turned it back around for approval.

"Nope. I'm not great at lying. I lied to my guidance counselor once and couldn't sleep for three nights."

"Wuss." He smacked his lips and gave it another shot, taking his time, but no longer reading his work.

Finally, he handed the phone back, and she read the message he'd constructed. "*Great to hear from you, but not the best time for me. I've met someone and am concentrating on our relationship right now. But hope you're out there killin' it with the other lady chicks. Do lots of lady kissing.*"

"Not bad. You had me up until lady chicks." She amended the last section. "*Hope you're well and we can catch up soon.*" She glanced at Billy. "That sounds a bit more like the friend zone, yeah?

"Not if by *catch up*, you mean..." He raised his eyebrows to punctuate.

"No. I don't." She erased the last sentence and tried again. "*Hope you're well. Take care.*"

"Probably better. Don't add a heart. Or any topless women."

She squinted at him. "What kind of emoji does *your* phone come with, Billy?"

Joey Wilder appeared on the path just as she hit send on the message, which she would reuse as needed later.

"I'll let you chat with your client," Billy said and headed back inside, break over. "Hey, Joey," he said over his shoulder.

"Billy the Kid." They'd been lab partners back in the day.

Ryan shaded her eyes against the late morning sun and stood. The day was beautiful and amazing aromas from Gabriella's truck wafted all over the property. "Hey, Joey."

"How's it going?"

Ryan nodded. "A few minor setbacks with the appliances, but I think we have it all sorted out." She pointed to the ground. "I got your email about the walkway not extending as far out as you were hoping, so I have my guy coming back this week to add to it."

"Happy to hear it. I don't want to take too much of your time, but I want to be sure we're on track for our soft opening." Joey's blue eyes sparkled. She was great at dealing with people. "We're inviting about fifty of our VIP wine club members on the fourteenth to coincide with the release party for our chardonnay."

"Right. I remember, which was going to be quite the push."

Joey's grin didn't waver. Positive assumption. That was friendly Joey Wilder. "Do you still think it's doable?"

She hesitated, knowing they'd be cutting it close. The release was just over three weeks away, and Gabriella was already hiring staff and setting up trainings, cutting into any chance of overtime in the space. "I think it's *possible*, but it also means we have no cushion. If anything else sets us back—inspections, permits, a water leak, a nuclear attack—we're a no-go, and I'd hate to screw up your party."

Joey rocked back on her heels, her blond hair bright in the sunlight. "I think we have to risk it, right? I'm counting on you." A pause. "In more than one sense."

Was that a nod to Ryan's personal life? It had been a couple of days since comfy couch night with Gabriella, and she imagined as a close friend, Joey might have been given the skinny. "I have the best of intentions and big plans." A pause for emphasis. "In more than one sense."

That earned a bright smile. "Good. And listen, I really appreciate you sticking as close as you could to our budget. I've heard horror stories."

"Well, that's not how I like to handle things. I plan for the hiccups, and it tends to pay off."

"In more than one sense?" Joey asked. Then she dropped her shoulders. "Okay, I'll stop with the code. I know you and Gabriella are moving into a new lane, and you and I have known each other peripherally since high school days, right?"

Ryan nodded.

"I'm looking out for my friend. She has the biggest heart of anyone I know, and I want to make sure this isn't some shiny thing you're following until you get bored and want to be back up for grabs at the Scoot on a crowded Thursday. That would wreck her and me."

"You just said so many words."

Joey swallowed. "I know. Tends to happen when I feel strongly about something. I apologize."

"No, it's okay. I'm glad you did." Ryan ran a hand through her hair. "Just give me a chance, okay? I promise I'm a good person with zero interest in being up for grabs on a Thursday or any other night of the week."

"She just sent blow-off messages to women hitting up her phone," Billy said, craning his head around the entrance. He cringed. "I was eavesdropping. I can admit to that."

"We know," Ryan said with a bounce of her eyebrows. "But I was doing okay out here."

"Were you, though?" Billy asked. He looked at Joey. "I helped her write the message. Telling the other chicks to kick rocks."

"You told them to kick rocks?" Joey squeaked, horrified.

"What? No!" She passed Billy a stand-down look. "He's paraphrasing, being a dude. Ignore him."

Billy nodded. "I'm a total dude." He nodded a few more times, his body still not entirely visible, giving him a creepy floating head vibe. "I'm gonna get back to varnishing again. Lonzo misses me."

"Hell, no, I don't," they heard a voice from inside say.

"Gonna leave anyway," Billy said. "I miss Lonzo."

"Good call," Ryan said calmly. She refocused on Joey. "So, here's the thing. You and I are on the very same page." She shifted, deciding to just go there. "And I don't know how you'll feel about this, and you can totally decline. I'd understand. But maybe we can all do something together soon? Madison, too, of course."

Joey hesitated on that last part. "I'll work on that. Madison is… protective. Becca and I would love to, though."

"Great. I'll check with Gabriella." Ryan leaned against the brick pillar, and she decided to just go there, take it one step further. "Is that all we're talking about? Madison is just being protective?"

Joey shrugged, but the unease that appeared on her face said a lot. "You'd have to ask her."

Ryan nodded, thinking that at this point, she'd leave those conversations for Madison and Gabriella. Didn't mean she didn't feel a pit in her stomach wondering if she had competition in that arena and worried about her ability to compete with someone like Madison. "Not really into confrontation with someone's ex, you know?"

"I remember that about you. Always calm. Always kind." Joey

descended the steps. "I'm gonna add dinner at Tangled to our release invitations. You'll get it ready. I know you will."

"Ah, a gambler."

"I didn't say I wasn't nervous."

"I have your back, Joey. We'll make it happen."

Five hours later, Ryan ran home to shower and returned to Tangle Valley at sundown with a bundle of wildflowers she picked near her lake house. She'd spent time finding the right color combinations that would look best in Gabriella's cottage and next to each other, careful not to rush the process. She pulled her truck along the path and parked it off to the side, in front of Gabriella's place. She took a seat on the folded down tailgate of her truck, flowers in a jumble beside her, and sent a text. *Delivery for you. Beep. Beep.*

Moments later, the door to the cottage opened, and Gabriella, long dark hair in a ponytail, stepped out in cutoffs and a green T-shirt that looked perfect against those hazel eyes, making everything in Ryan light up at the sight. She waved happily.

"What is this?" Gabriella asked suspiciously. But the huge grin that enveloped her face said she liked the surprise.

Ryan lifted the bouquet she'd assembled. "I don't know how you feel about flowers. We haven't discussed that yet."

"I love them."

"They remind me of you, so I couldn't imagine not making the introduction."

"Wow. They're gorgeous," Gabriella said and took the long stems in her arms, cradled in the crook of her elbow. "Are these from Possum's Blossoms? I love how they have the most heart-clenching arrangements. Why are so many things around here named after rodents?" She waved off the question and focused on the flowers. "Just look at these. They did a great job."

"Those are from me. I picked and assembled them. Though I agree. I like a good possum arrangement."

Gabriella pulled up short. "You did not pick these beautiful goddesses." Gabriella leaned her hip against the open tailgate. "You build things, tear things down, hammer nails, get dust on your face."

"And pick flowers."

"Who are you?" Gabriella said, studying the bouquet and beaming.

"There's a gorgeous field near my place. In the spring, the colors send your heart into your throat. I'll show you sometime. Just after four, you can get the most gorgeous photos."

Gabriella blinked as if discovering a new planet in her backyard. "You're a photographer, too?"

"No, a dabbler. I like black-and-whites. Something about the rawness of shadow." Ryan grinned, not minding the assembly of all the things she loved. "I guess I like the diversity, and it's fun to share it with you. How was your day?" She gestured to the spot next to her and Gabriella hopped up as the sun fell slowly over the fields to the right.

"I had a very somber Stefan working in the truck with me. He's seventeen and has decided the world will never understand him."

Ryan exhaled. "Oh, Stefan. It really does get better."

"We talked about outlets. He agrees that cooking is a great one, so he's going to help out beyond just the internship hours he owes the high school. He'll be back Saturday morning for service, and I'll be teaching him how to make potato gnocchi." She shrugged. "He has the chops to be good."

"You don't know what a difference a mentor like you makes in that kid's life. I speak from experience."

Gabriella nodded. "I'm starting to see that. I could probably use him here and there at Tangled, too. Would get him some good experience backing up some career chefs. I've got three hired, you know. Keith, Nadine, and Joy. The dream team."

"I did not."

"Keith's a transplant from back east. From my culinary school days. And the other two are both young female chefs who have promising résumés from Portland's food scene. I'm lucky. My food army is looking sharp, and they've embraced my menu enthusiastically. It means I can take time off here and there and know the place is in crackerjack hands."

"I've never worked in a restaurant, so please let it slide that I don't know this, but you'll be the head chef?"

"Executive Chef, but yes. I'll expedite some nights, jump on the line and cook others. But with only twelve tables, we're not a big operation. I'll be a jack-of-all-trades, visiting tables, updating specials, and managing the restaurant on a daily basis, not just the food."

"Damn." Ryan faced Gabriella and pulled a bent leg up onto the truck bed. "You must be a skilled multitasker."

"You have to be when you grow up in a household like mine. Four girls, my parents, and two aunts in a thousand square foot walk-up. Imagine my father, bless him, and all those women with different trajectories in that tiny space."

"Now that sounds like a party."

"That's a polite characterization." She blew a loose strand of hair off her forehead. "I learned early how to roll out my pasta, listen to my sister go on about her boyfriend, feed the dog, and watch *General Hospital* all while bumping into eighteen people." She laughed. "Anyway, those were excellent skills for a chef to develop, and they're hopefully just as good for running that place." Her gaze fell on Tangled in the distance and lifted to the eaves of its beautiful roof. Soon there'd be a sign in front and, not long after, people arriving for a rustic Italian meal prepared by Gabriella and her new team. Ryan couldn't wait.

As if reading her thoughts, Gabriella squeezed her shoulders together in excitement. "Will you come to the soft opening?"

She blinked. "Oh. Um, I thought Joey said it was for the winery's invited VIPs."

"And our own. You're mine, by the way, and you're formally invited."

Ryan absorbed the declaration that made her heart clench and her palms sweat. She wasn't accustomed to feeling this way. She loved it on one hand, but it also felt like a lot to lose. Terrifying. How was she supposed to get used to this? "Then I'm there," she said simply and finally, at long last, kissed the lips she'd missed. It had been days. Gabriella tasted like strawberries, which she decided must be her lip gloss. Ryan prayed she'd never stop using it. They pulled back slightly.

"Hi," Gabriella said, searching her eyes as if memorizing them.

"Hi, back."

"You should have led with that move."

Ryan laughed quietly. "Filing away for next time, because I always seem to want to kiss you."

"Then do." Gabriella leaned back on her hands, her ponytail swaying from the motion. "Now tell me about your day."

"Boring. Lots of sweeping. Some demo work on a job across town. I worked with the outdoor guys on your walkway. It's longer now, and the slight curve really does make a nice difference when you approach the restaurant."

"I saw. I love it. What are your plans for tonight?"

"I thought I'd grab a slice of pizza and make some progress on a bench I'm working on."

"A bench, you say?" Gabriella looked thoughtful, sitting up again. A sparkle hit behind her eyes, and she grinned. "Want company?"

Ryan pulled her face back, intrigued. "You'd be into bench making?"

"I'm a pretty good cheerleader is all I'm saying."

Well, that certainly took her places. She banged on her truck, not one to miss her chance. "Hop in."

## CHAPTER TWELVE

By the time they took the eight-minute drive with the windows down out to Ryan's lake house, the sun hung much lower in the sky with only an orangish-pink sliver showing. It would be dark within twenty minutes. Gabriella loved the mystery that came with dusk, the anticipation of the evening ahead. Tonight, there was a slight breeze rustling the trees, and the temperatures had dipped from the warmer afternoon, making the night feel like it came with possibilities.

The truck pulled to a stop in front of a wooden two-story home along the most picturesque lake. Gabriella stared, struck by what they'd just come upon, the beauty, the simplicity. She'd not been out this way before, but this stretch of land on the outskirts of town was…beautiful. From a short distance away, she listened to the lake lapping against the small dock extending from the back of the house.

"This is where you live?"

Ryan slid her hands into the back pockets of her faded, sexy jeans and looked around. "For about four years now. Saved everything I had and built this place slowly over time."

"I'm sorry. I thought you said you built this entire house. Say the thing again, and I'll listen more carefully."

"You're cute."

"You're off topic. But thank you. The house. Go."

"Well, I wasn't the only one who laid hands on it. My crew came out when I hired them, and my contractors. But I definitely have a lot of my own blood, sweat, and love in this place. Kinda my baby." She shrugged, sheepish and endearing. Gabriella wanted to kiss her then and there. "At least, that's how I think of this place."

"With very good reason. It's stunning." Gabriella wrapped her arms around herself. "You should be thrilled with how it turned out."

"Thanks." Ryan seemed proud of her work but still humble.

Gabriella studied the two eaves, one above each window. Gorgeous. The large front porch with two rocking chairs, probably built by Ryan, stood in invitation. She grinned, inhaling, as if that would allow her to hold on to this place awhile. Ryan's home came with a serenity the likes of which Gabriella had only seen on TV. *House Hunters* or some kind of travel destination show. But she'd never met someone lucky enough to actually live like this.

"Tell me you go out there," Gabriella said, taking Ryan's hand and dragging her to the side of the house for a better look at the dock.

"Every day. Sometimes I start and end the day there. Dale, too."

"That dog is your shadow."

Ryan's lips tugged with affection. "My lazy shadow. He sleeps more than any other animal I've ever known and eats a ton, too."

"I think that Dale just happens to appreciate the pleasures life has to offer. I envy him. Sometimes I think I should do more of that."

"Command pleasure?" Ryan slid her arms around Gabriella's waist. "I vote yes. In fact, I can, you know, help." They stood quietly for a few moments, and then Ryan asked, "So you like it?" She shifted her weight, uncharacteristically. That's when Gabriella understood how big a deal this was for Ryan. She was nervous and cared about Gabriella's opinion of her home. A lot, it seemed.

"I'm in love with this place. I might steal it from you, if you're not careful. Have my own little parties on that dock with Dale, the big lazy lover boy."

"Don't you dare tell him about these plans of yours. He'd kill me dead in my sleep for that kind of chance with you." Ryan moved behind Gabriella so they could face the water together and wrapped her arms around her from behind. God, the fit on them was perfect, the most natural thing in the world. She leaned back against Ryan as a grin spread across her face.

"Maybe you can come, too. Maybe."

Ryan offered a squeeze. "Oh, my night just got better."

They watched the gentle drift of the current just yards away. The sun was all but gone now but still added a touch of a glow to the water's surface. Achingly beautiful. Gabriella made a point to memorize the moment. "Do you bring people out here much?" She didn't want to be jealous of Ryan sharing this view with others, but it crept in anyway.

Ryan gave her a squeeze from behind. "Oh, I think you might be asking if I bring back women, specifically."

"I just imagine it's likely. It's your house. Why wouldn't you show it off? Entertain."

"No."

"No, you don't entertain when they're here?"

"As in, no, it's not something I've ever done." She went quiet a moment. "In fact, I can't remember bringing a date here ever. Just Billy mostly. Lonzo came once. My mom comes by."

Gabriella disentangled herself and turned so she could see Ryan's face. Their height difference was noticeable. She liked it. "That can't be true. One or two. Or five. At least."

"No." She shrugged, all nonchalant and matter-of-fact. "I've not brought a woman back here. Well, until tonight."

Gabriella grappled with that, nearly speechless. "Then why am I here?"

"Why do you think?"

"Because I invited myself?"

Ryan turned her around and threaded their fingers together, palm-to-palm. "I only bring the important people to my home. It's personal. A part of me."

Gabriella felt that sentence square in her chest. Her heart thudded pleasantly, like when you received good news that you didn't know you were waiting for. "I'm a VIP?"

Ryan quirked a smile of concession. "Yeah, okay? Yeah."

Gabriella placed a kiss on her chin, squeezing her waist. Ryan looked down, and Gabriella shifted that kiss straight onto those gorgeous, full lips. "I'm honored. But can I ask a question?"

Ryan stared down at her. Most specifically, at Gabriella's mouth. "You can try. My attention is elsewhere."

"When do I get to see the rest of it? Most importantly, your kitchen. I can tell a lot about a person from their kitchen."

Ryan laughed. "Then you shall never see mine."

"You better show it to me right now. I'm not even kidding." She jabbed at Ryan's ribs, making her dance.

"Fine, but you have to stop that and never do it again." And then as they walked, "Don't you dare open my fridge. I don't think I could withstand the horrified look on your face."

"A ketchup bottle and jar of jelly?"

Ryan hesitated. "I think there might be some yogurt, too."

"Praise the heavens for that, at least."

The rustic quality of the home extended to the indoors as well. The living room ceiling soared with wooden beams across the length. The kitchen was all warm brown wood. Tall cabinets stretched high, and a generous island stood in the middle that she imagined to be a great workspace. She ran her hand along the smooth countertop before moving on to the beautiful gas stove. "Tell me you use this thing. It's too pristine."

Ryan chewed her lip. "I can boil spaghetti."

"Oh no. Ryan."

"Don't you worry. I pop a mean can of sauce. As in, wow. I'll show you sometime."

Gabriella inhaled and blinked without moving any other muscle. "You're killing me softly. You have all of this. You have to use it. Have to."

"I'll try harder if you promise to give me some protips."

She liked that idea very much. "I could pencil that in. I've been told I'm an excellent teacher."

Ryan's eyes darkened. "Don't. Teachers are my weakness."

She met Ryan's gaze unwaveringly. "Filing that one away."

She continued to wander the space with Ryan following and occasionally tossing in narration. The furniture in the living room was mostly gray leather with cream colored accent pillows, a nice touch that lightened the interior. A big-screen TV hung on the wall, and Gabriella took note of a PlayStation on the console below.

"I like first-person action adventure games," Ryan confessed. "But that's a secret between you and me."

Gabriella shook her head in amusement, as the hobby went right along with Ryan's pleasure-seeker tendencies. "Is it okay?" she asked, gesturing to the hallway. "I don't want to invade your space, but I'm in love with your house. It's more *you* than I could have even constructed in my imagination."

"Please," Ryan said and gestured ahead. "And I take that as a compliment."

Gabriella found the master, the only bedroom on the first floor, and turned on the light. It was spacious with a four-poster bed, again made of wood. The bedspread was beige and fluffy and looked like you could sink into its depths and sleep for days. "Totally Ryan's room."

"That's why I love it so much here. All of my favorite things."

That's when Gabriella noticed Dale lying in the back of the room on his oversized dog bed. His head lifted, and he blinked at them. "We interrupted his evening nap, which is not to be confused with his morning nap, or his midafternoon nap, or his late-afternoon nap. Eventually he'll move to the couch and stretch out on his back. Mark my words."

"He enjoys life. Like you."

"You hungry?" Ryan asked him. His answer was to stand and lick his chops. "Fair enough. Come on, you adorable lug."

Gabriella laughed as Dale trotted happily right past them and headed to the kitchen where he turned in circles. Slow circles because this was, after all, Dale, who had his own leisurely pace for most everything he did. As Ryan prepared his food, Gabriella opened the fridge. Ryan froze. It honestly wasn't as bad as she had led Gabriella to believe.

"You've got quite a bit in here actually." She scanned the items and opened the freezer, finding even more, including some frozen chicken. Promising.

"Do you have cooking wine?"

"If it's not expired, it should be above the stove. Why? Do I fail a test if I don't?"

"Not a chance." She stood next to Ryan and squeezed her hand. "I thought I'd sauté us a nice chicken with a white wine butter sauce. I'm starving." She headed to what looked to be the pantry and saw a sack of potatoes on the ground. "Toss in a few pan-fried potatoes. I'd add a salad, but you don't seem to have any fresh veggies."

Ryan looked conflicted. "You don't have to cook for me. You're my guest."

Gabriella leveled a stare. "Are you hungry?"

"Definitely."

"Good. I'll make us a quick dinner. Nothing fancy, and you can work on your furniture project until it's ready. I'll come get you. Dale can assist." The dog looked up from his bowl curiously.

"I don't know what I've done to deserve this," Ryan said with wide eyes, "but it's the best offer I've had in a long time." She leaned down for a lingering kiss that left Gabriella a hot-and-bothered potato slicer moments after. When Ryan emerged in a formfitting navy tank top and faded overalls that she'd only fastened on one side, her stomach went tight and everything reacted. She was able to glimpse more of Ryan's body than ever, and it was simply off the chart. Subtle curves, perfect skin, and an athleticism she only imagined came from her morning run, genetics, and her very physical work environment.

"You okay?" Ryan asked, approaching the kitchen island. She raised an eyebrow.

"Me? I'm completely okay. Why do you ask? I'm just potato central over here." She left off the part about potato central being engulfed in flames. Lustful waves of them.

"The knife's in midair," Ryan said, gesturing to Gabriella's right hand where she, sure enough, had her knife raised and frozen mid-slicing motion, as if suspended for all time. She laughed it off and finished the motion.

"I was just, um, thinking through my dish. That's what chefs do."

"Or checking me out. Does potato central have HR?" Ryan grinned and the dimples came out to say hey. Damn those things.

"No. We most certainly do not."

"Good. Then I won't report you for…whatever that was."

"Just me noticing your new wardrobe. You look…good, I guess." She grinned as she focused, with everything she had, on wedging those potatoes for the pan she had heating behind her on the stove.

"Oh. Well, thank you, I think?"

"Hot," Gabriella tossed up, before going back to her project. "Fine. Okay? You look fantastic, and sexy, and I just really, really like the idea of you now heading out to make a desk or something."

Ryan came and stood over her shoulder, the heat from her body caressing Gabriella's. "Does it help that I'd kinda rather stay here and watch you toss ingredients together like a boss, because I happen to find your skill in a kitchen a ridiculous turn-on?"

She grinned. "Not gonna lie. Helps a lot. Now, go."

Forty minutes later, Gabriella carried two plates of white wine chicken and potatoes to the garage, which Ryan had apparently transformed into her own personal woodworking shop. Along the back wall rested lumber of all shapes, sizes, and colors, which she interpreted to be Ryan's stock. In the center of the room, Ryan knelt over a couple of sawhorses, protective glasses in place, as she cut through a thick piece of wood with a circular saw. Given the noise, she didn't seem to have heard Gabriella enter, and that was ideal because now Gabriella could linger unnoticed and watch her work.

Ryan's focus was laser sharp, and she bit the side of her lip, likely part of her concentration process. She'd pulled her hair into a ponytail since leaving the kitchen, which exposed the delicious column of her neck. Some sort of indie band played on the beat-up radio resting on the nearby workbench. Gabriella set the plates down next to it and approached slowly. It only took a moment for Ryan to notice her presence, pause her work, lift her glasses, and smile.

"Sorry. You been there long?"

She raised a happy shoulder. "A minute or two. I like watching you work. A lot." Not a lie. It did things to her. She gestured to the wood. "That looks like it's going to be a fantastic bench."

"You think?" Ryan stood. "It's going in my mom's backyard this time. She wants to watch the birds out there."

Behind Ryan stood a rocking chair, a duo of small matching tables, and a four-shelf bookcase. "Wow. You've been busy."

She nodded and wiped her forehead with the back of her hand. "Working out here on my own stuff helps me clear my mind. Process problems one nail or screw at a time. If you didn't know, I tend to get in my own way."

"I didn't. Seems to me that you often get what you want."

Ryan watched her. Tension pulsed between them. "Do I? Maybe I just chase the wrong things." Ryan caught sight of the plates. "That smells amazing. I might fall to my knees and cry."

Gabriella reached for the plates and brought one over to Ryan, complete with silverware stacked on top. "For you. Should still be hot, though I did get distracted on my delivery route."

"We're eating out here?"

"Did you have somewhere better in mind? Convention always has us eating at a table and chairs, but food should be consumed in any and all environments is what I think."

"Well, then. Field trip dining it is." Ryan looked around, snagged a sheet of plywood, and set it on top of the pair of sawhorses. She grabbed a couple of concrete blocks from the corner and set them on either side. "There. Table for two. You inspired me."

"And now we get to enjoy this awesome space." She took a seat on her respective block and set the plates on the wood. "What do we call it? Ryan's Fun Furniture Farm?"

"Yeah, that's exactly what I call it." She took a bite of the chicken and chewed slowly, finally pointing at her plate as Gabriella waited for the verdict. "How did you cook this amazingness so quickly in my kitchen with my food? My food doesn't turn into this."

"Your stuff did. It was quite agreeable to the transformation, really. A little bit of this, a dash of that, and we have dinner. The magic of food preparation is real. You should hop the train."

"I'll hop your train." Ryan slid a bite of chicken in her mouth playfully.

"That sounds like an offer, but I'm eating right now," she said sweetly.

"It was meant to be a chicken compliment, but I like the way you took it better." Ryan winked, and Gabriella took note of how much she enjoyed this. Them. Their dynamic. The easy teasing. Eating sautéed chicken and potatoes in a converted garage on a couple of blocks of concrete while they flirted. She could resist this all she wanted, but it felt right. It felt good. What was the point in continuing to come up with reasons it could all fall apart down the line? Right now, who the hell cared? She vowed then and there to lean in to every positive thing Ryan brought to her life, and she was going to start with those kind, thoughtful, and gorgeous blue eyes. She grinned up at them.

"Train hopping doesn't sound at all bad. In fact, I like the philosophy."

The smile dimmed slightly on Ryan's lips, and her eyes seemed intrigued. She held Gabriella's gaze, and it felt like the temperature rose eight degrees in ten seconds.

"Try some more of the potatoes," Gabriella said quietly.

Ryan's eyes lingered on hers for another long moment before she did as she was asked and slid the fork into her mouth. Gabriella waited, knowing that nobody did the center of a pan-fried potato quite like she did. The perfect amount of char on the outside, a slight crisp, and a soft, heavenly center. Ryan closed her eyes as she chewed slowly. Pleasure seemed to wash over her. She took a second bite, and Gabriella paused her own meal to watch what was turning into quite the show. Sensual and decadent. It made her want Ryan in the worst way possible. The intensity of Gabriella's desire washed over her like a tidal wave she had no ability to fight or control.

"I don't know how you did this, but you disappeared for a few minutes, and now I have these." Ryan gestured to her plate. "I'm now imagining you in other arenas. You work fast and effectively, I imagine."

"Sometimes. Other times, I like to go slow."

They ate for a few moments, stealing glances at each other, which

was impossible not to do because Gabriella loved the way Ryan enjoyed food. She demonstrated her enjoyment with every part of her,
making her the best kind of human.

"I might be imagining you with less on," Gabriella said, raising
her gaze. Yeah, she went there.

She watched as Ryan's features went still. Slowly, her face dusted
with pink, which then blossomed to red. Her blatant come-on had
affected Ryan in a way she'd never witnessed, and Gabriella basked in
her newly discovered power.

"Really?" Ryan said, almost like she wasn't sure where the other
words were. It only fueled Gabriella's fire.

"Mm-hmm. It's not the first time, either," she said simply and took
a final bite of chicken. Wouldn't be needing the rest. She set the plate to
the side in a deliberate manner.

Ryan tilted her head. "You've never said that before."

"I've never felt so compelled." A pause. They exchanged a charged
look. She raised a shoulder. "Until now."

The song on the radio shifted, and with it, Ryan stood, walked
around to the other side of the makeshift table, and offered her hand.
"Come here."

Gabriella stood and an electric guitar cranked just as Ryan caught
her lips with a level of passion that encapsulated everything that
had taken place over the course of the last two hours. The looks, the
touches, the kisses, the insinuations. Good God. That was good news
because Gabriella was there, too. No sweet nothings required. As they
kissed, she let any and all reservations go. She flashed to Ryan on the
ball field, Ryan in her tool belt, Ryan walking down the damn street,
and her center ached. Her underwear was wet and her cheeks felt hot
and all she wanted in the world was Ryan to do something about that,
fast. Her tongue was in Ryan's mouth, and her arms wrapped around
her neck as need clobbered her. The move brought their bodies together
in dizzying payoff. Her breasts were pressed to Ryan's, making her
wildly aware of her own nipples and how sensitive they suddenly
were. Ryan's hands were on the move. Into her hair. God. Down her
back. Under the front hem of her shirt. Yes. They were walking as
they kissed until she smacked up against something. The wall. Perfect.
The resistance allowed for so much more friction and access to…
everything. She inhaled sharply when her shirt was pushed up, and a
breathy Ryan stared at her breasts beneath the fabric of her sky-blue
bra. She placed her palms against the wall, enjoying the objectification.

The throbbing between her legs increased exponentially. She felt that gaze everywhere. To help things along, she pulled the shirt over her head entirely and let it drop to the floor. Ryan did the rest, unclasping her bra and freeing her breasts, which fell immediately into waiting hands.

"Gabriella," Ryan said softly.

Ryan saying her name while touching her so intimately felt like everything. She nodded, granting permission, and they were off. Ryan lifted a breast, dropped her head, and pulled the nipple into her mouth. Gabriella saw stars, threading her fingers through Ryan's hair, guiding her gently. Ryan continued to lavish attention on first that breast then the other. Her teeth softly grazed each nipple, offering a welcome release. Her tongue traced circles. Her lips kissed her skin with expert precision. To no surprise, Ryan was really, really good at this. Finally, she couldn't take another moment. When Ryan seemed content to continue what she'd started, Gabriella intervened. "No, no, no. I need you." Ryan raised an eyebrow in a question she had no problem answering. "Now."

Ryan didn't hesitate. She went to work unbuttoning Gabriella's jeans. In less than two seconds, she stepped out of them, leaving her standing in a garage in only her black panties and not a stitch else. Ryan ran her fingertips over the outside curve of Gabriella's hip, causing a shiver. She trembled and closed her eyes. With one hand behind her waist and Gabriella's shoulders against the wall, Ryan reached between her legs with her other hand. She stroked Gabriella through the fabric softly, and after all the buildup, it nearly brought her to her knees. "I've got you," Ryan whispered. Amazing. The rush. The pleasure. Her body responded in ways she hadn't been prepared for. Gabriella needed more desperately. Ryan didn't seem to mind. Her lips landed on Gabriella's neck, and she kissed down to her collarbone. As Gabriella inhaled sharply, Ryan lifted her head and met her gaze. Once they connected, she nearly toppled over the edge. Ryan expertly moved the slip of fabric to the side and touched her fully. Gabriella's eyes fluttered closed, and she pressed herself into Ryan's hand, asking for more, over and over. She didn't have to wait long, and when Ryan began to stroke harder, she moved along with her, the rhythm taking her higher and higher. She opened her eyes to see Ryan watching her breasts move with each thrust. That did it, sending her bolting into oblivion. She shattered, shocked by the intensity of pleasure that rocketed through every part of her, taking over control of her body entirely. Her voice strangled as she cried out and rode Ryan's hand until the very last amazing shred of pleasure ebbed.

"Ryan," was all she managed when she returned to herself moments later. She still gripped Ryan's shoulders for support.

"Hi," Ryan whispered, wrapping her arms around Gabriella, enveloping her. Ryan ran her fingertips up and down Gabriella's back, giving her a moment to compose herself. She placed a soft kiss on Gabriella's shoulder. She felt cherished, protected in a vulnerable moment. Once she felt like herself again, Gabriella straightened, slid her hands beneath Ryan's jaw, and ran her thumb across her full bottom lip. Going up on her toes, she caught that mouth in hungry declaration, claiming it for herself, and already making plans for the things she wanted to do next. "Take me to your room."

Ryan blinked and her eyes went dark. Gabriella allowed herself to be led by the hand through Ryan's home as she clutched her clothes to her bare chest. Dale lifted his head briefly, as they passed through the living room, then rolled onto his back for another snooze.

Ryan's bedroom was dark. Ryan must have thought so too and switched on a small lamp across from that gorgeous four-poster bed. Gabriella approached her from behind and ran her hands from her waist to her stomach, caressing her softly. "How is your skin so soft?" she whispered, turning Ryan around to her.

Ryan didn't answer. She seemed captivated, her gaze elsewhere, and then Gabriella remembered how little she had on. "Eyes up here, tiger," Gabriella said, satisfied when Ryan complied. She unhooked the one side of the overalls that was fastened and watched them fall to the ground, leaving Ryan in slinky black bikinis that made Gabriella's mouth go dry and that blue tank top, the one that had been teasing her with glimpses of cleavage for the past hour. "Take off your shirt," Gabriella whispered, loving everything about this driver's seat, the issuing of commands. Ryan swallowed and wordlessly slid the tank top over her head, leaving a black bra that left little to the imagination. "That, too," she said. Ryan exhaled and unhooked her bra, letting it join the rest of her clothes on top of the dresser. Gabriella feasted on what she saw, the reality of Ryan's body waiting for her. The subtle curve of her hips juxtaposed with surprisingly round breasts. Gabriella stepped forward and traced the outside of one with a fingertip. "Look at you." She kissed Ryan's neck and then the underside of her jaw, going up on tiptoe. She saw Ryan grip the dresser, which was fine. For now.

She palmed a breast and then two, sucked the nipple into her mouth. Ridiculously satisfying, all of it, but she had designs on so much more.

"Fuck," Ryan hissed and dropped her head back. Her dark hair fell with her, thick and gorgeous, her neck on display. Gabriella kissed and licked the column of it.

But those breasts called her back, and she was a woman on a mission. Gabriella took her time with her mouth, lost in a haze of lust. She hadn't let herself go, so unrestricted and free, in a while. Tonight, she did just that and reveled in the effect. With her teeth she skated across Ryan's nipple and listened to her murmur her approval. "I need you on the bed," she said in Ryan's ear. Her answer was swift. Ryan took a seat on the edge, leaving plenty of room for Gabriella to straddle her lap. Gabriella slid off her last bit of clothing and did just that. Ryan nodded when Gabriella began to roll her hips. "Yes," she breathed. Ryan adjusted herself beneath Gabriella, Ryan's hands on her bare back, pushing up against her, seeking purchase. This ride was only a momentary detour. Gabriella had a larger goal.

She pushed Ryan gently onto the bed and followed her there. Kissing down her body, she purposefully allowed her hair to trail behind her, caressing Ryan's skin. Ryan moaned, and she savored the sound. Gabriella settled herself between Ryan's legs and kissed her through her underwear and felt her squirm. Set squarely on a goal, she slid the bikinis down her legs and eagerly kissed those gorgeous legs up to Ryan's inner thighs. She then touched her delicately with her tongue, smiling to herself when Ryan jerked. "Hold on," she murmured, going back in. She went slow, excruciatingly slow if she did say so herself. Soft circles, lazy passes, until the sounds Ryan made told her it was time. She zeroed in on the one spot she knew would send Ryan off the bed and went to town with her lips, her tongue until Ryan's body went rigid and her hips lifted. Gabriella raised her gaze to watch the beauty in front of her writhe with pleasure she'd provided. Satisfied, she crawled up the bed and braced herself on her forearms over Ryan, who reached up and moved a strand of hair out of her face.

"You've been holding out on me."

Gabriella shook her head, proud. "I don't know what you're talking about."

"You seem sweet and innocent, but…"

"Oh, I am. I'm just a few other things, too."

"Heaven. Jesus. Lord."

Gabriella shook her head. "Not here right now. I am, though." She settled her body on top and eased her thigh between Ryan's, pulling a hiss.

"I did not expect to be worked over by a chef until she made me see nothing but stars."

Gabriella grinned slyly. "Well, who does?"

Ryan grabbed her by the waist and flipped them. It was Gabriella who gasped this time.

"Not that I'm complaining." Ryan grinned down. "I hope you don't have anywhere to be tonight."

Gabriella shook her head, more than captivated by where she already was. "My night is open."

To say that she had the most satisfying sex of her life that night would be accurate and a gross understatement. Ryan took her places she'd only read about, and she had a feeling she'd returned that favor. They were asleep in each other's arms by two a.m., and when the sunlight woke them just after seven, Ryan smiled. She opened her mouth to speak, but Gabriella silenced her with a finger upon her lips. Ryan passed her a curious look but complied, content to lie there and run her fingers up and down Gabriella's back as she held her. Finally, when the requisite ten minutes passed, Gabriella raised herself up.

"I don't talk for the first ten minutes of the day."

Ryan blinked. "Did you lose a bet with someone? That's so sad."

"No," Gabriella said with a laugh. "It's just a thing I have. It helps me get my thoughts together, and I suppose now it's kind of a superstition."

"A silent ten minutes, huh?"

"If I can manage it, yeah."

Ryan pulled Gabriella more fully on top and caressed her ass with both hands.

Gabriella raised an eyebrow. "It's only minute eleven, and you're already objectifying me?"

"Yes," Ryan said with a single nod and proud grin.

With her dark hair laid out behind her on the pillow, she was just as gorgeous in the morning as any other time of day. Maybe more. Gabriella kissed her and moved her hips in a slow circle that had Ryan closing her eyes. "I can get behind that."

## CHAPTER THIRTEEN

The day had been a long one, possibly because Gabriella hadn't gotten a ton of sleep the night before, but the memories had certainly kept her smiling to herself, like she had the most wonderful of secrets. As she worked, she touched her lips on occasion, remembering the impassioned kisses. And Jolene kept her on her toes. She was beginning to recognize repeat customers, who specifically came to the vineyard for lunch, which she took as a sign of success. They truly were meeting a need in the community, apart from the ongoing tourism. Her food was beginning to have an impact and generate buzz. Inspired by the Biddies and their now wildly successful joint Instagram account, Gabriella decided to create an account for Tangled, apart from the vineyard's social media presence, and showcase picturesque shots of her dishes to get folks excited about the upcoming opening. After plating a gorgeous pork belly and rosemary mash, she took a photo of it paired with an oversized glass of dolcetto, the beautiful hillside in the background, and threw it up there. Joey reposted it, and the followers started rolling in. This town really did pass things around like wildfire. She wondered absently as she plated a round of toasted ravioli if Ryan had seen it.

Once she'd gone to food war and won for the day, Gabriella decided that a glass of pinot grigio sounded refreshing as hell and headed over to the tasting room after ditching her chef's coat for jeans and a purple T-shirt with the words *Maybe Later* scripted across the front. The soft fabric only contributed to her happy place, and oh, it was happy. She took a seat at the bar and grinned at Loretta. "One glass of the good stuff. Put it on my tab, bartender."

Loretta laughed and held up an open bottle of the white wine Gabriella had pointed to, and she nodded.

"First of all, not a bar, you weirdo," Joey said, walking down the counter after pouring a tasting for a group of guests. "Second of all, you don't have a tab. You drink for free here. Why can't you remember that? You're part of the Tangle Valley family now, and until you start drinking cases at a time, we can carry that expense for you."

Gabriella grinned. "I'll work on free wine acceptance in my spare time." She accepted a generous pour and took a sip. Bliss in a glass. Why hadn't she always lived and worked on a vineyard?

"You're all glowy. Why? Oh my, you're also tired, aren't you?" Joey said quietly, moving out of earshot of a group of guests down the bar. "I know the glowy-tired combo. I've lived it. I still do."

Gabriella grinned from behind her glass but said nothing.

"Did you happen to have an extra-sexy sleepover last night?"

On one hand, it felt in poor taste to kiss and tell, but on another, she would have murdered Joey full-on if she'd withheld details all those months back when things were coming together with Becca, aka Sexy Execsy. It was her friend duty to reciprocate, wasn't it? Plus, she really, really wanted to.

She set her glass down. "There might have been. It might have been amazing, and I might want another sleepover again really soon."

"She's a tiger, I bet," Loretta said casually and strolled back to the guests with an open bottle of dolcetto for their next tasting.

Gabriella stared after her and pointed. She looked to Joey. "Sometimes I just don't see her coming."

Joey nodded. "She's not what she seems."

"Indeed, she's not." With Loretta out of earshot, she lowered her voice. "She might be having a few sleepovers of her own."

"Gasp and awe. With who?" Joey whispered, coming closer.

Gabriella made sure Loretta was busy. She was. "I'm not positive, but I'm a sneaky detective currently on the case. I suspect your uncle Bobby."

Joey blinked and paused. "No. That can't be right. She used to have a little thing with my dad. Just a flirtation, but he and Bobby are so different, you know? Plus, Loretta's all talky and into fun things. Bobby is just quiet and happy with a ball game on TV. Plus, he rarely says much, the lovable lug."

Gabriella held out her hands, realizing her suspicions were just brushed off. "I think they have a clandestine romance, and I get this sense that it's fiery. Decadent." She sat back and let that bomb fall.

"With Bobby." Joey grappled. She blinked. She looked down the bar at Loretta as if to try it on. She turned back, befuddled. "God, if they have a secret, clandestine thing, I'll be so mad."

"No, you won't," Gabriella scolded. "You'll be happy for them."

"Well, yeah, but only after I'm epically mad at being excluded."

"Which will be brief. We have to stop giving each other hard times for what our hearts want."

Joey nodded, and understanding sparked. "That statement is about Madison's reaction to you and Ryan the other night. I heard the awkward details and have to say I'm impressed you survived. I would have exploded into a thousand pieces in that very moment and floated into outer space. Yet here you sit."

Gabriella frowned. "Specific."

Joey nodded. "I've thought it through. It's a whole thing. We don't have to explore it." She waved it off. "But you. Madison. Ryan. Let's get back to that."

Gabriella sighed. "It was less than ideal, having Maddie walk in on what was a very...personal moment, but it should have been something we could have laughed off, you know? But JoJo, it was weird. She totally flew off the handle. You should have seen it, unnecessary and irrational."

Joey winced. "And human?"

"Yeah, but I didn't do anything wrong." Gabriella stared at her, adrenaline pumping. She tried to control it. "Are you taking her side? Level with me."

Joey held up her hands. "Not at all. I love you both equally, but it's...maybe more complicated than you're allowing for."

She deflated, not in the mood for anything that was going to kill her happiness buzz. "Because of our history."

"Yeah. It's weird for her. She said as much to me."

"Really?" Gabriella pinched the bridge of her nose, absorbing the news. "I thought we were so far past all of this. We've been friends way longer than we were together. Did she say anything else?"

"Not in word form."

"Joey."

She relented. "But I can tell it's on her mind because I speak Madison. My instincts say that seeing you with Ryan is bringing up some...confusion."

Gabriella had to sit with that one because it hit her with a thud.

She was aware of the fact that Madison wasn't a fan of Ryan's, but she thought it had more to do with how protective she was. Nothing more. "Well, this is news. I wish she'd talk to *me* about it."

Joey sighed. "Madison is smart and kind and funny. But she's a precision girl. Not big on emotions or their discussion. At least as it pertains to her own."

"You don't have to tell me that part."

"Right, right. I forget."

Gabriella swallowed. "So you think she's jealous. God, Joey, she would never in a million years want me back. We were so mismatched it was ridiculous."

Joey took a moment, likely deciding where to step and clearly not wanting to betray Madison. "I think the heart can get disoriented when faced with new information."

"Meaning Ryan's appearance has caused her to question things all over again."

Joey shrugged and excused herself down the bar with a look of apology. A couple had arrived and would need Joey's attention. Their robust voices reverberated through the room, a sign this wasn't their first stop on their tasting venture. Alone now, Gabriella sipped her pinot grigio, daydreamed about Ryan, and worried about Madison. Her conflicted heart alternated between sputters of happiness and concern, but what was there to do?

The situation was certainly not perfect, but then, what in life ever was? She sipped and sighed and repeated the process. In the end, she didn't have absolute answers. All she could do was be kind, be patient, and hope that, in the end, she'd know how to balance everyone and their feelings.

Tall order.

❖

"What about over there for the overflow spice shelf you asked for?" Ryan asked, pointing to a spot on the wall of the nearly finished kitchen at Tangled. Her workday was over, but she was in no hurry to head home. She had her arms around Gabriella because she seemed to always want her arms around Gabriella. It was just part of life these days. The soft opening was almost upon them. Ryan was going to miss spending her days just yards from the woman she thought about constantly. Hell, she'd subbed out work on some of her other jobsites simply because she wanted to be more present on this one. Something she'd never thought she'd do. But you realized what was important when your life completely changed for the better, the way Ryan's had.

Gabriella studied her shelf placement idea, leaning back in to Ryan. "No. I'm thinking over there, just above the backsplash."

She eyed the area. "But you're short. How are you going to reach anything on a shelf that high up?" That earned her an elbow in the ribs.

"How dare you, ma'am. I'm not that short." Gabriella stalked over, stood in front of the grill, and pretended to toss ingredients into an imaginary pan with some muttered *boom*s. Ryan held in her smile at this entire scene. "*Pow*," Gabriella said louder, gaining momentum and tossing some key element into her invisible pan. She turned up an imaginary burner and added in some new ingredients. "*Waha.*"

"Waha?" Ryan squinted.

"Shhh. It's a real thing."

"I don't think it is."

Gabriella ignored her, shimmied a bit, and shook her hips as she tossed more of her invisible whatever-it-was in the air and caught it with, yes, her invisible pan. Was this really happening? Finally, after a couple more pows, booms, whams, and wahas, she pretended to reach for something on the invisible shelf in question. When the action wasn't seamless at all and interrupted her flow, she deflated and turned. "Okay. Don't gloat, but you might be right about the height issue."

Ryan uncrossed her arms and let them relax at her sides. "Imagine that. You'd think I'd been doing this awhile or something."

"That's gloating," Gabriella said, betrayed. "We had a strict deal."

"We really didn't."

Gabriella leveled her with a look. "Don't stand there looking hot while you argue with me, either. Don't do it."

"I'll do what I want," Ryan shot back. She loved when they got into challenge mode, which was such a fun part of their relationship. She pointed to her original suggested spot on the wall, a little farther to the side, but lower. "There, for the shelf?"

"I think there. Yes."

The overly exaggerated look of contrition on Gabriella's face was too much, which forced Ryan to lean way down and gather her into a giant hug. "Oh, you're too cute when you pout, and now you must be smothered in affection."

"Am not. I'm dramatic, but I'll take the smothering anyway."

"That, too." Of course, the hug had to escalate to kissing against that stove, and then kissing against the large prep counter, and then a little under the shirt second-base action against the fridge, with Ryan's hands under Gabriella's shirt, which had Ryan too turned-on for her own good.

She exhaled, running her thumb in a circle around Gabriella's taut nipple, and struggling with the aching much lower on her own body. "I will never get tired of touching you."

"What does it do to you?" Gabriella asked quietly, biting her lip. "Are you wet right now?"

Ryan dropped her head back because hearing Gabriella talk dirty to her in a kitchen was too much to absorb. "I'm not answering that. But yes." She nuzzled Gabriella's neck, breathing her in.

"You might change your mind about the touching thing. We're still early."

"Trust me on this." Another kiss, during which Gabriella's hands cupped her ass, sending Ryan to places even beyond uncontrollable high school lust. "Nobody has ever affected me the way you do." A kiss, slow and thorough. "I think I just gave you a lot of power."

Gabriella smiled against her mouth. "But I like power." A nip. "A lot. I could work with power." She pulled Ryan's hands from beneath her shirt and held them behind her back as they kissed, demonstrating control. Sweet Lord. Good things really did come in small packages. Sexy as hell ones with gorgeous hazel eyes, thick dark hair, and breasts that had her under some kind of spell. She thought about them way too often and at inopportune times. The grocery store line. Client meetings. The DMV.

"Where did you come from?" Ryan asked in awe.

"We've been over this. Jersey City, so don't mess with me, small-town Oregon." She threw in a touch of a Jersey accent she didn't normally have.

"Oh, we'll need more of that."

"Yeah? We could maybe work something in." Gabriella grinned and released Ryan's hands. "You'd like my sister Teresa. She exaggerates her accent to match the people on TV. Makes her feel saucy."

Ryan said, "Maybe one day I can meet them."

Gabriella threaded their fingers. "We've talked about them visiting someday. They would fall in love with the Jade. Maybe when the restaurant is up and running successfully."

An idea hit. "Maybe we should stay at the Jade some night."

"Why would we ever do that when there's a breathtaking lake

house with a dock, a lazy dog, and a really comfortable king-sized bed I already have fantastic memories of? Another option? An adorable cottage on the grounds of one of Oregon's most respected vineyards."

"You had me at bed. Either one of them. Which we skipped the first time in favor of a dusty garage."

That pulled a laugh. "I have a feeling we can make up the lost time."

"Tell me that's a promise."

"You have my word." Gabriella looked around. "How do you feel about breaking in this kitchen before it goes into service?" She slowly lowered the zipper of Ryan's jeans.

"Here?" Ryan asked. Her stomach tightened and her thighs went weak.

"Here."

"Isn't this currently *my* place of business, though?"

"Aren't I kind of your boss? Could be a scandal in the making." Gabriella raised a saucy eyebrow and slid her hand inside Ryan's pants.

She was a goner.

Just a short time later, she was a highly satisfied one.

## Chapter Fourteen

A table for five at the Crown Jewel, the restaurant nestled inside the Jade Resort, was generally difficult to snag on the weekend. In fact, guests booked well in advance of their trip. Luckily, Becca Crawford happened to be one of their five and had arranged not just for last-minute reservations, but for a primo spot along the floor-to-ceiling windows, with a sunset view of the surrounding wine country. Gabriella was impressed and excited to be there, ready to sample the kitchen's cuisine and unwind with Ryan and her friends all together, a first.

Becca was the last to join their group, having just dashed over from her office off the lobby. Appearing in a killer off-the-shoulder black dress, she must have taken a moment to change from one of her traditional power suits. Gabriella watched as Joey accepted a kiss and gave her girlfriend a subtle once-over. Gabriella exchanged an amused glance with Ryan.

"You look fantastic," Joey said quietly.

"Not as good as you do," Becca said back and then regarded the table with a winsome smile. "Hi, guys."

Gabriella, Ryan, and Madison all grinned and greeted her back. The get-together was Ryan-inspired and arranged by Joey, which couldn't have made Gabriella happier. She was pretty sure this was Ryan's way of trying to smooth things over with Madison, who seemed pleasant enough tonight. That boded well, right? Honestly, she and Madison hadn't spoken much more than pleasantries in passing since their run-in. Occasional movie nights and group hang-out sessions in the tasting room after closing had slipped away. She knew it stemmed from the strain between her and Maddie. She just wasn't sure how to fix it. Maybe tonight was a good start. After all, everyone was dressed up, happy, and ready to eat amazing food.

"Ready for the restaurant to open already?" Madison asked, taking a sip of her water. She'd pulled her dark blond curls up tonight in an elegant twist and wore a sleeveless blue dress, making her seem more sophisticated than Gabriella was used to. She looked gorgeous. Gabriella would have to be dead not to register that.

"So ready. I keep checking my watch, and we're still weeks away." Gabriella sipped, too.

"I can imagine the wait is killer."

"It is."

They were too polite, and that made everything feel weird. This was *Maddie*, for heaven's sake. But with Ryan on her left and Madison on her right, Gabriella felt like she inhabited some alternate version of herself. Thank God the sommelier arrived and introduced the wines Becca had selected for the table.

Becca leaned in and addressed Madison. "Joey asked for some of the French varietals we got in last week. I hope you don't mind a pivot from Tangle Valley."

Madison waved off the disclaimer. She was a pro and a connoisseur. "I love new wines. I'm in."

They listened to Bruno, Becca's awesome sommelier, present the wine with a few tasting notes. "I think you Tangled lovelies are going to like this particular blend." He winked at Joey, who had become his friend, given that Tangle Valley was now featured as the house wine for its local connection to the resort.

"What got you interested in winemaking?" Ryan asked Madison a few minutes later, as Bruno poured for the group. She wore a sleeveless black blouse tonight that she'd accented with a long silver necklace to go with black pants she looked amazing in. Sleek and beautiful. Gabriella was proud to sit next to her.

Madison tilted her head back and forth. "I guess I have Joey to thank for that. When we became friends back in elementary school, I spent most of my afternoons at Tangle Valley until my mom would call me home for dinner." She smiled at Joey across the table. "I followed her dad, Jack, all around the place, watching everything he did. Taking notes in my Justin Timberlake journal, which is confusing now for a whole separate reason."

Joey nodded, enjoying the memory. "He called you his plucky

shadow because you refused to go away and asked so many questions. Good questions, he said, if I remember correctly."

"And you?" Madison asked. Gabriella couldn't help but notice that she hadn't looked at Ryan when she'd asked the question, instead inspecting the color of the wine. "With the construction?"

Ryan smiled. "Oh, well, I was always interested in how things were made. I'd examine toasters, bookshelves, everything. Drove my parents crazy. I eventually started teaching myself, and it went from there until I was old enough to get a job and assist a local contractor. We're kind of similar in that way, I guess. Knowing early where our interests fell."

"We're not that similar," Madison said flatly. She swirled her wineglass and took a delicate sip.

Ouch. Gabriella passed Ryan an encouraging smile, or at least tried to, but Ryan's gaze was firmly on the tablecloth.

"Well, you're both great at what you do," Joey said, trying to save them. She looked around expectantly. "What's the special tonight?"

"I believe it's a citrus grilled pork chop with polenta and a garlic mash," Becca said, jumping right in. Bless them both. A for effort.

"You have the most magical words," Gabriella said, focusing on the food. She was a recent fan of this chef, brought in from Chicago when the resort opened, and there was no way she was passing up that pork chop. "Decided. The special. What are you having?" she asked Ryan, who surveyed the menu.

Ryan offered a small smile, which meant she was rebounding. "Is it wrong that I'm gravitating to the burger?" She seemed embarrassed.

Gabriella shook her head. "Not at all. I bet it's wonderful."

"Remember when we'd hit up restaurants back east along the wine trail?" Madison asked. "I'd always let you order for me because you knew what would be good or in season. I guess that means I'll have the pork chop, too."

Gabriella turned to Madison, slightly uneasy about the reference to their past, which felt pointed. "Good call."

Ryan closed her menu. "You know what? You make a good point. I think I'll have the special as well."

"Convenient," Madison said quietly, the corners of her mouth tugging. This wasn't like her.

Ryan stared at Madison, who seemed not to notice. Gabriella watched the muscle in Ryan's jaw tighten and placed a hand on her leg under the table. Ryan covered it with her hand and gave it a squeeze.

Becca, Joey, and Gabriella did what they could to keep the conversation lively and afloat, but it was honestly exhausting navigating through the palpable tension. Perhaps this dinner hadn't been a good idea after all. She wouldn't have predicted the obvious strife.

They were a couple glasses in and discussing plans for the chardonnay release when the entrées arrived. Everything looked fabulous, the plating and the presentation superb. Gabriella couldn't wait to try the food. The Crown Jewel was bustling, full of lively tables as the little lights of Whisper Wall twinkled below them in the newly fallen darkness. But their table was strained, and what a shame that was. It should have been the perfect evening out with friends. Maybe they'd find a way to recover.

Ryan picked up Gabriella's hand and placed a kiss on the back of it. "How long did the two of you date?" she asked, indicating Madison in the conversation as well.

"Us?" Gabriella, surprised, looked to Madison and back. "Four months. Nearly five," she told Ryan.

"It was a memorable five months, though, wouldn't you say?" Madison laughed to keep it light, but it was anything but. The wine had loosened her up.

"Apparently not," Ryan said quietly and began to eat. Oh no.

"I'm sorry?" Madison asked, still smiling pleasantly, her wineglass practically dangling from her fingertips.

Ryan turned and looked Madison square in the eyes. "I just meant apparently it wasn't *that* great in the end, since you two called it off. What was it you said?" Ryan asked Gabriella. "That you two make better friends, right?" Ryan went back to her meal, and Gabriella now wanted to crawl under the table, furious at both of them. Ryan could have let the earlier comment go. Should have.

"We've definitely found what works best for us," Gabriella said in what she hoped was a measured voice.

"Maybe." Madison set down her fork in thought. "As for back east, I think our lives just weren't aligned at the time. But it was serious. We practically lived together and talked about getting married. Remember that?" she asked Gabriella casually, as if reminiscing about a fun movie they'd once seen.

"I love this wine," Joey said loudly, too loudly. "It's so fruit-forward and fun."

"Isn't it, though?" Becca said, leaping into the conversation with gusto. "I love wine that isn't afraid to say, *Here's my fruit. Just take it.*"

She looked at her glass with hearts coming out of her eyes. Those two were trying so hard.

"What has it been for you guys?" Madison asked Ryan. "A few days? That's a good handful of hours. Admirable."

Madison knew damn well it had been much longer, and Ryan had known trivializing the past would get under Madison's skin. It had worked. These two were destined to fight it out at this dinner table, and Gabriella wasn't sure how much more she was prepared to sit through. She wasn't into childish. She set down her loaded fork. "I have an idea. Why don't we enjoy dinner? Talk about interesting things. How about that game tomorrow? The char on these brussels sprouts. Anything."

"Who's playing?" Becca asked. "The popcorn alone gets me there, but the game is fun, too."

Ryan glanced up. "Otters versus Muskrats. Round two."

Joey moved to make the face but read the room and abandoned ship halfway through.

Gabriella jumped in. "We're approaching playoffs, which is really just one championship game. So the records are really starting to matter. Should be quite the game." She directed her comment to Joey and Becca, the only people she felt like speaking to at the moment.

"My money's on the Muskrats," Madison said.

"They do have a killer third basewoman," Ryan added. At least they were agreeing on something. Ryan smiled at Gabriella. "And in addition to your killer arm, you also make the uniform look great."

Madison looked around Gabriella. "Score one for feminism."

"What did I say?" Ryan asked. She looked to Gabriella, concerned. "I didn't mean to offend you. You're fantastic on the field."

"It's fine," Gabriella said. "You didn't."

"Of course not." Madison shook her head and set her empty glass down, reaching for the bottle in the center of the table. "You didn't say anything that isn't typical Ryan."

A pause. "You think you know a lot about me." Ryan couldn't seem to let that one go.

Madison shrugged in half apology. "Well, the whole town does. Objectively."

That went too far. Gabriella dropped her fork with a clang. "That's enough. Both of you." She turned to Madison. "This was supposed to be a nice night out for all of us, and you immediately started in, already playing offense." She turned to Ryan. "And you fed right into it, matching her, and behaving just as badly." She took her napkin from her lap and deposited it on the table. She looked across the table to Becca and Joey, who had sympathy and horror written all over their faces. "Thank you for arranging all of this for us. Please let me know what I owe you."

"On me," Becca said.

"Very generous." Gabriella smiled in gratitude. "I think I'll walk home a little early."

Ryan stood. "No. You don't have to speak to me, but I'm at least driving you there. It's dark."

"Fine."

"Hey," Madison said quietly, tugging on her wrist.

"No, Maddie. I can't right now," she said without even looking back. She had no idea what was happening to their relationship, but there would come a point where they'd have to figure that out. It was not, however, going to be tonight when her blood was set to boil over.

They rode the short distance to Tangle Valley in silence, pulled up to the cottage, and Ryan turned off the truck. Gabriella got out as fast as she could, still shocked and angry.

"I'm sorry," Ryan offered, following her out.

Gabriella stared into the night, hands on her hips. "You should be."

Ryan came around the truck, energized. "She's wrong about me, and I couldn't just sit there and take it." She touched her chest. "You know me."

Gabriella nodded. "I get it, Ry. You play hard, you love hard, and you're authentic. Mostly, that's wonderful. But I need you to work with me as far as Madison goes and hold your tongue to keep things from getting worse."

Ryan looked at the sky, exasperated. "I know. I should have."

"She's important to me, whether you like it or not. That means to keep the peace, you have to behave. Both of you do."

Ryan looked at her. "How important?"

"What?" The implication was surprising.

"How important is she to you, exactly. That's what I need to know." Concern was written all over her face.

"Oh God," Gabriella said, letting her head drop back in frustration. "Seriously? It's not like that."

"Are you sure? Because she's not. That much was clear tonight. She's not as over you as you seem to think, and what I need to know for myself is how much of that might be lingering for you, as well."

She refused to examine the question. She couldn't. "She was just pushing your buttons, Ryan. I think she's playing aggressively in the sandbox because she's worried about you breaking my heart."

"Yeah, well, after tonight, I'm worried about you breaking mine." Ryan blinked, and her big blue eyes carried undeniable fear.

Whoa. The sight affected Gabriella in a big way, and her anger slowly evaporated. She hated seeing Ryan this way, sad and vulnerable. She'd come to understand, the more they'd spent time together, that Ryan was a great deal more complex than she'd ever given her credit for. Ryan felt things deeply. She was kind and generous, and a little timid of the world, too. The last thing Gabriella wanted, however, was for Ryan to be afraid of *her*. She released whatever negative feelings remained, needing more than anything to reassure Ryan and feel close to her. She covered the short distance between them.

"Hey," she said quietly, trying to reset them.

"Hi." Ryan held up her hand, and Gabriella placed her palm flat against it. Their fingers intertwined, and she felt her world snap into place.

"I, Gabriella Russo, have no plans to break your heart. In fact, the more I get to know it, the more I happen to like this heart. Want it around mine some more. Because it's a good heart." She looked up at Ryan. "Crazy, no?"

"Insane." She shook her head in wonder. "I never imagined a you."

The sentence took Gabriella's breath away. She could tell Ryan meant it, that it wasn't just a line. "I can safely say the same. Ryan Jacks, you are definitely one of a kind. Wait. I don't know your middle name. How have we gotten this far without one?"

"Lenore. After my grandmother on my mother's side."

"Get out." Gabriella shoved her. "My middle name's my grandmother's on my mother's side."

"See? Two people named after their grandmothers are clearly meant to make trouble in this life together."

Gabriella met Ryan's gaze. "I like the sound of us making trouble. Ryan-speak for being adorable and romantic."

"You speak Ryan well." She sighed. "I'm sorry my mouth got away from me. I wish I could say it was the first time."

"Thank you. I accept your apology."

"That easy? I feel like I owe you push-ups or a pint of ice cream or maybe just my undying affection. Which will you accept?"

"So many options there," Gabriella said, folding her arms.

"I'll also apologize to Madison the next chance I get. Who knows? Maybe she'll decide I'm not so bad after all."

"Let's hope for that." Gabriella tried to remain positive, even though doubt and confusion still hovered. "Over time, I tend to think she'll come around."

"*Over time* means you're planning to keep me around."

Gabriella shook her head in weary amazement. "No matter what I do, I can't seem to get rid of you."

"Then I'm doing something right." Ryan paused. "I could make her a table." The corners of her mouth pulled.

Gabriella shook her head. "I'm not sure she deserves one right now. You're both in time-out."

"Me? I thought I was forgiven. Let me out. I'll be so good." Ryan flashed the Bambi eyes, and that was a problem. She loved the Bambi eyes. Was a sucker for them.

"Maybe later."

Ryan tilted her head. "Later feels very far away."

"You're so impatient."

"Only when it comes to you. Is your favorite color yellow?"

"Yes." Gabriella eyed her. "You're trying to distract me."

"No way. I would never dare. I'm in time-out. I just need to know." She gestured to the cottage behind them. "You have a lot of yellow in your house, so I thought maybe it was your favorite."

"Well, you would be right. Blue is second. Followed by green. Red's a little further back."

Ryan stepped into Gabriella's space, and the air around them inched up a degree the way it always did. "Red must have done something. Is it in time-out, too?"

"It runs a little…hot." At the use of the word, Gabriella felt it. She touched Ryan's shirt absently. "Maybe you can come inside. Maybe."

Ryan kissed her. "Still a maybe?"

"Don't know." Gabriella's lips tingled. "Might need more evidence."

Ryan grinned and obliged, offering up a kiss she wouldn't soon forget. "Can it be a yes? I really want it to be a yes."

"You are a convincing kisser." Gabriella went up on tiptoe, wrapped her arms around Ryan's neck, and held on to her for several long moments. She closed her eyes at the feel of Ryan's heart beating against her own. "We'll figure it out. All this."

Ryan nodded. "I know."

She took her hand and walked them into the cottage, emotionally spent. They found each other wordlessly that night. She explored Ryan's body slowly, caressing every gorgeous inch of her, keeping track of what sent her to wonderful places and what she responded to most. She'd found her new favorite hobby, learning Ryan.

"I have no idea how you do that," Ryan said, tossing her arm over her eyes as she recovered from her second time. Gabriella grinned from between her legs, kissed her way up Ryan's chest to her lips, settling on top and staggering their thighs.

"You give the most wonderful signals. That's how."

She still hadn't opened her eyes. "Then you're the fastest study ever. Prodigy status."

"Ry. Look at me so I can see those baby blues."

"I can't. You killed me."

Gabriella nipped at her neck and moved her thigh upward a tad. "Not yet I haven't."

Ryan opened her eyes and her lips parted. "Good God."

"Good? Nah. Let's shoot for great."

After all, the night was young.

# CHAPTER FIFTEEN

R yan swung by the Biscuit that morning for a quick coffee on her way to Tangled. She'd pushed an extra two miles on her run and decided she deserved a butter biscuit with bacon jam as well. Wouldn't you know it, there were those older women all clustered together at their standard table. The Biddies were hard at work on whatever it was they did—wreaking social havoc, she guessed.

"Well, hi there, Ryan," Thelma said with a wave. "How's that house across from mine on Blue Bird Cove coming along? I saw your guys out there this week."

"Yes, ma'am. That was us." Ryan approached their table with her take-out bag and to-go coffee, and one for Gabriella. "We should wrap up within the next three days. Just a little remodeling in the kitchen." She tilted her head and eyed them playfully. "You spying on us, Thelma?"

"Never in a million years," she scoffed, then turned to her friends. "I'm spying on my *neighbors*." They all laughed, and she sipped happily from her mug, probably scoring big points on the Biddy scoreboard.

"Who's that for?" Birdie, the gentlest one, asked, gesturing to the spare coffee. She was softer spoken and harder to resent.

"I'm headed out to the job at Tangle Valley, and I know Gabriella's a big fan of the coffee here."

"She's also a fan of yours," Maude offered and looked at the others like she'd just dropped a mic. Damn, these women didn't even hide their mischievous ways anymore.

Ryan grinned through it. "I can't speak to that, but I'm definitely willing to deliver a cup when I can."

"As long as Madison LeGrange doesn't beat you there." They smiled proudly at one another.

Ryan squinted and ignored the fact that the coffee was burning her hand through the cup. She always forgot those sleeve things. "Why would you say that?"

"They were quite the item back in upstate New York, weren't they? When Gabriella worked at that restaurant near Madison's vineyard. I heard it was quite a romance. Hot and heavy."

"True love," Janet, their fourth, offered.

"Who told you that stuff?" Ryan asked.

"More like who hasn't," Janet replied. The other Biddies nodded and added their wholehearted murmurs of agreement. Meanwhile, everything in Ryan deflated. Her stomach dropped, her spirits plummeted, and the bag she carried hung limp at her side. Madison again. Perfect Madison.

Maude sighed. "They were star-crossed lovers. Like Romeo and Juliet but without the poison and death."

"Shame it ended," Janet added.

Thelma leaned in. "Not sure if it's over or not. Brenda Anne at the Nickel has her doubts. She said so."

"Well, Madison is quite the catch. She was on the cover of that magazine about winemakers in the Fruit Loop," Maude said, pointing at her friends in reminder.

Birdie nodded along. "I also heard Madison is big on romantic gestures. That's sweet. Don't you think that's sweet, Ryan?"

"Yeah." Ryan glanced down at Gabriella's coffee in the cardboard tray and felt like the floor beneath her was starting to slide away. Her list of accomplishments was significantly shorter than Madison's. "I'm not sure it was as serious as all that, but I better head to work."

"Tell Ms. Russo that we can't wait for that restaurant to open up," Maude called, in her always wobbly voice. "I love Italian food."

"Yeah, I will," Ryan said, but her mind was racing, already elsewhere assembling the pieces of gossip.

"And don't worry about Madison LeGrange. You're a hottie, too," Birdie said across the restaurant. The Biddies laughed at the audacious quality of sweet Birdie's comment. Ryan attempted a smile and then left the café, grateful to take a great big inhale of fresh air. What she needed more than anything was to get to work and keep herself busy before her brain attacked itself wondering about Gabriella's past with Madison and whether it really was the past at all.

Yet turning off her thoughts at this point seemed almost impossible.

Her feelings for Gabriella had never been more apparent than in this moment when it felt like she had the capacity to lose her. Whoever argued that love was wonderful and amazing and worthy of a million song lyrics had certainly never felt the terror of losing it. Wait. Love wasn't a thing. At least not yet.

She blinked.

Was it?

Ryan wasn't convinced she was in love with Gabriella. She wasn't the type to fall for someone so easily and, in fact, had never been in love at all. But then nothing about Gabriella was typical.

She pulled her truck onto Tangle Valley's property, followed the winding road up the hill, and paused at the top, as always, for a breather. When she saw the gorgeous expanse of land below, she took a deep and slow inhale as reality crashed in. "I think I'm in love with her," she said to no one. Dale whined from his spot in the back seat and she laughed. "You and me both, bud. I didn't see this coming, and I'm not sure I recommend it at this point." She turned back to the view and knew that in spite of her worried, lovesick heart, she had a restaurant to prep. The soft opening was creeping up, and there were a lot of small things she needed to correct before inspection. She'd get out her standard checklists and get to work.

But first...

"For you." Ryan placed the coffee just beyond the window of the food truck, inside of which Gabriella seemed to be massaging a mountain of meat on a cutting board.

"How did you know I was dreaming of Biscuit coffee?" Her hazel eyes lit up. "Hi there. Was waiting for you."

"I took a chance." She smiled. "Hi."

Gabriella held up her meat-contaminated hands like a surgeon in gloves and leaned close to the window for a kiss, which Ryan happily savored. "How was your night last night?"

The answer was *lonely* because she and Dale had stayed on their own at the lake house instead of where she'd rather have been, with Gabriella. "I had a good night. Watched a Dodgers game and then did some work in my shop."

"Did you wear the sexy overalls? Say yes and make my morning."

"Yes," Ryan said.

"You okay?" Gabriella asked. "You seem, I don't know, distracted or melancholy. I can't decide which."

"Just trying to organize myself for the workday. I want to check in on Billy and Lonzo at Tangled, but then I have three other jobs to get to."

"Oh." Gabriella's smile dimmed, and everything in Ryan hated it. "Yeah, of course. I didn't mean to keep you. I know you have a lot going on."

"You didn't keep me. Nothing like that."

"Okay. Well, that's good."

She cringed inwardly because they were off on a weird, overly polite path now, and it was all her fault. She took a steadying breath to wipe the slate clean and fix this. "My mornings will always be better for seeing you. Always."

Gabriella's eyes softened. "Even with meat hands?" she asked meekly. "Cause I have meat hands."

"Especially then." She pointed behind the truck at Tangled. "I have to get my crew set up, but I'd love to see you after."

"Well, you will. We have a game. You'll probably lose." Damn, Gabriella was beautiful when her competitive side showed and her eyes got that spark of determination. She loved the damn spark. She loved all of her.

"That's right. I almost forgot."

"Muskrats don't," she said and pretended to tap her temple from six inches away while making that strange rodent face that always made Ryan laugh. "There or square, Jacks."

"Like I'd miss a chance to see you slug a ball and run around in a circle. Catch you later, Meat Hands Russo."

"My meat hands bring all the girls to the yard," she called after Ryan, who felt lighter for their exchange. She shrugged off the Biddies' comments, at least for now. She and Gabriella were really good together, and that should be the only damn headline.

❖

Gabriella had an hour before she needed to get ready for the ball game, and she knew what she needed to do. It had been a handful of days since the difficult dinner at the Crown Jewel, and she and Madison still needed to talk.

With nerves aflutter, she found Madison in her office, the one that used to belong to Jack Wilder when he was winemaker. But Madison had made it her own, organizing the clutter and using technology to cut back on the endless notebooks and binders Jack had relied upon. The door stood open, but typing something diligently into a spreadsheet,

Madison hadn't heard her enter. For a moment, Gabriella simply watched her work. Madison wore her work glasses, which, back in the day, Gabriella used to love on her. Smart, sexy, and businesslike all in one. That had been a different time, a different them. Right? Hadn't it been?

"Knock, knock," she said finally.

Madison looked up and took off the glasses. A smile. Good. "Hey. Didn't see you there."

"Didn't want you to for a moment. You were so focused." Gabriella leaned against the door. "Hi, back. Is this an okay time for a chat?"

"Uh-oh," Madison said, making a point to look guilty. "I guess I should have seen this coming, and I totally get it. Everything you're going to say I've likely said to myself, just with a lot less charisma."

"There's nothing coming other than us maybe finding common ground."

"Why don't we take a walk? I haven't done that today, and I like to look in on the fruit."

"I'll follow you. The fruit will appreciate our visit, I'm sure."

Maddie led the way through the vines that had truly started to flourish over the past couple of weeks, bursting with green grapes. "These guys look like they're on track, not that I know anything about them," Gabriella said, touching the small buds of fruit.

Madison stared down at the vines. "The warmer month has been great, and the dry spell we've had is really going to boost the sugars. I think we're in for a nice balance." She sighed. "I hope for another couple of weeks like this one."

"I'll hope with you." They walked a bit. "So…dinner the other night was certainly something."

Madison nodded. "I hate that we made you leave." She shook her head and looked over at Gabriella. "I was beyond childish. I can admit that."

"You definitely kicked it off."

"I'm really sorry."

Now this was the Madison she recognized, and she took advantage of the opportunity. She wanted to understand where Maddie was coming from, what had propelled her. "You don't like Ryan. That much I understand. But—I have to ask—is there more to this? It's starting to feel like perhaps there is."

Madison nodded and took a moment, staring up at the sky as

they walked. "I honestly didn't think so at first. I didn't like the things I'd heard about Ryan, how she was out all the time, her flitting from woman to woman on a whim."

"I'm not going to argue that I like those things, either. But I do believe that people grow and change. Don't we all?"

"I hear you. But it's *you* we're talking about, and my standards are different."

Gabriella took a deep breath and admitted the truth. "I'd likely be protective of you, too."

Madison laughed. "Trust me. I know that for a fact. You're a bulldog when people you care about are at stake."

"Fine. Guilty."

"But over time, maybe I've come to see that my behavior might be rooted in something a little deeper."

Gabriella rolled her lips in, nervous, but didn't say a word.

"I thought I was long done with us, you know? The romance part anyway. We weren't a good fit. It was obvious as hell." Madison shook her head, looking distant and confused. "But what if we gave up too soon, and it just took Ryan coming into your life for me to see that?"

"Madison." She paused their walk and turned. "You're forgetting what it was like. We hit daily roadblocks. It became a passive aggressive, unproductive way to live life. I adore you, and you adore me, but I think what we're dealing with is you watching me in a relationship for the first time."

"What if it's not just that?"

Gabriella blinked, terrified of the question.

"Because I've tried that on and it doesn't fit." Madison held up a reassuring hand. "I'm not trying to disrupt anything that you have going. I will apologize to Ryan at the game today, even. But maybe what I'm feeling is legitimate. I promise."

"Oh, Maddie." This wasn't at all what she was expecting, but it wasn't what she'd feared most. Joey had hinted at it. But never did Gabriella expect Madison to admit to having feelings for her again. The sky felt too big, and the sunshine too bright. She wasn't sure what she was supposed to do with this information because the world felt foreign. She needed to say *something*, though. She just wasn't sure what. "I would never say your feelings aren't valid. But we weren't a good fit from day one. And there's Ryan, who has been a surprisingly good fit."

"I know." Madison lifted her shoulders and let them drop. "I didn't say it made sense. But you and I are different here. We're on the same page. Wouldn't you agree?"

Gabriella opened her mouth and closed it again because there was truth to that statement, and it left her lost. "Madison."

"I know. I get it."

"It's just that—"

"You're not in the same space."

Gabriella nodded and met her gaze. "I'm sorry."

Madison afforded her a brave smile, but it was for show only. It didn't reach her eyes. "Hey, don't be. I'm ridiculous. We've always known that." She gestured to the grapes. "I should stick with what I know best, these guys."

"You're my best friend. I would fight off a tiger for you, you know that?" She opened her arms and Madison moved slowly into them.

"I know. And I've been such an ass lately. That's gonna stop. I promise."

Gabriella held her close. "I just want us all to get along and for it to not be weird and—"

"It won't be. I think it's good that we talked." Madison stepped out of the embrace. "I'm just a little all over the place."

"Okay. Well, I'm here. I'm still me, if you need to talk anything out."

"I'll remember that. And I'm really sorry if I made this weird."

"We're fine."

"Are we?" Madison exhaled. "Good. Maybe we can get back to regularly scheduled programming. Group movie nights and hanging out in the tasting room. You can even bring Ryan. I'll behave."

"I'd like that, Maddie." Gabriella gestured behind her. "Should we head back?"

Madison hesitated and studied the expanse of vines. "You go ahead. I'm gonna continue my expedition."

Gabriella nodded and watched Madison continue the walk alone. As if sensing she was being watched, Maddie called out, "Stop watching me. I'm being a scientist, not a sappy overthinker."

"Promise?" she called back.

"God, yes. I'm super-smart, okay?"

"*Right.*" Gabriella grinned, recognizing their friendship peeking out at her once again. She nodded. Things were going to be okay. They'd get there. She sighed. But if that was true, why did her heart hurt?

❖

It was the bottom of the fourth, and the Muskrats were giving them quite a game. What usually would have played out to at least a five-run lead was a nail-biter that left Ryan with a pit in her stomach. She loved and hated the suspense.

Gabriella, as expected, had led her team to a new level of confidence. They yelled louder, ran faster, and leaped for balls they normally would have assumed lost to them. It was Gabriella's turn at bat, and she made a show of warming up her arm with a series of swings that told the pitcher she meant business. Ryan filled with pride. That was her girl out there, showing everyone how it was done. Next, she moved on to hoping her girl *did not* get on base. Powell Rogers had been pitching balls all afternoon, and Ryan felt nervous he'd walk another batter. Gabriella had other plans and knocked the hell out of the first pitch, ball or not. It sailed over the second baseman and dropped into center field. Brenda Anne bungled the stop with an "Oh, crap," and Gabriella passed first base, headed to second, before doubling back when Brenda Anne got it together at the last second. That left her on first base. With Ryan.

"Hi, sexy first basewoman," Gabriella said, not taking her eyes off Clementine, up to bat next for the Muskrats.

"I can't fraternize with you," Ryan said simply. "I'll lose my focus."

"Oh, have a little fun," Gabriella said quietly. "You look hot today. How many miles did you run? Five?"

"Stop that, you saboteur," Ryan said. "My head's in this game."

"You'll probably lose anyway. Better to flirt."

Ryan couldn't resist her. Even the familiar smell of Gabriella's watermelon scented soap had her at attention. "Fine. Maybe I could take you out sometime."

"And maybe I could take your clothes off."

Ryan blinked, lost in a haze of imagining just that. The bat cracked, and in an unlikely turn of events, Clementine drove one past third. "Gotta go, Otter," Gabriella said and shot off. It took everything Ryan had to get it together and make the play to nab Clem out at first. She passed Gabriella a *How could you?* look, only to have her blow a kiss from second base. Forgiven.

In the end, the Otters managed to squeak by, putting them one step closer to the championship game. Ryan was happy to see her mom clapping in the stands as she approached.

"Looking good out there, but maybe keep your eye on the ball and not the runner." Her mom smiled sweetly.

"Did I just get roasted by my mother?"

"Totally did," Billy said, on his way past to Wrigley, who'd been keeping Joanna company.

"I saw you watching that girl who is a cook," Wrigley said with a smile. Joanna hooked a thumb at her as if to say, *See?*

"Yeah, well, I was set up," Ryan said meekly.

"Joanna!" Ryan turned to see Gabriella emerge from her team meeting in the dugout and move instantly to embrace her mom, who lit up like the Fourth. Nearby, she saw Maude the Biddy snap a photo, which would likely hit Instagram before nightfall.

"I had no idea you could play like that," Joanna said, beaming. "You're like a professional with a whoosh and that zigzag deal to avoid the tag at home." Her mom mimed a throw and swing and slide.

"Let's not get crazy," Ryan said. "She's okay."

"You're good too, sweetheart," her mom said in total pacification.

Ryan nodded. "Oh, thanks for remembering I exist, Mom."

"No problem, kiddo."

Gabriella turned to Ryan with a grin and shoulder nudge. "Good game."

"I had to keep up with a wily little Muskrat. No easy feat."

"I'd say you held your own pretty well. Took home the big W."

"She was watching you," Wrigley called out to Gabriella. Billy playfully covered his child's mouth.

"Nice game, guys." Ryan turned to see Madison sitting four rows up on the bleachers. Joey and Becca were next to her, and both waved happily. Gabriella shot them the muskrat face, and they, of course, reciprocated.

"Hey, thanks," Ryan said to Madison, grateful for the gesture. "They made us work out there."

"Made it exciting." Madison stood. "Do you, by chance, have a sec?"

Ryan first glanced around to make sure Madison was speaking to her. Next, she looked to Gabriella, who offered a conservative smile. "Uh, yeah, I do."

Madison nodded, hopped to the ground, and led them a few yards away where there was a quiet spot to talk on the grass. "Listen, I was an ass the other night and had no right to be. I wanted to apologize. That's definitely not the person I want to be."

Ryan took off her cap. "I appreciate that. I wasn't any better, and I'm sorry. You mean a lot to Gabriella, and that makes you important."

"Can we work on a clean slate?"

Ryan smiled, not one to hold a grudge. Life was way too short, and she'd always believed Madison was a good person underneath her distrust. "Done. I don't hold on to stuff."

"Good. And if I haven't said so, Tangled is looking amazing. You guys surpassed my expectations, and Gabriella seems over the moon with the place."

"Thanks." She was proud of the project herself and planned to use photos from it in her portfolio and advertising materials. "Before we know it, we'll be ready for our inspections. I believe Joey is on top of the permit side of things."

"You guys okay over here?" Gabriella asked nervously from a few yards away.

"Why would you even need to ask that?" Madison scoffed. "I can't imagine what would make you nervous."

"Seriously. I'm offended," Ryan huffed. "Us?"

Gabriella, looking amazing in her yellow and white uniform, rolled her eyes. "Lord help me."

Because Gabriella had hitched a ride to the game with her friends instead of bringing her own car, she rode home with Ryan. They drove with the windows down and the music up.

"My mom couldn't get over how great you were." Ryan grinned, enjoying the night.

"She's incredibly sweet. Does she know…about us?"

"Well, not everything, but the basics. She's really happy. About where this is going."

"And where is that?" Gabriella asked.

The air racing through the cab of the truck picked up as Ryan accelerated. She had no idea what to say, what wouldn't make her look like an idiot making things up as she went. "We're right here. In this truck. Enjoying this night. Isn't it great?"

That pulled a wide smile, and Ryan's heart sang.

"It really is." Gabriella placed her hand on Ryan's leg and gave it a squeeze. "Why is it that I can just breathe when I'm with you?"

Ryan chuckled. "Sometimes when I'm with *you*, I have the opposite problem. Not that I'm complaining."

"No, I get that part, too." Gabriella shook her head, as if searching for the words. "My world feels better with you in it. That's the main idea. Problems roll off my back. I can just be."

Ryan let the comment settle. She didn't want to blow it by trying to say something as amazing back and failing, so she kept it simple. "Can our worlds go sit on my dock and talk about our days?"

"Only if there's a little bit of smooching as the sun goes down."

Ryan picked up Gabriella's hand and kissed it. "Sundown kissing is a market that you have cornered."

And as the day came to a close and the sun touched the waterline in the distance, Ryan wrapped both arms around Gabriella, who sat next to her on the dock, bare feet dangling.

"I love the sound of your heart beating," Gabriella said and kissed the underside of Ryan's jaw softly, absorbing the warmth from her body.

"It's all for you." Ryan meant every word. She'd never experienced any of these feelings before, but one definitely floated straight to the top. As she held this woman in her arms, there was no doubt in her mind that she'd fallen in love. Now, the question became, was she alone?

# CHAPTER SIXTEEN

Thank God, Knead Me had a drive-through window. Gabriella had called in an order for a loaf of fresh focaccia bread that she planned to sample alongside an amazing batch of olive oil from Olive You, a specialty shop in the town square. She was essentially auditioning vendors and thrilled to see her local list coming together so nicely. She almost couldn't wait to get home, put on her comfy clothes, and return a call to her sister Angie, who'd left a check-in message earlier that day.

"Thanks, Elise," Gabriella said, taking a deep inhale of the brown bags as she placed them in the passenger seat next to her. Her car smelled heavenly and she planned to enjoy the next five and a half minutes, taking as many deep inhales as humanly possible.

Fifteen minutes later, with her glorious bread and olive oil snack by her side, her call with Angie was in full swing.

"How is it working with your ex, though?" Angie asked. "I always thought she was the one, you know?"

"I guess I did at one point, too. We're great friends, and I mostly love working with her."

"Mostly?" Angie asked. She heard the concern hit.

Gabriella didn't know where to begin. She had every intention of being open and honest with her sisters about this new development in her life because thus far, they knew nothing. "The truth is I'm seeing someone who's become pretty important to me."

Her sister gasped. "Do the others know?"

Gabriella grinned, acknowledging the four-way sister competition that never really went away. "No. You're the first I've told." She could just see Angie gloating.

"I can't believe you buried the lede. We've been on the phone ten minutes already. So it's a triangle?"

Gabriella balked. "No. But Madison hasn't been as go-with-the-flow as I would have imagined."

"She's still in love with you. I'm bettin' on that," Angie said matter-of-factly. "I'm telling you. She's the one."

The words alone made Gabriella go still. "No. No. It's nothing like that. This is just Madison getting confused."

"Huh." Angie softened. "Well, who's the new person?"

Gabriella did her best to be breezy and casually dipped a piece of bread in the oil. "Her name is Ryan, and she's the contractor renovating the new restaurant."

"Oh, as in she works with her hands," Angie said knowingly. "I see now. She comes with tools."

Gabriella nodded, even though Angie couldn't see her. "And she makes furniture on her own time."

Angie chuckled low. "But is she hot outside of the sexy job?"

Gabriella took her time before selecting a photo of Ryan on the porch in front of Tangled from the ever-growing collection on her phone. She wore jeans and her white Level Up Contracting shirt. The sun was shining, she had her hair down, and the dimples were both out. One of Gabriella's favorite shots that she looked at before bed on the nights when they slept apart. She fired off the text to Angie and waited.

"That's her?" Angie asked.

"Yep."

Angie paused on the line. Gabriella imagined her taking a moment to survey every detail of the photo. "I'm fanning myself. She's the most glamorous construction worker I've ever seen."

Gabriella grinned. "Except she's entirely no-frills. She just wakes up like that. It's not fair. Except now it is, because I get to wake up next to her and benefit."

"That's a definite bonus. I'm glad you're having some fun. "

Gabriella told her sister about softball, Ryan's mom, her lake house, and how sweet Ryan was to Dale.

"That's all well and fine, but has the other shoe dropped?" Angie went big sister on her. "She sounds too good to be true, and we all know what that means."

Gabriella nodded as she made her way to the couch, prepared to be honest. When she talked with her sisters, who knew her better than anyone on the planet, she didn't have to pretend or sugarcoat. Yes, they'd speak their minds, but maybe she needed to hear it. "Well, she's five years younger than I am."

"Matty is seven years older than me," Angie said, referencing her husband. "It doesn't bother me at all."

"Okay, well, she's also been known to play the field. She's never been big on committed relationships. In fact, she's stayed away from them for the most part." She winced and waited.

"Red flag," Angie said, automatically. "Nope. Nope. Nope."

"Is it?" Gabriella asked. "She says she's ready. That I make her want something different."

"You gotta be careful. I don't trust those types. Been there. Done that." Angie had been divorced once and didn't mince words about her hound dog ex-husband. "Especially not when you have someone so nice and dependable like Madison." Her voice took on a wistful quality when she said that last part. Gabriella frowned. This wasn't what she was hoping to hear.

Gabriella swallowed and explained. "My heart is dragging me to Ryan."

"You sure?" Angie asked. "You don't ever wonder if you and Maddie should give it a go now that time has passed? You've both grown and matured. Smart and dependable, that one. I heard she was on the cover of one of those lifestyle food and wine magazines in the Finger Lakes."

"Yeah, she was. She's been all over the wine world." Gabriella was about to say something that she'd not fully admitted, even to herself. But it was there all the same. "Sure, I wonder. More now that Madison's mentioned it, the concept of us, but I'd tucked that part of us away, Ang. We broke up for a very good reason, and we're the same people even though our lives have been transported across the country."

"I don't think that's it. She's not as exciting to you as this Ryan is," Angie said. "I get that. But sometimes, safe and a little less exciting pays off in the end. This isn't a sprint. It's your life. Plus, it's *Madison*, and the whole family loves her."

Gabriella blinked up at the ceiling, her head swimming. Those words hit her harder than she'd expected. Why was this Madison thing messing with her head? Would Ryan wind up burning her in the end? Did Angie have a point? Maybe she was on the wrong path and needed to take a good hard look at her life. She reached for her glass on the coffee table and took a swallow of wine. Maddie's wine. "You were supposed to help settle me down, not pose more questions than answers."

"It's your decision," Angie reminded her. "But if you're asking?

I vote for keeping an open mind about Madison. That's all. I want you to be happy."

"I love you and the rest of the family to the end of the Earth, but we're not voting on my life."

"Okay, fine. Then show me more of the hottie's photos," Angie commanded. "You'll come around to my side sooner or later."

Gabriella laughed and tried to ignore the second part of that statement. She sent more photos of Ryan and regaled her sister with more stories of the two of them, halfway trying to persuade her that Ryan was, in fact, amazing. Later, as she cleaned up from her successful focaccia bread audition, Gabriella couldn't shake Angie's words from her head. She usually trusted her sister's wisdom, relied on it. In fact, Angie had never steered her wrong. Did that mean Ryan *was* too good to be true? She refused to give too much attention to the sinking feeling she couldn't seem to lose. She texted Ryan good night and stared at her favorite photo before bed—Ryan looking over at her with a sly grin, on a brief break at the jobsite—running her thumb across it in contemplation. There was Ryan. And now Madison. Why was this more complicated than it needed to be? With a deep sigh, she switched off her bedside lamp and vowed to figure it out. Just not tonight.

# CHAPTER SEVENTEEN

A week after they'd cuddled on her dock, Ryan woke up in her very favorite spot in the world, next to the woman who had her heart. She kissed an exposed shoulder and molded her naked body to Gabriella's, squinting at the time on the digital clock on her bedside table. They'd been silently snuggling for more than ten minutes, so she was safe to speak. Somehow the silence was nice, though. They still had a little time before her official alarm, but Ryan wanted to get a jump on what would be a busy day because she had several new client consultations lined up and an estimate in addition to managing her active jobsites.

"You're so warm. I love it," Gabriella said, snuggling back against Ryan.

"And yet I have to get up."

"No, you don't," Gabriella said in the cutest voice ever. She turned in Ryan's arms and faced her, sliding one arm around her waist. She blinked up at Ryan with those big hazel eyes she adored. "Today is canceled. I checked."

"Well, if you say so." Ryan kissed Gabriella's forehead as sunlight peeked in on them. "I guess we'll have to just stay here forever."

Gabriella, who had proven herself to be a fan of mornings for a variety of reasons, some of them adult, palmed Ryan's breast. The sheet revealed a glimpse of one of Gabriella's breasts, and that sent a whole separate kind of good morning vibrating through her system. "We'll need something to do to pass the time."

Ryan bit the inside of her cheek and closed her eyes while everything in her slowly came alive, thanks to Gabriella's roaming hands. Her fingertips drifted down Ryan's body, lightly skimming her stomach. They brushed the tops of her thighs, tickling them. Her stomach muscles clenched, and she began to ache pleasantly, which she knew had been Gabriella's goal. "Oh, you have definite plans, don't you?"

"Mm-hmm." She ran her nails back and forth against Ryan's inner thigh, and then ever so slowly let them brush over her most sensitive spot, causing Ryan to jerk. Gabriella did it again, grinning proudly, and again, each time taking Ryan to new heights, and quickly, too. She'd always been extra-sensitive in the morning, and Gabriella knew it. With her thumb, Gabriella lightly pressed and Ryan was gone, falling into that oblivion of pure pleasure, her hips tight and her body enjoying every second of it.

"Apparently not everything was canceled," Ryan said, once she'd recovered. Every damn muscle in her body hung loose and happy. In actuality, she only had a few minutes before she needed to be up and moving, but these were not minutes she planned to waste, as she dipped her head and caught Gabriella's nipple in her mouth.

"Well, Miss Jacks, whatever are you doing?" Gabriella asked in her best Southern accent, which made the morning all the more fun. Everything was fun with Gabriella. "Oh, I do declare."

Following showers, a few more stolen kisses, and coffee in Ryan's kitchen, they were ready to face their respective days.

"I'm nervous," Gabriella confessed and blew on the contents of her mug. "I feel like this opening has a lot riding on it. I want Joey to be happy."

Ryan quirked her head. "What do you have to be nervous about? Everyone is going to love the place and the food you turn out. You never miss."

"I know. But what if they don't?" She touched her chest absently. "This feels like a really big time in my life."

Ryan came around the counter. "Look at me." She wrapped her arms around Gabriella's waist. "I've seen the look people get on their faces when they're trying your food. It's a little slice of heaven for them. Do you know what else? People love everything about the vineyard, and they will love Tangled just as much." She raised her arm in punctuation. "Hell, even if it was an awful looking place, they'd love it because that arancini thing is addictive." She moved a strand of hair off Gabriella's forehead. "You have absolutely nothing to worry about. We have some big deliveries coming in this week, then some detail work, followed by inspection. We're good to go. Nothing to worry about."

Gabriella exhaled slowly. "Thank you for the pep talk. I think I needed it." She shook her head. "I have no idea how you have the capacity to talk me down in a manner no other human being has been able to do." She seemed to search for the words. "It's almost as if you're able to look into me and know the words I need."

"I think you might be giving me too much credit, but I do think that I get to know you better every single day. And I love everything about you." She heard the use of the one word she hadn't meant to voice out loud and panicked. Dammit. Now what? Gabriella would think she was some love-drunk kid who didn't understand that real relationships took time. They date for a couple of months, and all of a sudden Ryan's in love? She watched as Gabriella's features subtly reacted. She wasn't sure, but Gabriella might have pulled out of her arms slightly. She tried to fix it, to backpedal. "I just really, uh, like where things are headed."

"Me, too." Gabriella blinked up at her. "But things got weird just now. What was going on in your head?"

Ryan, panicking now, had no clue what the right thing was to say here. She wasn't good at this, lacked polish, finesse. She disentangled them and looked around as if thinking about something else. "Oh, nothing. I just got distracted."

"I think you got spooked when the word *love* hit just now. It's okay," Gabriella said, looking half defeated, half annoyed. "You don't have to be afraid to use the word in passing. I'm not going to pin it on you or hold you to it in other regards."

"That's not it at all," Ryan said, releasing her and walking to the sink to wash out her cup.

"Then what is it?" Gabriella leaned back against the counter, careful smile in place. "I don't understand why you can't just admit that it spooked you."

"Why are you focusing on that word?" Ryan asked nonchalantly, totally flying blind now and feeling like an idiot. She was overcompensating but couldn't seem to stop. "Would you rather I say I'm head over heels in love?" She added a laugh to make it seem lighthearted, when really all she felt was a terror she desperately sought to mask. How did they get here?

Gabriella stared at the ground as if taking a minute. "No. I don't need you to say that at all. But..."

"What?" Ryan asked, shutting off the water.

"It would be nice if it wasn't such a joke to you. Something to laugh about in the kitchen on a Saturday morning when all I was doing was asking a question."

"You can ask me anything you want." Ryan closed her eyes and regrouped. "And it's not a joke. I'm so sorry it came off that way. I think"—she stared at the ceiling, desperate for a way to explain herself—"that I don't always know where we're at. And this is all so new that—"

"You're out of your comfort zone."

"No."

"Listen, I understand." Her voice was flat, devoid of emotion in a way Ryan had never heard from Gabriella.

"This isn't going well."

Gabriella laughed but it sounded near sarcastic. "I'd have to agree."

She slid her hands into the back pockets of her work jeans, aware she was already late for her first job. "I'm figuring this all out in real time, you know? So please try and cut me some slack?"

Gabriella nodded, softening a tad. "Yes, okay. I can do that." She checked the clock on the microwave behind Ryan. "You guys better get outta here."

Seeing Ryan reach for her bag, Dale leaped to attention and arrived at her side. She gave his head a pat and looked back up at Gabriella. "This feels weird. Are we okay?"

"Well, it was. But…yeah. We're fine." Her eyes didn't say so. In fact, she looked shaken. This rocky patch in the road left Ryan with a pit in her stomach. She leaned in for a soft kiss, which Gabriella obliged. It also didn't ring true. She'd hurt Gabriella by not being forthcoming and hated herself for it. Ryan wanted nothing more than to proclaim how in love she already was, but that seemed like a tall building to leap from now. She knew without a doubt what her feelings for Gabriella were, but saying them out loud, especially when Gabriella hadn't yet indicated her own feelings, was beyond terrifying. But she likely needed to find a way at some point soon and decided to be on the lookout for the right moment.

"You free for this week's walk-through later today?" she said.

"Yes." Gabriella's arms were folded. She seemed closed off to Ryan now, and that hurt. "Just give me a call when you're ready, and I'll walk over."

"Will do."

She grabbed her bag and her dog and headed out with a last sad look back at Gabriella, who she'd clearly upset. Ryan drove through town central to her estimate full of regret and feeling nauseous. It didn't matter how scary it was—she owed Gabriella her honesty. Maybe she was the only one in love, but you know what? Who cared? Later that night, maybe they'd sit on the dock and have a candid conversation. Her heart thudded heavily at the mere idea, but she could do this. She would. Too much was on the line, and she didn't want to regret another moment.

❖

"Jolene, I don't want you to feel left out when I start spending more time at the restaurant than I do here. You're still just as important, and just as cute." She shrugged as she bagged up her remaining fresh spices and placed them in the small refrigerator. "We'll need you for lunch service still, and the interns will get valuable experience once they take over more."

Gabriella had finished lunch service and sent Chelsea home for the day before she got the call from Ryan to head over for their walk-through. She gave her workspace a final wipe down, ditched her apron, and headed to Tangled. The outside of the restaurant was nearly finished. She paused and grinned up at the newly painted sage and dark brown building, the scripted sign placed at the roofline, elegant and simple. The small adjacent parking lot was also nearly complete, and she imagined it filled with cars. She followed the newly installed sidewalk up to the door, imagining herself a patron of the restaurant and enjoying the elevated rustic feel, which reminded her so much of Italy her heart squeezed. Inside was just as beautiful and warm. She liked that the dining room was small but with enough space for each of the tables to feel set apart. Well, at least they would when the tables went in. They were holding them for delivery until the floor went in, which should be anytime now. Soon aromas would flood this room, and servers with trays would whisk hot plates to diners.

"There you are," Ryan said with a smile. It was good to see her. After their difficult conversation that morning, she'd done her best to push the larger message out of her head: Ryan wasn't ready for any of this. Because maybe it was easier to ignore that little voice in her head for now. And the voice of her sister. And half the town, who likely believed Gabriella was set up for heartbreak in this scenario.

"Let me show you what's new this week." They walked the perimeter of the room, and Ryan showed her the new light fixtures along the wall, which looked even better in person, the texture they'd added to the paintwork, some of the automation that gave them lots of options for different music and lighting schemes. The security system had also been installed, along with the refrigeration systems for the uprights and the walk-in. She glanced down at the dusty floors, marked with paint and drywall. Most of the tile had already been ripped out to make way for a speedy installation. It stood in stark contrast to the rest of the room.

"Shouldn't the floor go in soon?"

"Yes, that's our last big hurdle." Ryan looked down and touched the top of her head. "I was actually expecting delivery yesterday. Sometimes they're a little loosey-goosey, so I'll check in with them, make sure we're on the schedule for today or tomorrow." She offered Gabriella a reassuring smile. "We'll sneak in just under the wire. Keeps things exciting, right?"

Gabriella's eyes went wide. "Exciting is one way to put it. You really think we'll make it if the tile doesn't arrive until tomorrow?"

"I do. In fact, I'll call right now."

Ryan stepped outside to make the call, while Gabriella strolled the restaurant's interior, pausing at the shelves behind the bar that came with a subtle backlight for presentation. A nice touch. She was already starting to organize how she'd set up the spirits.

Ryan stepped back inside, but her entire demeanor had changed. "Not today?" Gabriella asked, already sensing the worst. She was seriously worried about their timeline.

"Apparently the order went in wrong, and they had it down for delivery this same time next month."

Gabriella took a moment. "Well, what does that mean? Can they just adjust the date and make it happen for us? We paid a lot of money for that specific tile."

Ryan shook her head, her face stricken. "It's coming from Idaho and they don't have available trucks."

Gabriella didn't understand what was happening. "A refund, then, so we can pivot to something available in Portland."

"The company is small, and because the error was on our end, they're not willing to work with me on a refund."

"Our end. What happened?"

"I toggled the date wrong. All on me."

"Ryan. God, seriously?" Her hands went to her hips as indignation flared. "Incredibly professional. Thank you. And you didn't check in with them until now?" Gabriella's emotions were firing without any control, and dammit, she needed someone to blame. Ryan had definitely played a part. She *was* reckless, sloppy. How was she supposed to explain this to Joey, who had gone out of her way to market the upcoming event to their wine club clients? The invitations, which included dinner at Tangled, were already out, and the RSVPs were rolling in. They'd been so close to the finish line and now this.

"I know. I know. Fuck," Ryan said quietly. She pinched the bridge of her nose and turned back. "I'm so sorry. But please know that we can find a way to fix this." Ryan moved to her in a show of comfort, and Gabriella took a decided step back. A slap would have stunned Ryan less. The look on her face would have normally slashed at Gabriella, but not today. She was too far gone. Crushed. Angry.

"Maybe. Maybe not." Gabriella stared at the shredded floor as it existed now. "But we were barely going to make our inspection as things stood."

Ryan rolled her lips in and seemed to be thinking a mile a minute. Finally, she sighed. "Yeah, I know." She leaned against the bar in defeat. "Dammit."

"Hey, you guys." Madison stood in the doorway with an earnest expression on her face. Kind, responsible Madison. She walked straight to Gabriella, compassion in her eyes. "Hey, you okay? You don't look it."

She didn't even think. Gabriella turned to her, helpless, and then Madison had her. Wrapped in a hug, she let the tears make an appearance. She couldn't seem to stop them as her hopes for her opening vanished on the heels of what had already been an emotionally difficult morning.

"It turns out we won't be open for the wine release after all. We have no floor and no way to get the materials here in time."

Madison winced and whispered quiet words to Gabriella. "It's okay. I'm so sorry this happened, but it's going to be all right in the end. You know that, right? Ryan is on top of it."

Gabriella turned back to Ryan only to see her white as a sheet. She didn't say anything for a long moment, almost as if she'd seen a ghost. Gabriella remembered herself then. Madison's arms were around her. They *still* were. What had started out as a friend's hug was now Madison full-on holding and comforting her. She took a step back and cleared her throat. "I suppose I need to find a way to get it together." She dried her tears. "No one died, right."

"You're allowed to be upset," Madison said.

Ryan turned away, her forearms resting on the bar. "In the meantime, I'll make some calls and see if there's anything to be done." Her eyes were sad, flat, and carried defeat.

"Ryan," Gabriella said.

"Yep?" For the first time Ryan looked her square in the eye, and Gabriella had no clue what in the world to say. It felt like there was now an ocean between them. Their undercurrents had risen to the surface and now engulfed them. It wasn't what she wanted, but at this point, she just felt along for the ride.

Gabriella started to speak, then gave her head a shake. "Nothing. Let me know what you find out."

"Of course. I'll make the calls in my truck. Give you guys space," Ryan said without looking at them.

Once they were alone, Madison frowned at her. "I hate that this happened. I know how excited you were."

"Thanks, Madison. After all this work, and now we're not going to make it." She shook her head in disbelief. "It helps to have my friends holding me up."

"Anytime you need it." Madison gestured behind her. "Ryan okay?"

"I'm not sure. Part of that is my fault. We had a weird morning and then…" She gestured to the shambles of a floor. "Now, this."

"If it helps, Ryan seems just as gutted."

"It's nice of you to stick up for her." She smiled. "New, in fact."

"Yeah, well, I'm working on it. So far, so good."

They shared a smile, and it felt comfortable, and Gabriella needed comfortable desperately. She took note of it for examination later. Madison continued to orbit her thoughts, and she should pay attention to that, right?

She found Ryan outside, leaning against the tailgate of her truck. After a pretty uncomfortable bout of silence, Gabriella took the initiative. "I'm sorry I blamed you. I know you didn't do this on purpose."

"Just my irresponsibility." Ryan smiled ruefully. "Seems to be a theme. You think I'm irresponsible in my personal life and now my job, too." She straightened. "I get it. I'm no Madison, famous for her brilliance and rock-solid dependability. Put together and well respected."

Gabriella closed her eyes for a moment, frustrated. "It's not a comparison."

"Isn't it?" Ryan's eyes flashed.

This wasn't the time to have this conversation, and now Gabriella shifted to anger herself. "I can't believe you're taking the events of today and making them about Madison and me."

Ryan sighed. "I don't mean to. It's probably better if we just—"

"Yeah. Respective corners." She took a breath. "I'm gonna go clean up. Long morning and afternoon."

"I'll be here. Trying to turn all of this around."

Gabriella walked the path home, amazed at what a difference a few hours could have on her day. She thought about waking up in Ryan's arms that morning, laughing and deciding on canceling the day and losing themselves in each other. If only they *had* canceled today.

Then again, maybe everything happened for a reason. Was this the universe's way of grabbing her by the shoulders and pointing her in the direction she should be heading? With her heart and head in a war for the ages, she walked the path to her cottage, searching for answers that simply weren't there.

## CHAPTER EIGHTEEN

Ryan sat on her dock alone with her thoughts, a beer, and her dog, who'd already taken a lap through the lake and now lay spent on his side, wet and happy. She was so angry at herself and gutted over the huge misstep at Tangled. She planned to pull some really long days if she had to and call in a few favors, but she needed to be realistic. It might not happen. They had a little more than a week until Gabriella wanted to host the wine club members, so it would take a miracle to pull this off. Didn't mean she wasn't determined to make it happen.

What struck her most? Phone silence today from Gabriella. On a normal day, they would have lit up each other's phones, chattering throughout the day. Yet other than a couple of back-and-forths about next steps for the fiasco, Gabriella had gone silent. Ryan blinked, numb, her gaze fixed on the horizon. The sky glowed purple and orange as the sun escaped this horrible day. In the midst of the turmoil, she'd learned a few things. Gabriella still thought of her the same way she had when they'd met, in spite of all Gabriella'd learned about her, in spite of all they'd shared. Her heart was crushed when Gabriella, *her Gabriella*, raced to Madison's arms when things got hard. How was that possible? Ryan now knew one thing for certain—she wasn't cut out for this, and the farther she let herself go down this path with Gabriella, the worse the damage was going to be when it was all ripped away from her.

Over the next few days, Ryan worked until her body cried out for relief. Some of the subs she needed weren't available at the drop of a hat, so she filled in on drywall, floor patching, painting, trimming, anything and everything that put her ahead of schedule on her other jobs so she could step away for a couple of days on behalf of Tangle Valley. Finally, she hopped in her rental truck and hit the road east.

Four hours into her drive, her phone rang. Gabriella. Ryan clicked her phone on to speaker. "Hey."

"Hey, you." Gabriella's voice was cheerful, almost as if nothing had changed. How was that possible? "Haven't seen you around much."

"I know. I had a lot to get done before my road trip."

"Road trip? Where are you headed? You didn't say anything about a road trip."

"I was getting around to it. I'm heading to Idaho to see a man about some tiles."

Gabriella went quiet. "Ryan. Really? You're driving there yourself?"

"I figure it's the only way it's going to get here in time."

"I didn't mean for you to have to go so far out of your way. Literally. But that's very thoughtful of you."

She smiled. "I want to make it right."

"Speaking of what happened, do you have a moment?" Gabriella asked. The nature of the question made Ryan's stomach flip over and her shoulders go tight. *Here we go.*

"I have hours."

"Great." Gabriella took a breath and leaped right into it. "I don't like the way I reacted a few days back. I cast a lot of blame your way on what was an innocent mistake, and I want you to know that I recognize that. I'm sorry. Sometimes when you're shocked by what's in front of you, you lose your ability to see things, I don't know, rationally."

"I appreciate that," Ryan said and smiled weakly. This would normally be the moment in the conversation where she melted like a Popsicle on a hot day, thrilled to be speaking to Gabriella and taking in everything about her. She didn't allow that to happen today. She couldn't because her head was full of the Biddies' gossip session, the disappointment in Gabriella's eyes a few mornings back, and the way she fit perfectly into the arms of Madison LeGrange like she belonged there. So now, Ryan held back those reflex emotions and focused on the practical, shielding her heart, which was much more fragile than she ever knew. "And with a little luck, we'll be able to rebound from this."

"You honestly think we can?"

"Have you ever seen me give up?"

Gabriella chucked. "I can easily say that you never do."

The conversation felt easy again. Good. They shared a comfortable moment of silence.

"I really miss you, you know," Gabriella said.

"I know. I miss you, too," Ryan said. She didn't think about how much, though, and that helped her not feel it so acutely. So had working all the long hours.

"I know you're going really hard right now, but maybe it's too hard? Billy said you were on a job until close to ten last night."

"Yet you didn't check on me. My phone was quiet."

Gabriella sighed. "I was trying to figure out what to say."

"And what you wanted to do. I know. I get it."

"What does that mean? Do about what?" Gabriella sounded puzzled.

"Well, you have options, right?"

"Aha." Understanding seemed to strike. "Well, I don't want options." Gabriella exhaled slowly and audibly. "We had a rough couple of days, yes, but I'm not ready to walk away. Not even close. I don't give up either, Ryan."

"Yeah. Okay." But she had trouble believing it in the long run. Her heart was flattened and showing no firm sign of rebound. She tapped the steering wheel. "Traffic is picking up. I should go."

Gabriella didn't hesitate. "You're not being yourself right now."

"I know. I'm sorry about that. I just have a lot on my plate."

"When are you home?"

"Tomorrow night."

"Then let's get together then. Let me make you a late dinner."

"If you want." Ryan tried another smile to soften the tone of her voice. She had no interest in punishing Gabriella, but everything in her told her to find a way to distance herself in the name of self-preservation. She wasn't capable of walking away, but she had to take steps back. The chances of Gabriella sticking around when the love of her life lived just yards away were feeling slimmer and slimmer. Madison would likely use this opportunity to swoop in and play caretaker-best-friend, and then they'd ride off into the vineyard together, realizing they never should have parted ways. It made Ryan want to cry and doubt everything she once thought they had. She was such an idiot for proceeding so blindly.

Instead she lost herself on the road and in loud music. Eyes forward. Heart stashed away. Back to what she'd known all along.

She arrived back at Tangled the following night and unloaded the tile with her crew, exhausted and with very little left to give. After they'd locked up, she made the short walk to Gabriella's cottage where they'd agreed to have dinner and found Gabriella sitting in front of her cottage. "Hey, there. Good news. It's here."

"I owe you for this," Gabriella said with the warmest of smiles.

"You don't." Ryan glanced behind her. "But to be honest, I think I'm too tired to be much company tonight. Gonna chill with Dale. Can we do dinner another time?"

Gabriella stood, caught off guard. "It's me. I don't care how tired you are. Ryan, you don't even have to speak. We can just be in the same room together. Maybe kiss." She met Ryan's gaze. "I think it's about time we make up, don't you? Remember what's truly important in life?"

"Of course, yeah." She tried to buy in to that. Every part of her wanted to spend the evening with Gabriella and for them to be okay now and forever, but she was learning things about herself as she went. One of those things? Love and giving herself to another person maybe wasn't for her. She thought back to just six months ago when she'd been unattached. Yes, she'd been a lot less fulfilled, but she hadn't been living in fear, a shell of herself, waiting for the inevitable other shoe to drop. She hadn't been so dependent on another human being that she couldn't breathe at the thought that they would someday turn to their best friend and realize that's where they really belonged. And of course, that's what she fully imagined would happen at any moment now because her mind was a cruel place to dwell at three a.m. when sleep evaded. She made herself look at Gabriella, really look at her. "But maybe this isn't the night for it."

Gabriella's gaze shifted away from hers and back. "Yeah. Okay. Are you, though? Okay. It's been days, and you don't seem like…you."

"Just the long drive taking it out of me. That's what this is." She forced a smile, leaned down, and kissed Gabriella softly on the lips, realizing that she needed to get it the hell together. She was trying here, but not getting very far. They couldn't go on like this. She needed to figure herself out.

"I'll call you in the morning." Gabriella squeezed her hand and smiled. She was also trying, and that meant so much.

"I'll be there."

"Oh. Can I say good-bye to Dale?"

Ryan softened and her heart squeezed unpleasantly. "Yeah. Of course."

She watched as Gabriella came off the steps and sank to her knees, prompting Dale to trot on over, head low, clearly looking for some love. He got it. She cupped his big, dopey face in her hands and spoke quietly to him. He licked her nose and she kissed his cheek. They'd become

quite the duo over time, and that made Ryan sad for reasons she refused
to fully examine.

"Good night, Gabriella."

"Yeah. 'Night, Ryan."

❖

Gabriella checked her watch and moved into double time like a
mall walker on a mission. She had a meeting with Joey and Madison
to coordinate their efforts for the release party. Most of the details were
already in place, but with so little time remaining, it was time to circle
back and make sure all was on track for Saturday afternoon. She passed
the storage shed and caught a quick glimpse of Bobby. She opened her
mouth to say hello and realized he was in a lip lock for the ages with
none other than that sneak, Loretta! She'd been right! She pointed and
gasped, and for emphasis re-pointed and gasped, arm outstretched. She
looked around, vindicated. Yet there was no one to witness this torrid
love scene but her. Typical. She huffed. Hands on her hips, she watched
them a moment before feeling intrusive and heading to her meeting.

"I'm late like a rabbit down a hole, but I have like fifteen good
excuses, none of them being Loretta and Bobby sucking face in the
shed. Except, oh yes, one of them is exactly that."

Joey squinted at her. "This again? C'mon."

"Yes, and I'm right, so suck it, bitches."

Madison raised her gaze in curiosity. "We're bitches now. That's
new."

Gabriella shrugged. "I tried it on. Felt weird. So take that, weirdos."

"Much more you." Madison went back to her laptop.

"Did you actually see them?" Joey asked.

Gabriella, done trying to convince the world, turned the key in
front of her lips. "You know what? With that kind of attitude, you'll
have to find out for yourself. Maybe I saw their lips pressed together in
a jumble, maybe I didn't."

"Well, someone's sassy today," Madison said with a slight incline
of her head.

Gabriella sulked. "It's a whole thing. I won't bore you with the
details. Let's talk refreshments for this thing so I can chase my troubles
away with my food fantasies." Gabriella was beginning to understand
that maybe Ryan's pulling away wasn't just about the delay on the
jobsite, and sooner or later they'd have to discuss it. They chatted

here and there about surface level things. The weather, softball, the restaurant. They touched, but only in a PG-13 manner. Once in a while, they flirted. Ryan was infinitely too tired to see her at night, though… which seemed weird.

"Is this a Ryan thing?" Joey asked. "It's morning, but we can break out a nip of sangria." She headed behind the bar, probably already in search of a growler full.

Gabriella waved off the Ryan idea. "It's dumb. I'm probably overreacting, but she's not really available anymore. I miss her. A lot." She glanced at the clock. "It's late morning. Haul out the fruit wine."

"Ryan's been working night and day out there. I heard the floor went in and looks fantastic. Does she sleep?" Madison asked. "Because anytime I pass Tangled, the maroon truck's out front, and she's in there, lights on, working."

"And that drive she took? Quite the gesture," Joey said. "I think she's really trying to make all of this up to you. She seems guilt-ridden."

"Maybe." Gabriella shrugged. "I don't like the idea of her working so hard, but she's not talking to me much about it, or about anything for that matter. We're the masters of small talk."

She remembered their last conversation at dinnertime yesterday, when Gabriella swung by to drop off a chicken parmigiana for Ryan's meal. If Ryan was going to work so hard, she needed to eat. No arguments. She'd channel Grandma Filomena and shake a fist covered in flour if she had to.

Ryan stared in appreciation at the plate, complete with a leafy green salad and roasted peppers. "You are so sweet to go out of your way. You didn't have to do this." She lifted the tent over the plate and shook her head. "Looks amazing. I'm drooling."

"Least I can do for the hard work. I'd feel better if you took a break, though." She looked around at the dining room, now gorgeous, with tables and chairs dotting the beautiful tiled floor. "You've made amazing progress. The place looks like it could open today."

"I'm fine," Ryan said with a grin.

She'd been doing a lot of grinning lately, but they didn't feel authentic. She knew Ryan's real smiles. The lazy, sexy one, the sincerely touched version. The having a blast version was one of her favorites. This fake polite model? Less than convincing. She'd seized on the word then and there.

"You're extra polite these days. Stop it."

Ryan stole a bite of salad before replacing the tent over the plate and silverware. "I can't. Joanna Jacks raised me." She winked, a deflection.

"Fine." She gestured with her chin. "How are those arms holding up? They're my favorite, you know." She came around Ryan and placed her hands on Ryan's shoulders, feeling her tense beneath her black T-shirt. She applied pressure and felt everything in Ryan begin to surrender. Now this felt better, the contact, the slow relaxation. She continued to knead Ryan's shoulders, her arms, her neck. For better access, she slipped her hands beneath Ryan's shirt and laid her hands on bare shoulders and felt Ryan sit up straighter.

"As much as I'm in heaven, I gotta get back to work." Ryan turned around. "Thank you for my amazing dinner. I'll be out of here soon." Then a thought seemed to strike. "Oh, I meant to tell you. Everything's in order for the opening. We passed our inspection with a little hiccup on a grease interception issue, but we were given some wiggle room to correct the problem, and it's done. You have the permits, and you're good to go for Saturday."

Gabriella blinked. "We are? You didn't even tell me they were coming out today. How did you get us scheduled on such short notice?"

"I called in a favor, a big one. Small towns do have their benefits."

Gabriella burst into a smile and launched herself into Ryan's arms. "I don't know how you managed to pull this off after this major a setback, but I owe you." A kiss. God, it was a good one. Another. "Want to stop by my place afterward?" Gabriella whispered against Ryan's mouth. "You don't have to stay over, and we can be quick. In fact, I like our quickies. We're good at them."

Ryan glanced behind her. "Let me see what time it is when I finish up."

"But we're *inspected*. We're ready. What more could you have to do?"

"There's still a lot of cleanup involved. My guys aren't the tidiest when they work. Surfaces, floors. I want this place to sparkle before I hand it over for good. I'll give you a call when I'm done."

"Okay. Deal."

Surprise, surprise. Ryan finished up later than she'd planned and just headed home so as to not disturb Gabriella. Disturb her? Since when was that even a thing? Ryan had taken pleasure in rocking her world daily, so Gabriella wasn't buying it. In fact, she was beginning to understand that what she'd feared all along had happened. Ryan had gotten bored with her, and Gabriella had become the little puppy chasing at her heels. Not the position or the person she wanted to be at all. She could ignore the writing on the wall all she wanted. Didn't make it go away.

Sitting at the meeting with her friends, she still had no answers. "We're existing, I guess. But that's about it. She placates me. I think she's over it. The new, fun part is over."

"I hate that," Madison said, her eyes on her screen. She shook her head. "You deserve more."

"Yeah, sometimes I hope it's that she's honestly just overworked. But then it feels more like I've lost my shiny sparkle. Angie said this would happen just recently. She called it, and I blew her off."

"I don't know what's going on with Ryan," Joey said, squeezing her hand, "but I know I don't like what I see it doing to you."

"If you say so." If Ryan's feelings had changed, there wasn't much Gabriella could do. She swallowed back the emotion that threatened to engulf her at the very real possibility. A lump arrived in her throat, the room felt intensely small, and tears threatened. "Why don't we get started on our meeting?" A distraction about now would be nice.

"You guys, I have minor news."

Gabriella gestured to herself. "Lay it on us."

"I just wanted to let you know that I think Becca and Skywalker might become a more permanent fixture around here."

Gabriella widened her eyes. "Becca's moving in?" A normally thrilling bit of news somehow didn't hit the way it should have. It sat tightly on her chest. She brightened anyway. "That's fantastic."

"I knew this was coming," Madison said. "Happy to hear it."

"Thanks, guys. She's giving her landlord notice tomorrow that she won't be renewing her lease on the house." Joey made a face that said she was both nervous and excited. "Just a big step is all. We practically live together anyway, right? She's my person, so it's time to make this a little more official."

"You two and that dog are going to be so happy you won't be able to see straight," Madison said.

Joey relaxed and beamed. "We are, aren't we? I know big steps always freak me the hell out, but nothing has ever felt more right. I know my dad would just love her."

"That's how you know it's real, because it feels right." Gabriella identified with the feeling, and at the same time, everything in her worried it would never be hers again. "Did you pull out a Jackism from his box of sayings in preparation for this big decision?" It was a practice Joey had come to rely upon after discovering a box of sayings Jack Wilder had left behind when he passed.

Joey laughed. "Yeah, and just as expected, it was so awful that it was awesome. *Wine-ding roads sometimes lead straight home.*"

"I love that one," Madison said, meeting Gabriella's gaze purposefully. "It resonates."

"It's perfect," Gabriella said back.

Joey nodded. "When someone makes you feel as much as Becca does, you don't let that go. You take the big leaps, so that's exactly what I'm doing."

Gabriella internalized those words and tucked them away. *When a person makes you feel...*

Madison nodded her approval. "You've always been a risk taker, buddygirl. It's just nice to see you extending that to your love life these days."

They got down to business. Gabriella presented her menu for the sit-down dinner. Prosciutto and arugula pizzas for each table upon arrival, garnished with freshly shaved Parmesan. Next up would be a caprese salad with fresh mozzarella. For their entrée, each diner would then have the choice of her chicken scaloppine, shrimp carbonara, or Tuscan rib eye followed by a flourless chocolate cake that made you want to fall off your chair.

"Can we have that for lunch?" Joey asked.

"No way. Gives you something to look forward to." She scrunched her shoulders. "I'm just hoping to christen the place properly, and I think this menu might do that. A few greatest hits, you know? You guys approve?"

"Wholeheartedly," Madison said. "And we can do a pairing with each dish and feature the chardonnay, of course, since it's the vintage's big day. I'm thinking with the mozzarella?"

"Great minds," Gabriella said, closing her notebook. "And my culinary kids will have bites going from the truck during pickup times for the wine. Chelsea's been advised not to speak to guests about her teenage love life. I can't promise she won't forget that rule."

Joey couldn't have looked more pleased. "I don't know what we did before you. This is so exciting I almost need to dance with this happy glass of sangria." She swayed as if listening to bluesy music.

"Without me? Oh, you'd probably be wandering the vines, aimlessly scavenging for morsels."

"I'd probably have found very few, which is why I'm keeping you for all time. We'll never starve again."

As Gabriella left the meeting and returned to Jolene, she stared proudly at Tangled standing in the distance, just itching for customers. Next week, she'd be out of the truck and back in the kitchen where she belonged, with her staff there with her. She had a handful of servers well into training with the front-of-house manager, as she stood there. Her life was about to change, and she couldn't have been more ready. She wanted so desperately to share it all with one person in particular. Gabriella's heart ached at the very real fear that wouldn't happen.

# CHAPTER NINETEEN

Today was the day, and God, it sure felt like it. Everything seemed to sparkle. Even the toothpaste looked extra chipper as if acknowledging the importance of the hours ahead. Gabriella woke early and laid out her outfit for the release, a floral sundress with a modest-heeled sandal. That was for later. First she put on work clothes including her chef's coat to start early preparation with her team for tonight's dinner, which would take place promptly at six p.m., following the afternoon's outdoor festivities. They were lucky the sun had played along and decided to attend. Taking a deep breath and enjoying their first time all together in Tangled's pristine kitchen, Gabriella took the reins to address her team, three chefs who would work on a rotating basis, all of whom were present for the big dinner tonight, to make sure everything was prepared to perfection for their VIPs.

"Opening a restaurant for the first time is a dream come true for me, and I'm happy that each one of you will be here for the journey. We have so many nights ahead of us to learn from each other and grow as a team here at Tangled. I don't know about you, but I can't wait to get started on service alongside each of you." Heads nodded. Kevin, her friend from back east, grinned at her with pride. "We have some hungry diners coming our way in just a few hours, so let's roll up our sleeves and prep the hell out of this food."

"Yes, Chef," all three said nearly in unison. Already working together, it seemed.

She laughed. "Let's do this."

Normally, as proprietor and executive chef, she'd leave the prep work to her kitchen, and would do so in the future. Today was different. Gabriella's role would be a combination of expediting plates and jumping in where needed, right there on the line with the rest of her staff. She wanted to be present for every part of Tangled's big debut, and if that meant slicing vegetables, she was more than happy to slice the hell out of onions.

In no time at all, it was time for the party. When she arrived in her sundress for the release celebration on the lawn in front of the tasting room, having made the Superwoman-quick change in three minutes flat, there was still a spring in her step and a smile on her face. She was immediately handed a glass of the guest of honor, the new chardonnay. Loretta sent her a wink along with it. Did she know that Gabriella knew about her and Bobby? The saucy little minx. She must!

"All ready to dazzle tonight?" Joey asked, beaming. She was their hostess today and looked beautiful in a sleeveless emerald dress to her knees, her blond hair pulled back on the sides, flowing and perfect.

"I've never been more prepared. The team and I have gone over the menu and its prep at least a dozen times. Oh, and later, I've got Ryan sitting with the Biddies at the table next to you and the Tangle Valley folks. She'll be good at controlling them. Who knew the Biddies were members here?"

"Oh, they'll sign up for anything, those four. Professional joiners. Any chance to be invited to things is worthy of a quickly written check, which they still use. But I'll be happy to look in on Ryan. Make sure she's okay." But Joey was immediately pulled into conversation with the mayor and her husband, which gave Gabriella a moment to take in the sights and sounds of the event. She took a deep breath and ordered herself to try to relax, enjoy herself. Take it all in.

The vineyard grounds were buzzing with wine club members, all present to get the preview bottles of the new vintage of chardonnay, Madison's completion of Jack Wilder's work. It would only be a few months before Madison's work would stand on its own with the release of the dolcetto, and she knew Maddie was ready to spread her wings and establish herself fully at Tangle Valley.

An acoustic band played standards from the patio, and Gabriella beamed as she watched her kids, the culinary students, move from guest to guest with trays of small bites they'd prepared themselves in the truck, with a little bit of supervision from Gabriella. They even carried the trays the way she'd instructed them for optimum balance. In front of the tasting room, Loretta and several of the part-timers stood behind a table and distributed wine orders to the waiting line of guests. Some were picking up entire cases, while others were fine with the two-bottle score that came with their membership.

In the midst of the celebration and all the responsibility Gabriella had on her shoulders, she still longed for nothing more than to lay her eyes on Ryan and have her there by her side. She bopped her head to the music, sipped the crisp, refreshing wine, and scanned the faces of the guests for any glimpse of Ryan, who for some reason, was still nowhere to be found.

❖

Dammit. Just fucking dammit. Ryan sat in her truck, in the parking lot nestled alongside the tasting room at Tangle Valley, paralyzed. She gripped her steering wheel and stared over at the cheerful-looking release party happening fifty yards away. She'd chosen an outfit she thought would suit the occasion, slim-fitting white pants and a red top her mother had always loved her in. Her hair was down, and she'd allowed a lazy curl. Yet she couldn't seem to make herself exit the damn vehicle. Or find any air. She swallowed, and her heart thudded into overtime. She was out of her league with all of this. A kid playing grown-up and Gabriella would notice at any second and laughingly dismiss her. The thought crushed her.

"What's going on in there?"

Ryan blinked, turned, and found Becca Crawford standing outside her open passenger-side window, looking in with a smile. "Just getting up my nerve, you know?"

Becca didn't hesitate to jump into the truck without an invite, take a seat next to Ryan, and close the door. "I feel the same way before big events. I have to pep talk myself into them. Sometimes in the mirror. I'm not making that up."

"I would never have guessed that about you. You're always put together and confident."

"Yeah, well, so are you."

"Not in this moment." She sighed. "Today matters a lot to her." Ryan swallowed and stared at the leather steering wheel, the tiny spot that was worn through more than any other. She ran her thumb over it. "She should have all her people there with her."

"And that's not you?" Becca passed her a confused look.

She sighed. "Little bit of that syndrome happening. What's it called again?"

Becca nodded. "Imposter syndrome. You think of yourself as an imposter with Gabriella."

"I didn't used to. But"—Ryan shook her head—"I feel like it's turning into a charade. This is never going to work. We have amazing chemistry and this great friendship, but Gabriella and me? How?" She had no idea why she was laying all this on Becca Crawford, of all people, but she was here, and kind, and there wasn't much Ryan could do to stop the words anyway. They fled her lips.

"I know why you're saying that, but you don't know what I know."

"What's that?" Ryan asked.

"You've never seen the way she looks at you when you're not watching."

Ryan swallowed, absorbing this new information, clinging to it like a life jacket in deep waters. "I haven't."

"It's amazing really." Becca shook her head in wonder. "Like you were the very person responsible for hanging the moon that lights up the night. As if she just can't quite believe you're real."

Ryan stared down at her hands. "God, I want that to be true. The only problem is that I've seen her look at someone else the exact same way." She raised her gaze. "And I'm bad at this, Becca. It was one thing to put myself out there when I was first getting to know her. I could give of myself and be transparent and let her in, but the way I feel now? It's so much more. My feelings for her could swallow me whole." She shook her head ruefully. "I can't do that. I can't be that person, or I'll drown."

Becca tilted her head to the side and regarded Ryan with kind eyes. "I think you're selling yourself entirely too short. Love is scary. I'm not going to argue that point." She caught Becca gazing across the lawn at Joey, who was grabbed by one of the attendees in a handshake-cheek kiss combo. "And sometimes it doesn't always go the way you want it to. Been there. But what I've found is that sticking it out through the hard times can be the most satisfying payoff imaginable. The two of you grow stronger for surviving the rough stuff."

Ryan smiled at the idea. It sounded great in theory, and God, why shouldn't she take this ride with Gabriella and see where they ended up? It might be the decision that changed her life forever. This moment right here. "Is that what it was like for you? Terrifying until it wasn't?"

Becca's eyes lit up. "Yes, I think that's entirely accurate—maybe even more so for Joey, who'd been burned by love in the past." Ryan ruminated on that one for a moment. She remembered when Simone left Joey on their wedding day. She hadn't been in attendance, but the town had talked all about it for months. Looking at it through the lens she had now, the personal experience with real love, she couldn't imagine that kind of hurt. Who invented this kind of vulnerability, and how could she find them and shake them? Hard. None of this felt fair. "I envy Joey. I don't know how she found the courage to try again after that. I don't know that I could have."

"I think if what you have is worth it, there's really no other choice." Becca smiled. "Now I'm gonna get out of here and go support my girlfriend. Will I see you soon?"

Ryan took a deep breath and nodded. "Thanks for the pep talk. I needed it."

"Anytime. And Ryan? I mean that. Don't be a stranger."

She felt her chest grow tight. "I won't. Promise."

She watched Becca, decked out in a navy maxi dress and looking like a million bucks, stroll casually to the party. But she belonged there at Joey's side, and Ryan couldn't say the same about herself at Gabriella's, no matter how much she wanted to make that leap.

She fired up the ignition and pulled slowly out of the parking lot, leaving the vineyard, Gabriella, and the best parts of herself in her rearview mirror. The farther she got from Tangle Valley, the more powerful the emotion that descended. Her hands shook as she gripped the steering wheel, and hot tears that she was wholly unaccustomed to streamed fast down her cheeks. She choked on a sob, having never felt more defeated, alone, or helpless in her whole life.

❖

The release party moved into its second and final hour. Wine flowed. Everyone laughed a little louder as a result. The sun began to fall, and the beautiful colors from its setting blanketed the gathering. Gabriella took in smiles, the fun everyone was having. She joined in, greeting the people she knew and introducing herself to those she did not. All the while, she longed for Ryan to hold her hand on this momentous occasion in her life. A day she'd always remember. She made sure to snap a few photographs to commemorate the event. She smiled next to Joey as a guest snapped their photo with the restaurant in the distance.

Moments later, she glimpsed a woman with dark hair, but there was a small circle of people obscuring her view. She craned her neck as hope flared, everything in her relaxing now that she'd found Ryan. When the woman stepped into the open, she saw it was Becca instead. She saw Gabriella, smiled, and moved toward her. "So, are you excited?" She kissed Gabriella's cheek and gave her a warm one-armed squeeze as she held her glass of chardonnay.

"Are you kidding? I'm ready like a soldier about to head into battle," Gabriella said. "Only the battle is with food, and we can't lose because we're all friends anyway." She shrugged happily.

"Well, when you put it that way, bring on the war." Becca laughed. "I'm really looking forward to the meal. Did you find Ryan?"

Everything in Gabriella perked up. "No, but I've been searching for her. She's here?"

"She is." Becca frowned and looked around. "I ran into her in the parking lot, but that was quite a while ago. I thought surely she'd have found you by now."

"No." Another scan. Nothing. "Was everything okay? It's not like her to just not show up and not send a message."

Becca nodded, but there was something else there, too. Her eyes carried concern, and she shifted her weight. "I'm sure she's fine. Maybe she forgot something and had to run home." She glanced away, nervous. It wasn't like Becca to be.

"Becca, what aren't you telling me? Just say it. It's written all over your face."

She exhaled. "All right, fine. She was having a hard time with all of this."

Gabriella squinted. "All of this? One of the biggest days of my life? I don't understand."

"I think it might be larger than just today."

Gabriella rolled her lips in as understanding settled. "This is about *me*." God, that felt even worse. A wave of nausea hit, and her hands went numb. She flexed her fingers.

"This is about *her*," Becca said carefully. "Vulnerability is new for Ryan, and she's learning that it can be frightening and—"

"You know what? That's totally okay. I don't need to hear any more. I have an important meal to prepare." She gave Becca's forearm a squeeze. "Thank you for letting me know. Now I can concentrate on what I need to."

She walked away without waiting for a response, holding back the emotion until she was a safe distance away from the gathering.

Once she was alone on the path, she let the tears escape for the short duration of the walk to the kitchen, *her* kitchen. She reminded herself of her leadership status, wiped her eyes, took a commanding breath, and joined her team, already hard at work.

An hour later, her dining room was full for the first time. Servers in white starched shirts filled glasses and took entrée orders. Gabriella had never heard the room carry such activity. For the first time, it felt alive, bursting with energy and anticipation. Tonight, they'd serve the entire room at once, bringing out one course at a time along with the wine pairings. But first, Gabriella wanted to welcome her guests and kick off service with an address to the room. When the diners saw her stand before them in her hopefully still starched chef's coat, the room went quiet before erupting into applause. She felt the warm blush hit her cheeks and smiled back at them. As her gaze moved over their faces, she paused on the empty chair, the one she'd personally selected. Her heart hurt badly, but she had no ability to indulge it right now, and held that smile firmly in place. When the applause faded, Gabriella began to speak.

"First of all, hi." That pulled a laugh. Some people waved. "I'd like to officially welcome you to Tangled and tell you how pleased I am that you're here. You're the first guests to grace our tables in what I hope will be a long stay at Tangle Valley. If you like the food, tell your friends." Another laugh. She placed a hand over her heart. "What I'd like to share with you is how special today is for me." The emotion welled and her throat ached. "I'm realizing a dream in this very moment and each one of you is a part of it. Every chef imagines opening a restaurant and the Wilder's have given me the chance to do just that in a town I couldn't be more in love with. Please know that your meal tonight was prepared with love. Now onto business." Smiles abounded as the first course appeared from the kitchen, just as they'd rehearsed. "I see the servers are bringing out prosciutto and arugula pizzas for your table, family style, to be paired with the Tangle Valley pinot grigio, which will be coming around shortly. Enjoy your evening. I'll check in with you later." More applause as she exited and the meal kicked off.

When she got back to the kitchen, there was no time to catch her breath. She had four more courses ahead of her and didn't plan to drop the ball. She worked with determined focus, and sure enough, she and the chefs in her kitchen found a productive rhythm, calling out to each other in a communication win, surprising her how few hiccups there were, given it was their first true test.

Ninety minutes later, when the tiramisu plates were empty and set aside, the buzz from the tipsy, happy diners was overwhelmingly positive. She stood at the door, shaking hands with her guests as they exited, accepting the occasional cheek kiss, and inviting them back for a more traditional dining experience in the future. All vowed to return.

Once the guests had gone, Joey hugged her, eyes glistening. "Amazing."

Next was Madison's turn. She took both of Gabriella's hands, beaming. "I'm serious when I say, Gabs, that tonight was another level. One of the best meals of my life."

The compliment meant so much to her that she felt the pride bursting from her chest. She grinned. "Well, I hope to bring you many more. Can I just say thank you for being here? Both of you." She teared up because she needed people in her corner and these guys had been there. "I mean it."

Joey slung an arm around Maddie's shoulders. "We might be here every night if you're not careful."

"They'll have to wait for a reservation," Becca said. "Your staff was taking them down like crazy after dinner. People already want back in and want to bring their friends."

"They do?" Gabriella hadn't anticipated a clamoring, but she'd take it. Hot damn. They'd open for official business in just five days, but she felt ready now. Tonight had given her that confidence.

It was here. At long last Tangled was a reality, and apparently it was happening at exactly the right time. She needed a positive distraction from her crash and burn love life. Even just touching on the thought now, gutted her. Tonight should have gone differently. She'd had so many fantasies about opening the restaurant with Ryan, who'd been such a big part of the process, by her side.

The truth was maybe she didn't know Ryan as well as she thought she did. Maybe learning all of this now was a good thing, before they got in any deeper, before the hurt became immeasurable. As she stood alone in the kitchen after every last soul had finished for the night, she realized in the midst of the acute ache in her chest, she was already too late for that.

And immeasurable was an understatement.

❖

It was after midnight when Ryan heard the sound of tires on the gravel road out front. She'd been sitting on that dock for who knew how long at that point, still dressed for the event, still ashamed of herself for not being able to get out of the damn truck and show up for the person she loved, someone who deserved it. She'd thought about a beer but wasn't confident she could stomach it. Instead, she'd sought out her thinking spot where she could look out over the water. The light from her back deck was enough for her to glimpse its gentle motion.

Something in her was breaking, and she wasn't sure how to stop it. The water carried no answers, no matter how long she sat there.

She blinked at the sound of a car approaching. Who was out this way so late? She turned and in the glow of its headlights saw a familiar Jeep pull into her driveway and park behind her truck. She felt sick. Panicked. Guilt-stricken. Now what? How was she supposed to explain herself?

She found Gabriella knocking on her door when she came around the side of the house, slid her hands into her back pockets, and sighed. "I'm sorry."

At the sound of her voice, Gabriella turned and stared. "You look awful."

"Thanks." A pause. "How did it go?"

Gabriella's steely gaze seemed to pierce right through her in its intensity. "I'm here to tell you that you don't get to ask that."

"Well, I'm asking anyway, whether I'm an asshole or not, and trust me, there's no mistaking that I am."

Gabriella didn't acknowledge her words. "You also don't get to wander in and out of my life whenever it suits you. I'm putting an end to that now. You don't get to hear how my day was, or what I'm thinking or feeling, and maybe you don't even care." She waved her hand dismissively. "Totally fine. But you're the one who's missing out, because I have a lot to give." Her voice cracked on that last part, and her face crumpled.

Ryan felt those words to her core. She couldn't move. She couldn't speak, but she understood that the best parts of her life were slipping through her fingers, and there was nothing she could do to change any of it. *Just get through this part. Just get through this part.* "I know that," she said. "You're wonderful."

"But not enough."

"Of course you're enough. But maybe I'm not the person for you.

I'm not good at sitting around and hoping I am, and I fear that would be my existence."

"I guess you're not. Because my person? They don't just walk away when things get hard, when they get a taste of something that maybe requires some work or patience or a little understanding. So I think we're in agreement there."

Even in the dim lighting, she could see Gabriella's eyes flash new fire. She wasn't just hurt, she was angry. Ryan was, too, at so many things. Herself for her behavior, Gabriella for representing something she desperately wanted but was too afraid to hold on to, the universe for not equipping her to fight for what she wanted even if it felt like a losing battle.

She raised her shoulders and dropped them. "You are right about all of that. There's nothing I can say."

"That's okay." Gabriella took a step back. "I didn't come here for you to talk. I wanted you to listen, so that maybe one day you'll wake up and realize that you missed out." She gestured around her. "But I'll leave you to your world the way I found it. The way you like it. Out here all on your own." She shook her head. "What a shame."

The truth of those words nearly took Ryan down. She forgot to inhale as the startlingly accurate declaration smothered her. She watched Gabriella Russo, the only woman she'd ever loved, stalk to her Jeep and drive off into the night and right out of Ryan's life for good, looking damn beautiful in the process.

## Chapter Twenty

A s for beer, there'd been three. Turns around the dance floor, four. Number of times she got that sinking feeling she couldn't shake? Too many to count.

Ryan was out for the first time in a month, and though it felt a little strange to be in the middle of a crowd of people, she also found it weirdly comforting to slide back into her old persona and hide behind that mask while sitting at the bar at the Scoot, catching up with whoever strolled by. Midsummer brought with it warmer temperatures, which made the throngs of people a little more noticeable as they packed into the place on a rowdy Friday night. The bar was beyond busy, the music loud, and the dance floor crowded as hell. All things Ryan loved. At least, she used to. Her goal was to recapture a little of that life, in the hope that she'd find her footing yet again.

Simply existing wasn't as easy as Ryan had hoped.

She'd been moving through her days on automatic pilot. Wake, run, work, and repeat. She'd avoided the common areas of Whisper Wall, and unfollowed the Biddies' Instagram account so she wasn't bombarded with town gossip and photos, especially when she was likely a subject. But Ryan was hurting and afraid of how much further she'd sink if she stayed home any longer. She had no idea what was going on in Gabriella's life, and that left her feeling adrift and sad. Joey had paid her for the work she'd done at Tangled, and that left her daily ties to Gabriella firmly cut. For all Ryan knew, she and Madison had ridden off into the sunset together, or maybe Gabriella had Ryan's face on a dartboard. Maybe a one-two combo of both.

"What are you all sour about tonight?" Patsy asked. "Glaring at the liquor on the wall. Lips rolled in. It's not your best look."

Ryan forced herself out of it, sat back, and grinned. "I would never want you to think so. I adore you—you know that, right? You're my family."

"There's the Ryan I know. Where you been?"

"You ever just need some time away, Pats? When the world just seems to suck so hard that you need to hide out until you can hit reset?"

"Only happened to me once, and that was when Dennis Davidson broke my heart. I thought I'd never be the same again." She paused with a cold one in her hand for a guy down the bar. "Now that I think about it, I never was. We come out of those things different people."

Ryan raised her longneck. "Can't argue with that."

"She's here, you know. If that matters."

"Who?"

"Your Dennis Davidson. But definitely prettier. What else can I get for you, sweetie pie with cute freckles?" Patsy asked a customer down the bar as she delivered that beer to his friend.

Ryan, through her three—almost four—beer haze, took a moment to register Patsy's meaning. When she did, she turned in her chair and scanned the place, something she hadn't done in over an hour. Thank God, there was no sign of Gabriella, because she wasn't sure she was ready to face—

"Ryan." She turned to her right, and there she was, inches away, looking and smelling amazing as she leaned against the bar, signaling for service. The world began to move at a different speed. So did Ryan's brain as it stutter-stepped its way to a response.

"Hey. I wasn't expecting—What are you up to?" The gorgeous hazel eyes that haunted Ryan were staring back at her, live and in person, making this much harder than she anticipated. As if programmed to do so, everything in Ryan lit up with excitement the second Gabriella had appeared. It had been an alarming reflex, and when reality crashed in, the disappointment was every bit as jarring.

"Up to? Just a beer," Gabriella said, cool, calm, and unaffected. She wore a purple sleeveless top and jeans molded to her perfect curves. "Maddie and Joey's friends are in town." She pointed across the bar to a high-top table where Joey, Becca, Madison, and an attractive brunette Ryan had never seen before sat. A second later, Carly Daniel arrived at the table. Shit. She'd not returned Carly's message that she was in town and would love to get together. Her good friend from childhood kissed the lips of the brunette, which meant she'd brought Lauren along.

Another happy couple. Wonderful. She'd try to find the courage to say hello in a bit.

"Looks like fun. How are you?" Ryan asked. Another reflex. She had to know.

"Me?" Gabriella produced a winsome smile. "Never been better. Honestly, life is *good*." She gestured to the beer in Ryan's hand. "You enjoy, now." Patsy appeared, and Gabriella ordered a round for the table, and behind Ryan, where the group of friends had gathered, life went on without her. She took in every laugh and raised voice that floated over. The group was having a fantastic time. She wondered how long until Gabriella and Madison decided they should give things another try. Good for them. Didn't mean Ryan had to sit around and wait to see proof. She decided to call Carly later and apologize, closed out, and stood to head home, only to find herself face-to-face with Lana McCarver.

"Well, look who's here. Been a while," she said quietly to Ryan. Her gaze carried compassion. "How are you? I heard about the whole thing with the chef. I'm sorry."

"Hey, Lana. I'm fine." She wasn't. Not even close, but she was working on finding her footing. It had been a tad easier before Gabriella appeared live and in person to remind her exactly what she'd given up.

"You don't look it. You've lost weight and your eyes are dull. That's okay, though." This was not the Lana who was looking to flirt or hook up. This was Lana, her friend, and she appreciated the difference because she could use a friend about now. "I was worried about you but also didn't want to reach out if you didn't want to hear from me. These things can be tricky."

"You should have called. I'd have picked up." It would have been nice to have a friend to confide in. Sure, there'd been Billy to an extent, but he got uncomfortable when things got too heavy. She'd avoided her own mother, because she likely thought Ryan was a bonehead for not fighting for Gabriella and would tell her so in no uncertain terms. Maybe she was a bonehead. All she knew was that it seemed that she was on some kind of journey with herself, only her view of the road was dim, and she'd forgotten to turn on her headlights.

"Want to grab a cup of coffee? That little diner with the burgers on eighth is open late." Lana held up her hands. "No strings. Promise."

"Best offer I've had in a while."

Twenty minutes later, they sat in the back booth at Blue's Burger

Box. The food was greasy as hell, but the coffee, as plain as it was, was always served hot.

Lana set down her cup. "I have to be honest. I never once pegged you as someone who would want to settle down and couple up."

Ryan looked at the wall on which she saw a cartoon hamburger flashing jazz hands. "I have to be honest. I didn't either." She shook her head. "I take that back. I wanted it to work so badly, but I started to realize that I was going to lose out. When you put your whole heart into something, you have to trust that other person won't smash it up. I'm not sure I can do that."

"Oh, so you're a chicken?" Lana's green eyes danced in challenge. "Who the hell knew?"

"Knock it off. No. I'm just…not built for it."

"Okay, it's all coming together. The Biddies put out there that you two were in a magnificent love triangle for the ages."

"God."

"And now you tell me that you're a running-scared chicken, which means that you just surrendered the woman you're in love with to your romantic rival." She nodded. "I read a lot of romance novels."

Ryan hesitated because that was a lot. Of course the Biddies had weighed in, but she had no capacity to focus on that now. The rival part had her going. "You know that written in the stars mentality we're brought up on in movies and books?"

"Of course. The meant-to-be factor. Endgame romances are popular for a reason."

Ryan nodded. "At first, I was certain I was a part of one of those couples. Who would have guessed it, right? Me. And it was probably the most wonderful thing that had ever happened to me, but as time went on, I started to doubt myself and lose trust in what we had." She exhaled and ran her thumb along the handle of her mug. "Then something clicked. I got it. I wasn't part of the endgame couple at all. I was the pining away, tragic secondary character who would disappear in the third act."

"And Madison and Gabriella were the stars of the show."

Ryan lifted a shoulder. "Madison definitely fits the part more. I do construction, and she rubs elbows with the wine elite. Why prolong the inevitable? The sooner I got the hell out of the way, the quicker they could realize their lost love, and we can get to the credits with my sanity and emotional well-being intact. At least shreds of it."

Lana sipped from her mug. "This is deep for coffee."

"Yeah, well, I'm apparently boring now. It's what I do." She shook her head. "I actually like it, which is frightening."

They shared a quiet laugh.

Lana leaned her chin on her palm. "She's done a number on you, and I have to be honest, I'm not sure that's a bad thing." She winced. "Not that I didn't like you before."

"Oh, sure."

"No. Listen, I've always thought you were hot." She laughed quietly. "You know that part. Just a little aloof and unanchored. We had fun, though."

"A lot of fun." Ryan could admit to that part. She and Lana had been carefree and light. There was a mutual respect between them.

"I filed for divorce. The paperwork part. It's been a year and a half since I moved out. It's time."

"Wow." Ryan blinked. "You're almost official. What now?"

The tiniest of smiles hit. "Don't tell the Biddies, but I'm seeing someone. A woman in Portland." She held up her hands. "Nothing serious yet, but there's chemistry there. Potential."

Ryan picked up her coffee cup and touched it to Lana's. "Look at us, growing up and moving on."

"I'd really like it if we could stay friends, though."

"I think we already are."

Lana closed her eyes. "This is now officially a Disney sitcom." She looked around. "Is there an underscore happening?"

Ryan laughed. "Nothing seems to surprise me these days." She dropped her head back. "Fuck."

"No, no, no. You can't say *fuck* on Disney."

"Darn it all."

"Better."

After that night, the weirdest thing happened. She and Lana actually did set out to become better friends. When Ryan had low points that week, Lana picked up the phone. When Lana had relationship questions, she talked them out over ice cream with Ryan, who now had a little bit of experience to draw from. Their physical chemistry had all but disintegrated in the face of their mutual support system, and for the first time, Ryan felt like she might find a way to recover. Not thrive, but manage.

A couple of weeks after their encounter at the Scoot, Ryan passed Gabriella in front of the Nifty Nickel near town center. She swallowed back the excitement-melancholy combo that hit in that order. "Some serious shopping going on there." Small talk was probably the way to go. No reason for them not to be friendly, even if this whole thing felt so incredibly wrong. They were doing the right thing for both of them.

Gabriella's eyes landed on hers and held for a moment before she offered a smile. She lifted the bags. "Just a few seasonal items for decor."

"Oh, the restaurant."

"Pshh. My cottage. I plan to make it look like a living, breathing summer picnic site if it kills me." They shared a laugh, which was a remarkable thing. It felt like years since they'd laughed together, rather than the month-plus-change it had actually been. She shifted her weight, not sure what to say next. This had never been a problem for them.

"Sounds about right. Business is good, then?" The question was a formality and so sterile. The sentence contained none of the words she wanted to say. Hell, she even knew the answer already. Tangled was killing it and was currently the talk of the town because with a twelve-table dining room, reservations were hard to come by. Rumor had it the place was booked into early autumn.

"Yes, and I've received so many compliments on the craftsman-ship, so that credit goes to you."

"Nah, I just follow orders."

Gabriella's smile faded, and she really looked at Ryan. "You haven't been to the ballpark."

"Right. I took a few games off. I'll be back."

"For the championship. It's getting serious. Otters versus Muskrats. Gonna be epic. They might even break that snow cone sales record."

Their two teams had emerged and would meet in the big game. "Anything I can do to help the snow cone cause."

"Oh, of course. Take care of yourself, Ryan," Gabriella said and slung her bag over her shoulder, strolling the street like she owned the place. Hell, as far as Ryan was concerned, she did. She watched her go, struck by the fact that Gabriella seemed cheerful, put together, and had clearly moved on. Gone was the anger. Gone was the hurt. She saw in front of her a confident, happy woman. Somehow that slashed at her even more.

"Hey, Muskrat?" she called. Gabriella turned with questioning eyes and paused near her Jeep. "I miss you." She shrugged, feeling weak and helpless for giving in. So what? She could be an idiot for a brief moment in time. "I don't know if that's wrong to say."

Gabriella flashed a half smile, but it faded fast. "Then don't."

Ryan nodded and swallowed the uncomfortable lump that rose in her throat, accepting her new unfortunate normal. Damn love and everything that came with it.

❖

"Hi, guys. I'm Gabriella Russo, executive chef. May I ask how your meal was tonight?" Gabriella asked an adorable couple in the back corner of the dining room. Service tonight had been challenging as she'd been down a chef on the line when Nadine called out for a migraine. Somehow they'd muddled through and did their best to turn out quality plates regardless of being shorthanded.

The customer gestured to his plate. "I don't know what you did to the rib eye, but the Tuscan spices were out of this world. Perfectly cooked, too."

"The spices are all my secret, but I'm so pleased to hear you enjoyed it."

His date picked up the empty bowl in front of her and grinned. "You can see I hated the shrimp fra diavolo."

"I can tell," Gabriella said. "I'll let my staff know."

She thanked them for coming, handed off the empty dish to their server, and moved on to the next table. Gabriella made a point of speaking to each of her guests personally to ensure their experience was everything she hoped it would be. The night had been a hard one, but she was pleased with her team for pulling together. Plus, the Gorgonzola cream sauce on the special had been out of this world.

The restaurant closed at eleven, and Gabriella made it out of there just after midnight, leaving Keith to oversee cleanup. "All right, guys. Enjoy tomorrow with friends and family, and we'll be back up on Tuesday."

Joy danced in a circle. "Not that I don't love working with you killers, but I need a day to lie on my couch and not move."

Gabriella could identify. All she wanted about now was a glass of wine and some time to relax. She could head back to her empty cottage and try to stay out of her own head, which was not a fun place these days, or she could join her friends for the tail end of movie night in the barn. Although the weather was warmer during the day, the nights were gorgeous with a welcome chill. Yep. Staying busy and distracted was the name of the game lately, because as angry as she still was at Ryan, she missed her even more. She still turned in her bed halfway expecting to feel Ryan's arms move around her, her body pressed to Gabriella's in warm comfort. She also missed their talks late at night on Ryan's dock, and looking into those dark blue eyes that seemed to see straight into her. Her anger didn't seem to be much match for the memories her mind clung to, and what her heart still acutely yearned for. Movie night it was.

Exhausted as hell, she slipped into the old barn quietly, surprised to see a black-and-white film on the makeshift screen. She recognized it after a moment as that Hitchcock film, *Rear Window*. She'd seen it once at a festival Mariana had dragged her to for her college film class. Gabriella was confident this had to be a Madison pick and eyed her astutely. Without a word, Madison lifted the light blanket that covered her lap and shoulders and Gabriella wordlessly slipped under it next to her. Honoring the silence, she waved to Becca and Joey, who were snuggled up like two bugs in a love-struck rug. Joey blew her a kiss, and they watched together as Jimmy Stewart grew more and more suspicious of his neighbors. The warmth from Madison's leg against hers was a comfort, and she felt her eyes getting heavy as they moved toward the film's denouement. Madison must have sensed it and opened her arm, offering Gabriella her shoulder. "Come here," she whispered.

While it felt completely natural in one sense, she hesitated. But why? She had been feeling so lost and adrift, and this was her friend offering her a shoulder to relax against. She snuggled in and sighed, relishing the comfort and familiarity. Did she notice Becca watching them with interest from across the room as Madison pulled her in a tad closer? Most definitely. Did she have the energy to worry or overanalyze? Not tonight.

The energy in the room had definitely shifted, however, and when the film ended, it seemed like Joey and Becca were late for something important that likely didn't exist.

"Remind me never to spy on the neighbors I don't have," Joey said, motioning to the screen and scurrying to pick up the empty wineglasses and bottle.

Becca did the same for the popcorn. "Right? Nothing but trouble. Talk about tension in that one."

Madison laughed and sat up, releasing Gabriella who felt the loss of warmth immediately. "That's what I love about it. Perfectly paced. Hitchcock knows how to use a lengthy pause to antagonize us."

"And trust me, I'm antagonized," Joey said, overexaggerating the statement. She was trying too hard to be normal and failing miserably.

"Thanks for letting me join late," Gabriella said. "Just wasn't in the mood to turn in yet."

"Oh yeah, sure," Joey said in a voice that was higher pitched than her usual.

"So glad you made it over," Becca said, clutching various glasses and bowls like a thief making a getaway. "'Night, everyone."

And just like that the two of them were out of there in a very strange instant. "I'll walk you home," Madison said with a soft smile.

"Nope. I'll walk you." The extra air would do her good.

"Deal."

They strolled in silence for a bit. She felt so comfortable walking alongside Madison. She thought the world of her, and maybe she should try and open up her mind to…revisiting more. The problem was she was a confused mess with a broken heart and a lost sense of direction. This probably wasn't the time to plunge into something that—She didn't have a chance to complete the thought because in an instant Madison took her by the hand, pulled her in, and kissed her. Stunned, Gabriella stood there and accepted the kiss, receiving it only. It was a foreign feeling, but it wasn't. She'd kissed Madison hundreds of times in their past. Yet she hadn't expected to on this particular occasion. And then, wham. Why was she sorting through all of this now, mid kiss? Keeping that open mind, she ordered herself to relax into it and allowed the kiss to play out, even participating. Yes, that's how people kissed. Two-way. She stood taller and took Madison's face in her hands and kissed her back some more. And then it was over.

They stared at each other in the pale moonlight, Madison's eyes searching hers. "I didn't know I was going to do that, and I'm honestly a little rattled. Not like me not to think things through first."

"Yeah. Same. The rattled." A pause, and then, "Was it—?"

"You don't have to—"

"If you think that was—"

"No, I'm not upset or anything, just—"

They laughed. "You first," Gabriella said, rocking back on her heels.

Madison held up her hands as if clearing the slate and starting over. "While I didn't expect to do that, I'm glad I did. That's the thesis statement."

"It was nice," Gabriella said, terrified to analyze it any further. Madison made her feel safe with two feet on the ground, and that counted for so very much when everything in her world resembled a never-ending roller coaster of highs and lows. "I don't know what I'm doing right now, though. Does that make sense?"

"Complete sense. I wouldn't expect you to."

"I can't make promises I don't know if I can keep."

"I don't need you to," Madison said. "Tonight was nice. Maybe tomorrow we'll feel differently. The complete opposite. I'm prepared for go-with-the-flow if you are. No requirements attached. No promises needed." She touched the back of her head. "Honestly, I'm making this up as I go."

Gabriella took her hand because she cared so much about Madison she could hardly stand it. She was kind, and hard-working, and yes, very beautiful. She heard Angie's voice in her head, telling her what a catch Madison was and how she was the kind of girl you settled down with. Maybe they *had* been hasty when they ended things. She'd led with her heart recently, and that hadn't ended up so great. Maybe it was time she led with her head. "Fair enough. Let's see about tomorrow when tomorrow gets here."

Madison grinned conservatively, took a step back, extending their arms until she finally let go of Gabriella's hand. "Good night, Gabriella. Sweet dreams to you."

She watched as Madison took the three steps up to her porch and disappeared into her cottage. Alone now in the silence of the night, her thoughts immediately shifted to where they always did. Nope. She shut down the images of Ryan's cheeky grin, the feel of her amazing foot rubs on the couch, and acute memories of their passionate nights together. Ryan Jacks had to remain in her rearview mirror. She'd come too far in life to let roller coasters and butterflies confuse the big picture. Steady and boring and dependable was the way to go.

## Chapter Twenty-one

Gabriella never imagined that she'd look forward to Mondays, but after the week she'd had, she'd twirl in a circle in the middle of the damn vineyard just to have some time off, and Mondays, when the restaurant was closed, gave her just that. The kids had the food truck running to perfection for the daytime visitors, and with the scaled down menu she'd provided them, they were fully within their abilities to produce simple quality food for the guests with a little oversight from her.

She'd slept in and spent the afternoon transforming her cottage for summer, using the cute decor she'd found at the Nickel. Plants, flowers for her window baskets, and even new tie-back curtains with a few more splashes of color for the season. As late afternoon shifted to early evening, she found her way to the tasting room for a relaxing glass of chardonnay and maybe a little friend time if anyone happened to be around.

"Put it on my tab," she told Joey, who graciously poured her a nice glass. The golden color of the wine always impressed her with its unique beauty.

"You have no tab here, and you know it. You have to stop requesting one."

"No way."

"The least you can do is catch me up, though." Joey placed a hand on her hip and regarded Gabriella expectantly with a raised eyebrow.

"Fair enough, only I have just as many questions as you do." She stared at the glass as if it carried answers.

"Did you sleep with her?"

Gabriella's eyes went wide. "With Maddie? No. I promise. We kissed. That's all."

Joey's hand relaxed off her hip. "And how did that go? Because I have to be honest, I did not see that coming, and I worry. For you. For her. I mean, what's going on here? The world feels weird."

"With Madison and me, our differences always got in our way. We'd argue over the stupidest things—organizing a refrigerator, what time to leave for a party, how we approached our work-life balance. But you know what? I can handle stupid disagreements and the way we misalign if the important things are all accounted for. Someone who I respect and care about, who also feels the same about me. Someone who will be there through the good and bad."

Joey held up a hand. "Maddie's a rock. I completely agree. But in that entirely well-thought-out statement, you left out one very important word."

"And what's that?"

"Love. You can find an amazing combination of traits, put them all together, but they may not equal the most important sum of all."

Gabriella reflected on the words, but only briefly. "There was a time when I would have agreed with you. But love stirs the pot. It confuses the larger picture, and I'm not sure love is at the top of my priority list right now."

"Well, that's the stupidest damn thing I've ever heard you say." Their heads swiveled to Loretta, who'd moments ago been polishing wineglasses down the bar. She moved toward them with purpose, setting down the glass in her hand. She had her gray hair in a knot at the back of her head, which made her green eyes blaze more noticeably. "I've always thought you were a smart girl, too, but I can't listen to you spout words that are, simply put, ridiculous."

Gabriella was shocked but held her ground. "That's because you're caught up in it, too."

"Love? Damn right I'm in love, and thrilled, because it changes life for the better."

Joey's eyes went wide, and she looked from Gabriella to Loretta.

"Told you," Gabriella said, pointing at Loretta. "She's a smitten kitten for your uncle Bobby."

"And do you think I *planned* on falling in love with that baseball cap wearing fool?" Loretta asked with fire. "Absolutely not. I fought it with everything I had, just like I'm watching you do now, but when I finally came around and said, okay, I'll do the scary part, it's been the best time of my life."

"You and Bobby are real?" Joey squeaked, still absorbing.

"Yes, they're real," Gabriella practically snapped. "I've been telling you that they're a couple of make-out bandits for weeks now. They're sneaky, too. The sneakiest of kissing bandits, and dammit, you need to listen to me more."

"We do kiss quite a bit. I can admit." Loretta touched her lips as if reliving one of those stolen moments now.

Joey blinked. "I just thought you had it wrong, mistook what you'd seen."

"Trust me. I'm aware," Gabriella said. "The bandits set me up."

"Why not just tell us?" Joey asked Loretta, softening.

Loretta shrugged and grabbed a dish towel to twist for support. "Well, at first I wasn't at all happy about it, so I didn't want you to know. You'd think I'd lost my mind. Then, when I was happy about it, sneaking around felt clandestine."

"She means hot," Gabriella supplied, ignoring how sizzling her own love life used to be.

"Hell, yes," sweet little Loretta said. "But I told Carly when she was here, and she was very much in support. She'll be back for the wedding next year and is picking up the tab."

Gabriella's jaw dropped. Joey sputtered on a sip of water. "I'm sorry. What?" Joey asked.

"We're getting married. Your uncle and me. He presented me with a real pretty ring last week. He said I could tell you." She turned with purpose to Gabriella. "We had our issues, plenty of stumbles, but we hung in there, and now we're getting hitched. Love is the *secret ingredient*, not the problem. I firmly believe that." She leaned across the bar, feisty. "That means love is the one part of the equation that can't be left out—do you hear me?"

"Disagree. Tried it. I'm jaded now."

Joey nodded knowingly. "You've tried it that way? That means you were in love with Ryan. That you *are*."

A pause. She wasn't sure what to say. She'd never admitted that out loud, but of course she was in love with Ryan. But that would fade with time. Wasn't that what people said? All wounds healed, and hers would, too. "I guess I am, but it's temporary, and just because it doesn't smack me in the face when I'm with someone else, doesn't mean that relationship couldn't be every bit as satisfying in the end."

Joey and Loretta sighed in unison like Gabriella was a hopeless case of naivety. Loretta went back to work with a disapproving shake of her head, and Joey looked into Gabriella's eyes. "I know you're upset.

I know Ryan really hurt you, but don't screw up your entire life over it. Maddie is wonderful. We both know that. But is she your person?"

Gabriella tried to smile at her friend for caring, for reaching out and offering advice, but she couldn't quite manage it because of the painful ache in her throat. Instead, she nodded, absorbing Joey's words whether she wanted to or not. And finally, "I guess we'll see."

She spent the night at home on her own, and as she lay in bed, she surfed her phone idly, checking out the happenings of her friends and neighbors. Angie had posted a photo of her and their older sister, Teresa, in a water gun fight like they used to have when they were kids. She grinned and scrolled. On the Tangle Valley page, Joey had posted a gorgeous shot of the sun setting over the vines. She scrolled and went still. The Biddies' page had a shot of Ryan and the same woman she'd seen her talking with at the Scoot not too long ago. Lana something. She was standing on top of a bench in town center, and Ryan was looking up at her, laughing. She wanted to put the phone away, to get the image the hell away from her, because everything in the photo gutted her. She felt ill and shaky almost instantly. That's when she saw the caption: *Sassy summer brings out the romance.*

The romance. She looked at the photo again. Saw the mirth in Ryan's eyes, the way her mouth turned up in laughter.

Needless to say, Gabriella didn't sleep that night. Ryan was moving on, plain as day. It was time she did the same.

❖

"Sounds like you had a rough one," Lana said, after hopping in Ryan's truck parked in front of her apartment complex. Ryan needed a pick-me-up after a rough go of things at work, and chilling with Lana would definitely help.

"I screwed up a work order, and my guy painted the wrong wall. Not only that. He painted it red. Bright red, which was meant for a child's racer room across town."

"Damn."

"Yeah. As you can imagine, the client was less than thrilled with his living room and had quite a lot to say about it. I had to hold the phone away from my ear."

"Shall we grab a beer and lament your attention to detail and the fact that I'm falling in love with Tasha and wildly unsure how to tell her?"

In the course of their recent friendship, Ryan had received an earful about the whirlwind romance between Lana and Tasha from Portland. She'd nodded and listened and supported, and in exchange, Lana had done the same for her. "I'm all for that discussion, but I'm thinking ice cream instead. I'm becoming an ice cream addict and must be stopped. But not today."

"Your addiction is my good fortune. Onward to the good stuff."

The parking lot at Maraschino's was hopping, the way it often was in the early evening. The sun wasn't quite down, and families were all over the place now that school was out for summer.

"Name your poison," Ryan said, as she swung open the door to the shop, a throwback to soda fountains of yesteryear. Most of the blue leather booths were occupied, and the line for counter service was long, but Ryan was undeterred. Nowhere to be, and ice cream soothed the soul.

"Oh, I'm going with a hot fudge sundae all the way. You?"

Ryan didn't hesitate, feeling a tad lighter already. "Banana split because I love the way they layer the whipped cream. They make sure you never run out."

Lana grinned. "It really is in the details, isn't it?"

The bell above the door dinged as two new customers entered, and a casual glance over Ryan's shoulder had her chest tightening. As the two approached, Madison's gaze landed on Ryan's and they exchanged a pleasant enough nod. Gabriella, at her side, already came with a smile. One that dimmed when she saw Ryan. Then Lana.

"Hey, guys," Madison said. That's when Ryan saw it. They were holding hands. She swallowed, understanding that they'd just run into Madison and Gabriella on a date. She felt sick, and hurt, whether she had any right to or not. She flexed her fingers, which had gone numb. Gabriella released Madison's hand and folded her arms, looking every bit as uncomfortable as Ryan felt.

"Well, it's awesome running into you two like this," Ryan said in an overly cheerful tone. She turned up the wattage on her smile. "Nice night, no?"

"It is. Enjoying my night off." Gabriella eyed Lana and seemed to make a choice. "You're Lana. We haven't officially met. Gabriella Russo." She raised a hand in greeting.

"Oh, I've heard so much about you. Nice to meet you officially."

Gabriella winced. "That sounds dangerous."

Ryan shook her head. "Not at all. Right, Lana?"

"Quite true. Only good things."

The line inched forward, and they faced ahead, which bought Ryan a moment of reprieve. Everything about this felt wrong, and she wanted to scream or toss a chair. That's when she felt an arm snake around her waist and rest there. Lana. She smiled up at Ryan and leaned against her. What was going on here? This wasn't customary of them at all. Apparently Lana was putting on a show, and Ryan wasn't going to stop her. In fact, behaving like a child, she leaned in to the touch.

"What brings the two of you out tonight?" Gabriella asked loudly.

Ryan turned back, breaking contact with Lana. "Just thought it would be a nice way to spend some time together."

Gabriella narrowed her gaze. "Oh, so this is a new development?" She looked from Ryan to Lana expectantly, not really backing down an inch.

Ryan stared. "Lots of those going around, it seems." She didn't know why she was being petty, but she couldn't seem to stop herself. Her emotions were like a runaway train, running over logic, maturity, and grace.

Gabriella lifted a shoulder. "New seasons and all. Why not?" The only one not smiling like this was the happiest of occasions was Madison, which Ryan had to give her credit for.

"You guys have plans for the weekend?" Lana asked.

Madison and Gabriella looked at each other. Gabriella looped her arm through Madison's. "I have a feeling we'll be playing it by ear. You guys?"

"We usually decide in the moment," Lana offered.

The line inched forward. Ryan and Lana were close to the front now. The seconds ticked by with excruciating tension. When it was time to place their order, Ryan exhaled in relief. She considered pivoting and taking it to-go, but her pride refused. Because the tables were full, they grabbed two stools along the corner of the bar and waited. Ryan eyed the room, trying to predict the next thirty minutes of her life, and realized that the only two available seats were the stools catty-corner from theirs at the bar. Fuck her life. Seriously? No.

As if on cue, Madison and Gabriella, ice cream in hand, surveyed the room briefly before learning of their fate. They exchanged a look and made their way over reluctantly, probably wishing they'd realized before ordering.

"We meet again," Madison said, as they sat.

"Meant to be, I guess," Lana chimed in. She looked down at her sundae. "You need to try this." She took a spoonful of ice cream and offered it to Ryan, who stared, stunned. Not knowing what else to do, she accepted the bite Lana fed her and felt even more awkward when Lana dabbed an errant bit of hot fudge from Ryan's lip with her forefinger and licked it after. She caught Gabriella watching the scene with interest. If Ryan's goal had been to make it look like she'd moved on, she was likely succeeding. Only, it wasn't at all true.

While Ryan and Lana made small talk, discussing their days and Ryan's opinion that available carpenters were scarce in the area, Madison and Gabriella turned to each other, staggering their knees and speaking quietly. They appeared cozy, intimate, like any other couple enjoying a night out. Okay, so this was something she was going to have to get used to seeing apparently, this fucked-up torture show. When Gabriella gave Madison's hair a playful tug and Madison blushed, Ryan had had about all she could take.

"You done?" she asked Lana, sliding her own dish across the counter. "Let's maybe get outta here."

"I'll follow you," Lana said quietly.

Gabriella looked over her shoulder as they stood. "Leaving? I guess the night is young, right?"

Ryan couldn't play this game any longer. She looked to Gabriella in exasperation. "Look. This is not a—" She sighed. "You know what? Doesn't even matter. You two look like you were made for each other and for ice cream and a long, wonderful life. I wish you nothing but happiness. Me? Just trying to get by."

"You're doing quite well," Gabriella said tightly.

"Come on," Ryan said to Lana, realizing there was nothing she could do to make this feel any better for any of them. "Have a nice one, guys."

"You, too," Gabriella said with a tight jaw and zero eye contact.

Madison rolled her lips in but said nothing, finally bowing her head as if waiting for the moment to pass.

They walked to Ryan's truck quietly, only the rest of the world felt exceptionally loud, aggressive, and foreign, like Ryan had just wandered onto a movie set and didn't know her lines.

"You okay?" Lana asked. "That was a charged scene back there."

She placed a shaky hand on top of the hood of her truck. "I will be." She looked at Lana ruefully. "I guess they're official now."

"Sure looked like it to me." Lana winced. "What a way to find out. You don't deserve any of this, Ry. Honestly, just forget they even exist."

She shrugged. "Maybe I do deserve it. I pretty much gave up, didn't I? Madison didn't."

"Yeah, well, Madison is not you. Gabriella's loss. Want me to drive?"

Ryan, still dazed, tossed her the keys and came around the passenger side. As they drove with the windows down, Ryan looked over at Lana. "Thanks for having my back. I mean, the romance part was a little unexpected but…"

"I don't know why I did that. Just got so protective of you and had to do something." She grimaced. "I'm sorry if I've complicated everything further."

"It's okay. You're a good friend." She sighed. "Speaking of, aren't you heading to Portland tonight?"

"Yep." Lana lit up at the thought of seeing Tasha. "I need to pack a quick bag and head that way. We're going to just stay in tonight, and I can't think of a better way to spend time."

"Sounds nice," Ryan said, refusing to think about it too much. Not when she missed comfy nights like that so much she couldn't pull in a proper breath. The soft jokes, the flutters when she held Gabriella close, the amazing sex, and, just as important, sleeping next to Gabriella, inhaling her, holding her through the night. There had been nothing better.

After dropping Lana at her place, Ryan hopped in the driver's seat and headed for home. Only the idea of replaying the run-in at Maraschino's eighty times over didn't carry much appeal, so she turned her truck around and headed back into town.

Half an hour later, the loud music from the Scoot and the whiskey she'd tossed back helped dull the ache. "Another, please, Pats."

"You got it. Glad you came by tonight, sweetie," Patsy said with a grin as she passed.

Ryan raised her empty glass.

"Ryan fucking Jacks," Heather said, leaning sideways on the bar and regarding her.

"Heather," she said back conservatively.

"Figured it was time for us to bury the hatchet."

"I had no idea there was one." A lie. They'd left things on bad terms in the parking lot of the cocktail launch.

"There doesn't have to be."

"Good." She was beginning to really feel the effects of the alcohol, and that was good. Exactly what she needed. Patsy slid her a double, and she tossed back another gulp.

"Oh, hey. It's the little contractor from hell."

Ryan frowned at the snide tone and characterization. She turned to see Lana's ex, Scott McCarver, three seats down the bar. That fucking guy. The stools between them opened up and they had a clear view of each other. "What's up?" she said nonchalantly. She raised her glass and turned away from him.

"You know she's a home wrecker?" he shouted. To who she wasn't sure. She didn't know Scott very well, only what she'd heard from Lana. He was uptight, particular, and had a tendency to lose his cool without warning. A winning combo.

"You heard what I said. Can't keep your hands to yourself." He jutted his chin out to Heather. "She married? Whose life are you tanking tonight?"

"You've got me confused. I didn't even meet Lana until you guys were separated and living apart." She said it louder than she probably should have. Whiskey.

He stood up. "Bullshit. You're a damn liar. You're probably ruining this girl's life right now."

"Settle down, bro," Heather said, straightening. "This has nothing to do with you."

He approached, on unsure footing. Ryan looked away, refusing to engage with someone drunk, irrational, and just mean. She knew she'd never trod on anyone's marriage ever, and that was all that mattered. "Why are you ignoring me?" She could feel him standing behind her stool. Heather took a small step back but otherwise held her ground. Ryan had to give her credit. She was scrappier than she'd have guessed. "Hey, bitch. I'm talking to you." Scott was getting louder now, but no one seemed to notice because the music still topped him.

She took another swallow of her drink and regarded him over her shoulder. "You're drunk. Go home and sleep it off."

"What did you just say to me? Who the hell are you? You don't tell me what to do." He grabbed her shoulder gruffly and turned her around on her stool. She stared at his hand still holding on to her and shoved it off.

"Knock it off," Heather said. Her hand was trembling, but she held out her arm anyway to warn him away. "You just need to calm down is all. I think this is just a misunderstanding."

"Get your hand out of my face," Scott slurred, swiping at it. He grabbed Heather by the wrist and yanked her out of the way, causing her to stumble. Heads began to swivel toward them. When he continued to move in Heather's direction, Ryan got concerned. She stood and placed herself between the two of them, catching Scott and shoving him away. She was angry and felt like she had nothing to lose. If this asshole was going to play this way, she'd play smarter.

Scott steadied himself and glared at her with bloodshot, angry eyes. "A couple of stupid bitches," he shouted.

"I guess that's how your ex-wife likes 'em." It was a cheap shot, and she should have kept her mouth closed, but she was drunk and pissed off. Scott lunged for her, but she was ready. She hadn't thrown a right hook since kickboxing class years ago, but she threw one now and nailed him straight in the eye. He stumbled, stunned, just in time for a couple of guys to intervene, grabbing Scott's arms and holding him back when he lunged forward. He continued to shout at her with his eye scrunched closed. She was corralled away by Patsy and her bartenders but could hear Scott yelling over the music from the front as she apologized to Patsy.

"Completely fine," Heather said. "Thanks for that. I didn't know what he was going to do."

Ryan smiled warily. "I could say the same to you."

Patsy shook her head. "He's been looking for a fight. Not the first time he's caused trouble in here lately. I think his divorce is kicking his ass."

Ryan could identify with his pain, though she'd never take it out on someone else. She craned her head to check on his status and caught red and blue lights peeking through the open door. Fuck her life.

"Ryan?" the approaching officer asked five minutes later. Only it wasn't just any officer, it was Tuna Terry from high school because that's all he ever brought for lunch. "Can we chat about what happened?"

She exchanged a look with Patsy and followed Terry out of the place to see another officer talking with Scott. Fantastic.

"Start at the beginning," Terry said.

"I was sitting at the bar and he started yelling from three stools down."

Terry sighed and nodded, attempting a little bit of sympathy.

She finished the story while Terry took notes. The problem? There were enough witnesses that saw her deck him without seeing all the threatening behavior that came first. Whether it was fair or not, she was starting to see how this was all going to play out, and it wasn't good.

"Really sorry about this, Ryan, but you threw that punch in front of half the town." It wasn't entirely a surprise when her hands were cuffed behind her back. Luckily, she saw that, across the parking lot, Scott's were, too.

"You'd have done the same," she told him.

"Just between us? Probably," Tuna said.

Phones came out from the gathered crowd as she was placed in a squad car for the first time in her life. Her friends called out their support.

"Not your fault, Ryan. They'll sort it out."

"Hang in there."

"Love you, Ry."

"Self-defense. We all saw it."

Oh yeah. This would make for quite the juicy story. She gave it an hour before the Biddies scored a copy of one of those cell phone photos and plastered it all over Instagram. She shook her head and swore. The last thing she saw was Heather mouthing the words, "I'm so sorry," as she was driven away from the neon lights and straight to county lockup.

Ryan was going to jail.

## CHAPTER TWENTY-TWO

The sun had yet to make any kind of appearance, but Gabriella was up with her coffee, having not had the best night of sleep. The one-two punch of an evening had left her with the weight of unwanted emotion sitting square on her chest like a concrete block. So she sat on her porch watching the lightening sky, wrapped in her favorite comfy sweater, and contemplating all she had in her head and heart.

There was Madison. When she'd gone in for the good night kiss the evening prior, Gabriella had placed a gentle hand on her chest. "Maddie. I can't."

Madison had exhaled and offered a slow nod, internalizing the words. "I thought you might say that." She raised her green eyes to Gabriella's. "You're in love with her, aren't you?"

"Yeah. I am." She couldn't deny it. Not to herself and not to Madison. The things she felt for Ryan Jacks weren't ideal, helpful, or comfortable, but they were the truest feelings she'd ever experienced, never more startlingly clear than now. The ice cream run-in from hell had been painful. When Ryan's gaze landed on her holding hands with Madison, it had been like a knife in her chest, and she seemed to relive that moment over and over. The look in Ryan's eyes. The sadness. Then the world had flipped upside down entirely when Lana wrapped her arms around Ryan's waist. It was wrong, all of it, and she had to stop pretending otherwise. "I thought maybe this"—she gestured between them—"was something I should explore, that you and I were maybe a little more realistic than Ryan and me, but..." She shook her head. "I don't think it's something I can just dictate."

"No. I suppose not." Madison's eyes carried disappointment, but she attempted a wobbly smile anyway. "I guess a person can't help who they fall for." She sighed. "I don't think she's ready, Gabs."

"Yeah, me neither. It's not like I'm about to chase after her."

Madison scratched the back of her neck. "If you do, I'll support you." She swallowed as if trying to hold back tears, which only made Gabriella well up because she cared so very deeply for Madison, who never cried, ever.

"Maddie, I'm so sorry."

She shook her head. "Ah, don't be. You're being honest, and that's all I could ever ask for."

Gabriella nodded as tears made their way down her cheeks. "I wanted to try. I did."

"We're just not quite the right fit. It probably shouldn't be a news flash."

"But we're important to each other, and that will never change. Do you hear me?" She heard the ferocity in her voice that matched her affection for Madison.

Madison stared up at the tree in front of Gabriella's cottage. "I hear you. It's true. We are."

Gabriella took an earnest step forward. "Look at me." Madison did. "Your fit is out there. I can feel it as clearly as I can feel the air around us. She's just waiting for you to find her."

"Yeah," Madison said, seeming unconvinced. She shoved her hands into her pockets. "Or maybe not. That's okay, too. Not everyone has a happily ever after." She kicked at a pebble. "I should go. Let you enjoy the rest of your night." She turned.

"Maddie," Gabriella called, after a moment of watching her walk. She went after her, and when Madison turned, Gabriella wrapped her arms around her neck and held on. "I love you. You know that, right?" They both knew what kind of love she was referencing. The deeply felt love for someone hugely important, the closest of the close, who you don't want to move through life without. Madison LeGrange was family.

"Love you back," Madison said, squeezing her. "Now let go of me, so I can stroll back to my place with my dignity intact. I can't get all sentimental," she scoffed, back to playful Madison. "It's not my best look."

"The grapes would never let you live it down."

Madison tilted her head. "What about you, though? Are you going to be okay? I could feel that tonight was hard on you."

"I keep thinking things will get easier with time. That's not happening. She doesn't deserve it, but I can't stop thinking about her, missing her."

"Well, maybe there's something to that."

Gabriella balked. "No way. You saw them tonight, cuddly and cute."

Madison shifted her weight and looked like she was debating whether to say something more. She opened her mouth and closed it again before finally going for it. "If you want my opinion, what we saw tonight was a show. Manufactured. Those two didn't go together at all. Notice Ryan never really participated and kept stealing glances at you every other minute." She shrugged. "For what it's worth, anyway. 'Night, Gabs." She turned and headed off down the path.

Gabriella watched after her, trying on what Madison had described to see how it fit, not sure it even mattered. The idea did make her feel a tiny bit better. She bit the inside of her lip, frustrated that the relief felt like a much-needed salve. If only it hadn't eventually worn off, leaving her tossing and turning throughout what felt like a very long, very warm night. She'd thrown the covers off early that morning and wound up here on the porch, in the dark, nursing a now cold cup of tea.

She sighed and scrolled her phone to see what the rest of the world was up to. Her breath caught when a photo from the Biddies' account showed Ryan in—wait, were those handcuffs? She scrolled back. At first, she thought it had to be a joke and scanned the caption which simply read, *Uh-oh*. She dove into the comments to learn it wasn't a joke at all. Ryan had apparently gotten into it at the Scoot with some rando. What in the world? Worry hit. Then anger. Finally, unable and unwilling to sort through more of her warring feelings, she threw on a pair of jeans and a T-shirt, grabbed the keys to her damn Jeep, and headed straight to the jail.

❖

Jail was not that far off from what Ryan had seen on television. She'd started the night in a cell with three other women, two of whom were drunk as hell and one who stared silently at the wall. Then two hours later, Ryan was moved to a cell of her own where she'd spent the night leaning against the concrete wall, closing her eyes when she could. Had it not been so late, she'd have called Billy or her mom, but the idea of dragging either one of them out of bed to this kind of news hadn't seemed like the kind thing to do. Plus, she had no idea how she would face her mother after this. Small-town scandals tended to linger. She expected a metaphorical smack to the back of her head in the form of a long lecture, probably with visual aids and finger wagging. She deserved it.

"Hey, Ryan, you're sprung." Austin Tyler, the twenty-four-year-old who used to occasionally crew for her before signing up for the police academy, opened the door to her cell. "Sorry about all this."

"So you guys see the error of your ways? I was literally just trying to keep the guy from hurting my friend." She was so tired it was almost hard to argue at this point.

"That's not for me to decide," he said. "But your bail's been posted. You're free to go after you sign some paperwork. The charges will be reviewed, and we'll be in touch."

"They're gonna stick?"

"Between you and me? I doubt it. But your ride is just through those doors."

Dammit. Her mother probably heard what happened and drove to the station in humiliation and anger. Guilt engulfed Ryan, heavy and thick. How much furniture could she make over the course of one weekend to make it up to her mom?

She followed Austin to the front of the police station, signed the necessary paperwork at the window, and turned. Gabriella faced her with her arms folded. She wore jeans, a white T-shirt, and a navy-blue hoodie that looked so soft Ryan wanted to collapse into it. Her hair was down with gentle waves past her shoulders, and after the night she'd had, Gabriella looked too good to be true. She also looked really, really angry.

"What are you doing here?" Ryan asked, bleary and wondering if she was hallucinating.

"You don't get to ask the questions, Rocky. I posted bail, so let's get out of here."

Ryan nodded her thanks to Austin and followed Gabriella out of the station. Once they were safely in her Jeep, Ryan turned to her. "Thank you. I'm honestly shocked, but appreciative."

Gabriella nodded. She hadn't turned on the ignition yet, and the car was quiet. The morning sunshine hit the dash. "Not that you deserved it. You actually hit a guy?"

Ryan scrubbed her face. "He was coming at us, and I was several drinks in after running into you living your fairy-tale ice-cream life and I"—she shook her head—"snapped."

Gabriella faced her fully. "Well, you can't do that. You can't just snap. Something could have happened to you, and what am I going to do then?" She said it with such conviction that it tugged at Ryan's heart. It meant she still cared. Really cared. Gabriella's eyes searched Ryan's. "I don't know what's going on with you, but you have to get it together. Do you hear me?"

She bit her lip. "Easier said than done these days."

"No," Gabriella said, emphatically. "That's such a cop-out, and I'm tired of your cop-outs."

"What does that even mean?" Ryan heard the frustration in her own voice. After the events of the night before, no sleep, and no food, her coping skills were nonexistent.

"When something is hard, you decide it's unattainable." She hit one hand perpendicular against the other to emphasize her point.

"You're talking about us." Ryan shook her head, emphatic. "Which is so untrue."

"Damn right I am," Gabriella said. "What? You don't think so?"

"I was trying to do the right thing and get out of the way. You're the one who went and fell for someone else. That's not something I can control."

"Are you insane?" Gabriella asked. Her eyes brimmed with tears, and Ryan's lips parted in surprise.

"Well, am I wrong?" she asked meekly. She couldn't stand to see Gabriella sad, and it took a lot not to pull her in and not let her go.

"You don't get it. You still don't." Gabriella touched her chest, her heart, and took a moment to gather her words. Her voice was slow and unsteady. "The only person I've fallen for is sitting right here in this Jeep. She went to jail last night for being a hothead, and she broke my heart when she deserted me in every sense possible. So there."

Ryan was speechless. No. That couldn't possibly be true. All this time she'd imagined an amazing love story between Gabriella and Madison, and relegated herself to being merely the roadblock that got in their way. How was it possible that she had been more than that? She rejected the idea. "I admit that I wasn't there when I needed to be. But in the end, I didn't leave you. It was the other way around." The reply was weak at best.

"Oh, Ryan." Gabriella shook her head. "You don't have a clue, do you? How very unfortunate." Gabriella started the Jeep and drove them out of the parking lot in melancholy silence, each lost in their own thoughts. But Gabriella didn't take the farm road that would take them to Ryan's lake house. She also skipped over the shortcut to the Scoot for Ryan's truck. Instead, she drove them straight through the center of town to the drive-through window of the Bacon and Biscuit Café. Ryan watched in surprise as she ordered four bacon and butter biscuits and two large coffees.

"What are we doing?" Ryan asked, as they waited on their order.

Gabriella looked agitated. "You're bound to be starving. I'm not sending you home exhausted and hungry. It's against everything I stand for."

"You're angry at me, and you're buying me breakfast?" With the window down, the amazing aroma of freshly baked biscuits wafted through the car and almost brought Ryan to grateful tears.

"Yes, I am. Dammit." Gabriella squeezed the steering wheel. "Because that's who I am. An angry feeder."

"Not going to argue."

"Good."

They retrieved the warm bag from Clem, who smiled and waved at Ryan through the window. "You okay?" she asked. Clearly Clementine had not missed out on the newly minted gossip, but then the Biddies were likely present in that very building, dishing over coffee and sass.

"Yeah. Long night, but I'm good now."

Clem glanced at Gabriella and smiled as if to indicate all was right with the world, seeing the two of them. "I can see that. You guys enjoy the morning."

"It's a beautiful day, isn't it?" Gabriella said and pulled away from the window with a wave. They drove in silence to the lake house, and when they pulled off the gravel road into the drive, Ryan looked over at Gabriella, unable to hold back the question a second longer.

"When you said that you fell for me, did you mean in love?"

Instead of answering, Gabriella sighed in exasperation, opened the door, stormed out, placed her hands on her hips, and looked out at the calm water.

Ryan watched her a minute before joining her there. "Gabriella." The feel of her name leaving Ryan's lips was like a welcome caress. She'd missed saying it.

Gabriella turned, both hands placed on the small of her back. Her earnest hazel eyes found Ryan's and held on. "Yeah, I did mean in love."

Ryan swallowed as the weight of the declaration came over her. She had trouble believing it, but Gabriella had never been anything but honest with her. She let it sink in.

"But that's the tricky thing." Gabriella smiled through the obvious pain. "Love is a two-way street, and what could be the best thing ever to happen to a person becomes the worst when that love isn't returned."

Ryan didn't think. She didn't try to understand anymore. She came up behind Gabriella wordlessly and wrapped her arms around her. Gabriella bristled, nearly shrugging out of the touch at first, but then her body relaxed. Gabriella gave in and leaned back against Ryan. After a bit, her arms covered Ryan's, and Ryan and Gabriella stayed that way, watching the sun hover over the water in some kind of free pass of a moment, conflicts shelved and hearts honest. Having Gabriella in her arms, knowing that they loved each other, was everything. She marveled for a moment. Maybe they could actually do this. But not yet. She needed to say the words first. Her stomach flip-flopped at the scary concept, and her lips nearly vibrated in anticipation of the words.

"I better go," Gabriella said, disentangling herself. Without looking back, she returned to the Jeep, grabbed the biscuits and a coffee for Ryan, placed them on the driveway, and climbed back inside.

"Hey, wait a sec."

Gabriella shook her head. "No more waiting."

Ryan's entire being sagged in defeat. If there had ever been a chance to fix what had gone wrong between them, it had been in that moment. Yet she'd failed to open her damn mouth.

Gabriella pointed a finger at her through the open window. "And if I ever hear about you getting locked up again, not only am I going to leave your ass in jail, I will personally kick it when you get out. Do you hear me, Ryan Jacks? You're too good for bar fights."

Ryan eased her hands into her back pockets and bowed her head. "Loud and clear. And thank you for...today, busting me out. The breakfast. You didn't have to."

"I did not." Gabriella popped her sunglasses on and with a final wave drove away. Ryan watched her Jeep wind down the lonely road back to civilization, and along with it, her whole heart.

## CHAPTER TWENTY-THREE

I'm sorry, what?" Lana asked over the phone, incredulous. She was still in Portland, having stayed the night with Tasha. Because she'd set her phone aside, she was just catching up. "Scott came after you. Are you serious?"

"Yes. He was angry as hell, but that's not the point."

"And you both went to jail?" Lana asked.

"That's what I said. I heard from the chief, and he says the charges are in the process of being dropped. Just waiting on the formality."

"Hell, I leave for a short time, and the world goes crazy. Sorry, back to your thing. Gabriella has thrown you for some kind of loop. Proceed."

"Big time." Ryan paced the length of her kitchen, with Dale following behind her, changing direction when she did. Lazy as he was, he was a loyal dog who knew when times were rough. It was Tuesday evening and she'd had hours to mull over her morning with Gabriella. "She said that she fell in love with me. Did you hear that? Love." Ryan shook her head. "So that means she might still be in love with me. How long do those things last? You know, in normal people?"

"Well, I would think a long time. So you hit him? You hit Scott?"

"Yeah, I'm so sorry. I wish I'd handled it differently, but he was not backing down. Apparently, I've seen a few too many movies."

"I'm impressed."

"But what do I do?"

"I think you make sure you get the assault charge dropped, first and foremost. If you run into a hiccup, set up a meeting with the DA. I don't know much about this stuff, though."

"About the love. I can't stop thinking about it."

Lana laughed. "Gotcha. What happened to Madison?"

She swallowed. "I don't know."

"Huh. This is complicated. A love triangle. It's like *The Young and the Restless* over there."

"Definitely the restless part." Ryan heard the front door open, and in a matter of moments, Billy, the enjoyable dope, appeared with a six-pack of brewskis in his hand.

"Hang on. Billy's here. I called him for reinforcements." Dale ditched her and jumped in circles around his work buddy.

"What did I miss?" Billy asked, placing the beer on the counter and then scratching Dale behind his ears vigorously. "Oh, that's right. You're a criminal."

She held up a finger. "A misunderstood innocent. But there are bigger fish."

He looked around. "Awesome. I'm starving."

"No," she said, closing her eyes. She returned to Lana. "So far, he's not helpful. Save me."

"Is this about the thing you texted?" Billy asked. "Chef-oh-la Gabriella? I say close your eyes and leap. Was thinking about it on the car ride over here. What else do you have going for you?" He looked in boredom around her empty living room. "I like her. She's a knockout with a fantastic rack and probably makes great snacks. Great snacks go a long way."

Ryan adjusted the phone. "He's being a guy. I need guidance. Putting you on speaker." She looked to Billy and put the phone down between them. "It's Lana."

"Does she know you threw down with her ex last night? *Bam*," he said, imitating a punch. "I can't believe I missed it. No one got the swing on video, either. I asked around."

"Would you focus? This is my life we're talking about." She heard the foreign desperation in her voice.

"Yep. Got any chips?"

She pointed at the cabinet, and Lana chimed in, "Well, does knowing that Gabriella's feelings match yours change anything for you? I feel like a therapist right now. I should look into a license. And smart glasses."

Ryan replayed Gabriella's confession. *Yeah, I did mean love.* Her eyes had confirmed it. Ryan had been so surprised, affected, and rattled since she'd heard the words. "I think it's making me look back over everything we've said to each other with new eyes. It all comes with a different meaning, and I can't stop my mind from racing. I'm literally pacing in my kitchen right now."

"It's true." Billy munched chips from where he sat on top of her marble counter. "What if you just misinterpreted everything and screwed it all the hell up? I've done that before. A lot."

She closed her eyes. "That's the first helpful thing you've said since you arrived."

"Hurtful." He went back to his chips.

"Well, is he right?" Lana asked. "Did you screw it all up?"

"I don't know. Probably. Yes." Ryan ran a hand through her hair, which was likely a jumbled mess from having done the same eighty times that day. She thought how much Gabriella would have loved it and felt that familiar flutter in her midsection. Why was she fluttering again? The thought of Gabriella these days made her stomach feel sick and uncomfortable. Was this a sign that she now had hope that they could be...something? "I decided that Gabriella would be happier with someone else."

"Damn right, you did," Billy said and turned his cap backward. "Wasn't your call."

"I've never done this before, okay? I was winging it." She felt her eyes go wide as the full brunt of understanding swept over her like an enormous tidal wave. "But we were actually really happy together." She touched her chest. "I'd never been that happy in my entire life. What if she was that happy, too?"

"Imagine that," Lana said.

Billy nodded. "Everything was fine and you tanked it."

Ryan blinked, her chest tightening and her brain screaming. "What do I do?"

"Nothing. You live with your sorry choices." Billy grinned. "Kidding. Tell her you're sorry."

"I think it's gonna take a little more than that," Lana offered tentatively. "I saw her body language at Maraschino's. Totally closed off to you. Uncomfortable as hell."

"Because I really hurt her." She sighed and pinched the bridge of her nose, forcing herself to be honest. "I'm a stupid asshole."

Billy nodded. "But a likable stupid asshole. She'll see that."

"Call her," Lana said.

"No." The idea terrified her now. All she wanted to do was go back in time, scoop Gabriella into her arms, and not let go. She shook her head, imagining Gabriella looking for her at the restaurant opening and realizing she wasn't there. It wasn't Madison that Gabriella had been looking for that day. "I honestly don't deserve her, you guys. I should just move to an island somewhere and never speak to women again."

Billy winced. "Likely expensive to execute."

"Listen, you're a mess," Lana said. "And I wish we could do it for you, but until you find the courage to pour it all out to the one person that matters, you're just spinning your wheels."

Billy pointed at the phone. "This lady knows her stuff. Did I hear you were single?" Billy asked the phone.

"Sorry, buddy," Lana said. "Got a wonderful woman."

He shrugged. "Always too late."

Ryan smiled. In spite of her own catastrophe of a life, the gratitude she felt for her friends overwhelmed her. She smiled. "You guys are great."

"Duh," Lana said.

"Born great," Billy proclaimed with a proud grin. "What's the verdict? You driving over there tonight?"

She scoffed. "No, um, I don't have a plan. But I'm seeing her tomorrow at the game."

"Ah, yes, the Beavers," Lana said.

"Otters," Ryan countered.

"Same thing."

"If only." Billy laughed like a sixth grader, in rare form tonight. "Gonna be one hell of a game now."

Ryan nodded and rolled her shoulders, nervous, excited, and zeroing in on possible ways to explain herself, knowing this was going to be an uphill battle, too important to lose.

The stands at the ballpark were packed like pickles in a jar, with just about everyone in town in attendance. The line at the snack bar snaked around twice with the smell of nacho cheese and hot dogs settling pleasantly over everything. Kids ran around with snow cones. Gabriella grinned as she threw the ball to Clementine in the practice field, loosening up her shoulder and hoping she had the magic they'd need to win this championship game. She wanted it bad. Ever since joining the Muskrats, Gabriella relished feeling part of a team. With the restaurant in full swing and kicking her ass, days like today were a nice escape. She just hoped she'd do her team proud. Whisper Wall bragging rights were a hot commodity.

She tried to not think about the fact that Ryan was back on first base after a two-game absence. She also banished thoughts of how sexy she always looked in that red Otter uniform. She certainly didn't steal a glance at the other practice field to remind herself or swallow when she did.

"You ready for this?" She turned to the chain-link fence to see Madison resting her forearms on the top.

"A Muskrat is always ready for battle." She grinned, happy they were finding their equilibrium again. Madison seemed to get it, and of course she did. She was Maddie, all logic and understanding with a kind heart to boot. "You sticking around?"

"No chance I'm missing the rodent showdown of the century. Joey's grabbing me a giant pretzel, and then I'm settling in to scream a lot. Practiced in the car. I now have the perfect combination of shrill and intense."

"Holding you to it."

"Okay, have fun. Don't screw this up."

"Hey!"

"Kidding." A pause. "Not entirely."

Madison dashed off, and minutes later, the umpire called for the start of the game. The first three batters had decent showings, with two on base with one out. Gabriella was their cleanup and approached the plate with her game face on. As kind as she always tried to be, she left it behind when at the plate. She'd drill that ball straight through the skulls of every person on the Otter roster if that's what it took. Okay, she wouldn't really do that, but the ferocity of the thought kept her focused and competitive.

*Crack.*

She connected with the second pitch and saw the line drive bypass everyone in the infield and land squarely in deep right. As she took off for first, Stephen the cowboy, who must have been a substitute, hurled the ball to Ryan. Gabriella overran first base a millisecond before the ball landed in Ryan's glove.

"Safe," Byron the umpire yelled. She grinned at him, having always enjoyed the French fries he put out as grill master at I Only Have Fries for You. She still used that garlic seasoning he recommended.

Her eyes connected briefly with Ryan's. Ryan didn't have her normal overly confident game face on. It surprised her. Instead,

Gabriella was greeted with a softer stare that left her off-kilter. Clementine strolled to the plate.

"I'm really sorry about the other morning," Ryan said as Gabriella led off, her gaze firmly attached to her destination, second base.

She shrugged off the comment. "No idea what you mean." *Second base. Second base. Second base.* Clem swung and missed.

"You told me that you'd fallen in love with me, and I don't even know if that's the case anymore, but if it is—"

"Ryan," she said, glancing over her shoulder, "we can't do this right now. Game. Focus." But it wasn't like hers wasn't rattled now. Clem held her ground on pitch two, and the umpire called a ball. Gabriella sucked in a breath, unnerved and drawn back to the morning at Ryan's house.

"I have to do this right now," Ryan said. "I can't go another minute."

"Fine. What is it?"

"I have tell you that I love you."

*Crack.* An infield fly that, strangely, no one caught. Gabriella should be booking it to second, but instead she turned and looked straight at Ryan, her mouth open in shock. Distantly, she knew Clementine was headed to first base, but she couldn't seem to move.

"You can run," Ryan said with a soft smile. "In fact, you should."

Gabriella blinked, remembering herself, and took off. Clem was an easy out at first, and with the bought time, she made it safely to second. It wasn't like she could concentrate on the game, though. Not now. Not when her entire world was just tossed into the air with this new piece of information. And where did her damn muscles go? She couldn't feel them.

Two innings later, with the Muskrats trailing two runs to the Otters' four, Ryan hit a double that eventually brought her to third base and Gabriella. She didn't waste time. "Why didn't you tell me?"

"When?" Ryan raised a shoulder. "Everything was a mess."

"When you *knew*. A month ago. Last week. The other morning. Anytime, really."

The Muskrat fans went nuts when a strike was called at home plate. Ryan looked at Gabriella, and those blue eyes made everything in her tighten. "I should have, but I'm bad at this. I'm worried I'll keep being bad at this."

Gabriella nodded, then winced. "Maybe I wasn't so great at it either. God." She marveled at all of their missteps. The confusion, the head games she'd played with herself, the outside opinions that she'd allowed in, Ryan's pulling away, the Madison factor, all of it.

*Crack.*

Gabriella held out her glove automatically, and the line drive landed squarely in the pocket. Three outs. Gabriella tossed the ball to the mound and headed to the dugout, leaving a dumbfounded Ryan alone on third. "How did you catch that?" Ryan called after her. "We were mid-conversation."

"I just stuck my hand out." Second nature because she was too caught up in her thoughts to focus.

Gabriella hit a single on purpose her next time at bat and with shaky hands asked another question of Ryan the second she landed on base. "What made you tell me about your feelings now? I don't get it." Her head swam, and she needed answers.

"Because I can't imagine going another day without giving one hundred percent of what I have to you," Ryan said, adjusting her cap. "I want a second chance. I'm terrified of it. But I want it all the same. Says a lot."

*Crack.*

Dammit. Gabriella took off running, but inside it felt like something was taking root and blooming. She ran on lighter feet, knowing now that what she had with Ryan had been real. It didn't solve the uneasiness she felt about any kind of future, but it settled her heart. As she rounded the bases to home, she let herself wonder about the possibilities. In a helpful turn of events, the Muskrats had a stellar inning, which gave her one more shot at bat. Living on emotional and physical adrenaline, she landed on first base.

"Do you hate me right now?" Ryan asked right away.

Gabriella straightened, foot still on the base. She didn't know what came over her, but in that moment she had to act. She grabbed Ryan by the face and kissed her with all the jumbled feelings she had in her. Ryan murmured quietly in surprise and sank in to the kiss, grabbing Gabriella and hauling her in. God, the wonderful familiarity, the heat, the tension. Gabriella reveled in all of it.

*Crack.*

The crowd went wild, and though distantly Gabriella was aware of Clementine running toward them yet again, she couldn't seem to pull away from the heaven that was Ryan's lips.

"Run, Gabs, you kissing bandit!" Joey's voice. "Run like the wind."

"Get a room," someone else yelled, followed by laughter. Ryan smiled against her lips, and everything in Gabriella sighed happily. The world felt right. And damn good. She had no idea what any of this meant, other than that they loved each other. What she did understand, however, was that Clementine had now arrived at first base and the ball had joined her, landing just behind Ryan with a thud.

"Gotta go," Gabriella said, pulling away and finding her breath.

"I give that a ten of ten!" Monty the cowboy yelled from his spot next to Becca, who whistled loudly with two fingers.

Gabriella bolted, and to her credit, Ryan took her time retrieving the wayward ball. Gabriella rounded second base and, feeling gutsy, continued to third. Apparently, the goodwill ran out, and Ryan beamed the softball, beating her to the base by a millisecond.

"Outta there," Byron yelled, throwing his arm back and then forward with, okay, way too much gusto. The Otter fans went wild because it was the final out of the game.

"Might take it down a notch," she whispered to him.

Didn't matter. The Otters had taken the Whisper Wall championship. The Muskrat supporters sat down in defeat with a collective *awww*. Gabriella took off her hat and waved to the crowd in apology as she trotted to the dugout. She caught Madison smiling in quiet support from the stands, which was a relief. Next, she glanced over her shoulder to see Ryan backing away from first base with a genuine smile on her face, her focus not on her celebrating teammates but on Gabriella. No trace of softball smugness or playful gloating. Ryan looked so very happy, and that made Gabriella happy. A chain reaction because they were linked. She could pretend she had control over that, but she didn't. The connection that ran between them was alive and well, and she'd unleashed it fully right there on first base in front of the whole damn town. She'd examine the repercussions later. For now, she smiled apologetically at her teammates, who were forgiving enough to let her off the hook for her antics.

"At least you got a little action out of it," Bruno said with a gleam in his eye.

Clementine laughed as they bumped fists. "And by proxy, so did the rest of us. Damn."

They gathered together as a group, and Clementine gave them the requisite good game talk. "We came out. We played hard. We were Muskrats until the end." She studied their faces intently one at a time. "We've missed out on this championship game for three straight years now. But we made it here this time. Next season, we're gonna win. Now put those hearty Muskrat paws in here and claim the pride you've earned. Hold those whiskers high."

With hands in, they chanted, "Muskrats for life!" and erupted in cheers. The crowd echoed their sentiment, and someone broke out the beer. Her team had lost in a stomach clencher that had been mostly her fault. But it was a beautiful summer evening, and she felt the goodwill of everyone around her. She glanced across the field at the Otters' celebration. Gabriella didn't have the answers to the questions her heart was asking of her, but she was open to searching for them.

# CHAPTER TWENTY-FOUR

There were some moments you held on to forever, and Gabriella grabbing Ryan and kissing her was definitely a keeper. Though her spirits soared, Ryan hadn't spoken to Gabriella after the game. Perhaps, for the best. Maybe they needed space to process the new developments. She'd gone to Pizzamino's with Billy and a small group of her teammates, accepting their ribbing, because really what else should she expect?

"Ry, can you pass me the menu, or do you want to make out first?" Billy asked, serious faced.

"You're hysterical," she said.

From down the table Brenda Anne nodded. "I generally make out with my competitors, too, Ryan. It's how I keep the Nickel in business."

She gasped, because being dragged by Billy was one thing, but wholesome Brenda Anne was another.

"I can't help it," Ryan said. "Sometimes you have to seize the moment."

"She sure seized your face," Billy said around his slice.

"I think you two seized a little more than a moment. I had my stopwatch out," Brenda Anne said into her beer. "Those games should come with a PG-13 warning."

There was a rumor that the Tangle Valley crew had headed to the fry shop for drinks and dinner. It took everything in Ryan not to innocently swing by. It was like she couldn't tamp down her anticipation. She needed to fast-forward and learn how this damn movie ended. An hour later, she showered and changed and drove to Gabriella's beneath the stars with the windows open, allowing her hair to dry in the night air, speakers blaring as one must on such an evening.

Only when she arrived at the cottage, Gabriella was nowhere to be found.

A little disappointed, she let the music continue to play through the open windows as she sat on the steps in front of the cottage, content to wait forever if she had to. This was the love of her life, and she wasn't about to sell her short for another moment in this lifetime. Gabriella Russo deserved the sun, the moon, and the stars, and Ryan was hell-bent on giving them to her.

It was around forty minutes later that she heard the trickle of overlapping voices coming up the walk. When she saw the four of them approach, Ryan stood, nervous as hell but determined to be brave no matter how terrified. She focused fully on her love for Gabriella and refused to let herself think about all that could go wrong in the next thirty minutes. She'd imagined every last one of those scenarios on the drive over, hearing Gabriella's voice explain away that kiss in a million different ways.

*It was the excitement from the game. Doesn't mean anything's changed.*

*It was a really nice moment, Ryan, but I'm afraid that's all it can be.*

*Oh, the kiss? That was just to distract you at first base. I'm sorry if it confused you.* That one was Ryan's second least favorite, next to *Madison and I are still giving it a shot. I'm sorry.*

She heard them all in a jumble as Gabriella and her friends approached, still laughing and talking over each other.

"I'm just saying"—Joey's voice was immediately recognizable—"that if you'd listen to me, you'd understand the importance of a fleeting glance across a crowded room."

"Mine always come off as stalker-like." Madison.

Gabriella laughed. "Only eight women have said that. Don't worry."

Was the group heading to Gabriella's to continue their evening and Ryan had just completely crashed? She panicked and glanced behind her for a hidden door to escape through. Nothing. Instead she shifted her weight uneasily and raised a hand. "Hey," she said to the group, but her eyes were trained on only one person. "You weren't home, so I thought I'd wait."

Joey and Madison exchanged looks, and Madison gestured with a head to her cottage back down the path. They'd picked a new gathering spot.

"We'll let you talk," Becca said and gave Gabriella's shoulder a squeeze. Gabriella nodded, but her gaze hadn't moved from where Ryan stood on the steps. Ryan searched her face for answers, but her features gave nothing away.

"Hey," Gabriella said once they were alone. "Didn't expect to see you."

Ryan nodded and swallowed. "Yeah, well, pretty sure I wouldn't sleep tonight if we didn't talk." She lifted a hand as Gabriella ascended the steps and took a seat. "Sorry about the blurting on base."

"Sorry about the kissing on base."

"Yeah," Ryan said with a half smile and rapidly heating cheeks.

A pause. "No, I'm not," Gabriella said with determination. She turned and looked at Ryan head-on, that stare unwavering and mirroring her delivery.

Ryan exhaled. "I was worried you'd regret every second. I haven't made things easy."

"You think?" Gabriella asked. Her mouth turned up on one side and her eyes went wide. She shook her head. "What are we going to do with ourselves?"

"Beware of the self-fulfilling prophecy."

Gabriella turned to her. "Is that what got you? You decided we were doomed, so we were?"

Ryan looked out at the darkened fields in front of them, highlighted partially by a dusting of porch light castoff. "I'm about to confess everything." She leaned back on her hands and stretched out her legs. "Are you ready?"

"I think so."

"I thought I was sent to you so you could figure out your feelings for Madison. I decided she was everything you ever wanted, and I never would be. In doing so, I proceeded to act like the asshole of the century, which did what?"

"Pushed me straight to Madison, who's entirely wrong for me, who doesn't have my heart."

Ryan held out a hand. "Self-fulfilling prophecy."

Gabriella walked down the steps and turned back to her, thoughtful. "The problem is you didn't account for the other variables."

"Like?"

"That I'm a human being with free will, and I get to decide what I feel and what I want."

"Right," Ryan sighed, as dread descended. She'd taken all of those liberties and more. "I get that now."

"And Madison and I are great *friends*. We're not meant to be more."

Ryan nodded and sat up straight, ready to go there. "And what about us?"

"At first I thought we were silly. Then thought we had potential. Finally, I understood we were so much more than anything I could have hoped."

"Before deciding how foolish you'd been."

"Yep. That."

"And now?"

"And now I wonder."

"I love you more than words describe." Ryan leaned against the railing, looking down at Gabriella. "And I don't want you to wonder. I want to show you that you weren't wrong." She looked skyward. "Before the believing you'd been foolish part, which I'd like to erase from the history books."

Gabriella shook her head slowly. "I don't want to erase it. I think we need this knowledge to reflect on in the future. Listen, Ryan." She took two steps forward. "You weren't the only one who could have done things better. I got in my own head and let outside opinions influence me. I took out my anger on you when it seemed we wouldn't hit the cut-too-close soft-opening. I fully see my part in all of this, and I don't plan to forget it. Don't you dare, either."

A small smile teased Ryan's lips. "And what might we need this knowledge for, moving forward?" Gabriella was indicating a possible future, but she'd yet to say so. "What might we do with it?"

Gabriella placed her palms on the back of her hips and looked coy. "We could, maybe, I don't know, try and be better."

"That simple, huh? Be better?" Ryan was already walking to Gabriella, who was too damn far away. She wanted her close. She couldn't imagine ever not wanting that.

"I didn't say anything about simple."

Ryan exhaled and paused a few feet away. "I was afraid of that. I can admit that…all of this—"

"All of this? Nope. Say it."

Ryan nodded and started again. "I can admit that *love* is harder than I would have expected. It makes you feel happy, and crazy, and afraid, and vulnerable, and I wasn't prepared." She paused. "I am now. Bring on all of it."

"You sure about that?"

"As long as I know you love me, I can take on anything." Ryan tilted her head. "But what about you?"

Gabriella didn't hesitate. "I want to be wherever you are. I just need to know that you want us just as much as I do."

"Trust me. It's more."

"You already won the softball game," Gabriella said with a grin. She inclined her head to the side. "Why are you still over there? The scary stuff is over here."

Ryan grinned and her whole being relaxed in happiness as she erased the distance between them. Was it possible she glowed? She'd never done that before, but it was feeling likely. "Come here," Ryan said and pressed her forehead to Gabriella's. "God, I love you," she whispered.

"I love you, too," Gabriella said quietly. The most wonderful words. Ryan memorized the sound. They eased her soul and made it sing. For a time, they simply stood there, breathing in the same air and savoring the feeling of being in each other's arms once again.

"Kiss me already," Gabriella whispered.

Ryan laughed quietly and did as she was told. She lowered her mouth to Gabriella's and kissed her, feeling everything in her warm when they came together. She knew, as sure as she knew the sun would rise, that nothing could come between them again. This woman was it for her, and she was so damn happy about it her chest ached.

"Did I mention I love you?" Ryan asked.

Gabriella answered quickly. "No."

"I do."

She grinned. "You do what?"

"I love you."

"Then let's do this some more. Every damn day." Gabriella kissed her again. Slowly. Expertly. It awoke a thing in Ryan she'd forgotten about. Her temperature climbed, and her heart rate tripled, and there was a very recognizable aching coming from much lower. "Suggestion. Take me in there."

Ryan closed her eyes, acutely aware of Gabriella's breasts pressed against her. "I've always been open to suggestions."

"Maybe get a little box." Gabriella looked skyward. Playfully cute. Ryan wanted to eat her up, nuzzle her for days, and do scandalous things to her. All of it. "I've missed you."

"Really?" Ryan asked.

Those hazel eyes went dark. "Want to find out how much?"

Ryan had no idea when she'd set out for the softball game that afternoon that she'd have found her way back to Gabriella by the day's end. So much of life came in unpredictable packages lined with layers, complexities, and unanswered questions. She'd have to learn to trust more, to follow her heart instead of her fears. In the end, Ryan would give all she had to Gabriella, and then she'd give some more. All she wanted was to spend her days making Gabriella smile.

They kissed more on the sidewalk, on the porch stairs, in front of the door, and stumbling into the cottage, all hands and lips and eager hearts. While they tried to take their time, to go slow and savor the rediscovery, it was not to be. Gabriella had her naked and tumbling over the edge in the hallway just shy of the bedroom. She took Gabriella at the foot of the bed in a haze of heat and desire. Satisfied and happy, they laughed at their half-naked state as they lay side by side in the moonlit bedroom.

"I'm pretty sure your bra is around your waist," Ryan whispered.

"And your jeans are around one of your ankles. We walked in here like that?"

Ryan kissed the underside of Gabriella's jaw. "You think I can answer that question? You were topless, so my brain was busy."

Her gaze danced across the breasts that did her in every damn time. Her skin tingled and her lips parted. Gabriella followed her eyes, amused. "Such a breast woman."

"Except I'm not. Just yours." She shook her head, leaned down, and took a nipple into her mouth. Gabriella slid her hand into Ryan's unruly hair and exhaled sharply, pulling her in closer. That respite certainly hadn't lasted long. "Oh, here we go," Ryan said and slid on top, kicking off the jeans that clung to her ankle, with a laugh. She kissed her way up and down Gabriella's body as she writhed against the sheets. Ryan systematically removed every lingering piece of her clothing, so she could properly worship the body beneath hers. Absolutely beautiful.

Gabriella began to roll her hips, pressing up into Ryan, searching. "You're too good at this," she breathed.

"Too good is not a thing." Ryan kissed her neck slowly, her

collarbone, her stomach. She then kissed her inner thighs, first one then the other.

"Dear God. Feels like a thing."

"Should I stop?" Ryan asked with a grin against that gorgeous skin.

"Only if you want to die," came the answer, which even in the midst of passion, pulled a smile.

❖

Ryan decided to skip her run that next morning because when she woke to find herself in Gabriella's bed, her face pressed into Gabriella's hair that smelled so familiar of citrus and sunshine, she wasn't about to move. This was literally her heaven, and the idea that she could wake up to this every morning had her not only energized for the life ahead of them, but content to enjoy the special moments like this one. With his giant bowl of food and his access to her back deck, she wasn't sure Dale knew she was gone. Either way, she'd pick up the lug soon and see what Gabriella had in store for the day. Maybe she'd see if there was space for dinner at the bar at Tangled tonight. She could watch Gabriella in the kitchen if she chose the right stool, and she knew exactly which ones did the trick.

"What are you thinking about?" Gabriella turned in Ryan's arms, warm and wonderful. She glowed like someone who'd had amazing sex the night before. Ryan could identify.

"Excuse me. Has it been ten minutes yet?" Ryan asked, incredulous.

Gabriella broke into a sleepy grin. "Yep. I've been watching the clock."

"Sneaky. You were awake, and I didn't know it."

"You didn't answer my question."

Fair enough. "I was thinking about how happy I am. How different it all feels. I'm scared, but I'm also not at all. What were *you* thinking about, slugger?"

"How you effortlessly made me climax three times last night, and the ridiculous amount that I love you."

Ryan swallowed. "You were really thinking that?"

Gabriella kissed her chin tenderly. "And more. When I woke up and saw it wasn't all a dream, I got a little misty."

Ryan kissed her nose. "No dreaming. We're real."

"We are." Gabriella smiled and her eyes crinkled. "Let's eat lots of food today. Sit in the sun. Maybe have a glass of wine with whoever's about, and then maybe fool around before I go in to work."

"I think you've just described my best day ever."

"Shall we get started?" Gabriella asked. She stood up naked and beautiful and walked slowly into the bathroom, swaying her hips. Ryan nearly melted to a puddle at the sexy sight. She heard the shower. Grinned. Her cue.

With a deep inhale, she embraced the unending gratitude that swelled as she tossed the covers off and followed Gabriella. "I think we definitely should."

In the shower, Gabriella snaked her arms around Ryan's neck, went up on tiptoe, and grinned. "I've missed you."

"You won't have to, ever again."

The hot water fell against their skin as they shared a kiss that seemed to seal the promise. So much ahead. So much to look forward to. So much love to wrap themselves up in.

# EPILOGUE

*Eight months later*

It was what Gabriella called a lazy Friday night. Keith was heading up dinner service at Tangled so Gabriella could prepare for the big festival the following day. She had everything prepped and her signage ready to go, and was pumped for Tangled's first official food booth alongside the Tangle Valley booth. Tonight was hers, however, and she relished the opportunity to simply relax at home. She leisurely stirred her chicken and corn chowder, impressed with its heartiness. Stealing a taste, she closed her eyes and nodded. "Nailed it."

Ryan had been lying on the worn-in leather couch at the lake house, reading a murder mystery with Dale folded into a ball at her feet, commanding the last cushion for himself entirely. He wasn't shy about claiming sleeping space, that guy. "You always nail it. It's your gift." Ryan looked over her shoulder at Gabriella, who stood at the stove. "No one nails it as much as you do. Even me, who hammers them daily."

"You are too kind, peanut gallery. But seriously, this smoked paprika is a winner. Keeping it."

"Do we get to eat it now? Please say yes."

"No," Gabriella said and folded her arms. Ryan was barefoot in a combination of sexy-cozy, which meant Gabriella had to join her on the couch as ordained by the heavens. Given that there was no available space, she was forced to snuggle in alongside Ryan, who lifted her arm in welcome, a total hardship.

"But why?" Ryan asked. "You always make us wait for food. It's unlawful."

"Because right now, all of those amazing flavors are marinating and coming together as one. You can't rush perfection." She gave

Ryan's chin a soft shake. "Just look at us. We took time." They had, too. Sometimes Gabriella wondered what would have happened if they hadn't given things another try. It made her ill to consider that she could have missed out on this amazing woman, who had become the love of her life. They'd taken it one step at a time for the first couple of months, but for the past six they had been inseparable, moving with Dale between the cottage and the lake house. They knew they'd have to make their living situation official at some point, with the lake house being the obvious choice. Gabriella had never lived anywhere more peaceful in her life, such a contrast to Jersey and her city mouse upbringing. They spent hours each week drinking wine on the dock and watching the water lap gently, content to be in each other's presence and talk about anything and everything until they devoured each other most any night they weren't exhausted. And then? They cuddled until sleep claimed them.

Ryan grinned. "You always use us as an example to make me more patient. It's your trick."

"Does it work?"

She kissed Gabriella softly. "Yes. Because I love you and would wait forever for you if I had to."

"Just like you're gonna wait for this soup." Ryan sighed adorably, and Gabriella couldn't take it. "Stop being attractive. It's too much, I say. The sun is setting, the kitchen smells awesome, and my girlfriend is beyond sexy."

Ryan's eyes went wide. "How are you supposed to survive? Your life is taxing." She unbuttoned Gabriella's top button, which exposed a good portion of cleavage. "Now my life is." She glanced back at the stove. "Since the soup's busy…you're kinda free right now." She popped another button.

Gabriella gasped, scandalized. "Oh, I'm being seduced."

Another button. "Is it working?"

She sat up, straddling Ryan's stomach, her white shirt hanging open and her sky-blue bra now on display. Ryan reached up and cradled Gabriella's breasts through the fabric, making her instantly wet. "I'd say it's definitely convincing me to take a break."

Ryan sat up and pulled Gabriella's mouth down to hers. "I love it when you make soup."

The next day, the town came out in droves for Waffle Fest. Gabriella had come to understand that in honor of Whisper Wall, most of their festivals began with a *W*, which she was in complete support of. While Tangle Valley would be selling wine by the glass next door, Gabriella and Nadine had the full size waffle irons out and sold hot pizzelle waffles with strawberries and a dollop of mascarpone cheese. Gabriella drew on Grandma Filomena's recipe, and once word got out, they had the longest line at the festival.

"Sweet Lord sleeping on straw, this waffle is magnificent," Brenda Anne yelled to Gabriella with a smidge of strawberry juice on her cheek. "This is criminal."

"What's criminal is this line," Monty called.

Gabriella sent him a wink as she handed over a hot Italian waffle to Lucinda the chocolatier. Tangled was turning out to be the hit of the festival, and next to their booth, Joey and Madison grinned with pride. "You're really making a name for yourself in this town," Madison called to her.

Gabriella shook her head and regarded the line, her heart full at the welcome she'd received since arriving. "I just want to feed the masses. What can I say?"

As she worked, she caught glimpses of Ryan here and there as she walked with Billy and Wrigley through the festival, sampling food and perusing the different vendors. Just after two p.m., Gabriella handed over her apron to Chelsea, who'd become quite the little chef these days, and trusted her to assist Joy on the second shift.

Free and clear to frolic, Joey poured her a glass of dolcetto, and she wandered the grounds until she caught up with Ryan, who kissed her cheek with a smack. Ryan stood under a tree with Clementine, who sipped a beer with a smile on her face.

"Everyone's talking about you," Ryan said.

She looked around, exhausted but on a high. "I'm famous?"

"I hate to admit it," Clementine said, "but you drew much bigger crowds than the Biscuit did, and we surpassed last year's record."

"That's awesome." Gabriella offered a chef's kiss to the sky. "But I can't take credit for our reviews today. All my grandma's doing."

"What's the plan?" Ryan asked. "You up for some exploring?"

"I've been counting the minutes until I could join you. Kiss me real quick, so I get my fix." Ryan obliged and Clementine grinned.

"Stop being the cutest people ever," she said in mock exasperation.

Gabriella laughed. "We'll work on that." She tossed a thumb behind her. "Joey and Madison are switching out with Loretta and Bobby, so they're gonna walk with us. Cool?"

Clementine swallowed. "Oh. I'll let you guys hang out."

"No. We insist you join us," Gabriella said, looping her arm through Clem's. Right on cue, Joey found them, a big grin on her face.

"Waffle Fest has got to be the best smelling festival of all the fests," Joey declared. "The biscuits you guys are turning out certainly contribute. God, I never get tired of them."

And just like that, Clementine unlooped her arm from Gabriella's. Her cheeks went rosy red and she swallowed. "I've got to go. You guys have a good night." And before Gabriella could say anything in return, she was gone.

"What was that about?" Ryan asked.

Joey grinned. "I'm not entirely sure, but Madison's walking toward us."

"Well, well," Gabriella said. "I did not see that one coming."

"Because you didn't go to high school with us."

"Clementine had a thing for Madison in high school?"

"I've always suspected. Not that Maddie has any clue."

"Hey, guys," Madison said. Her dark blond curls were down, and she seemed carefree and happy. Three heads swiveled her way in knowing amusement. She squinted. "What did I miss?"

Gabriella smothered a grin. Oh, this could prove very interesting, indeed. "Oh, nothing. But, you know, maybe hold on to your love affair with Clem's biscuits."

As night fell and the music from the bandstand kicked into gear, Ryan wrapped her arms around Gabriella, and they danced beneath the stars, tipsy, happy, and in perfect sync. She sang quietly in Ryan's ear because she knew Ryan loved it. When their eyes met, they shared a kiss as the audience applauded the band. "This right here," Ryan said and closed her eyes.

"What does that mean?" Gabriella asked.

"I'm memorizing this moment because I've never been happier. Thank you for moving to Whisper Wall. Thank you for changing my life. Thank you for loving me."

Gabriella's heart grew as she looked up at the woman who was her everything. "Before you make me tear up any more, let's get out of here."

"Yeah?" She tucked a strand of hair behind Gabriella's ear. "Where should we go?"

Gabriella didn't hesitate. "Why, home, of course. Our home."

Hand in hand, that's exactly where they went, in love and ready to traverse the world together, for always.

# About the Author

Melissa Brayden (www.melissabrayden.com) is a multi-award-winning romance author, embracing the full-time writer's life in San Antonio, Texas, and enjoying every minute of it.

Melissa enjoys spending time with her family and working really hard at remembering to do the dishes. For personal enjoyment, she throws realistically shaped toys for her Jack Russell terriers and checks out the NYC theater scene as often as possible. She considers herself a reluctant patron of spin class, but would much rather be sipping merlot and staring off into space. Coffee, wine, and donuts make her world go round.

# Books Available From Bold Strokes Books

**Aurora** by Emma L McGeown. After a traumatic accident, Elena Ricci is stricken with amnesia, leaving her with no recollection of the last eight years, including her wife and son. (978-1-63555-824-1)

**Avenging Avery** by Sheri Lewis Wohl. Revenge against a vengeful vampire unites Isa Meyer and Jeni Denton, but it's love that heals them. (978-1-63555-622-3)

**Bulletproof** by Maggie Cummings. For Dylan Prescott and Briana Logan, the complicated NYC criminal justice system doesn't leave room for love, but where the heart is concerned, no one is bulletproof. (978-1-63555-771-8)

**Her Lady to Love** by Jane Walsh. A shy wallflower joins forces with the most popular woman in Regency London on a quest to catch a husband, only to discover a wild passion for each other that far eclipses their interest for the Marriage Mart. (978-1-63555-809-8)

**No Regrets** by Joy Argento. For Jodi and Beth, the possibility of losing their future will force them to decide what is really important. (978-1-63555-751-0)

**The Holiday Treatment** by Elle Spencer. Who doesn't want a gay Christmas movie? Holly Hudson asks herself that question and discovers that happy endings aren't only for the movies. (978-1-63555-660-5)

**Too Good to be True** by Leigh Hays. Can the promise of love survive the realities of life for Madison and Jen, or is it too good to be true? (978-1-63555-715-2)

**Treacherous Seas** by Radclyffe. When the choice comes down to the lives of her officers against the promise she made to her wife, Reese Conlon puts everything she cares about on the line. (978-1-63555-778-7)

**Two to Tangle** by Melissa Brayden. Ryan Jacks has been a player all her life, but the new chef at Tangle Valley Vineyard changes every-thing. If only she wasn't off the menu. (978-1-63555-747-3)